GHOST in the
SUNLIGHT

BY THE SAME AUTHOR
Queen of the Lightning

GHOST in the SUNLIGHT

KATHLEEN HERBERT

St. Martin's Press
New York

For Katie and Anna Jensen

Library of Congress Cataloging in Publication Data

Herbert, Kathleen.
  The ghost in the sunlight.

  Sequel to Queen of the lightning.
  1. Great Britain—History—Anglo-Saxon period,
449-1066—Fiction. I. Title.
PR6058.E623G5 1987   823'.914   86-24803
ISBN 0-312-00126-6
First published in Great Britain by The Bodley Head Ltd.

First U.S. Edition

10 9 8 7 6 5 4 3 2 1

LIST OF CHARACTERS

BERNICIA

Oswy, King of Bernicia, later King of Northumbria and Bretwalda (High King)

Alchfrid, prince of Cumbria, his eldest son by Riemmelth, later King of Deira

Ecgfrid, his younger son by Eanfled

Alchflaed, Riemmelth's daughter

Ebbe, Oswy's sister, Abbess of Coludesburh, later revered as a saint

Athelwold, Oswy's nephew, puppet king of Deira

Aidan, Bishop of Northumbria, later revered as a saint

Finan, Bishop of Northumbria in succession to Aidan

Ethelwin, leader of Oswy's war-band

Cadman, ealdorman of Westmoringaland and regent of Cumbria

Godric, a Bernician thane formerly Oswy's shield-bearer

DEIRA

Eanfled, daughter to King Edwin, Oswy's second wife

Oswine, her cousin, murdered August 20th 651

Hunwald, thane of Getlingas, Oswine's closest friend

Trumhere, a kinsman of the Deiran royal family, first Abbot of Getlingas

Romanus, Eanfled's chaplain

Grimhild, her bower-woman

Willibrord, Dish-Thane (steward) of the palace at Eoforwic

ELMET

Honesta, "Nest", a lady of Romano-British family, Willibrord's mistress

Bledri ap Iddon, an outlaw chief

WALES

Morfran, a hermit, formerly Lord of Iâl

Meilyr, his nephew

Madoc, Meilyr's elder brother, present Lord of Iâl

Stephanos, "Asyn", Morfran's servant

Sulien, Abbot of Llangollen

5

MERCIA

Penda, the heathen warrior king, killed in battle, November 15th 655
Cynwise, his wife
Peada, his eldest son, murdered April 17th 656
Cyneburg, his eldest daughter, Alchfrid's wife
Wulfhere, his younger son, later king of Mercia
Eadbert, a powerful ealdorman
Wulfrun, his wife, Peada's foster-sister
Winefride, her younger sister
Berhtwald, captain of her bodyguard
Helmstan, King's reeve of Leirceaster
Freawynn, a priestess
Aino, a wise-woman

GHOSTS

In a society based on tradition, and regulated by the blood-feud, both constantly repeated in stories, songs and poems, men and women found the shape of their own lives, even of their own characters, governed by their dead kin. The demands of the dead could force the living into actions which were sometimes against their own wills and feelings.

Riemmelth of Cumbria, Oswy's first wife, last heiress of the dynasty of Urien and Coel
Urien, the greatest king of Cumbria. In the Arthurian legend he is Arthur's brother-in-law
Coel Hen Godebog (Coel the Old, Protector) the ancestor of the Cumbrian House. It has been suggested that he was "Old King Cole"
Taliesin, Urien's bard, author of the earliest surviving Welsh poetry
Peredur ap Efrog, a Welsh hero. In the Arthurian legend he is Percival/Parsifal
Vortigern, the British High King whose employment of Germanic federates was blamed for the loss of Britain to the English
Cadwallon, the warrior king of Gwynedd who conquered Northumbria in 633
Edwin of Deira, Eanfled's father, the first Christian king of Northumbria who defeated Ethelfrith, Oswy's father. Killed by Cadwallon and Penda 633

Ethelburg of Kent, Eanfled's mother, daughter of St Ethelbert of Kent, the first royal English convert, and Bertha the Merovingian

St Paulinus, her chaplain, leader of the first mission to Northumbria

Ethelfrith of Bernicia. Last heathen King of Northumbria, Oswy's father. Massacred the monks of Bangor-ys-y-Coed at the battle of Chester 613

St Oswald of Northumbria, Oswy's elder brother, killed by Penda. 5th August 642

Offa of Angeln, an English hero of pre-migration times, ancestor of the Mercian House

Hengist, a Jutish hero, ancestor of the Kentish House.

Wiglaf, Beowulf's nephew and successor

Sigemund the Waelsing, a great Germanic hero. He appears in the Volsunga Saga and Wagner's 'Ring'

THE ROYAL HOUSES OF NORTHUMBRIA

BERNICIA

Ida
|
Ethelric
|
Ethelfrith m. Acha of Deira

Eanfrid	St Oswald	St Ebbe	1) Riemmelth m. Oswy m. 2) Eanfled
Talorgan of Pictland	Athelwold		of Cumbria	of Deira

Cyneburg m. Alchfrid   Peada m. Alchlaed   Ecgfrid   Elfflaed
of   of
Mercia   Mercia

DEIRA

Yffi

| Aelle | | Elfric |

Edwin m. Ethelburg	Acha m. Ethelfrith	Osric
of Kent	of Bernicia	

Eanfled   m.   Oswy   Oswine

The Fight for the North
651–656 A.D.

■ Roman sites
● non-Roman sites
† Monastic sites
═══ Roman roads

PICTLAND

STRATHCLYDE

BERNICIA

CUMBRIA

Eidyn
Coludesburh
Tuidimuth
Holy Island
Bebbanburh
Devil's Causeway
Atwall
Caer Luel
Gatesheafod
Idon
Tina
Penrith
Tese
Heruteu
Perscbrig
Stony Moor
Getlingas
Cetreht
Suala
Lastingaeu
Aldeburh
Deorwent
LONG HILLS
ELMET
Lonceaster
Weorf
Eoforwic
Yr
Calicaceaster
Ceasterford
Caldre
LOIDIS
Maerse
Weneta
Haethfeld
Manceinion
Doneceaster
Humbre
Don
Nene
LINDESSE
Witchale
Arnemeton
PEACLOND
The Lady's Bower
Lindcylene
MÔN
Caer Seiont
IÂL
Legaceaster
GWYNEDD
Dinas
Brân
Dyfrdwy
Llangollen
Northworthig
Treonta
Weligton
THE FENS
POWYS
Tomeworthig
EAST
ANGLIA
Leirceaster
Medeshamsted
Ceasterton
Saefern

THE SAXON KINGDOMS

ACKNOWLEDGEMENTS

The translation of 'Beowulf', lines 81–85, is by Kevin Crossley-Holland, 1968; Folio Society, 1973; World's Classics, 1982.

The translation of 'Propertius, Elegy IV xi' is by Gilbert Highet: *Poets in a Landscape*, Hamish Hamilton, 1957.

For the purposes of this story it has been imagined that 1300 years ago it was possible to go through the Castleton caves from the Peak Gorge to the Blue John Mine. The writer wishes to thank the guides to the Peak, Speedwell, Treak Cliff and Blue John Caverns for their courtesy and patience in answering questions and, in particular, Mr Keith Hague for a private tour of the Treak Cliff Cavern and some very helpful advice.

Peada's riddle on p. 173 is based on the letter-names of the runic alphabet:

Two needs	Need	N
Two oaks	Ac/oak	A
One ash	AEsc/ash	AE
Hail twice	Hail	H

Reassembled they spell Hana and Haen—Cock and Hen

CHAPTER
1

There had been no rain for over a month. Under the midsummer sun the land of Bernicia had become like tinder, ready to burst into flames at a single spark. The west wind, coming over miles of parched heather and dry, cracking bog, blew the sea-coolness back off the land as it threw back the crests of the white horses tossing and sparkling all the way to the Farnes and beyond.

Ever since the Mercian raiders came, the bower-maidens had been spending their time whenever they could escape from their tasks of weaving and embroidery—and the harrying of the Dish-Thane's wife—lounging in the sollar under the rear gable of the dead Queen's hall. It was unusually light and airy. The Queen had ordered many window-spaces to be made there, high and broad, regardless of the gales that came shrieking down from the Cheviots or across the northern sea. She had liked to sit there with all the shutters thrown back, during the brief respites when she was free from her duties of hospitality or state-craft, sometimes touching her harp and singing softly to herself in her own tongue, usually just gazing out over the waves. At that height the crash of the breakers at the foot of the crag sounded like a constant hushing. Gulls floated level with the windows or wheeled and flashed white against the sky. The Queen said that she felt as free as a gull herself, up there alone with the wind and the sea. Queen Riemmelth had been a Welshwoman; she was apt to talk strangely like that at times.

The girls were not yearning to feel like gulls. However, the sollar made a very pleasant refuge from the multiplying stinks of the countryfolk who had crowded into Bebbanburh when word came of a raid from the south. They had brought their animals with them and as much of their household gear as they could cart or carry. Now they were all camping in whatever shelter they could find among the stables, barns, forges, kitchens, weaving-sheds, brew-houses, bothies, vegetable plots and rough pasture that made up the royal city of Bernicia on the cliff.

These fugitives kept well away from the inner courtyard. They respected the royal halls, even though King Oswy was away on the Cumbrian border and his queen was nearly a year in her grave. This respect was impressed on them by the warriors of the garrison, who thwacked them with their spearbutts or kicked them out of the way if they got underfoot. The Queen's hall stood a little apart from the other royal buildings; it had a walled garth behind, with a herb-plot and a few stunted apple trees, so the girls were spared the worst of the filth and clutter beyond.

While they were in the sollar, the girls were also safe from the eyes and ears of the warriors. They could speak their minds freely, unwind their veils, untie the neck-strings of their shifts and pull their gowns up to their knees to let the air get to their skins. Though the wind, now heightened to a gale, was as hot as the blast from a smith's bellows, at least it dried their sweat and lifted their lank hair from their brows and cheeks. So the girls faced into it, turning their backs on the sea: placid Edyth, sharp Osburg and little Leoba, together with the traveller who had arrived unexpectedly from the north just before the raiders came and had been penned in with the rest of them.

They were so high up on the sheer crag that the Mercian war-band on the plain below shrank to insects. Those clusters of toiling ants were Bernician serf-gangs; the gleaming beetles were mailed Mercian warriors. Their king was watching them, waving an arm at moments to point an order. Even at that distance he showed as a mountain of a man, towering over the rest. When he walked he limped slightly, dragging his left leg, so he usually went mounted. He was no horseman; he sat on his mount while it carried him, rather than rode it, his feet nearly brushing the ground on either side. The animal, not being a war-stallion but a stump-legged, barrel-bodied Dales pack-pony, took the burden as just another sack and plodded on.

The girls glanced carelessly from time to time at King Penda the Mighty getting ready for their throat-cutting, or rape and slavery, with the same mild amusement they would have felt watching the churls at a cattle-fair down on the meadow. They were lifted high out of danger on Bebbanburh's great fortified sea-cliff; it had a spring of pure water at its heart.

Whenever raiders came—and in recent years Penda had come north every summer, driving deep into Bernicia just as he chose—the countryfolk would drive their stock in and the garrison would hurl the attackers from the gates with a rain of spears on their heads. Then everybody sat and feasted inside, while the gulls and ravens feasted outside on the dead and not-quite-dead that the enemy had not been able to get down from the crags. The raiders might make a few more attempts at the gates, until they got bored or began to sicken with the bloody flux from camping in one place. Then they went away again with the loot they had gathered on their progress.

This year, however, the Mercians had prolonged their foray. Having failed, as usual, to take Bebbanburh by storm, Penda was now fencing it in for a siege. He had rounded up the countryfolk who had not fled to the citadel in time or scattered into the hills and was forcing them to drag up the timber from their villages and farmsteads to make a barrier outside the gate and the landward wall. The defenders, much more securely walled-in by their own mighty stockade, looked down scornfully on Penda's ramshackle rampart, shouting insults and mock-advice. The girls sat and sunned their breasts like pigeons lazy with the heat.

Edyth raised her arms as if they were almost too heavy to lift, pushed her spread fingers through her sticky hair and sighed out a long yawn.

'If the warriors can share out captive women after a battle, why don't we get first pick of the men?' she asked sleepily.

There was a slight ripple of interest.

'I'd have that big fair one who led the last attack — he's got muscles like a bull,' said Osburg, waking up.

'And just as clumsy! I'd have that dark one who got right up to the gate and cut Ingeld down — he moves as light as a wolf.'

'Or a wild cat.'

'Or a fair-ground tumbler!' Leoba's plump little face suddenly crumpled into giggles. 'Penda's men should be good at tumbling by now, with all the practice they get, going head-over-heels down our rocks!'

There was a prolonged screech of laughter that left them panting and flapping their hands in front of their faces, then sinking back into restful silence.

'I saw a juggler once at the Hagustaldesham horse-fair,' said a dreamy voice. 'He set knives point upwards in the ground and danced between the blades, and all the while he was tossing coloured balls up and catching them. I swear he had a dozen going up and down between his hands and never missed one — you've never seen the like!'

'We'll see the like and better when King Oswy and our war-host get back here and take Mercians — only it'll be our knife-blades dancing between their legs!'

'And they'll miss all their balls soon enough!'

13

The laughter was shriller this time and more vicious; the heat was beginning to try their tempers.

'And *that*, Edyth, is why women don't press their claims after a victory. What use could we make of our captive men but pack them off to our farms with the oxen and wethers?'

'You need stallions in bed as well as in battle. There's no excitement riding a gelding.'

'And even less in being ridden by one — what do you think, Lady Alchflaed?'

The girl so challenged had taken no part in the talk and gave no sign of having heard the question. She was sitting upright, as still as an image in a shrine. In spite of the heat she was shrouded from neck to foot in a plain grey robe; her wimple was swathed closely round her head and throat. She was gazing straight ahead, over the ravaged plain, towards the line of hills on the horizon, outliers of the Cheviot.

Alchflaed's silence began to weigh on the other girls; they felt it as a rebuke to their bawdy talk. It made them uneasy, then resentful. Their voices sank to whispering.

'For shame! You shouldn't speak about such things — not in front of a novice!'

'She can't hear us — look at her eyes!'

'Even if she did hear, she wouldn't know what we were talking about. The holy sisters of Coludesburh don't even know how men are made.'

'What's she staring at?' Leoba looked scared. 'She's not watching the Mercians — you'd think they weren't there. She's not right — not canny —' Her voice was getting shrill.

'She's looking over at Gefrin, of course,' said Edyth calmly. 'How could the princess come to her mother's hall for the first time in her life and not be thinking of her mother's great deed, that time when the Mercians destroyed the palace there. It's no wonder Alchflaed cares nothing for sacks and sieges. Her mother was carrying her in the womb, remember, when she challenged Penda sword to sword and fought her way out with all Gefrin burning round her.'

'And lived wild in the woods like an outlaw for months after — though I daresay she took that lightly.' This was Osburg, the girl who had gloated over gelding the Mercians. She came from the north-western marchlands; for her, the Welsh were the hard-riding cattle-raiders who came over the border from Strathclyde. Her smile was sharp with spite. 'The Welsh — they should have been called the Woodwoses.'

14

But she had gone too far this time and failed to get her laugh. There was some furtive hushing and a hasty search for another topic. They all looked away from Alchflaed, who showed no sign of having heard them, out of the window on the landward side. Another load of wood was being painfully hauled up the slope towards the gate. Doors, roof-beams, the huge timbers of the water-mill at the head of the bay—the Mercians must have wrecked every homestead in miles to make their clumsy siege-work.

'I wonder what scares them most—our men coming down on them or King Oswy's war-host catching them from behind?'

'Well, they won't be getting the choice. The host can't be far away now. The Mercians will be caught between two fires.'

As if in answer to that word flames broke out of the Mercians' rampart, and a gush of smoke. A howl of jeering laughter arose from the stockade. A mock-sympathetic voice called to the Mercians to watch out, their dinner was burning. That was the last joke made in Bebbanburh for a long time.

There was another burst of smoke from the rampart—another—then another all along its line. Penda had ordered green wood and dampened thatch to be piled in front of his wall. Driven by the westerly gale the smoke poured over the stockade in smothering clouds. The defenders were taken unawares, blinded and choking.

Fire came leaping behind the smoke. The heavier timbers had been packed with brushwood that caught and consumed like tinder. Through the gaps that were left flames lashed out like whips and struck against the Bernician stockade. This was made of oak trunks, well-seasoned. They would not ignite easily but they had been scorched by the drought for over a month. If Penda's bonfire burned against them long enough, they would end by burning with it.

The Mercians had no mind to wait for that. They sent a hail of blazing arrows over the stockade to land where they might, starting more fires on the dry roof-thatch and among the store-sheds piled high with fodder. The panic they brought spread even faster than the flames.

The cattle inside the stockade were already uneasy, driven up from their familiar fields. The smoke and crackling of the fire maddened them. They broke loose and tried to stampede but were halted by the stockade and swung back in a goring charge. The farm-folk struggled among them, trying to beat out patches of flame, trying to get buckets to the well, trying to find and pick up their children. Women who had been sheltering in huts on the seaward side clutched their babies and ran to the northern postern. The gate-guards refused to open in case the enemy had worked their way up the crags and were waiting outside. The guards tried to drive the women away with their spearbutts; the wretched creatures stayed pressed up against the stockade, beating their hands raw in mindless terror.

Inside the warriors' hall, men who had been lounging off-guard paused over their drink and dice at the outcry, then leapt to snatch their weapons from the walls and rush to the point of danger. Once in the courtyard they were driven back and scattered by the swirling tides of confusion. Under the pall of smoke on the landward side they could not see where the main attack was coming, or even if their own men still held the gate. Some turned aside to help fight the fires; they couldn't make a last stand against the Mercians if they were being fried alive. Outside, with the western gale still holding their screen of smoke and flame in front of them, the Mercians had brought up battering rams and were smashing the gate in, unopposed.

Perched in the sollar, the girls stared down helplessly, like cottars trapped on the roof of their hut by a sudden flood, watching their homestead breaking up and being swept away underneath them. The thing that could never happen was suddenly happening. Bebbanburh was falling to the enemy. Their jokes about flesh-cutting and slavery were about to be played out— and they were the victims of the jest.

Little Leoba threw back her head and screamed. The girls were shocked into movement. They jumped up, clawed each other aside from the top of the stairs, tripped or stumbled down and fled from the Queen's hall to add their terror to the panic outside.

Edyth saw Wermund just by the door, trying to force a way with his shield-boss towards the gate. He was her lover; she threw herself at his sword-arm and clung to him. He cursed her but could not break her grip; she made him as useless as if a Mercian spear had pinned him to the hall timbers.

A rook that had been gorging in one of the granaries and taken flight too late plummetted on to Osburg's head. Its wings were already smouldering; it lashed out with claws and beak as she beat frantically at the stinking black mass, her face scored across.

The wiser gulls had already sheered away from their scavenging to the water's edge. After wheeling up and down along the shore-line they suddenly gathered themselves into a huge flock and fled shrieking out to sea, calling the disaster over the Farnes till the rocks re-echoed.

Slaughter! Slaughter! Slaughter! Bebbanburh is falling, falling, falling!

CHAPTER
2

Eighteen years ago, when Bishop Aidan first crossed from Holy Island to the Inner Farne for one of the rare retreats he allowed himself from the cares of his vast Northumbrian diocese, he had made a ring of stones round a hollow place. He piled them high enough to wall himself away from the sight of everything except one small circle of sky. He had made an island within an island. The tides of this world, even the blood-waves of his own bodily life, beat against it but were held outside, as the cliffs of Farne held off the battering seas.

His body was lying there now, limbs stretched rigid in the shape of a cross. His spirit, lightened by a week of fasting and ecstatic prayer, had soared up into the radiant silence of God.

There came a rushing wind, the beat of many wings, voices calling and wailing all round him.

Slaughter! Slaughter! Slaughter! Bebbanburh is falling, falling, falling!'

Bishop Aidan's spirit sank to earth. His body stirred, groaned, dragged itself forward to the ring-wall, clutching the topmost stones. His head lifted into the gale; his wasted, hollow-eyed face turned to the smoking cliff-top on the mainland. The greatest Christian kingdom in England was being broken; the royal city was falling to the heathen. He stretched his arms towards it in anguish.

'Lord! Lord! See what harm Penda is doing!'

Aidan had lived for a week in the worlds of the spirit. His eyes had not yet lost the second sight; this earth looked as thin as a veil. In the smoke clouds that were coiling over Bebbanburh, in the swirls of fire from its blazing thatch, he seemed to see the shapes of those who were riding into the doomed citadel over the

17

heads of the victorious Mercians. Woden, the one-eyed, merciless smiler on his eight-legged horse; his screaming waelcyriges drunk with blood, swooping down the wind like hungry ravens; his laughing, tricky servant with hair and fingers of flame darting from roof to roof.

Aidan rose to his knees, lifting his arms to the sky, forcing his exhausted spirit to rise again in an agony of prayer. He tried to empty himself, so that Power might flow back through him even if it shattered his body in passing. A second battle for the Bernician stronghold was being waged in the air above the flesh and blood struggle.

The west wind slackened, dropped, veered.

Alchflaed was alone in the sollar, at the heart of one of those odd moments of stillness that come even during the fiercest battles. The Queen's hall was furthest from the gate of all the royal buildings. Neither the fight nor the fire had reached it yet, though smoke was beginning to drift past its windows.

Alchflaed had not moved so much as her eyes when the girls fled in panic. She sat gazing at the distant hills. For weeks there had not been the lightest feather of cloud to touch them with shade but now one of them, the most westerly of the chain, was wrapping itself in rising folds of mist. As she stared, this hill lifted from the earth and came floating towards her.

It's the heat, Alchflaed told herself desperately. *I've sat too long in the sun—must get into the shade—my skull will boil over—go down—get someone to draw me a bucket of water and dowse my head—I'm brainstruck—*

But she couldn't escape, couldn't even raise a hand to shift her stifling veil from her throat and brow, couldn't take her eyes from that hill floating through the mist that was silvery with dawn light. Wisps of it reached out to her, swaying like a dancer's veil to the music of rustling leaves and the cool voice of a river. The enchanted hill was very close now; it had passed through the stockade, blotting it out. If she stepped over the window ledge she would not have far to walk to its foot.

The hilltop rose out of the mist into dawn sunlight. It was cone-shaped and circled with green ramparts. At the crest an outcrop of rock was gilded by the rising sun—or was it a golden palace she saw with one high tower? She blinked to clear her eyes; her ears were filled with the plashing of the unseen river, running fast over a rocky bed. Now it seemed that through the ripples she could hear the notes of the harp her mother had been used to play in that very room. Shadowy forms appeared in the mist; they were beckoning to her; she heard voices calling for her: *Alchflaed, Alchflaed, where are you? Come home! Come home!*

She got up and began to walk towards the window—only now it was a door opening into a country that she knew she had to reach. A step or two more and she would have passed through. One of the shapes had come to meet her; it loomed solid at the head of the stairs, waiting. The magic mist parted. Suddenly she could feel in her nose and throat that it was smoke. She heard the roar and crackle of flames on thatch, the clash of weapons, screaming. Bebbanburh was on fire all round her and she was face to face with a Mercian warrior.

Outside, the west wind slackened, dropped, veered.

The lull in the gale left the smoke going straight up. The hard-pressed and scattered Bernicians had a moment's chance to clear their lungs, snatch a few breaths and blink their smarting eyes.During the respite they saw how few Mercians had got in yet past the smoke screen; that the gate was only part-broken; that there was still a knot of their own men up by the stockade.

Wermund got free of Edyth by stamping on her feet and then putting his knee hard into her belly. He yelled to every man within earshot to rally to him and headed a charge towards the gate. At the same moment the wind rose again, but this time it came from the east, oversea from the Farnes. It raced ahead of the Bernicians, blinding and choking the foremost invaders with their own smoke, sending them recoiling into their own bonfire while it drove the flames back towards the main body of the Mercians, now massed outside for the final assault.

Inside the sollar, the man and the girl stared at each other. She saw that he was lithe and lightly poised on his feet, like a cat ready to spring. His helmet, which had a nose-piece, cheek-guards and a neck-curtain of ring-mail, gave him the head of a monstrous iron bird of prey, with dark pits behind the eye-spaces where something moved and glittered. Only the mouth was human; it was well-cut and supple, the upper lip shaded with black hair. She watched the mouth; it was smiling.

The warrior saw a woman whose smooth cheek showed she was young, but whose body was muffled in a loose grey robe and whose brow and hair were hidden in the folds of her wimple. He noted that her hands were soft, unscarred by serf's work; that the robe and wimple were clean and finely woven; that she had a gold cross set with garnets on her breast. A high-born novice, a thane's daughter with a sanctified maidenhead; one who would feel the shame of rape and slavery as a more galling burden even than an iron slave-collar. Good. He smiled, savouring it.

'Look what my luck has sent me!'

She stared at him, her eyes dull and blank. He thought she was frozen with terror, like a leveret with a hawk overhead. His voice hardened.

'Come here!'

Still she did not move. Her face gave no sign of understanding or even interest. He wondered impatiently if she were a lackwit, dumped into a nunnery by her wealthy family because no man would take her even with a dowry. He started towards her, when a strong gust of smoky wind took him in the eyes and throat. He checked, coughing. Feet were thudding across the hall below; Bernician voices shouting.

The Mercian listened, head turned and lifted like a hawk. He glanced over the nearest window-ledge and saw a flurry of fighting below, his own men driven back, the northerners underneath him. He threw his spear among them so that they scattered and turned, expecting an attack from the rear. He drew his sword and jumped straight on to the shoulders of one man, driving the blade into his back; leapt over the corpse as the next man rushed at him and stumbled across it; then vanished into the smoke and flames towards the gate.

Outside the stockade, with the flames surging in their faces, the front rank of the Mercians was breaking and trying to force a way back against the main body of their own men. Their king, still prepared to fight his way in, was blocking their retreat on his stolid pack-horse, like a rock in flood water, calling on Woden. Someone caught his bridle and pointed south over the plain, where the noon sun was glinting on helmets and spear points. The Bernician relief force was coming up fast. If the Mercians held their ground they would be trapped against the rock, with their own bonfire and the freshly-heartened garrison of Bebbanburh at their backs.

Penda shouted his orders; the attack was called off and the raiders headed westwards to the trackless wastes of the Cheviot.

*　　*　　*

The fresh sea-wind had blown away the illusion that had kept Alchflaed bespelled, just as it scattered the smoke. Her own lively wits came back to her. In fact, as she had escaped the brunt of the skirmish and the fire, she was in better case than anyone else in Bebbanburh at that moment. She thanked her rescuers and comforted Leoba who, though terrified, had cared enough about her to force one of the warriors and a couple of churls to come and snatch her from the flames. Then she went out to see what she could do to help.

There was plenty. The garrison had not suffered too badly during the assault because very few Mercians had got within spears' reach of them. Their wounded were not suffering too badly now, because Bebbanburh was a royal city and was royally provided, even though the King was absent. There was a skilled leech in the household and several cunning-women. There were stocks of new feather mattresses to spread for them in the warriors' hall, fine woollen blankets, clean linen to bind their gashes, a still-room full of healing draughts and salves, and many servants to fetch and carry for them.

Others were not so lucky; it was to these that Alchflaed turned. She had a fair, though not outstanding, knowledge of healing. Her aunt Ebbe, the foundress of the convent at Coludesburh, insisted that all her nuns and novices, however highly-born, should take their share of every task from milking to copying manuscripts. Alchflaed had served her turn in the infirmary, though she had no great pleasure in leechdom or herb-lore. She would far rather spend her time turning the colours and curves of flowers into patterns of beauty with her embroidery needle or ink-brushes than mash them shapeless with a pestle. Still, she was a kind-hearted girl and, when she was in her full senses, quick-witted and handy, so she was well able to care for the sick.

Osburg was lying in the bower behind the Dish-Thane's hall. Leoba had got her to bed and wiped her face before she went to find Alchflaed, but did not know what else to do for her. Osburg was sobbing over her ruined looks; Alchflaed got a sleeping draught down her throat then, when she was quiet, laid a cloth spread with salve over her cheek. She left Leoba to watch by the bed; in spite of her youth and babyish manners the girl had shown more sense and kindness than the others in the moment of trial.

The common folk had suffered most and, as usual, were considered least. Many of the fire-fighters were badly burned or injured by falling timbers. Bones had been broken when the cattle panicked; some of the men had been gored or had their guts crushed when they fell under the hoofs. Lost children were screaming for their mothers, who were screaming for them somewhere else. The Dish-Thane and his wife were too hard-pressed to pay heed to them. They had to oversee the needs of the wounded spearmen, at the same time as offering a fitting welcome to the royal war-band who had just ridden in to their rescue.

Alchflaed wasted no time in begging supplies for the churls; they would have been refused. She kept her eyes and ears open, tracked down what she needed, gathered a group of sturdy farm-girls and led them raiding the still-room and store-huts with a ruthlessness that would have done credit to Mercians. The household officials, seeing her hurrying to and fro, took it for granted that she was busied about the newcomers' comforts and did not interfere. In fact, the princess was the last person of note in Bebbanburh to greet the royal troops, though she soon learned from the excited gossip buzzing about her ears that they were led by her own brother, who was a complete stranger to her.

Prince Alchfrid was the heir of Cumbria, in right of his mother, the last of the native line. His father, King Oswy of Bernicia, always under attack from Mercia, had no mind to be threatened by rebellions and resentments in the powerful Welsh kingdom on his western flank. He had left his queen to deal with her own people. His son had been fostered among them in the household of his Horse-Thane, a nobleman of Welsh stock. All the boy's friends were sons of Cumbrian lords.

Alchflaed, who was a year older, had been brought up from birth in her aunt's convent in the north of Bernicia. She had seen her mother every time Queen Riemmelth had come to Bebbanburh; she had glimpsed her father once, her brother never.

The presence of this unseen brother was with Alchflaed all the time she worked among the stricken farm-folk. In kindness to them she hid her eagerness to be off and meet him, though every minute seemed an age. She kept her face calm and cheerful in spite of the things she was having to see and smell and touch. Part of her brain was busy with her own concerns, though, all the while her hands were trying to clean and soothe burned skin, bind torn flesh, splint broken bones and shift crushed bodies so that they could lie with a little more ease.

22

From time to time she had a quiet pause, after she had cautiously measured a draught of poppy-juice or henbane to deaden someone's agony and was waiting till the sufferer slept. Then she forced the eyes of her mind to look steadily at the strange vision that had come to her in her mother's room. She tried to understand it. Nothing of the kind had ever happened to her before: she was neither moon-touched nor gifted with the second sight.

Strangely, though she was convent-bred, she never thought for a moment of witchcraft or the devil, though these figured luridly in the homilies and warnings that had been poured into her ears during her education. As she remembered what she had seen, there was nothing ugly or frightening in it. The Welsh stories her mother had told her were full of haunted mounds that changed into enchanted palaces or opened gates into the Land of Youth.

It quite slipped her mind that the vision had nearly tempted her through the window to her death on the flagstones below and had certainly held her spellbound at the brink of capture. In fact, her only clear idea about the ending of her trance was that her brother had arrived with the relief force just as the hill came within reach of the window.

All the while I was watching that hill floating towards me, Alchfrid was riding nearer and nearer. And I was in Mother's favourite room—I thought I could hear her playing her harp—

Excitement rose in her; she felt sure she was on the track of the truth now.

It was a Sending. Mother brought me here, she wanted to give me a message. There's something I have to do. This was all meant to happen—even the Mercians were part of it. If they hadn't attacked Bebbanburh, I'd have left a week ago and Alchfrid wouldn't have come at all. We were meant to meet—we've lived all this while with the width of Britain between us, but now we're together—it's our fate—

She went cold, even under the glaring afternoon sun, as if a ghost had stepped out of its gravemound and laid a hand on her breast.

We two are the only ones with her blood in us. We're her life now—and the life of her House, that was ruling in Britain before the Romans came. And Alchfrid's the heir—if he dies without a son the House dies with him—except for me—

Suddenly everything whirled round her. She had to shut her eyes and grip the edge of her stool while she willed herself not to faint.

23

*That's what happened to Mother! Her brother was killled in a
border raid and she was left all alone with a kingdom to keep.
She's trying to tell me it mustn't happen again. I must step into her
empty place by his side—be another pair of eyes and ears for
him—watch and listen for any sign of danger or treachery that he
might miss by himself—if need be, take the blow that was aimed
at him on my own body. That's why she brought me here—to
carry on her work for her—to guard our House and her son—so
she can rest in peace—*

Still, she made herself finish the work in hand first. It did not
keep her long. The country folk had been picking up their
bruised bodies and gathering their battered household goods
with their usual grim patience. Alchflaed tied the last strip of
bandage, straightened her aching back and drew a deep breath.
Then she went racing up to the King's hall to meet her brother,
ready for whatever their linked fates would bring her.

Alchfrid's Cumbrian horsemen had a Roman look about them
that set them apart among the Bernicians. They were Roman in
the uniform crimson of their cloaks, Roman in the Chi-Rho
emblazoned on their shields and most Roman in the veiled contempt with which they were taking in their surroundings. This
contempt was felt most strongly by Prince Alchfrid himself,
though he was hiding it best, together with the anger that was
building up inside him.

He was angry that he had been too late to catch the Mercians.
He was angry that he and his men had been forced to waste so
much time putting out fires and rounding up cattle instead of
getting after the raiders. Alchfrid was very young. This was his
first campaign; he had dreamed of crowning it with glory by
killing Penda. Bebbanburh angered him; it had not conducted its
defence with the neatness and order he was used to in his weapon-
drill. The Bernician stronghold, littered and reeking of smoke,
full of grimy, dishevelled people rushing about and shouting,
manifested a squalor and lack of control that were truly barbarian. When a strange girl dashed up to him, her crumpled gown
hitched to her knees, sleeves rolled back over blood-splashed
arms, hair carelessly knotted up under a grubby veil, and hurled
herself into his arms calling him 'brother', he nearly forgot himself and showed temper.

'Good God! Are you—you're never my sister Alchflaed? What
are you doing here?'

He looked at her in horror. 'You should have known better than to run out into the fighting—you could have been hurt. You should have stayed quietly in the women's bower, however frightened you were, and set a good example to the rest.'

Alchflaed was gazing eagerly at her brother, hardly taking in what he said, only that he was showing concern for her. He was a young man to delight any sister's eye, very tall and finely made, with the jut-nosed, long-jawed Northumbrian face and hair so fair that it gleamed silver against his tan. He was like a prince out of one of the old hero-tales, Beowulf or Sigemund; but what nearly stopped her heart for a moment were her mother's eyes looking at her out of his face. No one else had eyes like Riemmelth's: deep blue and radiant as a summer evening sky, fringed with long black lashes. Thinking of those eyes dulled and shut for ever, with the coffin lid and the earth above them, was one of the lasting sorrows that had come upon her with her mother's death last year. Seeing them alive again was too great a joy; she leaned against Alchfrid, shaking with sobs.

'Don't cry, the danger's past. Go and get a clean gown from the Dish-Thane's wife, it looks so bad to the men for you to be running about in this state. She should have seen to you; I can't be watching over everybody in this place.'

He sounded impatient but patted her shoulder. 'We'll talk after supper—I must go now and try to bring Penda to bay.' His voice was bitter. 'It's almost hopeless. I've been delayed too long—I should have set out days ago, only Father—' He shut his mouth abruptly on what he had been going to say.

Alchflaed remembered her mission. She caught at his arm.

'You mustn't leave me behind—there's danger—'

'There's not the slightest danger to you now. Do you think I'd leave you if there were? You're far too valuable as a hostage for me to risk your capture. Now, go back to the women, there's a good girl, and don't hinder me.'

He turned away. She felt frantic, thinking of that young king, her uncle who had died before she was born, setting off light-heartedly to trounce a band of cattle-raiders and taking a chance arrow in his throat. She tightened her grip on his arm.

'No! Listen to me! We've got to keep together—'

'For shame! You're not a baby to be whimpering and clutching at its nurse's skirts every time she walks away! And I'm certainly not your nurse, to stay petting you while our enemies go where they like and do what they like in our land. Remember the stock you come from and try to act worthy of it!'

Alchflaed was beginning to feel that sensation of helpless futility that swamps people when they try to explain some dream or omen they know is important, to be met by blank stares or contemptuous boredom, and they sound like halfwits, even in their own ears. She struggled to sound calm and reasonable.

'I do remember it. That's what I'm trying to tell you. I won't hold you back from your work, I want to share it with you. I'm your sister—I want to help you, to ride by your side and—'

'Help me? What help could you possibly be, a girl? What help do you think you're being now, wasting my time with this unseemly nonsense? Remember what St. Paul wrote: *"Docere autem mulieri non permitto neque dominare in virum."* That means,' he condescended to her female ignorance, 'I forbid a woman to teach or to bear rule over a man.'

'Thank you, brother, I can read Latin. Our aunt, the Abbess, taught me.' Alchflaed was as shocked and angry as if he had spat on her. 'Did you throw that text in our mother's face while she was guarding your kingdom for you—and likely wearing herself to death to do it?'

It was her brother's turn to be shocked. His mouth was tight with temper; for a moment he could not speak. Some words Alchflaed had heard lately sprang to her lips; they had sounded in her ears during her vision.

'Our mother was carrying me in the womb, remember, when she challenged Penda sword to sword and fought her way out with all Gefrin burning round her. And if she could ride and fight as a waelcyrige why shouldn't—'

'Don't you dare use a word like that about our mother! Have you no respect for her memory?'

Alchflaed was appalled. The eyes that were so like her mother's were now looking at her with disgust as well as anger. What demon had set her quarrelling with her brother within minutes of their first meeting? With a pang of contrition she remembered her aunt Ebbe gently rebuking her for her pride in her sharp wits, warning her that if she let her quick tongue outrun her prudence it could rush her to destruction one day. Now it seemed to have brought her to the cliff's edge, wrestling with her brother. If they lost their balance they would be over. She withdrew from the brink.

'We're at cross-purposes, my dear.' She smiled at him. 'As you

26

say, there's no time to linger in chat. Believe me, I've no wish to insult our mother's memory, or hold you from your duty. God be with you and keep you safe—come back and talk to me when you can.'

She took his hand, touched it gently to her lips, then hurried away. Alchfrid found this sudden change as alarming as her previous unruliness. It made him suspicious. When he was at last ready to start on the track of the raiders—when he had seen his war-band's precious horses rubbed down and fed, got fresh mounts, talked over the lie of the land, chosen a group of Bernician warriors to come with him as guides, made sure that the walls and gate would be well guarded in his absence—he went to check what she was doing.

He found her, neat and seemly in a gown she had borrowed from Edyth, busy with some of the maids in a store hut near one of the weaving-sheds. They were sorting and counting out clean linen: fresh garments and new bedding for the Cumbrians. This was a good, womanly task; he gave her a word of praise and kissed her. She took it meekly, wished him Godspeed again and went on with her sorting. When enough time had passed for her brother to be well out of the fortress, she sorted herself a shirt and breeches and took them away with her, telling the maids to keep at their work.

Then she went to the weapon-store by the forge and fetched a spear. The smith thought it was an odd task for a maiden to be running errands for the warriors—but then, Bebbanburh was in a turmoil that day, everyone was putting a hand to the nearest job.

Alchflaed withdrew to the sollar in the Queen's hall and changed her clothes. Taking the spear, she went to the stables, chose a pony, helped herself to a coil of rope, whistled to a couple of wolfhounds to come with her. Then she rode quietly past the gate-guards with a nod and a smile as if this were something she did every day, and set off to follow her brother—and her fate.

The gate-guards looked at each other.

'Do you think we should stop her? There might be danger—'

'What danger? The Mercians have been running for two hours and more. They're all well away, and none of our own folk would dare to hurt her.'

'And as for stopping her, she's Queen Riemmelth's daughter— and not even Penda could stop that one!'

CHAPTER
3

About a mile inland there was a jagged outcrop of rocks, like splinters from the great cliff at Bebbanburh. Tucked into a sheltered hollow on top was a shepherd's hut, only a summer bothy, a frail circle of wattles thatched with fern. It had not been dismantled by the raiders; even if they had seen it, which was unlikely, there was not enough kindling in it to make it worth carrying down to the siege.

A warrior was standing just inside the hut behind the edge of the doorway—a heavy-boned, blunt-featured man with wiry light-brown hair. He was keeping as wide a watch as he could without showing himself, glaring from side to side across the hollow—westwards, where he could see the topmost boughs of a wood growing down the slope—eastwards, where a crack in the rim of rocks showed Bebbanburh on the horizon, with a haze of smoke still drifting round it against the hard-blue sky and sea. There was not a sound near at hand but the rush of wind through the branches; even the wood-birds were silent in the afternoon heat. Only from the east at times came a faint mewing of gulls.

A hoarse voice called from inside the hut, 'Is Meilyr coming back?'

The watcher turned, making a sign for quiet. A boy was sitting propped against the far side of the hut, one leg curled under him, the other stiff and roughly splinted to a lath with strips of rag. He was trying his best to look alert and ready for action, but his face was flushed and his eyes bright with the onset of fever.

'Hush, Edric, keep your voice down! No, there's no sign of him.'

He had only shifted his glance a second from the empty hill slope when someone stepped through the doorway behind him. The warrior swung round, reaching for his sword-hilt, then checked. The newcomer, who was as dark as a shadow and moved like one, was carrying a helmet full of water. He gave it to Edric, who drank greedily though the water was tepid and slightly greasy from the sweaty leather lining. Then he handed it to his companion, who said grudgingly, 'You took your time, Meilyr.'

'I followed the streamlet down to the river at the foot of the rocks. It must flow out into the bay past that mill we took to pieces yesterday.'

Meilyr had gone back to the doorway. He glanced for a second at Bebbanburh, then away to the west where the dome of the Cheviot showed ghostlike in the heat haze behind the moors.

'Ashferth, we're too near Bebbanburh for comfort. I went along that river to see what the going's like. It's cut a deep bed into soft earth. The banks are high and overgrown with trees. If we wade upstream, we'll come out on to the high moors as if we'd walked through a cave—we won't leave sight or scent for the Bernicians to come after us.'

Ashferth scowled. 'And what about my brother? He's in no case to go wading up rivers.'

'You go, Ashferth,' said the boy, eagerly. 'I'll take my own chance, I won't spoil anyone else's. I can hold the Bernicians off for a bit, give you and Meilyr a start.' He laughed. 'If I can't make a last stand, I can manage a last sit!'

Edric was thirteen; he had only just taken man's weapons and was playing the battle-hardened hero as best he could, mocking his own death like the warriors in the poems.

'Stop talking rubbish! D'you think I'd ever leave you to save my skin?' Ashferth glowered at Meilyr as if he had suggested it.

'I'm not asking you to leave him—what do you take me for? We won't be running a race, he's light enough for you to take on your back till I can steal a pony for him from one of the hill farms. I'll guide you; I'll hunt food for you—and when we get over the Cumbrian border I'll do the talking for you. Trust me to get us all safe home to Powys, and then the two of you can cross straight back into Mercia.'

Ashferth looked unconvinced.

'There's no cover up on the moors, we'd be like flies walking on a trestle-board.'

'No cover! There's cover in every gully, in every clump of heather and fern! There's cover in the shadow thrown by every rock. If you're with me, I can place you so the whole Bernician war-host could ride past within a hand's touch of where we're lying and never know we're there. You'll see!'

Meilyr was laughing. He might have been offering them a day's sport, but his dark eyes were uneasy as he watched the rim of the dell. He was a hunter: long days and nights in the wild had made him close kin to the creatures he loved and killed. His senses were as fine as theirs; the land spoke to him in the lightest scent of the breeze, the touch of air on his skin, the slant of grasses, the changing feel of earth and rock under his feet. Now, every nerve in his body was saying, *Get out. Enemies coming close. Get away before the trap closes.*

Ashferth's heavy face was stubborn.

'We couldn't do anything against the Bernicians out in the open, not even kill one of them. They'd spear or stone us down from a distance. We could make a good last stand here if they find us—they can only come through the doorway one at a time and stooping.'

Meilyr's patience was fraying to rags. When the joy of battle was on him he would fight, as Ashferth himself had said approvingly, like one of Woden's own, though he was a Welshman and a Christian. But to let himself be trapped in this little wicker cage when he could be free, matching his wits, his strength and his speed against all comers, with every hill, tree and stream in Bernicia as his ally—that was idiocy, not courage.

'A last stand! That's the one and only idea you English have ever had in your thick skulls about how to fight a battle—dig your heels into the ground like a badly-broken donkey and stay there till you're killed.'

'Do we so? Well, that's one charge we can't throw back at the Welsh—your heels move even faster than your tongues when you're getting off a battlefield!'

Ashferth guffawed at his own ready wit; Edric laughed with him.

Meilyr would have stayed with them, fought beside them and likely died with them if they had been trapped, since Ashferth—all honour to him—wouldn't leave his brother. But this stupid, undeserved insult broke his brittle temper. He snatched up his gear and whirled out of the hut. Ashferth blinked; then called him and lumbered to the doorway. The hollow was empty; there was not a sound or a stir but the rush of wind through the branches.

Meilyr whisked down the rocky slope like a fox; then paused on the brink of the little river he had found. To his left, it would lead him upstream, out on to the moors. To his right, it ran down towards the sea. He pictured the coast as he had watched it from Bebbanburh during the siege, as it could be glimpsed from the hut among the crags: a wide expanse of sand at low tide and, on the horizon a few miles to the north, a dot of rock at the seaward end of a low ridge of dunes. This, he had learned, was the island of the

Lindesfaran, the Bernicians' holy island. Bishop Aidan's monastery was there.

He decided that now he was unburdened of two heathen Mercian allies, he would begin his journey homeward by claiming a meal and a bed from his fellow Christians.

He stepped into the water and began to wade steadily downstream. The riverbed was reddish-brown sandy mud, where his feet sank but not so deeply as to clog his steps. In places, there were outcrops of rock; the chattering of the current against them, with the rustling of the wind in the reeds and overhanging branches, covered the sounds he made. After about a hundred yards he sat down on a broad slab of stone and unlaced his mail-shirt. He unfastened his scabbard before buckling his belt again over his leather jerkin, rolling the sheathed sword in the discarded byrnie. He pushed the bundle into a hollow down by the waterline under an arching bank, plastered it over thickly with mud, then washed his hands. The armour was well-made and very costly, but he could afford more if he ever reached his home. Neither mail-shirt nor sword would help him on his way there. They showed him to be a warrior and a nobleman. In Bernicia, where every thane would be known by name and probably by sight, that would mark him at once as an enemy. He couldn't take on the whole Bernician war-host single-handed, or even a mob of stone-throwing Bernician peasants, who would just batter him to death from a safe distance. He kept his hunting-knife; but his best weapons were in his quick wits and his plausible tongue—and in the three-cornered otterskin bag which he carried as carefully as a baby, guarding it from knocks and setting it down gently.

Having changed himself from a warrior to a wanderer, which he did without nervous haste or fumbling, Meilyr settled the hilt of his knife easy to hand, picked up his precious otterskin bag and set off again downstream.

Some ten minutes after Meilyr left the hut, its owners arrived back in a vile temper. They had spent the last week under the burning sun and the spears and whips of the Mercians, breaking down farms and hauling the timbers up the crag. They had eaten scanty food while the Mercians slaughtered and feasted on their stock. They had nearly been trampled to death in the Mercian flight and had been rounded up by Alchfrid's men to help in the clearing of Bebbanburh. Finally turned loose, they were combing the rocky ground to see if any of their flock had scattered and survived. They were in a mood to enjoy murder, preferably a wounded and helpless Mercian, and at last their luck had turned.

The Mercians got ready for their last stand; Ashferth inside the doorway, Edric propped against the wall to keep his brother's back if anyone came through the roof. However, the Bernician churls had been taught one useful lesson by their Mercian masters and had learned it thoroughly. They collected dry fern and brushwood, piling it into a circle round the hut, out of range of Ashferth's spear. He watched them helplessly—he couldn't come out after them and leave Edric open to attack; he couldn't charge out fast enough to break past them carrying Edric on his back.

When the circle was high enough, they fired it; the easterly wind, still blowing a gale, soon took sparks to the thatch and wattles, which flamed up at once. Not long afterwards, a blackened and smouldering figure leaped in the doorspace, shrieking, but fell backwards inside. The churls settled down happily to watch the meat roasting, but their lurcher bitch was uneasy. She kept making runs towards the slope where a thread of a streamlet trickled down to the burn, then coming back to whine at them.

Meilyr and the river moved among the last trees, past the ruins of the mill and out on to the shore. The river went on; Meilyr stopped, cursing. There was a bay about a mile-and-a-half long between him and the open sands; the ebbing tide had left an expanse of mud-flats through which the river twisted, to be met by another stream coming from the farther side. It looked just the place to be sucked under. He'd be lucky if he only sank to his knees, trapped like a fly in honey. He had no idea how deep the joined rivers were; likely too deep and treacherous for wading across, too shallow to swim.

Far out, the sand-bar stretched beautifully firm and gold, swinging north towards the refuge of Holy Island. He'd heard tell that you could walk over at low tide. There was nothing for it but to go round his side of the bay until he reached the sand-bar. This meant skirting the edge of the dunes above the mud-flats, a slow and wearisome journey as his feet sank in the loose sand.

It took longer than he thought. When he came on a coble drawn up in the shelter of the dunes and sat down in the boat's shade to rest, he was surprised to see how far he had come from the trees, though the sand-bar seemed as far away as ever. The bay was curving south, away from the island; the river swung round with it. He realised that every step was taking him back along the coast to Bebbanburh.

Why not? he thought. He could lie up among the dunes for the rest of the daylight. He wouldn't go thirsty; there was a freshet close by trickling out of the sandhills towards the river. Then he'd work his way down the coast after dark past Bebbanburh. He could move like a night-shadow, defy any guard or fisher to see or hear him. Next day, he'd come up innocently from the south as a travelling harper following the royal warband and claim the minstrel's privilege of honourable welcome and safe-conduct wherever he went.

Meilyr's eyes were gleaming at the pleasure he foresaw—to make the Bernicians entertain him as a valued guest in the very fortress where he'd cut down their gate-keeper. Then, too, he could take a closer look at that holy girl he'd nearly taken, see if he couldn't charm some life into that blank face. There were more ways—much more amusing ways—of capturing a woman than by the sword and the rope. He lingered on that thought, smiling. To spirit her off single-handed with her own goodwill—and she a novice—under the eyes and noses of the royal court of Bernicia, and then play hide-and-seek with the hunters over the Cheviots and down the Cumbrian border to Powys, with no weapons but a quick brain, a ready tongue and a hand skilled on the harp-strings. What an exploit—and what a jest against the English!

He had already begun to word a satire about it in his mind, when the sound of hoofbeats wiped the smile off his face. They were coming near, along the beach from the south, rounding the point into his bay. Then a gull skimmed into sight, flying low out to sea with a wolf-hound in pursuit along the shallow water. Meilyr dived into the coble, praying that the fishy stink there would smother his own scent if the hound came towards him.

In the flare of tempers when she met her brother, Alchflaed had pictured herself hunting down fugitives at his side, shielding him when the Mercians turned at bay, taking a blow that could have killed him on her own body, seeing her mother come smiling to greet her as she died.

This beautiful and moving vision melted like morning mist soon after she passed the gate, at the first sight of the Mercian corpses. The garrison had taken up their own dead for Christian burial; they had thrown their enemies down the crags. The gulls and crows had returned and were already quarrelling over shares at the tops of their voices.

Alchflaed comforted herself with the thought that the Mercians had a long start; scattered in the wilds of Bernicia they were as safe from her brother as he was from them. In the confusion of hoofmarks going in all directions she had no idea which way to ride after him. While she paused, the sea and wind called to her. She turned her pony beyond the heugh and went out on to the beach to the north of the rocks.

Beyond the tide-line the sands were firm for a gallop. For a while she forgot everything in the sheer joy of free movement after being cooped up so long—the clean scents, the sparkle on the waves, the sea-wind tugging her hair. In spite of the wind it was still cruelly hot; the spearman's thick woollen shirt and felted breeches were harsh and sweaty on her skin; her arm was aching with the weight of the spear. Unlike her mother, she had no idea how to carry it,much less wield it. She'd make a poor showing as a warrior.

She drove the useless weapon point down into the sand, hobbled her pony and left him to drink from a nearby freshet and nibble if he chose at the coarse grass among the dunes. Then she thankfully kicked her boots away, tore off her burdensome clothes and dashed into the sea.

First she swam straight out, charging the breakers that the east wind was rolling down the long sands, while the grime, stink and disgust of the siege were washed out of her. When she began to tire of the buffeting, she came back to the shallows, trod carelessly on a stone, hopped a one-legged jig with the agony, then turned upside-down and walked on her hands. She had once seen a tumbler do that at a cattle-fair and mimicked him afterwards to the joy of her foster-brothers and sisters, the ploughman's family at the convent grange.

Finding that she had not lost the knack, she went on to back-flips and somersaults, and finally set off bowling over and over through the shallow foam, her arms and legs like the spokes of a wheel tossing up a rim of sparkling drops. The hounds caught her mood and forgot their dignity, racing round in ever-widening circles, charging each other in the shoulders like puppies.

The Welshman had risen to his knees in the coble. He was lost to his danger, because for the moment he had lost himself. Ever since his childhood had ended, he had been siezed from time to time by a strange power—whether it was a spell or a curse he did not know, but only that it would kill him one day when it came upon him in a battle or at the moment when a boar charged. It

34

broke him to pieces like a crock smashed on a flagstone and each piece was a different man fighting to go his own way, with the real Meilyr lost and helpless. Now, while that carefree tumbler spun like the wheel of fortune between the elements of earth, air, water and fire, there was one man who simply wanted to get her down and get into her. This man was eager to wind his arms round that supple waist, set those nimble legs dancing to his tune, cup his hands round the firm curves of her breasts and haunches, let the scent and touch of newly washed skin whet an appetite that had been dulled in the past weeks on dirty, terrified peasant girls.

But while his body warmed and stirred pleasantly with lust, someone else was busy weaving a net of jewelled words to catch and hold her for ever inside that minute—*white foam-flower of Llyr's meadow—swoop of gull's wing on the wave—apple-branch in April rain*—Another person, the boy he'd been only a while ago, would have just liked to play with her, throw sticks for the hounds, dare her to a swimming race, see if he could pick up those tumbler's tricks, forget hatred, revenge and death.

One of the hounds, racing round to catch the other, passed behind the coble, caught his scent, then saw him and leapt towards him, barking a challenge. The other joined him and they held Meilyr at bay, though their training kept them from savaging a human unless attacked or given the order by their master. Meilyr made himself rock-still, knowing that his knife would be useless against their fangs and claws with the sheer weight they could launch against him from their gathered thigh muscles if they sensed the slightest threat or panic.

The girl glanced round when she heard them give tongue, then fled for her heap of clothes, threw her shirt on, buckled the belt round it, pushed her feet into her boots and hurried up to the coble with her breeches in one hand and her spear in the other. The inept way she carried it told Meilyr that here was no English waelcyrige. He could have mastered her even without his knife— if it hadn't been for those hounds. When she came near enough for him to see that her face was as enticing as her body, he cursed his luck to die without having her first. Knowing what he'd just seen, she'd set her hounds to savage him at once, and only finish him with her spear if she felt a touch of pity.

Even in these last moments, the wordsmith inside his mind was asking why bards only praised tresses black as a raven's wing or yellow as gorse, in endless repetition, but never gave a line to the autumn wealth of brown. This girl's mass of waves and curls had the darkness of oak woods but wherever the sun touched its ripples, he could see the varied coppers and golds of beech and bracken, even the paler glint of willows. Her eyes, large and wideset, fringed with long lashes, were dark hazel with greenish-gold flecks like dapples of light on forest pools. She was rosy from her play on the beach. If this was death, it had turned a warm and lovely face to him for his last sight on earth.

Alchflaed watched the stranger warily, trying to make out what he was. His clothes—thick, well-woven shirt and breeches, leather jerkin, boots of hide—were much like her own. He could have been a warrior out of armour, a hunter, a well-to-do farmer. He could have been one of the Bebbanburh household; she'd had no time to meet them all while they were holding off the Mercians—but then, why should he hide and why didn't the hounds know him?

On the other hand, he didn't look in the least how she had pictured a Mercian fugitive. He had no armour (the rust marks on his jerkin meant nothing to her), nor weapons beyond the hunting-knife that every freeman carried. He was not blood-stained or in tatters; above all he showed no signs of weariness or terror. True, he was wisely keeping still, crouched against the side of the coble under the eyes of the hounds, but this did not suggest either cowardice or servility. It was more like the deceptive quietness of a wild cat, choosing its moment to strike.

His face was as still as his limbs, yet it too had a sense of cat-speed and savagery from slanting brows and keenly-cut nose and lips. He was very dark, with thick curly hair black as Deiran jet and eyes of such deep brown that in the shadow they seemed to be all pupil. He was young, about Alchfrid's age; the fine shading of black on his upper lip and jawbone did not soften their lines, only added to his look of wildness.

The silence stretched as long as the shore; the stranger had a cat's patience. Alchflaed, emboldened by her hounds and spear, gave the first challenge.

'What are you doing here?'

Meilyr fought back the answer 'Enjoying your performance' and murmured respectfully, 'Hiding, lady. This part of the world hasn't been healthy for strangers these days.'

He had learned English from Mercians; now he deliberately stressed his British accent to hide the Mercian tones. There were many folk of the old race in Northumbria, from Elmet to Eidyn.

All the way on Penda's march north he'd heard echoes of the British tongue in the garbled names of places—Deorwent, Cetreht, Ros Low—calling up the ghosts of his people's lost kingdoms in the east. To the Bernicians, a Briton need not be an enemy to be speared or savaged by hounds as soon as he opened his mouth.

'Who are you?'

Meilyr had already decided against being a local hill-shepherd of British stock, who had been forced to haul timber for the Mercians. A hard-riding thane's daughter—her father must be powerful, those hounds were worth a fortune and there was gold on one of her fingers—she'd know every cottar by sight and name for miles around. He would be a Briton from Elmet, a Christian seized for service to the heathen horde, now escaped and making for refuge on Holy Island. He was about to begin a heart-rending tale when he saw her looking at his hands. Fine long-fingered hands that had never done serf's work. Before he could invent a revised version, she saw his otterskin bag and told him what to say.

'Why, you're a harper!'

To his amazement, she spoke in British, with a true accent and tone. She sounded as joyful as if she had just met a long-lost friend.

'My mother used to keep her harp in a bag like that—you must be one of her people. I could hear it in your voice even when you were talking English—she was a Cumbrian too!'

'Was she indeed?'

Meilyr's voice and eyes were alert, a hunter's who sees his prey coming close, unsuspecting. He was thinking, *You silly little bitch, teaching a stranger what he needs to know to cheat you.*

For the second time that day, Alchflaed was feeling that she had come near to her living mother. Alchfrid had Riemmelth's eyes, though the spirit that looked out of them seemed cold and alien. This stranger had the tones of her voice, the music in her fingers. There was something of her too in his night-black hair and unEnglish cast of features.

'True, lady, I come from west over the hills. I'd heard tell that King Oswy still welcomes our harpers for the sake of his queen, so I meant to visit Bebbanburh and offer my skills. But I found that the fort was under attack so I lay low. Your Bernicians will be spearing every stranger at first sight.'

Alchflaed smiled at him reassuringly. Meilyr wondered again why she looked at him as if they'd known each other for years, but judged that it was now time to give her a charming smile in return. In that second of silence they could hear shouts and tearing branches among the trees at the head of the bay.

A lurcher dashed out in the open, barking excitedly, circled, sniffing, then found Meilyr's track in the sand. She made a run at the coble but was faced by the hounds, haughty nobles, stiff-legged and bristling at the low-born intruder. She crouched, dragging her belly. Her masters came crashing out on to the beach after her, a group of churls to guess from their rough clothes and shaggy, matted hair. Their leader was a bulky, thick-shouldered fellow with a sullen, heavy-browed face; he was followed by two slighter men and a boy. They were armed with iron-shod shepherds' crooks and had knives or axes in their belts. The leader also had a jewel-hilted sword which he must have taken from a nobleman's corpse.

As they came out into the open, Alchflaed jumped to perch on the side of the coble, blocking Meilyr from their sight. He was crouching behind her at the bottom of the boat, his knife drawn, ready to spring out fighting at her side or put the blade to her back and use her as a hostage if she betrayed him.

Alchflaed sat calmly, watching them come, propping herself with her arm round her spear, resting her cheek against the shaft. The hounds showed their teeth, their hackles rising. The churls stopped at a wary distance. Once again Alchflaed gave the challenge.

'Who are you? Where do you come from, and what are you doing here?'

They were uncertain how to treat her, high-born and self-assured, but her sex and her scanty clothes emboldened them.

'We could ask the same of you, girl,' said the leader. 'Perhaps you'd like us to help you.'

The other men snickered. The boy let his glance run up her bare legs to the hem of her shirt, making clear that his mind was going further. Alchflaed's tone and expression did not change.

'I'm the King's daughter, Princess Alchflaed. I've come from Bebbanburh yonder,' she nodded towards the headland, 'to take the air and bathe after the siege.'

As she spoke her name, Meilyr caught his breath. Then, very stealthily, he lifted his knife and cut off one of the long tresses hanging down her back.

The hunters looked abashed and their leader's tone was slightly more respectful.

38

'You shouldn't be here alone, lady, with the Mercians on the loose.'

'Alone? With the royal household a few score yards away, to say nothing of Prince Alchfrid's horsemen! And the Mercians took flight hours ago.'

'Not all of them. We found two holed up in our bothy on the heugh.' He pointed to the southwest, where smoke was rising among the rocks. 'We burned it over their heads, but the bitch picked up a scent coming away across the hill. We lost it at the river, but we came downstream on the chance and sure enough, she found the track in the sands coming this way.'

'She found mine. I told you, I bathed. There was salt in my hair, I went up to wash it in the river.'

'Well, anyway, we'll take a look round while we're here.'

'There's nobody else on this beach. Do you think I'd bathe without making sure I had the place to myself? If anyone got out of your hut, he followed the river upstream on to the moors if he had any sense—that's the way the rest of them went. You'd better get back up there before you lose your chance of catching him. I'm going to bathe again while the sun's still up.'

The leader held to his purpose like a mastiff.

'He could be hiding among the dunes, lady, or lying low in one of the fishers' cobles. What would the prince say if we let one of Penda's rats give us the slip when we had him cornered?'

'What will the prince say when I tell him you found me undressed and wouldn't go when I told you? He'll have you flayed.'

The other men looked alarmed and inclined to back off; the leader stood his ground.

'I'll answer to the prince,' he told them, ignoring Alchflaed. 'He knows enough to heed a man's word over a woman's whim.'

'Oh, he knows more than that!' Alchflaed's anger blazed. Her womanhood had been belittled once today by her own brother; she wouldn't take it from churls. 'Let me tell you what he knows. He can read and write—he knows book-Latin, *gramarye*—and so do I.'

She lowered her voice to a hissing whisper. 'There's a book of shape-shifting runes, I've held it in my hands.' She curved her fingers into claws. 'I know what it teaches.' She smiled. 'There was a man went hunting with his dogs—like you today. He was thirsty, he heard running water among the trees,' she glanced at the river flowing out into the bay, 'and went to drink. And there,

39

where the sunlight streamed down through the leaves, he saw the Queen of the Woods, the Lady herself, bathing with the water drops like crystals on her breasts and thighs and her hair like a golden waterfall.'

She paused to let the the picture take shape behind their eyes.

'If he had bowed and passed on, thanking her in his heart for the joy of her beauty, her blessing would have been on him for the rest of his days. But he stayed to gape, gloating over her nakedness as if she were a slave in a trader's booth.'

She stared straight at the boy with cold menace; he went red and tried to look away, but she would not let him escape her eyes.

'The Lady saw him. She stooped and took a handful of water and threw it in his face.'

Alchflaed threw an invisible handful at her listeners, who blinked and ducked.

'For a second he was blinded and she vanished. He felt a terrible pain and weight on his head—he tossed in agony as branches of bone sprouted from his skull. He tried to lift his hands to his head but they dragged to the ground—they weren't hands any more, they were hoofs. He opened his mouth to cry out, to pray for mercy, but no words came—only the belling of a stag. But his cries were answered. The dogs came running, his faithful companions that he'd brought up from puppies and trained to pull down game for him. How their eyes glared at him, how the slaver dripped from their fangs as they rushed at him. He turned to flee, but their teeth were already sinking into his flank. They dragged him down, they tore his throat while he was still trying to call their names, they crunched his bones, bolted bloody gobbets of his flesh while his limbs still twitched with life—'

Alchflaed was watching it happen, staring at it in the space between the churls, forcing them to watch it as well. One of the men put his hand to his head as if feeling for antlers. The bitch, scenting terror, raised her muzzle with a mournful howl. The hounds lifted their lips and snarled. The boy sobbed. She made her voice deadly sweet.

'We know all about this, my brother and I. What do you think we could do to you for spying on me when I came to bathe?'

They were broken now and abject.

'Forgive me, lady—'

'It wasn't my idea—'

'We meant no harm—'

Suddenly, she was smiling and gracious.

'I know that. It's because you meant no harm—you were only trying to protect me—that I'm going to spare you and see you safe. Go home now. I'll make sure the prince knows about your faithfulness and rewards you. You needn't be afraid to leave me alone, I know how to guard myself. And whatever you do, *don't* look back, even when you think you're hidden by the trees. The ones I can summon don't need eyes or noses to follow a trail.'

The churls had no thought of looking back. They could not get out of sight quickly enough for their peace of mind. Alchflaed clicked her fingers to the hounds, who stalked after them to the head of the bay and sat down by the path through the trees. Only when the intruders had been out of sight for some time did she turn back to the enemy she had saved by her desperate mummery— why? Because he spoke her mother's tongue, had the same harper's hands, made her feel for a moment that Riemmelth could come back to her from the grave?

Meilyr had slithered to the bottom of the coble. He was lying comfortably at full length, with his head pillowed on his left arm. The lock of her hair was out of sight under his jerkin; he was playing with his knife.

'You told that very well.' She might have been some travelling story-teller brought in to amuse a chief after a feast. 'You could make a good living going round cattle-fairs.'

He meant it as an insult to one of her rank, to show what he thought of English royalty, but she only smiled.

'By the way, is Prince Alchfrid really a master of sorcery and shape-shifting?'

'Heavens, no!' Picturing the horror her orthodox brother would feel if he knew the character she had given him, she chuckled, and then felt guilty. 'But he can read and write, so can I—that's sorcery, to churls. And as for the book on shape-shifting, I'm ready to wager he construed his first Latin out of the *Metamorphoses*. Every schoolchild does, that's where I got the story. And you're not a Mercian and you're not on the beach, so what I told them was mostly the truth.'

'Like all the best lies.'

Suddenly he sprang up and vaulted out of the boat as light-footed as a cat and put the tip of his knife blade under her jawbone.

'Well, as neither of you is a magician, and your hounds are at the other end of the beach and not looking at us, there's nothing to stop me quietly slitting your throat and making off with your spear.'

She laughed at him over the blade.

41

'Nothing at all. But the hounds can run much faster than you as they follow your scent. And when they catch you, one won't sit and wait while you spear the other. Anyway, unless you go past them you can only go back to Bebbanburh or out to sea.'

'I can go to Holy Island.'

'You can't, not from the south. Did you think you could just walk along the sandbank? There's a channel nearly a mile across between the end of it and the island, and it's hellishly dangerous at any stage of the tide. And there are four more rivers coming out across the flats till you get to the ford.'

'So you think you've got me trapped.'

Meilyr's mouth was smiling as it had smiled when he fought his way out of Bebbanburh, but his eyes were not.

'By no means. See that twisted thorn tree by itself at the other side of the bay? The coast track starts there. It keeps to the landward side of the dunes and the sea-marsh, there are foot-bridges or stepping-stones across the rivers. It's easy to wade over Ros Low from here where sands are firm. You should get to the ford before the tide comes too far in—the monks have marked it with a row of stakes—but if there's any doubt you'd better wait overnight at their grange on this side.'

'Would the farmfolk take a stranger in? These are wild times in Bernicia.'

'Say you're a minstrel, come from Cumbria in the track of the prince's war-band. And here, take this—' she pulled off her ring and handed it to him '—everyone knows it, it's a royal jewel. You can say you had it as a reward for amusing the King's daughter. That's a good lie, too, as it's mostly truth.'

She was laughing again as she spoke, pleased at the neat way she had picked up and shared his jest against herself. Also, she had been lifted by a great wave of exultation that had swept her into making the gift. The ring had belonged to her mother; this meant more to her than the fact it was part of the royal treasure. Not all the gold in Britain could have bought it from her. Yet she suddenly felt sure that Riemmelth would have wanted her to give the ring, that her mother was very close to her at that moment— was herself drawing the ring from her finger and offering it to this harper of her own race. She laughed for joy.

Meilyr took the ring and slipped it easily on to one of his long fine fingers, bowing his head to show respectful gratitude. Inwardly, he was raging that he, a prince of the ancient race with bardic skills, should be treated like a tramping gleeman, while an

English pirate's daughter tossed him alms and jeered at him.

'Thank you, lady. I shall look for the chance to pay you back for this.' *And that's the truth too, my girl, as you're going to find out before long.*

He picked up his harp, turned and walked out towards the mouth of the bay. She watched him splash through the river, then make for the thorn tree. The sun was westering now; the Welshman's shadow stretched long and black towards the sea. Alone on the wide sands, he seemed small and defenceless against the whole of Bernicia, but he was walking easily as if he owned the land. She waited until he reached the track and vanished behind the dunes, but he did not once look back.

CHAPTER
4

The wind had dropped and the glow in the western sky was deepening from gold to flame when Alchflaed rode up the steep track to Bebbanburh. The gate-guards were waiting for her and called a groom to take her pony. Their eyes were curious but their manners respectful. She was told that the prince had already taken his place in the royal hall and the feasting had begun. He had given orders that food should be served to her in the Queen's bower and said that he would come to her after the meal.

She was glad; the long hot day had brought one shock after another, like a hail of blows. She could not have endured the hours of a royal feast: the great hall smoky with hearth fires and torches in spite of the heat; the smell and grease of roasted meat; the sticky sweetness of mead; the long speeches and shouted boasts. As she glided along in the shadows at the side of the courtyard, she saw that the hall's wide doors had been left open for air. She caught the notes of a harp and a voice chanting exultantly:

> 'Soon shall be the cry of ravens,
> hoar wolf's howl, hard wood-talk
> shield's answer to shaft.
> > Now shines the moon,

welkin-wanderer. The woes at hand
shall bring to the full this folk's hatred of us.'

The scop had chosen 'The Fight for Finn's Hall' as a fitting close
to the victorious defence of Bebbanburh.

Coming under the porch of the Queen's hall, Alchflaed felt a
slight lifting of her heart to think that at last she would have it to
herself for a while. When she had arrived—was it really a week
ago?—unheralded and unattended, she had had the Dish-
Thane's wife clucking over her, excusing herself needlessly for
being unready with her welcome, pestering her to choose some
food—would she wait for hot bacon pasties or take some slices of
roast beef cut from the joints in the warriors' hall, with a salad
from the herb garden—the maids were bringing some mead—or
would a convent-maiden drink milk? . . .

Alchflaed had tried in vain to stop her. That feat had been
accomplished by King Penda and his war-band, who arrived
while she was in full spate. But after that, while the siege went on,
there had been the girls chattering around her all day, whispering
and giggling in bed half the night.

Now perhaps in the silence she might hear an echo of her
mother's voice, the rustle of her gown.

She stepped into the spacious hall, unfurnished because
unused, but spotlessly clean. The high walls had been freshly
plastered white; they were bare, but the torch-brackets and
hooks for embroidered wall-hangings were burnished. The stone
flags had been washed but no rushes were spread. Trestles,
feasting-boards and benches were stacked neatly by the walls in
the side aisles. The double row of wooden pillars and the heavy
roof beams had their carvings newly touched with gilding. The
last rays of sunlight, coming from the unshuttered windows high
under the eaves, slanted across her way, picking out fantastic
shapes of monsters and heroes tracking each other through an
endless coiling of branches that were turning into snakes, or
snakes that were sprouting leaves.

Alchflaed walked up the hall to the dais, her feet tapping on the
bare floor, raising echoes that had never been heard when Queen
Riemmelth held court there. The echoes said nothing to
Alchflaed. She was in a rich woman's hall during the owner's
absence. It could have been any thane's dwelling, anywhere.

To the right of the dais, a door led through to the private
chamber, where a table had been set up and laid ready for her

44

meal. A girl from the kitchen waited to help her. Before she ate, she climbed the ladder-like stairs to the sollar to change out of her man's clothes. Her brother was probably angry with her for riding out without his knowledge; he had better find her meek and maidenly.

With the same idea, when she returned downstairs she forced herself to nibble at some oatcake and cheese, though her stomach knotted at the sight of meat. Though she had not eaten since morning she was now too tired to be hungry, but in courtesy she would have to offer the mead-cup to her brother and taste it with him. She did not want to disgrace herself finally by a fit of the giggles or vomiting.

When she heard steps in the hall, she sent the kitchen-girl away, saying that she would serve her brother herself. She was feeling more on edge than when she faced the Welshman or the churls.

Alchfrid was coming to the meeting in a good humour that had nothing to do with the beer and mead now flowing like a spring tide in the King's hall. He had drunk as sparingly as good manners, and his name as a warrior-prince among these barbarians, would let him. He was pleased with his afternoon. He had not caught Penda, but then he had not expected to. A ride across the moors with a fresh mount on a fine day could always lift his spirits; he was his mother's son in that at least. The captain of the Bebbanburh garrison, Wermund, had ridden by his side. Coming back at an easy pace, they had talked about Penda's attempt to burn his way in. Wermund spoke his mind forcibly about the girls' behaviour.

'The princess was the only one who had the sense to stay quiet in the bower and leave us to deal with the enemy. Not like those other stupid cows bellowing and bolting into us. They gave more trouble than the Mercians. Then afterwards, when they might have been some use, they'd either taken to their beds or they were bawling their eyes out.'

Wermund had got high words from Edyth, in front of some interested Cumbrians, about the brutal way he'd treated her; this still rankled.

'But your sister buckled-to, and did the work of six men getting things to rights. She's as good as a king's reeve, too, in handling the churls. You should hear them talk about her. They say you can always know the royal blood, shepherds of the folk.'

Alchfrid was pleased. He was too thoughtful to look down on

the common people or make light of their good word. Also, he realised he had spoken unfairly to his sister, and he was a young man who prided himself on his justice. He made up his mind to be gracious to Alchflaed at their meeting. He was even ready to grant her right to have a ride on the sands and only made ritual objections.

'You should have taken a couple of the men.'

'I wanted to bathe.'

'You should have taken the girls.'

'They were hard-pressed, clearing up after the attack.'

Remembering Wermund's report, he nodded benevolently. 'Well, I hope you feel refreshed after your bathe. These must have been very anxious days for you, while you were trapped here. What were you doing out of the convent?'

'Our aunt sent me to the Holy Island with some vestments and an altar cloth I'd embroidered, and to carry a letter to Bishop Aidan—only he'd gone on retreat to the Farne.'

Her brother smiled his approval. 'And what about your errand here? Did you see to it before the raiders came? Can I help you—is there anything else you must do before I send you home?'

'Errand?'

'Why did our aunt want you to come here? Or was it something for the monks?'

Alchflaed saw no reason to lie at this point. She rather welcomed the chance to talk freely to her brother about the matter closest to her heart.

'Nobody sent me—I was looking for Mother.'

Alchfrid looked startled and a little alarmed. She tried to explain.

'I wanted to be in the place where she had lived—where she died. Oh, Alchfrid, she went so suddenly—like the quenching of a torch—without either of us, her own children—' Her voice broke on a sob.

'I was away down the coast at Caerdurnoc, there'd been an alarm about sea-raiders. I came as fast as I could, the moment they brought me word she was ill, but it's over a hundred miles of the roughest land in Britain.' Alchfrid sounded aggrieved as if his sister had accused him of neglect. Her eyes were blind with tears.

'I was just thirty miles north, a day's sail with a following wind; a day's ride. And nobody brought me word. The bell tolled in the chapel, the Abbess called us to prayer—and my mother had gone out of the world with never a word between us.'

Alchfrid found his sister's outbursts of feeling burdensome, but did his best.

'You were closer to her at the foot of the altar than I was riding the moors to Bebbanburh, and giving her better aid than any doctor with your prayers. You helped her on her first steps to Heaven.'

She shook her head; that was cold comfort. 'It's not the same as being there, holding her in my arms, kissing her goodbye, *knowing* what happened.'

'Anyone would think she'd died alone in a ditch. She had a skilled doctor and cunning-women to attend her—you've met them here, you can see they know their trade. And Father was with her all the time.'

A sudden thought made him stare at her closely; his voice sharpened.

'Did you think she'd been neglected? You've not been hearing any stupid gossip—any tales about foul play?'

She shook her head. His irritation grew, but he forced himself to speak patiently, as to a spoiled and fractious child.

'Mother didn't forget you. You know she spoke about you near the end. She said you were to have her ring. Father took it from her hand and had it sent to you.' He glanced at her bare fingers. 'Our aunt's keeping it safe for you, that's right. You can offer it at the altar when you take the veil. And I don't grudge it to you in the least, though it's the royal ring of Cumbria, that's been worn by every king of our House since Coel Hen Godebog. So you see, there's not the slightest reason to feel jealous of me—'

'Jealous?' Alchflaed was so shocked that she could not say more for the moment. Her brother was pleased to have struck her dumb and pressed home his lesson.

'You see, sister, you cannot have everything your own way, just as you would like it. You have a duty to your holy profession, and to your royal blood, and these duties must always be your first thought. You gave me some very high-sounding words today about wanting to be of help. And now, thanks to you, some of those good men, who've been fighting so hard all this week to defend you, will have to forgo their well-earned rest. They'll have a wearisome ride late into the evening and hard lodging after.'

'Why?'

'Do you have to ask? Are you cold-hearted as well as selfish? I've got to get word of your safety to Holy Island, and then on to

Coludesburh. The good brothers will have been worried about you, to say nothing of our poor aunt. Did you never think of her?'

Alchflaed saw the Welshman trudging slowly along the twelve miles or so of rough winding track to the ford, caught up and questioned by the horsemen from Bebbanburh. He would tell the story she had taught him — to the very people in Bernicia who would know it could not be true. Likely they would spear him out of hand, but if he showed her ring — Dear God, why had she given him a thing so rare and precious? She must have been demon-possessed. Everything she had thought and said and done today had been under evil enchantment. Looking at her brother's self-righteous face, she knew he would hang the Welshman, not for having fought alongside Penda's raiders, but for wearing the royal ring of Cumbria.

She decided to confess the truth as far as it concerned herself. Her brother could not kill her and could not be much angrier with her than he was already.

'Nobody's been worrying about me, because nobody knows I'm here.'

'Don't be stupid. How could that be?'

She swallowed.

'I took my leave of the guest-master on Holy Island as if I were going back to Coludesburh. But I'd already told my companions I was only riding across the ford to see them on their way and then going back to the monastery. I said the librarian had offered me the chance to copy some passages from a book that my aunt wanted if I cared to wait another day. I told them I'd probably catch them up at the Tuidimuth ferry, as I'd be riding hard but they could take it easy. If not, I'd follow on when I was ready, so they needn't wait to cross the river. When they were out of sight, I turned south to Bebbanburh. I only meant to spend a morning here — I'd have caught the others up if the raiders hadn't come without warning. But nobody will be worried, because the monks think I'm back in Coludesburh, and my aunt will have been told I'm safe on Holy Island. So no harm's been done.'

'No harm!' Alchfrid was pale with fury. 'You wicked, deceitful girl, can you look me in the face and say "No harm" to a string of lies that would make Ananias and Sapphira blush? You've lied to the monks, you've lied to your own servants and got them to tell lies to our aunt! Do you ever speak the truth? How can I be sure you're telling me the truth now?'

As Alchflaed had by no means told the whole truth, she looked guilty and ashamed, though she was not in the least sorry that she had helped the Welshman's escape. She was therefore angry with her brother for making her feel guilt and shame.

'I'm sending you back to Coludesburh at first light tomorrow, under escort. I'll give them a letter for my aunt and I hope she orders you a whipping.'

His voice had risen; Alchflaed's voice rose in answer, and her temper with it.

'You won't need to send me; I won't stop another hour to be spoken to like that. And you can spare your men that wearisome ride that troubles you so much for their sakes. I'll take myself back as I came. And don't concern yourself to write to my aunt, I shall tell her where I've been and take any penance she chooses to lay on me—if she should choose to punish me for loving my mother's memory!'

'You'll do as I tell you!'

'You've no right to give me orders, you're not my king!'

'I'm your brother and I stand in the King's place. As your kinsman I've a right to restrain you from roaming round the country like—like some fair-ground juggler's trull, and degrading your family. You'll go back to the convent under proper guard if I have to lock you in here tonight and fetter you to your horse tomorrow!'

'So who's planning to degrade our family now?'

In the pause while Alchfrid tried to think of a retort, they heard someone stumbling over the stacked trestles in the hall. The Dish-Thane's voice said with unnatural loudness, 'Clumsy of me! It's getting dark, I should have brought a torch.'

Having taken a moment picking himself up, to make sure the prince and princess had taken his hint to stop shouting at each other, the Dish-Thane appeared in the doorway, red and breathless.

'Forgive me for breaking in on your supper, lady, but a messenger has just come with a letter for the prince.'

He stood aside to admit the newcomer, a tall figure in horsemen's leathers. Alchfrid was startled to see him.

'Why, Cynog, you must have set out on our heels! Is anything amiss in Cumbria?'

'No, lord. The King told me to give you this letter when you had finished dealing with the raiders.'

He handed over the parchment; Alchfrid broke its seal and unrolled it. Alchflaed watched him as he read. She was painfully

49

learning to translate his looks. When he was angered he did not flush and wave his fists about, shouting, as the warriors in Bebbanburh did. He went white and still, with his face as tense as if he were holding his rage on a leash like a hound. This was far more alarming than any amount of flailing and cursing.

At length he looked across at her. He would have given the world rather than deliver the news, but she would have to be told sooner or later and delay would be childish.

'It's an order from the King, with a message to our aunt. He says I am to bring you here from Coludesburh as soon as the country is quiet and all things in order. I am to tell you that as there has been no notice or time to prepare robes, you are to fit yourself out from the contents of our mother's chests which are stored here. Then we are to set out to meet him on the Deiran border.'

Alchfrid's voice was calm but he showed no sign of pleasure or affection at the prospect of her company. Earlier that day, Alchflaed had vowed that she would try to curb her quick tongue and not provoke him. But he had upset her too badly—and the retort was so tempting.

'I hope you're grateful for my help, brother. Thanks to me, you and those other good men who've been riding so hard all this week to defend me won't have to forgo your well-earned rest for another wearisome ride up the coast. Here I am, all ready to obey our father.'

Her brother had enough self-command not to hit her, under the eyes of the Dish-Thane and the King's messenger. He gave her goodnight, put a cold kiss on her forehead and walked out, signing the others to follow.

Alchflaed was left mistress of the battlefield, in triumphant possession of her mother's hall.

CHAPTER
5

At noon that day, as the gate timbers at Bebbanburh had begun to crack, King Oswy of Northumbria, the lord of that beleaguered fortress, had been out walking. In that quiet time of a royal day, between the council or weapon-drill of the morning and the afternoon's feast, he was strolling at his ease, enjoying the sunlight and the western wind. He was a tall man, very like Alchfrid in features and not looking much older at first sight. His flesh was as lean and sinewy as a hunting wolf; his well-kempt hair and beard had always been so fair as to look like silver. Only the lines deeply scored along his cheeks marked his age; his wary, sea-green eyes had never been young.

Oswy was making for the warning beacon that was always kept ready at the summit of the fell. Penrith watched the fords of the Eamot and Idon. At its feet the Roman roads went north to Caer Luel, south to Lonceaster and, most important of all, east over Stony Moor, linking Cumbria to the Anglian kingdoms. It might be supposed that the king had come to this high place to brood over the defence of his threatened kingdom. Nobody would have thought so, watching his tranquil face or listening to the calm tones of his voice.

He was with the two friends he trusted most, so far as he trusted anyone living. There had been one person whom he had let walk in and out of the closely-guarded stronghold of his mind as she liked. She had picked up his deepest thoughts like the jewels in her trinket-box, played at will on his heart-strings as she did on her harp. Now Riemmelth was dead and he kept the rest of the world at bay with no trouble.

He leaned against the beacon platform, gazing over the southern eaves of Englawud towards the tumbled mass of mountain peaks, the heartland of Cumbria. The kingdom had come to him as Riemmelth's dowry; he had married her to get it into his hands before he began to love her. A dark, difficult land and a dark, difficult woman, that could both suddenly gleam with elvish beauty.

One of his companions stretched himself on the warm turf, listening with lazy amusement as the others argued. This was

Cadman, ealdorman of Westmoringaland. As Alchfrid's foster-father he had been in effect the ruler as well as the war-leader of Cumbria since Riemmelth died. He was a Bernician of the ancient Welsh stock; his blood and well-tested loyalty made him useful to hold the Welsh kingdom and bring up its heir. Oswy was drawn to him as well by a similar wiliness and enjoyment of mockery.

His other friend could not have been more unlike. Godric was a stocky man with manners as blunt as his face. He had once been Oswy's shield-bearer. Though he was now a thane with wide lands and a respected voice in the witan, he would still give the King the rough edge of his tongue as he did when Oswy was a boy at weapon-training. He was doing so now.

'It's a branding shame! Folk are saying the Bernician war-host only knows how to move one way—backwards!'

'Which is why we've still got a war-host and don't pay tribute to Penda. Apart from Kent, we're the only kingdom left in England that doesn't.'

'Penda doesn't need us to pay him tribute. He just comes in when he likes and collects it himself.'

'He doesn't get all that much. There's plenty of space in Bernicia for folk to move their stock out of his road. Those who don't have the wit to budge in time should take a lesson from me. Tribute's a fixed sum, and the victor does the fixing. Also, those who pay it are called *subjects*, and Penda's not going to put that name on me. While my army's unbeaten, he can't.'

'That's all very well, Oswy.' Cadman was lying with his arm over his eyes against the sun. He looked to be asleep though his wits were awake. 'But we can't go on much longer boasting about Bernicia's unconquered warriors without doing some conquering ourselves. Sooner or later you'll have to come to terms with Penda.'

'Sooner or later I'm going to kill Penda.'

In a feasting-hall with the mead flowing, this hopeless claim could have been laughed down as a pot-valiant boast. Oswy made the remark as a matter of fact; he might have been telling them that he planned to build a larger hall at Bebbanburh one day.

'He killed my brother—hacked off his head and arms and staked them. Also, he fired my palace at Gefrin while my queen was in it. She had to fight like a warrior, and then skulk like an outlaw to save her freedom. She got the better of him, with her courage and keen wits. Still, he caused her such stress as no woman should have to undergo. So I'm going to kill him.'

He smiled at Godric. 'But I can't do it now. It's no use scowling at me like that, I'm not strong enough to fight him. If I risk a battle too soon and my army's destroyed, then Bernicia will be destroyed with it. And I'll lose my queen's land as well, instead of handing it on to her son.'

Godric was not appeased. 'A fine kingdom you'll have to hand on to the boy if you can't even stop an enemy crossing its borders.'

'To do that I'd have to cross its borders myself. You're not a fool, Godric, you know what would happen if I led my men south into Deira. Holy Cousin Oswine doesn't lift a finger to stop Penda crossing his land there to attack me, a kinsman and fellow-Christian—I don't suppose he could if he wanted to, but he's shown no sign of trying. So Penda can come up to the Tese before he sees the point of a spear and he's got over a hundred miles of quiet riding through Deira to get his loot back home to Mercia. But if I went so much as a mile over the border to meet him or chase him, the Deirans would take me in the back as soon as I joined battle.'

Godric looked glum. Oswy laughed and slapped him on the shoulder. 'I agree with you about these raids. They're a nuisance. It's time they were stopped. That's why I've decided to marry again.'

Godric almost jumped with shock; Cadman opened his eyes and sat up. Oswy enjoyed his effect in silence for a second.

'I've sent down to Kent to offer for my cousin Eanfled. As King Edwin's last living child the Deirans see her as their rightful queen. She can't rule on her own, of course, as a woman. I'm the next male heir through my mother, so together we'll have an unanswerable claim to the kingdom.'

'You've certainly got a lot of blood in common.' Cadman spoke with malicious enjoyment. 'Your grandfather killed her grandfather, her father killed your father—'

'Yes, it's high time to settle these feuds for the sake of both kingdoms. We'll join them, re-make a united Kingdom of Northumbria. Only, instead of killing to do it, like our fathers and grandfathers, we'll unite Deira and Bernicia in the holy sacrament of matrimony.'

There was one flaw in this neat and pious plan. Godric pointed it out, surprised that Oswy should have overlooked it.

'You won't either of you be the next heirs to Deira when Oswine marries and gets a son.'

'True. We'll both lose our claims unless Oswine should happen to die without a son.'

Cadman looked up sharply. 'Oswy, the Deirans will never accept you if—'

'If?'

Cadman chose his words carefully. 'If King Oswine should die in any way that they can blame on you.'

Oswy nodded with grave approval. 'And rightly so. I should be unworthy of the name of King if a kinsman of mine should die in any way that could be blamed on me.'

Cadman raised his eyebrows and smiled. Oswy went on in the same quiet, thoughtful tone. 'But if Oswine attacked me first, even the Deirans would grant that I have a right to defend myself and my land. That's my duty as a king.'

Godric roared with laughter. 'Holy Oswine? He'd never attack you, the bishop wouldn't like it. Remember that time Aidan scolded him in public and he burst into tears?'

'Oswine might think that he had a duty to take over in Bernicia. He's heard my rule is crumbling because I've failed to stop Penda. Think of this last attack on Bebbanburh—it took me a week to get troops up there and I didn't even go with them myself.'

Cadman chuckled. 'So that's why you held Alchfrid straining at the leash.'

'I've got your good training to thank that Alchfrid hasn't insulted me or rebelled against me—yet—but he wasn't far off either before I let him go. As Godric says, it's a branding shame on our warriors to let Penda range round Bernicia at will. No wonder some of them are talking of turning back to Woden. Oswine's heard that the Christians up here are desperate for help. Who better to bring it than Holy Oswine? Besides, he'd have to come in, to rescue Bishop Aidan.'

Godric was looking more and more puzzled. 'But—your rule isn't crumbling. Nobody's going to rebel. And nobody's talking about going back to Woden. Where did Oswine get all this drivel?'

Oswy looked vague. 'People talk.'

'I know we grumble but we'd stick by you against all Hell.'

'I've never doubted it. I'm sure every able-bodied man will rally to me when I call out the war-host. In fact, that's what I'm going to do. I'm calling the muster here. Nobody on the Deiran side will know about it. But we can be over Stony Moor fast on the Roman road and block Oswine's way at Cetreht if he tries to invade.'

Cadman shook his head. 'You'll never hold Deira if you take it by war.'

'I wouldn't be taking it by war, I'd be taking it by inheritance. I'm the male heir and I'd be bringing back Edwin's line with my marriage. Edwin's blood is what the Deirans care about most. Oswine was never more than a makeshift when Edwin's boys died in exile—given the choice, they'd rather have a man-eating fiend ruling them than a Bernician.'

'And if they can't find one of those, they'll take the next best.' Cadman looked unusually serious. 'They'll call in Penda, heathen or not, rather than you with Oswine's blood on your hands.'

'I don't believe for a moment there'll be anyone's blood on my hands. There won't be any fighting. Oswine will have come to protect Christian Bernicia—he could hardly start by slaughtering its Christian defenders, even if we weren't five to one against him. I shall have a war-host; he'll only have his troop of hearth-companions, because he'll be expecting to be welcomed as a deliverer. He'll retreat into Deira as soon as he sees my army and disband his warriors to prove he meant no harm. Then he'll call for Bishop Aidan to reconcile us.'

'So what gain would all that have made?' demanded Godric. 'We'd just be back where we started.'

Oswy looked grave. 'The Deirans won't like it. A king who gives the dare to another, then withdraws when the challenge is taken up, can't go back where he started. He's disgraced his name—and the name of every man who fights under his banner. Kings have been killed by their own war-bands to wipe out such a stain. In fact, it's usually the men who've been closest on such a king's hearth who raise their hands against him first.'

Godric was silent, rather bewildered. Oswy seemed to be telling them something that had already happened, an old story to while away the time before dinner. Cadman was smiling appreciatively. He never mentioned Oswine again, as if the Deiran king had already passed out of account.

'Do you think the Kentings will take your offer for Eanfled?' he asked.

'They already have. I sent some time ago. They were delighted to get her off their hands—a landless, dowerless exile isn't easy to dispose of. She's twenty-five years old, remember. I don't care about a dowry, it's her blood and ancestry I want. I've paid the Kentings well for her too—presents all round.'

'She's your first cousin—you'll need a dispensation.'

'I've already got one. I left all that to the Kentings and their Merovingian kinsmen—the Frankish bishops can get to the ear of the Pope quicker than I could. It was easy enough. Reconciling a feud between kinsfolk, linking two Christian kingdoms against the heathen—a truly blessed intention!'

'So you've got everything ready?'

'I believe I have.' Oswy unpropped himself from the beacon, stretched and laughed. 'All this talk and fresh air have got me ready for my dinner. Thank God, there's only one plea to hear before I can enjoy the feast your lady will have prepared for us. I always say Mildred keeps the best table in the northlands.'

He seemed to have shrugged off the cares of his kingdom, together with all thoughts about his new bride, and set a good pace down the beacon hill to Cadman's stronghold. When they entered the great hall, it was already thronged with Oswy's and Cadman's warriors, Cumbrian nobles, the priests who acted as their chaplains and clerks, a visiting bard with his retinue.

A stranger was isolated rather markedly in a pool of silence, a well-dressed man with a hard mouth and cold eyes. He had a group of his own retainers round him, looking wary and suspicious.

Oswy took his seat on the gift-stool and blandly asked the stranger, a Deiran called Hunwald, to state his case. It was a complaint about cattle-lifting over the Bernician border from his estate at Cetreht. Godric's head jerked sharply at that name; Cadman gave the stranger a long, appraising look. The Bernicians waited for their king to rebut the charge, or throw it back in the stranger's face with a counter-charge about Deiran thieving.

Oswy listened gravely and sympathetically. He promised to have the thieves tracked down and punished. He offered to make good all that had been stolen. Hunwald could pay himself back at his own valuation from the royal herds. He gave Hunwald a costly arm-ring and brooch as a personal gift in reparation for his trouble.

The Bernicians were puzzled but not angry. Oswy always had a good reason for the favours he gave, though these sometimes boded no good to the receiver. Cadman looked quietly amused.

The hearing was over; Oswy called for the feast to begin. Everyone took his place. Lady Mildred entered with her bower-maidens, the servants brought in the dishes. Hunwald was given the place of honour at Oswy's right hand. The King chatted pleasantly about the harvest, the hunting, his cousin Oswine's church-building, Bishop Aidan's latest visitation. Cadman noticed that the Deiran was not so glib as Oswy—sometimes his answers were halting and he forgot to smile.

When the main meal was over the stranger took his leave. He wished to cross Stony Moor before nightfall. Oswy kept up his courtesy to the last. While the boards were being cleared for the serious drinking and the bard was tuning his harp, he walked out to see the visitor on his way. Cadman satisfied himself that the Derians' horses had been rubbed down and fed; Godric had a few words with the escort that would guard them to the borderland. Oswy and his guest were left alone for a moment. Hunwald's eyes shifted uneasily.

'About my lands—'

'Yes?'

'There would be less chance of trouble if my lands came up to the Tese—less temptation to raiders, I mean. I wouldn't have to keep asking you—'

'Certainly. If my word was law over those lands, I'd see you were rewarded as you deserve.'

Smiling and gracious, Oswy watched the Deirans mount and ride down the hill. Cadman and Godric had come back to his side. Godric's forehead was wrinkled; his face had the look it often wore during a difficult riddle-game. If he thought he was close to the answer this time, he was not finding it amusing.

Cadman broke the silence that was becoming thundery. 'There goes one who has no cause to complain about his welcome. Who is he?'

Oswy said quietly, 'He's the thane of Getlingas. As I'm going to marry their princess, I'm glad of a chance to show goodwill to Deirans, especially one so close to King Oswine. He always stays with Hunwald whenever he comes up to ride his northern march.'

Godric suddenly broke out, 'I could spew!'

Cadman's mouth said lightly, 'That's not fair to Mildred, she feasted us very well, I thought.' His eyes meanwhile warned Godric to be quiet, but Godric would have spoken his mind with Woden's spear at his throat and all the waelcyriges screaming for his blood. He ignored the diversion and charged on.

'A man who betrays his own king is foul. It's bad enough in hot blood, after a quarrel or a wrong—but to turn on someone who loves and trusts you—Hunwald's kind stink like the unburied dead.'

'You're unjust. Hunwald has never betrayed anyone yet, to my knowledge. If he turned against his king, of course he would be unfit to live. Oswine is my mother's kinsman and I'm going to marry his heir. If anyone harmed him, I'd do my duty and avenge him at once.'

He looked at Godric's face and laughed.

'Don't worry, old friend.' He spoke quite gently. 'I wouldn't make you take any part in it.'

CHAPTER
6

The morning rise was by no means over; the fish were coming eagerly at the flies. The fisherman was having one of his best days, angling aloft on the water, dopping his deftly tied scraps of wool and drakes' feathers as if they were alive, playing and holding his catch with sense and skill. His servant had already taken six fine trout in the landing-net. On days like these, time stops for a fisherman. He is already in his own green-and-gold heaven, floating between the leaf-shadows and the clear, deep pool.

The servant had collected his patience to wait for hours when, without lifting his gaze from the water, the fisherman said quietly, 'My nephew is climbing the track under Craig y Forwyn. He will dine with me in three hours' time. Take me back.'

He handed over his rod and lay back on the cushions. The servant stowed his master's tackle, unmoored and took the boat downstream. As it moved from the shadows of the overhanging branches, the August sunlight blazed on the fisherman. He seemed to be tall; though it was not easy to guess the height of his body, lying down and clad in a plain, shapeless robe, like a monk's. His shoulders were very broad, his hands and arms were long and shapely. His head was massive, with strong handsome features and a high, wide brow framed in thick, tawny hair and beard, well-kempt and glossy. When the sun caught his eyes, their light-brown irides glowed like amber for a second before he closed his eyelids. The sun was harsh; it showed that the red-gold hair was tarnished with grey; the amber eyes were sunken; the flesh strained over the noble bones and deeply scored.

Behind his head, the dark figure of the boatman loomed like a shadow. He was also tall and very thin, but strong and wiry. His skin was tanned to leather and much calloused; his black hair and beard were rough and dusty with neglect though they had been kept hacked short. He was wearing nothing but a coarse shirt, with the end pulled between his legs and girt up in front with a piece of rope.

Some fifty yards downstream the trees parted and a patch of smooth turf came down to the water's edge, making an easy landing place. A litter stood nearby; four ponies were grazing while a couple of grooms lounged in the nearest shade. They jumped up when the boat appeared and ran to harness the litter. The boatman made fast fore and aft; then waited till the grooms were ready, when he stepped carefully over the side and crouched in the water. The fisherman mounted his back and rode him to the litter.

When he was once more lying on cushions with his eyes closed, the grooms led the ponies away from the landing. The boatman followed the litter carrying the fishing-tackle and the catch, which he had wrapped in dock leaves and placed in a wicker basket. The grooms did not speak to him; he was only a foreign slave, shipped into the port at Caer Legion, a stupid brute without wit enough to learn more than a word or two of the British tongue or even to remember his own name. The servants and farmfolk called him Asyn since he was his master's beast of burden; sometimes as an even crueller jest they called him Asen, She-Ass, for he had been gelded.

The group had turned their backs on the River Dyfrdwy and were making their way up to Dinas Brân on the hill-crest not quite a mile away. The hill was cone-shaped and stood alone between the Dyfrdwy and a wall of limestone cliffs that edged the mountains to the north-east. Lording over the river-valley, it had been a high and holy place for centuries before the Romans came. The valley tribe had circled its crest by ring upon ring of huge earth ramparts. The Romans disliked hill-forts; they had slighted the ramparts and ordered the tribe to keep to the valley farms. Now the ramparts were green walls of turf overgrown with gorse and fern. But the Romans had gone and the ramparts remained. Dinas Brân was still a high and holy place.

Inside the topmost circle was a signal tower, built in the last desperate days of the Empire, to send warning if raiders had broken past Caer Legion. Its height and its walls of well-dressed stone set it apart as alien. Joined to its western wall was a large eight-sided hall of timber, with a porch facing the sunset. Across a cobbled courtyard with a well in it was a small chapel; huddled against the rampart were a few bothies where the servants cooked and kept the stores; slept and stabled the ponies.

The litter drew up by the door into the tower. Asyn crouched and his master dismounted on him, then stood leaning on him like a staff while he gave commands about the meal, telling the servants exactly how much time they had to be ready when his nephew arrived. He watched them out of sight before he gripped Asyn's shoulder as an order to move indoors. When he began to walk, it was clear why he avoided being watched.

His body was bent and twisted to one side from the hips as if the trunk did not belong to the legs. These splayed out with every step as if they were indeed trying to go another way from the canted, straining body. The noble, leonine beauty he had while he lay still was lost, he became pitiful or ridiculous according to the hearts of those who watched him.

He could walk well enough in his fashion. If he had been a ploughman with a family to feed he would have been forced to work as soon as he could stand after his injury and his legs would have regained some of their strength. But he was Prince Morfran of Iâl and would have been its ruler but for the stroke of ill-luck that had befallen him. His bodily dignity was part of his life. Only the slave, taciturn and indifferent as a brute, watched and shared his struggles to dress, wash and relieve himself.

Nothing of this was to be seen or guessed when Asyn finally rang a little bronze bell and the servants came to carry his couch into the hall, now set out for dinner.

The floor was carpeted with fresh rushes, scattered with meadowsweet and honeysuckle. The stone hearth had been swept and the fire banked down with turf to make it bearable on a hot August afternoon. The roof was held up by a circle of eight massive posts made of oak trunks. They were beautifully cut like all the woodwork in the hall but quite bare of ornament.

Morfran's robe of undyed wool was equally plain, though well-woven and spotless. By contrast, the trappings for the feast were startling in their brilliance. Morfran was a monk of Llangollen and had withdrawn even further from the world to the life of a hermit, but he was also a prince of the ruling House. When such men entered religion they made their own terms. Morfran was austere enough in his personal life but he got some satisfaction from beauty. On rare occasions he had a visitor and it pleased him to offer an unexpectedly splendid welcome.

The bolsters and pillows on the two couches were fine purple wool stuffed with duck feathers. The table silver was old and Roman, chased with scenes from the Orphic mysteries. The embroidered wall-hangings were quite new. They had come from Constantinople stage by stage through the Pillars of Hercules and up the western seaboard to Caer Legion, where the traders knew that the 'Rich Fisher' of Dinas Brân had taste and wealth for such treasures.

There were six of them. Four showed Earth, Air, Fire and Water with their elemental spirits; the other two were the Moon and the Sun, embodied in the myths of Diana and Apollo. These last had been so heavily couched with silver and gold thread that they glittered in the sunlight streaming through the western porch.

The servants had hung the tapestries between the roof-posts, three on each side of the hearth behind the couches. The guest's place was to the south, where the Sun blazed between the crimson and flame of Fire, the russet and brown of Earth. Morfran lay under the gleaming Moon, flanked by the blues and greens of Air and Water.

There was a small table by the head of his couch; when the servants had settled him on his cushions they brought him wine and a gaming-board inlaid with gilt and silver squares. He had carved the playing pieces himself from walrus ivory; all his life now was in his mind and the skill of his hands. He passed the last hour of waiting by playing one hand against the other.

Exactly to the time he had predicted, there were hoofs on the cobbles, voices in the porch, the sounds of water being poured for hand-washing, a dark figure against the sunlight in the doorway. Morfran held out a goblet of wine.

'Welcome, Meilyr; you've a long journey behind you.'

Meilyr knelt by the couch to kiss his uncle, then drank to him. 'The longest road would be well worth tramping barefoot for one of your welcomes, Uncle.'

He looked eagerly round the circle of pillars at the hearth, the couches, the wonderful tapestries that seemed to quiver with life as the light moved on them, the board game. Nothing had changed. Dinas Brân was lifted out of time.

Meilyr took his place on his couch, where a table had been set for him. During the first part of the meal—bowls of broth and a

61

great platter of trout cooked in oatmeal—the uncle and nephew talked of general topics in front of the servants. Morfran described his morning's fishing; Meilyr asked for news of Abbot Sulien and the monks of Llangollen. When the main dishes had been cleared and they had settled to their wine and mead, Meilyr said he would serve his uncle. The servants went out. Meilyr brought his goblet and came to sit at the end of his uncle's couch. Morfran lay back on his pillows.

'You've come from your brother's court. How is Madoc?'

Meilyr laughed. 'Well, as ever. Madoc sits comfortably to life—he rides it easily, like his horses and his women.'

Meilyr and his brother, the present lord of Iâl, were on terms of good-humoured contempt. Meilyr saw Madoc as little better than a healthy animal who lived only for war, hunting and wenching.

Madoc thought that Meilyr was too clever for his own good, since he seemed to get little profit from his cleverness. He had a natural gift for composing in words and music, but would not settle to the long, rigorous bardic training. He had learned his letters quickly at the monastic school, but balked at submitting to monks' vows and discipline. He was a reckless and skilful fighter but took war as a chance for personal adventures and dare-devilry rather than a way to power.

After watching his younger brother suspiciously as he came to manhood, Madoc had decided that whatever Meilyr wanted out of life he did not want Iâl. Sooner or later he would become a bard or a bishop; either would be useful to have in the family.

The pain-lines round Morfran's mouth creased to a smile. 'The sun has always shone for Madoc. He was born while my sister still believed your father loved her.'

The laughter died out of Meilyr's face. 'Before she found out that his heart had already been eaten by that Cumbrian traitress —that she only had the ghost of a husband.' He stared at the blood-red dregs in his goblet. 'They knew what they were doing, the ones who named her Riemmelth, Queen of the Lightning. She blasted everything she touched. Not just my father's and mother's lives, but the hopes of all our people. She opened the gate to the west when she opened her legs to Oswy. What chance have we got now of winning back the east, with the English across the Long Hills, holding the land from sea to sea?'

'Yet you fight alongside the English. You've just marched with Penda.'

'Penda can bleed Northumbria white for us, he's done it before. Anyway, I had business of my own in Oswy's land.'

Morfran raised his eyebrows.

'I went to get a woman.'

His uncle burst out laughing. 'You must have been desperate. If you couldn't find a willing one in your brother's court there are plenty for hire in Caer Legion—or have you gambled all your gold away?'

Meilyr was too much in earnest to rise to the teasing.

'They've taken too much—the English. Our rich eastern lands, our great cities—Llundain, Caer Efrog, Caer Luel—all gone from us. Our princesses self-sold into their beds, to keep the title of Queen. Even our name taken, called "Welsh"—*foreigners*—in our own country. It's not to be forgotten or forgiven.'

'So?'

'So I decided to take one of their girls from Oswy's court, a woman to pay for a woman. Let one of their pampered creatures find out what it is to be a foreigner, lost in an alien land, alone in beggary and slavery, with not a friendly hand lifted to shield her from the whip or the fist!'

Morfran's face showed a distaste that had nothing to do with pity.

'Crude!'

Meilyr nodded. 'And meaningless. There's neither pleasure nor pride to be got from putting fear into a slavish heart. A woman worth breaking wouldn't break—she'd use her courage and wit to escape, or kill me, or herself.'

'So you went on a hopeless quest.'

'Far from hopeless. After all, I don't *break* my hunting creatures—my hounds, my horses, my falcons—they'd be no use to me if I smashed their bodies or their spirits. Think of my falcons. They don't love me. My hounds and horses do, but not my falcons, never as long as they live. But they come back to my wrist after a flight, and let me hood them and fasten their jesses.Why?'

'Tell me.' Morfran knew the answer, but he was interested in the talk and in the mood to humour his nephew.

'Because I know them. I've made myself know the hawk nature, what it is, what it wants. I can forethink their every move—and so I hold them by what they are in themselves. That's why they can never break free. And that's the way to hold a woman. Folk are never so well deceived as when you make them

63

cheat themselves. They only hear and see what they want, and never know that they're using their own wishes to build the trap that will catch them.'

'And what trap will catch your woman?'

'Curiosity, of course. I'm a stranger from another world. And some challenge to her pride in her cleverness and daring. And love—they all want love. She'll get none from me if she waits till doomsday. I could never love one of that race. But I can weave a web of words and music and dreams round her till she thinks I've promised her my heart and soul.'

He sneered. 'And then, when she's followed my whistle—broken with her own people and branded herself as my harlot—she'll wake up and find that she's put herself into lifelong exile for nothing, that she's in my power and I can hand her over to my stable-grooms when I'm tired of her. And when she weeps and reproaches me for cheating her, I can say, "How have I cheated you? What did I ever promise you? You made your own choice. Whatever's happened to you, you did it to yourself!" '

Meilyr was flushed and breathless as if he had just been through the very scene with the betrayed girl. Morfran was staring at him as intently as he would watch a trout rising to his fly.

'So you've planned your campaign to the very last word. Now you only need to get the woman to say it to.'

'I've already got the woman. Alchflaed, princess of Bernicia, no less.'

His uncle's head jerked with shock.

'Oswy's daughter?'

'Riemmelth's daughter. Who better to pay her mother's debt? She's already given me a ring.'

He stretched out his hand; then, as Morfran twisted and strained to look, he pulled off the ring and handed it over.

'A fine jewel, isn't it?'

Morfran balanced the ring on his palm and bent his head over it. It was made of gold, heavy and dark, worked into the shape of a dragon, its tail coiled to encircle the wearer's finger, its claws and unfurling wings gripping and guarding a large oval ruby, its head rearing over the top as a proud, threatening crest.

'A very fine jewel. But for the royal ring of Cumbria you would expect no less.'

He heard Meilyr gasp. 'What did you say?'

'The royal ring of Cumbria. The ring that the last Roman

governor of the North gave to Coel Hen when he made him Protector. Every king of that race has worn it after him. It was on Urien's hand when Morcant struck him down. It was on Owain's hand when he killed Theodric Flamebearer of Bernicia.'

He looked at Meilyr with calculation, like an angler just before he starts to draw in his line, gauging how the trout will thresh.

'Your father described it to me long ago. It's the ring Riemmelth would have given him to seal their betrothal, only she changed her mind and gave it to Oswy instead.'

Meilyr could hardly speak for rage. 'And that—that slut— threw it away on a chance-comer! She thought I was a travelling gleeman—said I could call it my pay for having amused her!'

He snatched up the ring; for a second he looked about to throw it in the fire, then replaced it on his finger saying grimly, 'I told her I'd take the first chance to pay her back—and by God, I will!'

'Be careful, Meilyr. Anger is slavery.'

Meilyr made himself shrug and smile. 'She isn't worth my anger.'

'You said you'd got her. Where is she? If you've left her in Madoc's court you won't have had her to yourself for long.'

'She's here.' He stretched his arm towards his uncle again. He was wearing an arm-ring, a double band of wrought gold set with garnets over a broad strip of brown silk braid. As he moved, the braid showed glints of copper and bronze.

'That's her hair.'

Morfran delicately touched the braid with his finger-tip, feeling the silkiness, watching the warm colours.

'She gave you that too?'

'I took it on my knife-blade without asking her leave. She never saw or felt it go.'

He laughed triumphantly. 'I've been looking into your books, Uncle.'

'I know you have.'

Meilyr gripped the bracelet with his other hand. 'So you see, I've got her. Here are her jesses. I can bring her to the lure whenever I want to take her.'

'Did you give her anything in return?'

'Not I. Didn't you hear me say she'll get nothing from me, not even a promise?'

Morfran looked down, so that his nephew could not see into his eyes. He was shaking inwardly with silent laughter.

You didn't look into my books long enough, you arrogant

young fool. You'd have done better to take your poor crippled uncle into your confidence. If you'd stooped to ask my advice, I could have told you that these bonding tokens have to be begged for and given willingly, whatever lies you tell to cheat the giver. And you have to get your victim to take something of yours, to set your seal on her. You haven't got Alchflaed of Bernicia tied by jesses to your wrist. She's free — you've bound yourself to her!

Meilyr saw his uncle's eyelids close and felt guilty.

'I've tired you, Uncle — talked the sun down over your head.'

Keeping his eyes shut, Morfran whispered, 'It's time to shut the doors and light the candles. I would be glad to sleep, I must confess, but there's no need for you to retire so soon. There's fire, mead and the gaming-board. You won't disturb me if you make harp music. Curig will sleep in the porch, he'll bring you anything you want. Ring the bell, please.'

The servants came, lit the candles and drew back the hanging behind Meilyr's couch to show his bed already made up on the sleeping dais, the feather mattress and pillows covered with fine linen and a chequered woollen blanket. Meilyr knelt to kiss his uncle; then the servants carried Morfran's couch through to the Roman tower and returned, shutting the heavy door behind them. Only Asyn attended on his master's retirement.

The ground floor of the tower was Morfran's study, where he kept his books and received Abbot Sulien or any other rare visitor who came to consult him. At one side, a ladder-like stair led to the loft. When the door was shut on the other servants, Morfran gripped Asyn's back and was hauled up.

The loft was Morfran's usual sleeping-place, though another stair led up to the beacon platform where he could spend nights watching the stars. Its trapdoor was closed tonight. Morfran's plain, narrow bed was ready, a heavy wooden armchair at its head, spread with cushions, and a stool to serve as a table. A black curtain hung across the middle of the room, hiding half of it from the stairs' head. Asyn lit a lamp and placed it on the stool, where he had already set a cup and a ewer of water. Then he went down to the ground floor, pulling the trapdoor over the hatchway behind him. He spent his nights lying at the stairfoot; his master would strike the trapdoor with his staff to summon him.

Morfran sank to the armchair and closed his eyes. He was desperately weary, also disturbed, as he always was when he spent time with Meilyr. Yet he still had a long and hard road to travel that night.

The first part of the journey led, as always, back through the last day of his life—that bright fresh autumn morning before Meilyr was born, when he had been as proud and wild-hearted and hunting-mad as Meilyr was now. He rode out laughing with a group of his friends, started a stag and brought it to bay after a long, blood-whipping chase, not knowing that a boar was couched in a nearby thicket. They dismounted; the boar charged; he was in its path. One companion shouted a warning, so that he jumped aside just as another hurled his spear at the boar. He took the blow in its stead. His hip had been shattered and wound-fever came on him before they could get him home. Everyone thought he would die—if only he had died!—they were busied too much in keeping him quiet and giving him the rites of the church, to torment him with the needless agony of bonesetting. When his body struggled back to life, it was maimed and twisted beyond repair.

That was the end of his heirship of Iâl. A prince had to lead his men into battle, to give a good account of himself in the hunt, to preside at councils and feasts with a lordly majesty that would set him beyond the merciless satires of enemy bards.

As for that other proof of kingly power, the potency that would assure the life of his land, the fertility of its crops and stock and womenfolk, he had never dared to test it—not even with a foreign slave, terrified and unable to talk about what happened; not with a well-paid whore from Caer Legion, pleased and interested to try her skills on the prince.

The disaster threatened Morfran's family and land. He was the only living son of his father's marriage. The old lord had been faithful to his wife while she lived; there was no bastard old enough to rule. All their neighbouring enemies were ready to strike as soon as the old lord died or sickened: to tear Iâl like crows on a corpse, to slit his helpless son's throat, to rape and enslave his daughter Angharad, or at best force her into a blood-stained marriage with her captor.

The old lord acted quickly. He had an elder sister married to a Manx chieftain. He asked them for their youngest son, Elidir, who had not yet taken a wife.

It was a lucky choice. Elidir had been the heir that kings pray for—strong, fearless, with a natural gift for war and statecraft, able to make men obey him willingly. He took a firm grip of Iâl. His cousins duly played their parts to support his rule. Angharad had fallen into worshipful love for her chosen husband almost from the moment she saw him. It was some time before she learned that Elidir only desired one woman, Riemmelth of Cumbria, with all the intensity of thwarted ambition, pride and lust.

Morfran had considerately left the court for the monastery; he helped Elidir when needed with his learning and penmanship. Abbot Sulien was fond of telling his flock that the House of Iâl had faced a sore trial but had overcome by simple courage and love. The Abbot had a mind like untrodden snow; also, his parents had given him to the church as an oblate when he was a little child. He was hardly aware that human feelings are rarely simple, least of all love.

Morfran sighed. He had tried not to hate Elidir. He had rather liked his cousin, had been grateful that under Elidir's protection his father had died in peace, his sister had lived in safety and honour. But the bitterness of his own fate had poisoned liking and gratitude; the poison lingered, though Elidir and Angharad were in their graves. Whenever Meilyr came to the hermitage, as he did more and more often, looking like the ghost of Elidir's youth, Morfran could hardly find a name for his feeling towards the boy. Was he the son he would never beget of his own body? Or something won back, or stolen, from Elidir? Or Elidir's own young self, who could now be mastered and ruled by Morfran's hard-won knowledge and power?

He shifted painfully in his chair. His head was beginning to ache, his breathing sounded like groans. These were not right thoughts for a monk—but he had entered religion without a vocation, without love of God or man, because only in a monastery could he go on living with some dignity.

He had been taught to read and write in Latin and had taught himself some Greek from an old grammar book. At first, he practised these skills as a way of passing the time, like tying trout-flies or carving gaming-pieces. Then the novice-master, whose waking hours were taken up with teaching and the copying of gospel-books, had asked him to list the contents of the old chest that was the monastery library. Llangollen was not a large, wealthy foundation, famous for its scholarship, like Bangor-ys-y-Coed. Its abbots and brothers had always been more given to prayer and pastoral duties than to book-learning.

Morfran found a strange jumble of texts, many incomplete, the flotsam of a sunken empire that had drifted in from the ruins of Roman forts. He discovered the *Pymander* of Hermes

Trismegistus; also a copy of *The Celestial Hierarchy*, with a very odd commentary and invocations to be used with the Names.

It began to dawn on him that there were ways of travelling that could take him faster and further than a swift horse on a Roman road—and a power greater than the Emperor's that he had still got the strength to wield if he could reach and seize it.

The bulk of the little collection had been brought to the monastery two hundred years ago by a wealthy landowner from Caer Gloiu, fleeing to the mountains with his treasures after Hengist's massacre. He had been one of Vortigern's councillors and had shared his lord's interests and pastimes. The novice-master told Morfran innocently that their benefactor must have been a mathematician with a leaning to geometry. His books were full of numbers and strange diagrams. It was after examining them that Morfran had decided to become a hermit, but he had kindly offered to take the books with him for further study.

Elidir had been generous with his cousin's lost lands. The old fort of Dinas Brân stood opposite the monastery on the other side of the river, only a short distance away. He had made it over absolutely, and endowed it with the rents of several rich farms. So Morfran had wealth, comfort and seclusion to follow the studies that brought him the fame of great learning and even greater holiness.

Years passed. Meilyr came as a pupil to the monastic school; he had always been drawn to book-learning far more strongly than his elder brother. He made a duty-visit to his uncle in Dinas Brân and was fascinated by his company; he felt far closer to Morfran than to Elidir and Madoc. When he began to dabble in his uncle's occult studies with the quick—too quick—cleverness he showed in everything he undertook, Morfran saw the chance at last to win himself a body as strong and agile as the one he had lost in his youth, inside which his own spirit could move and act.

It would not be easy. Meilyr had a strong vein of selfishness and self-confidence to protect him. On the other hand, it was not impossible. Morfran studied Meilyr as intently as one of his magical texts. Though his nephew never spoke about it even to him, he was well aware of those moments when Meilyr's selfhood splintered into fragments. Something had been flawed in him, perhaps from the moment of his begetting between a father obsessed and a mother embittered by the ghost of a cheated passion. A stronger will, armed with knowledge, should be able to invade and rule him.

Now that Morfran had forced himself to retread his path of life back to the present moment, he had calmed and mastered himself. He was ready to take up the problem of mastering Meilyr. This latest crazy prank of going to Oswy's court to steal a woman had been an act of his own free-will. He had not said a word to his uncle about his plan. Morfran did not like that, nor Meilyr's binding himself unwittingly to a stranger. Still, the fact that he was now bound, and by an act of his own choice, was something gained, particularly as the girl did not know her power or how to use it. He turned his thoughts to Alchflaed.

Getting to his feet, he took the lamp and went behind the curtain to the other half of the room. It seemed bare and unused; a chance visitor—but there were no chance visitors to this place—would have thought that the plain table, stool and chests had been stowed here out of the way because they were not needed. He set the lamp on a shelf, took a bowl of black Castor ware from one of the chests and filled it with water from the ewer.

Then he sat down at the table with the lamp behind him, keeping his gaze on the water. In his mind he touched the braid on Meilyr's wrist, felt its silkiness, saw the warm tints in the dark brown hair, unbound it and twined his fingers in its waves, then gently closed his hand on it. He was breathing deeply and steadily; with each breath he silently called her name: *Alchflaed, Alchflaed, Alchflaed.* . . He did not try to force his thoughts but turned his attention north-east, towards Northumbria.

There was a blurring in the watery mirror, then much shapeless movement that turned to scudding clouds and brief glimpses of pictures that vanished as quick as an eyeblink—a bare sandy coast with long rollers coming in on an easterly gale, a forest of great oaks with their branches thrashing; then the clouds parted and the full moon sailed out of the darkness. He may have drawn his breath too sharply and stirred the water; the moon wavered, for a moment her two crescents showed on either side of the full circle. Then the broken sparkles joined and the water began to glow till the whole cup was full of light.

Morfran was hovering over a landscape as if he were poised on hawk's wings. There was a high spine of moorland to his left with the sun sloping towards it, but below him was a valley with a clear stream running through, sheltered by gentle hills. There was a large steading on the rise above the stream; inside the stockade he could see a hall in the English style; its high gables and porch-pillars deeply carved, surrounded by bower, barn and stable.

The late sun gilded the thatch, the carvings and the rich grass in the water-meadows where cattle were grazing. It was the most peaceful place Morfran had ever seen.

Four riders came down the track from the north. The leader pointed to the hall and said something with a laugh. Morfran stooped lower to see him. He was tall and richly-dressed, unarmed but for a sword. His hair and beard were bright gold; he had large light-blue eyes. Morfran was struck by the serenity of his expression. He was not a very young man; he must have been at least ten years older than Meilyr yet seemed as much the younger. It was oddly disturbing to see a face so unmarked by life or passion, especially in a warrior of high rank. Morfran had seen that look on some monks.

The lord's companion seemed to be his armour-bearer; there was a mail-shirt lying across his thighs and a helmet at the saddle-bow, as if his master had disarmed during the ride. The other two men were guards or servants; they rode behind and carried spears.

As the riders forded the stream, someone in the steading must have seen or heard them. Men came to the gate and helped them dismount; the horses were led away to the stables; the lord's servants went with them. The lord and his armour-bearer walked to the porch; someone stepped out to greet them—a well-dressed man with a hard mouth and cold eyes. He made to kneel but the lord caught him up and embraced him. Then he unbuckled his sword and handed it to the master of the hall, who passed it to one of his attendants. The armour-bearer had also been relieved of his weapons. The lord flung his arm round the shoulders of his host and the two went inside the hall—

Morfran had only meant to do a little quiet scrying. He wanted to see the girl who had Meilyr's fate plaited into her hair, he had not intended to take any action. Even so, he was not usually careless. But Meilyr's presence, and the ordeal of travelling his life-path, had weakened him. He had been too impatient; he had not set a boundary or placed guardians. He was unprotected against what came next.

The picture in the water clouded and darkened; he expected a new scene. But the cloud began to rise from the cup, it thickened between smoke and slime. Tendrils of it brushed across Morfran's face, groping for his eyes and mouth, reaching round his neck. There was a disgusting stench; his entrails heaved but his stomach felt as empty as if he had not eaten for days. In spite of his longing to vomit, he was wild with hunger and that terrible helpless rage he had suffered when his mind first cleared of wound-fever and he knew he was trapped beyond escape in the prison of his body.

As the horror tightened its grip, a door was burst open suddenly by some force that tried to come through. There was a roaring of wind, sea-birds screamed in the distance, a raven croaked by his ear. He knew that the door must be closed and threw himself against it. For some moments he was nearly torn apart: the horror coming out of the cup held him from putting all his strength on the door; his struggle to close the gap pulled his mind from what was rising in the middle of the room. It was thickening and taking shape all the time, soon it would be beyond his control. All the while, he was being battered nearly senseless; his self-hood was being swept away as if it had been caught by a flooding river full of uprooted trees, he was drowning in cold mud—

With a last effort he got his mind free for a second, in which he made it shape the words of banishing and utter a Name of Power. The room became quiet. He was lying against the wall as if he had been thrown there; the bowl had been tipped over and its water was dripping from the table-top. The lamp still shone, but the only shadows in the room were from the furniture.

He listened. There was no sound from Asyn below or Meilyr in the hall. Nothing had disturbed them. The trapdoors in floor and roof were firmly shut. The door he had just slammed had been burst open somewhere else, perhaps in one of the other worlds. He knew he was closer to death than he had ever been since his friend's spear had pierced his loins. Still, he forced himself to sweep Dinas Brân, raised the Ring along its rampart and set it under protection. Then he crawled into bed.

Hell had been let loose in Northumbria. What had the English been doing there? He guessed at some unexpiated crime, some evil that stirred at the name of one of the Northumbrian royal House. Morfran had taken his studies and experiments far enough to know that the dead do not always stay sleeping in their graves. When a soul has been driven untimely from bodily life, going out on a stream of hatred, pain or fear, it may linger hungry and craving on the borders of this world, waiting for a chance to come back. Such lost souls are more powerful than the living, as they are free from the chains of time and space. Yet they are also weaker, because they lack a body to act for them. They will try with all the terrible power of their desire to seize one and win back a place in the land of the living—and they are as alert as hounds for the least scent of weakness or evil that will lead them to their prey. Something was tracking Alchflaed; perhaps it was tracking all those of her blood. Whoever, or whatever, it was could be called into dangerous awareness at the sound of her name.

For the space of a heartbeat Morfran was glad at the thought of the miles of mountain and moor that lay between Northumbria and Powys. Then his heart nearly stopped. What had tried to come out of the cup had not been a vision but a presence. It had known where to come. Such visitants did not need to use the Roman roads or the winding shepherds' tracks over the hills. They could travel on a path no wider than a hair's breadth—dark brown hair with autumn glints in it, set in gold and bound around Meilyr's wrist.

CHAPTER
7

The track from the north breasted a rise, then ran down to the ford. King Oswine of Deira reined in at the crest to savour the pleasure of coming to a friend's house and a warm welcome. The sun was westering over the moors above Sualadale. The little valley, sheltered by gentle hills, was brimming with sunlight gilding the thatch on Hunwald's hall, the ripples of the stream, the rich grass of the water-meadows.

Oswine turned to his armour-bearer, laughing with gentle mockery as he pointed to the hall.

'So here we are, Tondhere, in spite of your raven's croaking. A quiet ride behind us and a quiet rest before us.'

'You shouldn't have dismissed the war-band.'

'I keep telling you—I'm showing the Bernicians I hadn't gone north to attack them. It was just a mistake. Anyone could get on the wrong side of the border, up on the moors. We're not at war.'

Oswine had acted with the best of intentions, but it would be awkward to tell his cousin that he had thought the Bernicians were about to kick him out of his kingdom and was coming in to take over. He was neither a liar nor a hypocrite. He had told himself and Tondhere the courteous version of his advance into Bernicia several times during their ride south. By now he had convinced himself.

'Oswy could ask why you didn't stop to explain. It looked bad, turning tail like that when we saw their war-host. The men didn't like it.'

'I wasn't going to throw away the lives of my dear companions against a whole army. It's likely Oswy's restless and angry after this last Mercian raid. He could have struck first and asked questions later.'

Tondhere glanced uneasily over his shoulder, where the track went north to the Roman road over the moors. Oswine laughed again.

'Oswy won't come after us. He's got more than enough to do trying to hold his land against Penda. He'll never risk a war with us as well. I'll get Bishop Aidan to make all right between us. Now, come and get your dinner—you and your belly will stop grumbling after one of Hunwald's feasts.'

He put his horse down the slope to the ford. Tondhere and the two grooms who were the King's only escort followed him. As they splashed across the stream, someone in the steading must have seen or heard them. Voices called in the courtyard; men came running to the gate to help them dismount. The horses were led to the stable; Oswine's two grooms went with them, brightening at an offer of beer to wash their throats out before supper.

Oswine, followed by Tondhere, made straight for the porch where Hunwald had already come out to greet him. He made to kneel, but Oswine caught him up and embraced him warmly.

'Hunwald! It's good to see you!'

He unbuckled his sword and handed it to Hunwald who passed it to one of his attendants. Tondhere was also being courteously relieved of his weapons before the handwashing and the feast. Still talking eagerly, Oswine flung an arm around his friend's shoulders and the two went inside the hall. The steward himself was ready by the door with bowl and towel to attend on the King.

'I didn't send word ahead I'd be staying with you. Coming to Getlingas is like coming home. I knew you'd find me a mouthful of food and a mattress to sleep on!'

He laughed as he dried his hands, looking round the bright hall, its floor strewn with fresh rushes, its walls hung with embroidered cloths, its trestle boards and benches ready for the feast.

'I've come from the north—in fact, I went over the border a mile or two.'

Hunwald looked grave. 'I know. A rider came through on his way south and gave us the news. That was a bad business, my lord—coming up against Oswy's troops and having to back away in a hurry. The Bernicians will make an ugly story of it against us.'

They walked towards the dais. Hunwald's retainers were coming into the hall behind them; servants scuttled out of the way. Oswine was smiling with his usual unruffled serenity. If Hunwald had meant a rebuke, or a warning, the King did not heed it.

'It wasn't like that at all. I'll send a messenger to Bishop Aidan. He'll make my peace if Oswy's pride has been hurt.'

He took his place in the high seat with Hunwald at his right hand. Tondhere was respectfully welcomed on the warriors' bench alongside the leader of Hunwald's spearmen. Oswine signed for the meal to start. Turning to chat to his host, he saw that Hunwald was still looking gloomy and ill at ease.

'You're not still worrying about the Bernicians? It's not like you, Hunwald, to scare so easily. And you surely don't think I'd come here if I were bringing trouble and danger at my heels, to fall on you?'

Hunwald forced a smile. 'Forgive my poor spirits, lord. My wife was brought to bed of a son three nights ago. She had a bad time; she's still poorly—but she'd blame herself, and me too, if I spoiled your welcome on her account.'

Oswine was sympathetic. 'I'm truly sorry she's had to suffer, but remember what God's word says: "*A woman when she is in labour hath sorrow because her hour is come, but when she hath brought forth the child she remembereth no more the anguish for joy that a man is born into the world.*" ' His eyes beamed with pleasure. 'What luck that I should come just at this moment! I can bring a gift to my godson's cradle.'

Oswine's self-content wrapped him like a cloak against any chills of anxiety or fear that might be touching the other feasters in the hall. There was not much talk or laughter among the spearmen. Tondhere guessed they were brooding over the shame that had come to the royal war-band. He felt ashamed himself in spite of all Oswine's reasoning, and was not in the mood to make folk speak to him.

Hunwald's wife, of course, did not appear. The mead-horn was presented by his young daughter, helped by two bower-women.

The girl was edgy and clumsy, overset no doubt by the King's presence and worries about her mother.

Oswine tried to cheer her with thanks and praise, saying kindly, 'I won't trouble you long, my dear.' He was afraid she would disgrace herself by bursting into tears and earn her father's anger on his account.

The tense silence was broken by a tumult of shouting in the courtyard. A stable-hand dashed into the hall regardless of decent manners, yelling, 'There's a war-band coming— Bernicians!'

Oswine stood up. 'Tondhere, bring me my sword. The rest of you stay where you are.' He turned to Hunwald. 'I take this on myself. I'll go out and meet them, find out what they've come for. If it's myself, I'll surrender. No one else shall be in danger for my sake.' He smiled. 'If I don't come back, farewell, old friend.'

Hunwald had also risen; he caught both of Oswine's hands.

'You shan't go!'

The leader of Hunwald's spearmen had a friendly arm on Tondhere's shoulder. Suddenly Tondhere screamed out, 'Your back, my lord!' before his throat could be slit. Hunwald gripped Oswine's hands even tighter but the King had turned at the cry. The steward's knife took him in the side instead of the back, so he did not see his friend's face as he died.

The porch was thronging with armed men. The trampling and shouts outside told a large number were all round the walls. From the bower a woman screamed. Someone entered the hall. Hunwald had seen him before during his furtive visits to Bernicia; he was Ethelwin, leader of Oswy's war-band.

Ethelwin stood near the door, looking at the folk along the benches.

'Peace to this place! I've brought a message from King Oswy to his cousin. He's sorry they didn't meet earlier today, as they came so close. He'd dearly like a meeting, to have a friendly talk for the good of both kingdoms.'

He let his glance rest at last on the figure slumped over the table on the dais.

'If King Oswine is weary after his day's ride, or sleepy after the feast, I've brought the royal litter.'

He made a sign to the men outside and began to walk up the hall to the dais. The Bernicians crowded in after him, fully armed. Four of them were carrying a litter draped with a richly-embroidered coverlet. None of the feasters stirred. The few who had been in the murder plot were puzzling over the Bernicians' next move; the innocent were still stunned by their king's death.

Ethelwin advanced on Hunwald and the blood-stained heap by his side. He put his hand on Oswine's shoulder and turned his body to check that he was dead. Hunwald tried to smile but, meeting Ethelwin's eyes, the smile died.

The four bearers raised Oswine and laid him reverently on the bier, straightening his limbs, crossing his hands on his breast, smoothing his golden hair. They draped the rich pall over his body and carried him out, still in unbroken silence.

Ethelwin put his hand on Hunwald's arm.

'Come.'

Life came back into Hunwald's face.

'Where?'

'Just up the Roman road to Gretabrig. The King will want to see you. You're all witnesses,' he looked at the Deirans, 'that my lord sent a friendly message asking to meet his cousin. He'll want to know how his cousin died, as he's the nearest kinsman and heir to the kingdom.'

Ethelwin was not taking much trouble over his acting. The Deirans were unarmed but for their feasting-knives, and also outnumbered. Besides, to his mind, men who killed their own king were viler than rats. If it wasn't for Oswy's orders, he'd have barred the whole pack of them into the hall and burned it.

The screaming outside sounded nearer; there was a stir at the door, Hunwald's wife rushed in. She had been suckling her baby; her hair was loose, her shift unlaced, her swollen breasts were bare. She flung herself in front of Hunwald, her hem slopping in Oswine's blood, and clasped Ethelwin's knees. The daughter clung to her father sobbing. The Deirans stirred. Ethelwin sensed a surge towards him; his men levelled their spears.

'No blood,' Oswy had said, his eyes like the winter sea. 'If you handle it well, there'll be no bloodshed. And no woman or child is to be abused in any way.'

Oswy had spoken pleasantly; he usually did. Ethelwin knew he had better not handle it badly.

His mouth smiled. 'What ails you, lady? I'm just taking your good lord to come and clear this matter up for King Oswy.'

She searched his face, then looked desperately at Hunwald's warriors. 'Take your weapons and attend your lord.'

'And leave you all unguarded, lady? These are wild times. Don't worrry about your lord. There are enough of us to see him safe.'

'Oswy promised—' Hunwald's voice rasped as if it had got rusty from disuse. He swallowed, managed to raise it and keep it steady for his men to hear. 'He gave me his word, sitting at his table, drinking from the same horn—'

'He hasn't forgotten what he owes to you and to himself.' Ethelwin's eyes were on the crouching woman and the blood of the guest who had also sat at table and shared a mead-horn. Then he glanced at the Deirans. 'We're warriors, we all know what belongs to the honour of a warrior—and a king. But for the sake of your lady, to ease her heart, I swear by the head and hands of St Oswald—and that's an oath Oswy sets above his own soul, he'd flay and burn anyone who broke it—that no man shall take your life while you're in our care. No hand or weapon shall be raised against you. No harm shall be done you by blade or rope, fire or water. You'll not get so much as a bruise,' he smiled grimly, 'unless you've a bad seat on a horse.'

Hunwald made himself laugh, to calm his wife and keep up some sort of dignity in front of his men. It was for dignity, too, not even as a test, that he called for his sword as well as a cloak. The Bernicians did not stop him buckling it on; he knew the sword would be no use anyway. Oswy would keep an oath on his brother's head; they wouldn't come at him with weapons. Part of his mind even amused itself asking how Oswy would kill him: poison, a pillow over his face, getting a girl or a child to do it while he slept?

His wife had got to her feet and drawn her shift up over her breasts. One of her women had pulled off her own veil to cover her lady's head. Hunwald kissed his wife and daughter lightly, as for a brief absence; then turned and went out with Ethelwin.

The bodies of Oswine's two grooms were lying near the stable; they had been cut down as they tried to run to their lord's side when the Bernicians were sighted. The bier had been lifted on to a horse-litter; Ethelwin's mount was led up, and another for Hunwald. It was not one of his own beasts but a fine chestnut stallion out of Oswy's stud. The by-standers were being made to witness that Oswy had expected his cousin to be alive and to visit him in friendship. He had sent magnificent gifts, the litter and the horse, for Oswine to make choice of how he travelled.

The bier turned out of the courtyard. Ethelwin and Hunwald rode after it, but once they were through the gate, Ethelwin went to the head of the war-band, leaving Hunwald to follow the litter like a mourner, with the rearguard at his heels.

He took a last look at his home as they paused to ford the stream. His wife had come to the gate of the stockade with her arm round her daughter's shoulders. She watched the riders go up the track to the north; when they turned the corner round the hill-slope and went out of sight, she was still standing there.

The Bernicians kept silence all the way up the hill to the Roman road that went straight as an arrow's flight west over Stony Moor to Cumbria. After hardly more than a mile they came to a track on the left, that led south across the wooded hills up to the high moors above Sualadale. The litter moved on up the Roman road with most of the war-band. Ethelwin remained behind with Hunwald and his escort.

Hunwald asked no questions when they turned on to the track, nor when they left it for the thread of a path that twisted steeply up the hillside. They went single file, but the trees crowded too close and the undergrowth of fern and bramble was too dense for him to break away.

The earth was jagged with rocks that were larger as they climbed, great slabs from some rock-fall. At last they came to a wall of low cliffs and turned along the pathless ground at its foot. The horses were having to pick their way now, to guard their legs. Ethelwin drew rein and called down the line to halt when he came to a place where the cliff wall ran back into a narrow, sheer-sided cove. A streamlet trickled out from the far end, making the ground marshy. Near the source, a sturdy holly tree had rooted in a crack of the rock, leaning out over the water. Directly above it, looking as if it were growing out of the very crown of the holly, was a rowan. Every man there, even those who called themselves Christians, felt a moment's lifting of his scalp and a shiver down his spine to the loins, coming to a place that the Lady of the Wood had so clearly marked for her own.

Then the Bernicians dismounted; one of them came to Hunwald's side and took his sword from the scabbard.

'Get down.'

Hunwald thought he had accepted death, but the sight of his own sword drawn against him, the shameless oath-breaking, was too much.'

'You gave your word—'

'And we'll keep it.' Ethelwin nodded to his men. 'Gently now. See you don't hurt him.'

When he saw the slave-chain with its collar and manacles, his heart lifted. So this was how Oswy meant to save his oath. They would sell him furtively to some west-bound trader making his way down Sualadale and over the pass to Lonceaster. Oswy had likely fixed the meeting to hand him over even before his visit to Penrith. Slavery should be an end worse than death to a nobleman: but he was rich, he could offer ransom. He could find a Christian priest among the Welsh or Irish and explain his plight, get word to his wife sooner or later by one of the pilgrims.

Even when the Bernicians bound him to the holly trunk, looping and crossing the chain round it from the collar to the manacles on his wrists so that his hands were raised helplessly on each side of his shoulders, he did not struggle. Let them amuse themselves by tethering him like a beast till they handed him over to his new master. While there was life, there was hope—above all, hope of telling the story when he was beyond Oswy's reach, so that Welsh and Irish bards could take it up and hand it back to English scops, till Oswy's name stank throughout the islands.

Ethelwin examined the chain, then swung up to his saddle. He brought his horse in front of the tree so that Hunwald could see him.

'Bear witness, our king keeps his word. No harm has been done to you by blade or rope, fire or water, while you've been in our care. And no man will take your life. No one else will ever come here.'

The Bernicians rode away. For a while he heard their horses and the cracking of twigs as they pushed through the undergrowth. Then there were no more sounds from the world of men.

The wind from the moors whispered through the rowan, rustled the stiff holly leaves. A magpie chattered like a burst of mocking laughter; midges from the stream whined past his ear. Despair kept him from screaming; nothing human would heed him. There was no path; the ground was too steep for cattle, too overgrown for sheep. If some hunter caught a cry on the wind he would think it was a woodwose or an etin from the moors, and keep well away.

He stared ahead, over the matted treetops on the rocky slope, towards the wooded plain with its fertile clearings and rich farms all the way to the Tese, the lands he had sold his soul to gain. The terrible fury of the betrayed traitor ripped through him. He began to writhe, jump, pull, claw at his chains till the holly thrashed as if a gale was blowing. He was wild with rage at his helplessness; his home was barely three miles crow's flight over the hill—

Crows. Hunwald had seen them on battlefields and after

hangings. He knew what the faces of the dead were like under their beaks and claws—but he was hanged alive on his gallows. At that moment he fully tasted his death; it made him vomit the meal at which he had betrayed his lord. The stench and stickiness drew the flies to his mouth and neck; his tongue was foul, longing for a drink from the stream; his feet were cold and wet, sinking into the mud. He felt himself crumbling into a midden of separate pains, angers, terrors—soon there would be no more Hunwald.

He struggled to hold together, to keep his mind clear while he gathered his sufferings and willed them into one curse to throw at Oswy and all his line. May they all be betrayed by those they trusted. May they be trapped into living death. May they die alone in terror. May their names be blotted out from memory or prayer and may their souls be eaten—

Shadows swept over his head, there was a rushing of wings. He twisted his neck in the iron collar with a mad hope that his hungry curse had called some demon of the air to carry it to its victims. But it was only a couple of ravens, Woden's birds, who had perched on the edge of the cliff. They watched him for a second, then raised their wings again, coming for him.

CHAPTER
8

Alchflaed was wise in victory. She held tight to her gains and dodged the risk of another battle when she might lose them. She gave Alchfrid no excuse for changing their father's orders and packing her back to Coludesburh. She loved her aunt Ebbe and had always been happy in the convent, but now the thought of it was like a foreboding of prison. Her idea of freedom was that Welsh harper, strolling unconcerned across the wide sands as if he had all the world to choose his way. Soon she would be out in the world herself; if anything stopped her now she would smother.

While she was bustling to sort and pack her travelling chests from her mother's rich store of robes and jewels, she would find her feet tapping out a jig. Or she would suddenly break off, drape herself in one of her mother's embroidered cloaks and declaim some lines from the *Seafarer* as if she was a scop performing in the hall:

> '*Endless longing lures my soul to set out,*
> *to seek a foreign folk in a far land*—'

She never let her brother hear her. It had been her mother's favourite poem, but instinct told her he would think them no fit words for a woman's mouth. In front of Alchfrid she showed nothing but a housewifely concern that his men should have new shirts and well-aired cloaks for the ride south.

After a few days' wary truce, the brother and sister were brought together by the shock of the news from Deira. While Bernicia was still reeling from the Mercian attack, King Oswine had bought his troops across the border.

Alchfrid had barely time to get his men saddled up for a dash south to bar their way, when another rider brought word of Oswy's lightning move over Stony Moor with a Cumbrian war-host. Faced with overwhelming numbers, the invaders had retreated without striking a blow. Alchfrid was full of admiration.

'He must have known this attack was coming,' he explained to his sister at supper, mapping the country for her with pieces of oatcake and lines drawn on the table-top with his finger. 'That's why he kept me from riding here sooner. He didn't want to commit my troops before he'd sent out to gather the war-host. And all without letting fall one word, even to me, that might have given his plans to the enemy!'

Alchfrid was truly happy. He had very high ideas about a son's duty to a father and was always careful to speak of Oswy with respect. It was a relief to know that the respect was deserved.

Not long after came the dreadful tale of Oswine's murder by one of his own thanes, embittered at the shame of the Deirans' bloodless retreat. Oswine was unmarried and had no brothers or uncles to come after him. Deira might have fallen into civil war or been seized by Penda. Luckily, Oswy had kept his war-host close to the border in case of another Deiran attack. He was the nearest male heir of Deira, as his mother had been King Edwin's sister. He had claimed the Kingship, rescued his cousin's body for honourable burial and dealt at once with the killer.

This news made a great difference to Alchfrid. His sister could see it at once in the eyes and voices of the household. As well as his own Cumbria, he was now heir to both the great English kingdoms that side of the Humber. If he outlived his father he would be the most powerful man in the north. The fate of all Britain could be in his hands.

The most powerful man south of the Humber was Penda; it was not hard to guess how he would look at such a rival to Mercia. He was not giving Oswy any peace now; smashing at his land year after year until he could be killed or forced to submit. Surely Penda would do anything to destroy a united Northumbria before it could gather strength.

Kingdoms died with their kings; Oswine's fate had shown once again that they need not die in honourable battle. Alchflaed was quite sure now that she had been called to her brother's side by another will than her own. Her mother's spirit had called her to play a part, along with Alchfrid, in their father's work.

It was now urgent for them to join Oswy, but the bright weather suddenly broke in a shattering storm that roared out of the east, hurling the breakers up the sea-rock till the foam came over the stockade. Then, with the calm, came the worst news of all. Bishop Aidan was dead.

He died strangely. As soon as the Mercians had gone he had set out—on foot as usual so that the humblest serf or beggar could speak to him man to man—to minister to the stricken country folk. When his sickness came to him, he was at the royal estate a little to the north of Bebbanburh, but he would not let himself be carried up to the palace. He would not even go into the reeve's house nearby, or have himself lifted into the church porch. The folk put up a shelter of cowhide over him by its west wall; he leaned against a buttress-post and died there on the last day of August, only eleven days after Oswine.

Aidan had loved him; most people did, drawn by the almost childlike innocence of Oswine's nature. Folk said that Aidan had died of grief for the beloved King, that he had not wanted to live any longer in a world where the gentle-hearted were so foully betrayed. When the story crossed the Deiran border it took an uglier twist: folk said the bishop had not wanted to draw his dying breath under any roof owned by Oswy.

In spite of this grief, Alchflaed's spirits were dancing like the waves when she rode out of Bebbanburh at last on a bright September morning. There was a fresh breeze off the sea, the becks were brimful and sparkling after the rain, the moors were royal purple. She felt as if one of her mother's stories of magic and adventure was beginning, with herself as the hero of the quest.

It was a happy journey. She rode like a boy, in leather breeches and jerkin, sparing Alchfrid the burden of escorting a lumbering travelling cart and a flock of squawking maids. She took the little attendance she needed from the womenfolk in the thanes' halls where they stayed overnight. The young Cumbrian nobles in Alchfrid's war-band liked her for her beauty and good humour; her brother enjoyed her company more than he expected. She was intelligent and book-learned but had seen almost nothing of the world outside her convent on its remote headland. She had a great many questions to ask and listened with admiring interest to his answers, especially when they came to the great Roman road that led down to Deira. Here they could see more and more traces of the lost Empire. At last they came to the famous Wall and halted at the fort guarding the gate to the south.

Alchflaed was almost stunned. She could hardly speak her wonder, staring up at that barrier of finely-cut stone and thinking how it went right across Britain.

'It's true what the scops say:

"This wall is wonder, Fate felled it, Broken lie the cities built by giants—"'

She turned to share the verses with her brother and was startled to silence by the cold rage in his eyes.

'It should never have happened. This is what comes of heathen barbarism. Dozens of petty thieves calling themselves kings, tearing the land to pieces like curs snarling over the bones on a kitchen-midden. There should be one Church, one Law, one Emperor. Then this could all be rebuilt.'

For a moment Alchflaed saw Britain covered by square stone cities linked by straight stone roads. Armies marched endlessly along them, troops of men keeping the same step, wearing the same armour, all with the same face carved out of stone. She shuddered and nearly disgraced herself to her brother by saying 'God forbid!' aloud.

There was a farm in one corner of the fort where she was to sleep that night. Alchflaed strolled out towards dusk while her brother was inspecting the horses. Hens scuttled out of her way; an elderly collie followed her, nosing among the cowpats as she went towards the crumbling heap that had once been the fort commander's villa. Some of its roof held up, a couple of rooms were still used as pens and wood stores. Her foot kicked the litter to show a few scraps of coloured stone, a mosaic of grapes. One wall kept the shadow of a painted flower-garland. It was sad, as all lost beauty and splendour are sad, but it was only a heap of stones, nothing to break the heart over. The collie lifted his leg and pissed on the mosaic grapes. She remembered her brother's face and voice, looking at the ruins.

Alchfrid could break his heart for it. Alchfrid could kill for it.

She wondered with a stab of dread whether he counted their father as one of the *petty thieves calling themselves kings, tearing the land to pieces like curs snarling over the bones on a kitchen midden*; and if so, what he might do about it. She shivered and hurried back to the firelight and warmth in the farm-house.

During the last days of their ride south, the thought of meeting her unknown father grew in Alchflaed's mind until it blotted out everything else. She had been eager for it; she wanted a father. She also believed that knowing him would help her know her mother better, fill in the missing gaps of her life. Yet ever since she had passed through the Wall, the eagerness had been threatened by disquiet—a disquiet which the chosen meeting place did nothing to soothe.

Perscbrig had also been a Roman fort, but as it was on the frontier between Bernicia and Deira it had kept its usefulness and a sort of dignity. The reeves of both kings met there to argue cases of theft or damage, stolen cattle were held in pound till claimed, traders waited to pay their dues or to group together for safer travel. So there was ample stabling to be had inside the walls, well-appointed guest halls to sleep in, besides the reeve's fine homestead.

Though it stood on the northern bank of the Tese, Perscbrig was in Deiran hands. Penda had come that way too often to make it a restful or healthy spot for Bernicians. Oswy had not made any changes since he took the Kingship. He claimed to be the rightful heir of Deira and the faithful avenger of his cousin; he couldn't dismiss the reeve for being Oswine's man.

As soon as they entered the northern gate, Alchflaed felt a watchful hostility closing round the Bernician group. Nothing was done or said openly against them but everything that was said seemed to mean more than the words.

It was early in the day; they had arrived before Oswy, who was coming up from the south. The reeve apologised, quite needlessly, for the poor food and lodging he had to offer.

'We were taken all unawares—we aren't ready to welcome our new king.'

Alchfrid said courteously that everything was to his liking; Alchflaed smiled and murmured agreement.

'If the King had come this way a month ago he could have stopped at Getlingas,' went on the reeve. This was clearly what he had been leading up to say. 'There used to be good hospitality at Getlingas. But King Oswy can't go there now.'

'Why not?' Alchfrid's voice was sharp. As they neared the Deiran border there had been some ugly hints in front of his companions, who had repeated them.

'Because it's burned to the ground.' The reeve spoke with deep satisfaction.

Alchflaed was sympathetic. 'I'm sorry—I hope no one got killed.'

'All of them. His wife. His daughter. The baby at the breast. They were all in there, like rats in the standing corn. The gate was barred, not even the stock escaped.'

'Raiders?' Alchfrid was worried; he knew that raiders would never behave so wastefully. He dreaded that civil war was breaking out and was not sure that he could halt it.

'Deirans.' The reeve's smile was vicious. 'We've no time for traitors. Or traitors' friends.'

Alchflaed did not understand the hints but felt more and more uneasy. When she went to the women's bower to change her clothes, she refused a cold offer of help from the reeve's wife, then sank on her knees by the travelling chest, pressing her face against her mother's robes for comfort.

She had thought long and anxiously about wearing them. For herself, she loved the touch of them against her skin, as if Riemmelth had drawn her back into her arms, but she dreaded hurting her father. She could not give him the worst wound of all: he would not see Riemmelth's ghost coming to greet him. She was so unlike her pale, raven-haired mother that she did not even know she was beautiful. Her fear was that she might stir painful memories of happier, lost times.

So she set aside all the garments in her mother's favourite green; also a silver necklet that the Queen had always worn, though she had far more splendid jewels than that simple chain with a full moon pendant flanked by its two crescents. The brocade tunics from Constantinople, so heavily couched with gold and silver that they could have stood for armour, were far too magnificent for a night's halt at a fort on the marches.

Alchflaed chose a gown of russet wool, embroidered at the neck and hem with black silk and gold thread. The Dish-Thane's wife at Bebbanburh, helping her to pack, said that Riemmelth had never worn it, finding the colour unbecoming. It suited Alchflaed's warm autumn loveliness very well; with a triple necklace of amber and a saffron veil over her brown curls she looked glowing though her spirits were chill.

As she sat waiting for the sounds of Oswy's arrival, she had one of Riemmelth's green gowns still spread over her lap; she was fondling the moon-necklace, unwilling to put it away. Time paused; then flowed back across the years as she recalled how her mother had looked, that day in her childhood when she had caught her one glimpse of her father . . .

The Queen was visiting Coludesburh. When she came the Abbess always allowed the daughter full freedom from her lessons to be with her mother. That day, they had spent a lazy noon-time sitting in the convent herb garden. Alchflaed, who loved her mother's Welsh songs and stories, had asked yet again for the tale of Blodeuedd, the girl who had been made by wizardry out of flowers.

Butterflies floated in the air; the heat had brought out the scents of mint and thyme; it seemed as if Blodeuedd herself might take shape among the leaves and step out before their eyes. Yet somehow, for the first time the hopelessness of the story had caught Alchflaed more than the magic.

'It's a pity she left her man and went with another lover,' she said thoughtfully, rubbing a sprig of mint and sniffing her fingers. 'Why did she do it—was she wicked?'

'She liked the second man better.' Riemmelth's voice sounded sad, though her lips were smiling.

'But her first man got her back in the end, didn't he? Only by then he hated her.' Alchflaed shivered in the heat; her foster-mother said that meant someone was walking over your grave, wherever it lay waiting. 'If he didn't want her, why did he destroy her? Why didn't he just let them go away and be happy together?'

'Because they were living outside paradise.'

'What's paradise?'

'An enclosed garden. Where no evil or hatred can get in to destroy people. Like this one.' Riemmelth stroked her daughter's cheek. 'Dont let the story fret you, little one. It was all over long ago. You're safe in Mother Ebbe's house.'

Alchflaed didn't feel too sure; she glanced anxiously at the hedge that walled them in—it didn't seem to be a very strong defence. Just outside the entrance, at the top of the steps into the orchard, a man was standing watching them.

He was very tall; his hair shone silver-fair in the sunlight, like sand just washed by the ebbing tide. He was richly dressed: the crimson cloak thrown back from his shoulders was fastened by a huge square-headed brooch, his blue tunic was heavily embroidered, garnets flamed from the gold on his belt and arm-rings. He might have been called up by her mother's story to wait for Blodeuedd under the flowering branches — was he the treacherous lover or the vengeful husband?

Alchflaed jumped up, not sure whether she was going to run to the stranger or flee in panic. Her mother, who had risen at the same moment, caught her arm and whispered, 'Run and tell the Abbess her brother is waiting to take leave.' She sounded hurried and urgent; she kissed Alchflaed, then turned her round with a little pat to go towards the convent.

She set off obediently, but turned to shut the wicket gate behind her and took a backward glance. She saw her mother hurrying away from her down the gravel path, she was almost running — in eagerness or fear? — her green skirt flying above her ankles. The man gripped her by the waist and swung her round violently in the curve of his arm; the green skirt was smothered in a swirl of blood-red; she heard the man laughing. The two turned away into the orchard, their garments stirring the fallen blossom; they gleamed for a moment in the dappled sunshine under the apple-boughs, then vanished into the past . . .

Alchflaed found herself back in Perscbrig, clutching the green robe to her breast. She put it back carefully, with the silver necklace, into the clothes chest. A clamour from outside told her that the King's men had already ridden into the fort. Her legs felt weak as she crossed from the bower to the reeve's hall. She arrived at the same time as Alchfrid, who had been checking the gate-guards, and drew back behind him as they went in.

Oswy had already been greeted by the reeve and had withdrawn to the small chamber at the far end of the hall. He was sitting by the hearth; there was a table with a mead-flagon and goblets close by his hand.

'Ah, children. Come in, both of you, and sit down. Alchfrid, help your sister to mead.'

Alchflaed was dizzy; she had to draw a few quiet breaths and sip the mead before she could make herself look steadily at her father at last.

He was so like Alchfrid that he did not seem a stranger: a fine-looking man who took care over his clothes and his body, but with nothing showy or vain about him. His 'children' and 'both of you' had brought her into the welcome but his eyes and smile were for her brother.

'It's been a busy life since we last met. Is all well in the north? Did you have a quiet ride?'

'The ride was quiet.' Alchfrid hesitated. 'Father, I think you ought to know—there are stories—'

'When a king's killed there are always stories. Folk want somebody to blame.'

'Will there be trouble? They've already burned Hunwald's family.'

'That's between Deirans. I don't want trouble for us. I've just shifted our border down to the Don—that'll be no gain if Deira comes up in arms.' It was Oswy's turn to pause. 'We need a firm peace with goodwill on both sides, so I've pledged myself to marry Edwin's daughter. That should keep them quiet.'

Alchflaed felt sick with shock, then blamed herself for not expecting such news. Kings' marriages were part of their border defences. The marvel was that Oswy should have delayed so long in taking another wife—though Edwin's daughter was a prize worth waiting for. There had likely been some skilled haggling over terms.

Were you planning this, Father, while you sat by my mother's death-bed? Is that why your mind was too busy to think of sending for your daughter?

Alchfrid's face had not changed, only stilled. He spoke carefully.

'That is a very wise plan, Father. I hope it will work out to your happiness.'

Oswy laughed. 'Spoken like a dutiful son—but we've got to be frank it we're to work together now you're a man. A new queen for me means a step-mother for you—a son's happiness is at stake as well as a husband's.'

And a daughter's too, surely, when you put another woman in her mother's place?

'You've a right to know my plans. Cumbria's yours, of course, from your mother. And you're my eldest son and heir—no other marriage of mine can change that. But I haven't found it easy to hold Bernicia and Cumbria in double harness. Adding Deira will make it harder—but we can't do without Deira. This marriage will bind it to us while I live—but it would be a help to you when I'm gone, if you had a brother of Deiran stock who could rule it for you, as under-king. He'd be so much younger, you could mould him to your liking while he's growing up.' He grinned. 'That's supposing that Eanfled and I can get a son between us and that he grows up fit to rule. If he seems stupid or dangerous, I'll have him in a monastery before you can say 'oblate'.'

Did I seem so stupid or dangerous, Father, that you left me in a convent and never wanted me near you?

Alchfrid was looking and speaking more cordially. 'Thank you for being so open with me, Father. Be sure I shall do my best to be worthy of your trust.'

'I'm sure you will, my boy. That's why I'm trusting you to meet the new queen at Eoforwic and bring her north. At the moment the Deirans feel they've been beaten by treachery. I wouldn't dare go south without an army, yet that would look as if I'd come to take their princess by force. You're Prince of Cumbria as well as being my son. I want you to go to Eoforwic as Prince of Cumbria—that name won't remind them of feuds. Also, it will get our family life off to a pleasant start if you go to greet your new mother—and as your sister's the only lady in the royal family who hasn't taken the veil yet, I'm sending her with you.'

At last he turned to Alchflaed. He seemed to meet her eyes but she still felt he wasn't really looking at her.

'So, Alchflaed. You're looking very well. Life in Coludesburh suits you, it seems—you get on well with the Abbess?'

She was so glad to get some token of caring that she caught at it eagerly.

'Aunt Ebbe's very kind and the soul of patience over my lessons.'

He smiled. 'You don't make much trial of her patience. She writes me glowing accounts of your progress, says you're the best pupil she ever had. You must be very fond of your studies.'

'I don't care for all of them. But I love painting manuscripts and planning embroideries—choosing the colours and then seeing the shapes growing under my hands. And the chanting—how the notes draw out like threads of silk and weave in and out—'

'Good, good!' Oswy cut in briskly. 'I'm sure your aunt has told you that when you were born I meant to offer you to God in thanks for your mother's escape from Penda. But she was urgent that you should only take the veil by your own consent when you were old enough to know what you were doing. That's why I'm telling you this now. But I can see there's no doubt of your answer.'

Looking at her face, he could see a great deal of doubt.

'What's the matter? You say you're happy with your aunt. One day you'll succeed her as Abbess. Gifts like yours would be wasted outside the church. Where else could you use them?'

Alchflaed heard the Welsh harper saying: 'You could make a good living going round cattle-fairs.' She felt a great longing to shock her father, to make him look at her and know that she couldn't be bundled out of his way without question. She wanted to see his face when she told him, 'I've got more gifts than painting Gospel books or embroidering vestments. I can tell stories that hold churls spellbound. I can walk on my hands and turn somersaults. I could be a travelling glee-woman!'

She had enough sense not to say it; she didn't want to wreck her first talk with her father as she had wrecked her meeting with Alchfrid at Bebbanburh. Instead she made the time-honoured excuse.

'I don't think I have a vocation.'

Oswy was not interested enough to argue. 'Very well. I'll keep the promise I made to your mother, I'll fix a marriage for you. Earl Cadman's eldest son is a fine young man, he's a great friend of Alchfrid's as well as his foster-brother.'

Alchfrid nodded approvingly; Oswy spoke to him across Alchflaed.

'You'll need somebody reliable in Cumbria when you have to spend more time here in the east. I should settle him in Lonceaster if I were you — he can watch the southwestern marches if the Mercians attack from that side.'

The two men were smiling, pleased at this tidy and useful arrangement. Oswy glanced at the girl's unsmiling face. His voice hardened.

'Alchflaed, you've no mother to tell you this, so you'll have to take it from me. Marriage can be a painful and frightening business for a young woman if the man is rough or bodily disgusting. It can be worse for a princess, sent away to bedding and childbirth in a strange land where the womenfolk maybe hate her for old feuds' sake and wish her harm. I'm offering you a home in your mother's country, with a comely young husband of your mother's race. He's your brother's foster-brother.' He paused, then added quietly, 'And his mother was your mother's dearest friend. Mildred would be kind to any daughter-in-law, but she'll treasure you.'

Alchflaed was still silent.

'As near as possible, I'm marrying you into your own family.

Not many fathers would take so much trouble over a daughter's feelings.'

That was true; she had heard enough among the pupils in the convent and the women at Bebbanburh to know it. But she also knew in her bones that Oswy was not moved by the slightest concern for her feelings. With all the coaxing plausibility of a horse-coper hurrying to clinch a sale before the buyer had second thoughts, her father was trying to get her somewhere out of his way, where with luck he'd never have to see her again.

'Do I have to marry anyone?'

'Don't be stupid. If you don't take the veil, of course you have to marry. Once a girl becomes a woman, she must be a wife or a nun.'

By now Alchflaed was too hurt to care what she said.

'Or a whore.'

Her brother opened his mouth to give her a tongue-lashing, then waited dutifully for his father to speak first.

'Well, if your vocation calls you that way,' said Oswy, politely, 'you'll need no help from me.'

For a second their eyes laughed at each other; she thought delightedly, *He's seen me. We've met!* But he withdrew, saying coldly, 'This has been a most interesting and entertaining talk. However, I can't set aside the affairs of my kingdoms while we chat. I must ask you to make your choice.'

'How can I choose between one thing?' she asked bitterly. 'I only know the convent.'

'True. Well, you can give me your answer when you come back from Eoforwic. You'll have had your chance to look at the world while you're welcoming our new queen and bringing her to my bedside. Did you know her father, King Edwin, killed mine? Or that my grandfather took Edwin's sister at the sword's point and made my father bed her there and then to stake his claim on Deira? My mother celebrated her marriage on a cloak thrown down on the floor, while her new father-in-law ransacked the palace at Eoforwic looking for her brother to cut his throat. But I see I'm wearying you with all this talk of state affairs. Go to bed. I shall be leaving early in the morning, you needn't get up to see me on my way.'

So Alchflaed was sent out of the room like a tiresome child. Like a child, she took her mother's moon-necklace out of the chest and put it on, to comfort herself. From that night she wore it all the time, hidden under the neck of her shift, as a secret sign of revolt.

CHAPTER
9

There was no more friendly chat between the brother and sister as they rode south through Deira. Alchfrid was furious with her for her bold, immodest talk and her unreasonable refusal of her father's wise and kind plans for her future. She was nursing her bruised feelings and her resentment that her brother should join in treating her as a chattel. She would not flatter his pride in his knowledge, or humble herself, by asking questions about what she saw. This was a pity; when they reached Eoforwic she was sorely in need of his help and advice.

She had grown used to Roman forts and even Roman towns as they came down Deira Street through Cetreht and Aldeburh, but nothing she had seen could have prepared her for Eoforwic inside its ring of massive walls and towers.

As Eboracum, the city had been the capital and military head-quarters of the northern Roman province. Later, as Caer Efrog, it had been the fortress of Peredur, the British warrior-king. It was still a fine place, though the Britons lamented its tragic fall into alien hands—English pirates from heathen Germania beyond the cold eastern sea.

In fact, the city's first visitors from Germania had been federate troops brought in by Rome; they had joined in the proclamation of Constantine the Great as Emperor. When orders and pay had finally stopped coming from the south and the federates set up their own kingdom of Deira, they remembered the imperial glory and even kept it up as best they could, in their fashion. One of the wall towers had been rebuilt, roughly but strongly. The Deiran kings held court in the old principia, though some of its roof tiles had been replaced by thatch and open hearths had been laid in the middle of mosaic floors. King Edwin had flown Roman banners when he rode out and would not even walk down the street without a standard-bearer going in front of him.

Alchfrid was at home from the moment they rode under the northwestern gate arch. They went along the main street and turned into the pillared courtyard of the palace. This looked vast enough by itself to hold such townships or noblemen's estates as Alchflaed had seen. She felt herself shrinking; it was true what the scops said, the Romans must have been giants, like the huge stone images of themselves they had left amongst their stonework. She glanced sidelong at her brother and envied him, he was taking everything so much as a matter of course.

They were greeted by a large body of palace officials led by the Dish-Thane. Willibrord was a short fleshy man, whose red face and paunch bore tribute to the table he kept, though he was beginning to wither into old age. Her brother kept him busy with questions as they went into the palace: he wanted to know where and when the new Queen would arrive, the numbers of the palace guard, the state of order in the city. She gathered that he was going to see the guards' quarters, then ride out again to look at Eoforwic himself as soon as he had taken some refreshment.

He took little notice of his sister. Willibrord was courteous and gave some orders. She found herself following servants who carried her travelling chests into what seemed the heart of a maze. She got bewildered as they went along a colonnade, turned into a courtyard, entered a room that opened into four other rooms with doors in different corners, came out into a second courtyard and turned along another colonnade. She would not have been surprised to meet a flesh-eating monster at the centre of the maze and be told that she was its next meal. What she did meet was hardly more homely.

They arrived at another set of rooms that were in a bright and costly clutter of stools, carved and gilded chests, feather mattresses, fine bed-linen and trinket boxes, among which a flock of richly-dressed women pecked, fluttered and squawked. The servants set down her boxes, exchanged a word or two with the women and left.

Alchflaed had felt herself getting smaller the further she came into the palace; now she began to wonder if she was still visible.

She gathered that the rooms were being prepared for Queen Eanfled and that the women were the Deiran nobility. By rights, as the King's daughter in the King's palace, Alchflaed should have taken charge and given the orders. She was not so stupid or bad-mannered as to try, since she had no idea what they were doing, but she would have been very ready to take her part in the tasks and begin to know her companions by talking and laughing with them.

However, her hesitant offers of help were met with, 'Oh, no, not at all!' or 'Help do what?' spoken with blank smiling faces and eyes over her shoulder as the speaker went on with whatever she was doing. They all knew each other and were chatting busily about their own affairs or about other women who were not there.

'Did Goldburh say she'd bring the dried rose petals?'

'Breguswith can't travel till next week because of the baby.'

Alchflaed felt lost and alien; she did not know if she was meant to, or if they were truly too busy and excited about the return of their princess to see her. She sat down on a stool, out of the main tide, watching and listening, ready to make herself part of this new life when she understood it.

Some of the older women had been bower-maidens in the palace before King Edwin's death in battle nearly twenty years ago. They kept up a refrain of, 'In Queen Ethelburg's time . . . Queen Ethelburg would have it so . . .' which quieted any mutiny among the younger ones. Alchflaed saw that there was one elderly woman above all, who seemed to have taken it upon herself to order everything and set everybody else to rights. She was very thin, with a remarkably long stringy throat and a sharp nose. She had a way of blinking, then jerking her head forward as her scolding reached its peak, as if she were pecking at her victim.

The chief target of her attacks was a plump young woman with cream-pale skin and black hair, who was being accused and found guilty of shameful laziness and neglect. A set of hangings, partly embroidered by Queen Ethelburg herself, should have been brought out and had not been brought out. Blink, jerk. So where were they and why had the Dish-Thane not been told to see that they were ready? Blink, jerk. And if they weren't to be found, who had made off with them? Blink, jerk.

The victim took the harrying meekly, with downcast eyes, though she must have been a rich thane's wife or daughter. Her kirtle had a silk border; her full breasts were like a jewelsmith's stall with brooches and necklaces. When she was finally packed off like a slavewoman to fetch those hangings and be quick about it, she made a graceful reverence and said very gently, in a sweet, deep-toned voice, '*Boed iti ferwi ym mhair y Diawl, yr hen iâr grebachlyd iti.*'

Alchflaed was startled to hear her speak in British and even more startled to hear what she had said; she could hardly believe that the girl had called the masterful Deiran lady a scraggy old hen and told her to get boiled in the Devil's cauldron. When the Deiran pecked again, all unaware, saying, 'You Welsh think sweet words can settle everything, but see it gets done!' Alchflaed

95

had to choke a laugh. She drew a glance from a pair of eyes as bright and hard as jet beads while the girl went past her. That was Alchflaed's one moment of amusement; she was soon lonely and bored again. The women took themselves off on their various errands; she was left alone in the empty room. Soon there were no sounds in that part of the palace. She felt angry, then told herself that the Deirans would take for granted that she knew what to do next. She wanted to go in search of food and company, but dreaded making a fool of herself, offending the Deirans and shaming her brother.

'Left you all alone, have they?'

She jumped and turned to see the British girl smiling at her. She had brought a tray with a meat pasty, some honey-cakes and a flagon of mulled, spiced ale that smelled warm and comforting to Alchflaed's chilled spirits.

'Your brother's eating with the warriors. Didn't you know that? He wants to meet the palace guard. I thought you'd like a bit of supper.'

'You're very kind.' Alchflaed smiled gratefully. 'Who are you —what's your name?'

'Nest—Honesta. That's Latin, it means 'noblewoman'. I'm from Elmet. Funny name, isn't it—Noblewoman of Elmet? There's been precious few nobles in our country since King Edwin took it over.'

'It's a lovely name. I knew you were British.'

'Yes, I could see you understand our language.' Nest poured some ale, then leaned against the wall fondling her elbows, watching Alchflaed. 'I was only joking, of course. There's no harm in old Hildelith but she does go on.'

'I'm half British myself—my mother was a Cumbrian.'

Alchflaed was feeling much happier; she'd found a friend and an ally.

'Yes, but she married an English king, didn't she? So he got Cumbria and she got Bernicia. Very friendly. And now it's the Deirans' turn to be taken over, so we'll all be together, won't we?'

She smiled at Alchflaed.

'Where are they—those ladies who were here?'

Nest shrugged. 'Oh, they'll have gone off to pass their time. There'll be no big feast in the palace till the Queen comes.' Her mouth took an odd twist. 'They should be down in the cattle fair, it's a good place for them to be.'

'Oh, is there a fair?' Alchflaed looked up eagerly. 'I love fairs! I used to go at the seasons' ends with my foster-mother—she's the ploughman's wife at Coludesburh. My aunt's the Abbess there.'

'Is she indeed?' Nest looked at her thoughtfully. 'Suppose you slip down for an hour or so. There's nothing happening here.'

'Shall we go together?'

Nest shook her head regretfully. 'I've got my duties here—I serve under the Dish-Thane.' She looked at Alchflaed, gauging how much she would believe. 'But you'll soon meet the others. They were wondering if you'd like their company—but then they thought you wouldn't want to mix with them, as you're a Bernician.'

'Oh, is that why—?' Alchflaed jumped up, eager to go after the Deirans and clear up this misunderstanding.

'You'll want to get out of those riding clothes. Shall I help you dress?' Nest moved over to the travelling chests. 'What about this crimson kirtle? Crimson's a lovely colour, isn't it? So cheerful. And it's a beautiful day outside—warm as summer, and the sun'll be up for a while yet, so you won't need a cloak, just this pretty saffron veil. Oh, and here's some red ribbon to braid through your hair. You haven't had your ears pierced, you can't wear ear-rings, there's a pity! Still, here's an amber necklace to match your veil, and a couple of gold bracelets. You look quite festive now.'

She finished buckling on a pair of crimson leather slippers, stood up and looked at her handiwork approvingly. 'You just need some colour.'

'Colour?' Alchflaed thought she already looked like a sunset.

Nest opened a little ivory box that was fastened to her girdle-hanger among a cluster of keys, tools and trinkets.

'For your face, of course. Don't you know that no decent woman ever goes out without covering her face? But you've been brought up a nun, haven't you? You'd keep your veil wrapped round your head.'

'Oh, is that how it's done at court? I never knew.'

'You don't know much, do you—about palace life down here?'

'Nothing at all.' Alchflaed smiled frankly at her new friend. 'You'll have to teach me.' Nest's fingers were flitting nimbly over her cheeks and lips.

'You'll soon learn. Now, I'll just see you on your way—it's only a step. You go off and enjoy yourself for a bit. I'll have a room ready for you by the time you come back.'

Nest took her arm and led her back through the maze. It did not seem so hostile or bewildering this time. With a friend, someone who shared her mother's language, Alchflaed felt more at ease, ready to enjoy the wide world she had looked forward to exploring but which had seemed so bleak up to now.

There were few people about at that hour. None of them recognised Alchflaed as the rider in plain boy's clothes who had come in with the prince.

'Who's that with Nest?' asked one of the gate-guards as the two women went out into the street.

'Another nun of the same sisterhood, by the look of her,' said his companion, 'come to minister to Prince Alchfrid and his Cumbrians.'

Nest crossed the narrow street to a road that led downhill. Barely a hundred yards along, it passed through one of the gates in the great curtain wall. Here Nest paused, pointing another thirty yards or so where there was a crossroads and beyond it a bridge over a wide river. Startled, Alchflaed saw that across the river was another walled city. There was a straggle of huts, booths and pens around the crossroads; ships were moored at jetties along the river. Folk were milling round the booths and jostling on the bridge; she heard shouting and laughter and lilts of music; her spirits began to jig.

'Down there by the bridge—you'll soon find your company.'

'I wish you could come too.'

'I'll hear all about it later.'

Alchflaed waved to her new friend, turned and hurried down the hill. Her steps quickened, she was almost dancing, the red skirt swinging jauntily.

Nest watched her, smiling, without the least flicker of pity for what was going to happen to a convent girl turned loose and unsuspecting in a city that was even more crowded than usual by the cattle fair and by the hordes of loyally drunk Deirans who had come in to welcome their princess. Nest had heard the words 'Welsh whore' flung after her too often. It was going to be very amusing to throw the like insults back at those high-nosed Deiran bitches in the palace—and about one of their own royal family, too, just at the time of their great wedding they were all so pleased about!

She felt no kinder towards the girl because Alchflaed trusted her, still less because they shared the British blood and tongue. In Nest's view, Riemmelth of Cumbria had sold herself to one of the rich incomers, as many another woman had been forced to do.

Riemmelth had more to sell, a great family name and a kingdom, and so had made a better bargain. She'd got herself a wedding ring and an English kingdom, but for all that, she was a whore, just like Nest—and just like her daughter was going to be before the sun rose tomorrow.

It crossed Nest's mind that more harm might come to Alchflaed before the sun rose than a pricked maidenhead and mud on her name. She could lie with her throat slit in an alley, or be shipped overseas in one of the Frisian trading boats. What odds? How many thousands of women had been raped or hacked to death or dragged off to slavery by Irish and Saxon raiders since the Roman peace was broken? What difference would one more make, though she called herself a princess?

Nest laughed softly, then turned and went back to her service under the Dish-Thane.

CHAPTER
10

Eoforwic was two cities facing each other across the river. On one side was the fort, now the palace. The royal war-band had quarters there and King Edwin's church was nearby. On the other bank a shanty village of ale-shops and brothels, that had appeared almost as soon as the Roman army, had grown over the centuries into a great trading colony. Time, and the Deirans, had treated it more roughly than the royal stronghold but its sheltering walls and its port had kept it alive. Craftsmen found it safe to store their goods and tools there; local landowners had homesteads inside the walls and drove their stock in when fair-times or raiders arrived. The intrepid Frisian sailors, who would go wherever there was water to float a ship, brought in cargoes from the Baltic or Frankland—furs, amber and glassware in exchange for jet, mastiffs and slaves.

The autumn fair was ending but the folk stayed on to see King Edwin's daughter come back to her palace. Every thane and farmer with a hall in the city had been joined by kin and friends from the hinterland. Trade had never been so brisk. Frisian merchants, local craftsmen and travelling packmen were keeping their booths and stalls open for the extra profit. The ale-houses were crammed and noisy with healths to Eanfled and damnation to all Bernicians. And every minstrel, story-teller, juggler, rope-dancer and bearward in the north had been drawn like wasps round a honey-pot to the freest-handed audience they'd had in years.

Meilyr was sitting at the bridge-end, feeling the excitement flow into his veins, rising like the tide that was beginning to float the ships at the jetties. He had come as a travelling harper. In spite of his rage when Alchflaed had taken him for a gleeman, he knew it was too useful a character to refuse. The English court would be keeping open house for minstrels. He meant to get taken into the household of some noble, make his way back into Alchflaed's company and keep the boast he had made to his uncle, of seducing her and tricking her away into his possession. When he learned from the talk at the ale-booths that she was in the palace at that very moment, he knew it would be easy.

He took out his harp to test its strings and tuning, flicking out a little melody, not to please the throng but in sheer light-heartedness at the pleasure to come. Some of the youngsters nearby caught his mood, linked hands and began a chain-dance through the crowd, looping round stalls and pushing between groups of talkers. Folk were still in the good-humoured stages of drink; they laughed and joined the chain or stepped back to make a space for the dancers, clapping out the time.

Meilyr glanced up and saw Alchflaed coming across the space, in a red kirtle, with red ribbons in her hair, her face painted and smiling like a harlot. He thought at first it was her wraith, or his own thought taking shape on the air as thoughts can if the desire behind them is strong enough. Then he saw that the westering sun was casting her shadow and knew that she was truly there. She was obeying the tug of her leash, though he had not pulled it deliberately.

I've got her by the hair—she's mine!

His fingers quickened the tune, the last dancer caught Alchflaed's hand, the chain linked into a circle and began a reel. She joined in merrily, her red slippers twinkling like the notes of music, heel and toe, side-step, stamp, back-kick. Meilyr amused himself making her dance to his tune, remembering how she had danced on the sands, thinking of the lithe body under the red kirtle, the high breasts, the supple waist and rounded haunches, seeing in the brown curls cascading down her back the delicate cluster between her thighs.

When I own her I'll make her dance for me like that whenever I choose.

The reel flung Alchflaed into the centre, where she twirled like an autumn leaf in a gale. The other dancers stopped to watch, cheering and clapping. Meilyr whipped the tune into a fury and stopped. The crowd threw scraps of copper and silver, then broke up as crowds will, drawn to the next amusement. They saw the harper gather up his takings and toss them to the girl.

Alchflaed held out her red skirt to catch them, joining in the joke by playing the part of the minstrel's woman. The whirl of the dance on top of the spiced ale Nest had given her made her light-headed. She was not surprised to see the Welsh harper again. He was from her mother's world, like that strange summons that had come to her on the day she first met him. When he took her arm and pulled her towards the nearest ale-house, she laughed.

'I still don't know your name!'

'Meilyr. I know yours. You told it to those men on the beach — Alchflaed.'

'It means 'Sanctuary' in my father's language.'

'That's pretty.' In fact, the English name was rather distasteful in his mouth, he felt it harsh and alien. In his mind he had been calling her 'Afallen', remembering how, when he had watched her dancing naked at the edge of the waves in a sparkle of water drops, he had thought of apple blossom under spring rain. Changing her name was another token of owning her. Also, he could play with her in his verses without telling the world about her.

They stooped under the lintel of the tavern door. The air was thick with smoke, ale-fumes and the fug of frying sausages. After the loneliness and strain of the last few days, warmth and laughter wrapped her like a cloak. Meilyr put her on a stool with her back to the fire, got her some mead because less of it worked quicker than ale, set himself opposite her and began to weave his web.

Alchflaed handed him the beginning of the thread. 'Did you have trouble getting out of Bernicia?'

From the moment of seeing him she had spoken in British; it made a circle of solitude round them, though the hovel was crowded.

'Not the least. I got to Holy Island before the tide, had a meal and a bed in the monastery, talked Irish poetry with the monks, then went over the hills to Cumbria.'

He noted that she looked wistful at the name of her mother's land.

'And then you came back east for the new Queen's wedding?'

This was his chance, he took it with a charming smile. 'I came east for the hope of seeing you again.'

That's true, like all the best lies—remember, 'nghariad'?

'And what brought you to the fair, princess? Did you dream you'd meet me here again?'

He was eager to find out if she had any sense of being drawn to him, if she'd felt the tug of the leash without knowing who held it.

'I thought I'd find the Deiran ladies down by the bridge. One of the bower-maidens in the palace told me so—she helped me to dress properly and put colours on my face. Only I haven't seen any of them yet.'

'So I picked up the jewel they lost.'

Meilyr was curious; he thought: *The Deirans must really hate her and her family to play a vicious trick like that on her.* Then, with an odd little spurt of anger: *What was her fool of a brother doing to let her be decoyed out and shamed?*

Before he could ask any questions she said rather sadly, 'I suppose you'll be going away again, with all the other strangers, once the Queen's here.'

He nodded, wanting to see how she'd take it.

'Where will you go?'

'Wherever I want. A minstrel's at home anywhere. There's no border can keep us in and no locked gates to keep us out.'

He leaned towards her, eager and persuasive. 'Think. A minstrel's the only man who's welcome wherever he goes. When a king or noble arrives, the householders are afraid of being taxed. When warriors arrive, they're afraid of having their throats cut. When merchants arrive, they're afraid of being cheated. When beggars arrive, they're afraid for their stores. But whenever we come, they know they'll only get music and good pastime and laughter, with nothing to fear.'

Alchflaed thought of what happened whenever she arrived— her brother's shocked disapproval, her father's attempt to flatter and bribe her out of his way, the Deiran women acting as if they did not see her. She pictured Meilyr coming into a strange house at dusk, faces lighting up at the sight of him, cries of welcome, a place made for him near the hearth.

Meilyr could see from her intent face that he had caught her interest. She was busy building the trap that would catch her, as he had told his uncle, out of her own wishes. He smiled at her.

'I'll be bound you've never thought—shut away in your

convent — the sort of life we lead. Just for a few minutes, just to pass the time while you finish your mead, suppose you were someone like me. You'd set out, tomorrow or the next day, west through the Forest of Elmet where folk speak your mother's tongue. When you came to a chief's hall you'd be taken up to the high seat and served with the best of the flesh and the wine. You'd sing the chief's praises; then the chief would give you gold in thanks for the honour you'd done to his house.

'Or you'd come to a farmstead or a shepherd's hut and take your place in the ring round the hearth. You'd get your share of the broth in the cauldron, your hunk of cheese and oatcake. And then, over the ale, you'd spin your tales of adventure and enchantment till the folk would swear they saw the wizards and elf-women you told about, floating out of the peat-smoke.'

Meilyr had gone inside his own story; he spoke as if he really did live like that; for the moment he almost believed it.

'And if the night was too hot and close to spend under a roof, you'd make your fire in a glade to roast the game you'd killed, or eat the nuts and fruit you'd gathered. And you'd roll yourself in your cloak with the turf for your bed, the trees for your hall-pillars, the stars your candles and the nightingales to sing you to sleep.'

The mead was golden. It left the scent of the summer moors in Alchflaed's mouth and carried sunny warmth through her body while the firelight on the hearth behind her warmed her skin. Meilyr's face glowed at her out of the shadows, the reflected flames dancing in his eyes. Beyond him the low-roofed smoky hovel opened on to a wide sweep of mountain and woodland. She saw herself going over the hills and far away at Meilyr's side, from chiefs' halls to churls' huts, from fairs to forests, telling stories or dancing to his harp music, sleeping under the stars rolled in his cloak, wrapped in his arms —

All the while, her hard Anglian commonsense was telling her firmly that she was only playing with daydreams. The British half of her nature had been lost and lonely since her mother's death. It answered to the presence of her mother's people like a harp-string to a minstrel's fingers — but in a moment or two she must finish her mead and go back to the palace.

Then the memory of what it had been like there, alone and overlooked, chilled her even through the firelight and the mead. A princess had no choice, though; she was bound by her duties.

The word 'choice' reminded her that her father had kindly

given her one; she was bound to tell him what it was as soon as the new Queen was bedded. She could go back to the convent and stay there for ever; or be married off to a man she had never seen. Like Eanfled, shipped north into her kinsman's clutches with three generations of murder between them. Like Acha, thrown down on a cloak while her father's killers looted her home. Surely the only true choice she had was the one Meilyr was offering her—to walk out now and make her way in the world by her own gifts?

Meilyr was watching her like a hunter in a covert, who stills his breath while a young she-creature treads warily towards a hidden snare. Her eyes were tranced; he wondered what she was seeing—not that it mattered. *'They only hear and see what they want . . . Folk are never so well deceived as when you make them cheat themselves.'* She was doing his work for him.

He saw a shadow pass over her face, she was shivering. He changed his smile for a look of tender sympathy.

'You're lonely, aren't you? You've found no happiness in English palaces.'

After what she'd told him, what the Deiran women had done to her, that was a safe guess. She looked at him, startled that he should know her feelings. He held her gaze, his eyes glittering in the firelight and made his voice beguilingly soft.

'When you reach the western shore and look over the waves at sunset, you can't tell where this world ends. Sea and sky melt into each other, green and gold and rose. Clouds become islands and islands float like clouds. An Irish pilgrim told me once that if you sail out then to the west, you might find the Land of Youth. Winter never comes there, or old age or sorrow. The apple-trees bear flowers and fruit together. Centuries pass like hours, time goes by so lightly with music and dancing and laughter. Wouldn't you like to come away with me and look for that lost island, floating in the sunset clouds?'

Meilyr was hardly troubling what he said, stringing together odd scraps of poems and legends, weaving a web of words and dreams round her. By now he was sure he had caught her. There was no movement in her eyes, she no longer saw the life round her.

Alchflaed was watching the Land of Youth floating towards her out of the summer sky, forming into a cone-shaped hill crowned with green ramparts and a golden tower. She knew it; she had watched it drawing near to her in her vision that day at

Bebbanburh. She could hear the sound of ripples, there was a wide stretch of water parting her from the hill. But Meilyr was by the bank, standing in a boat. She reached her hand to him.

'Take me —'

'Why, look, it's Lightskirts!'

Three men had just pushed into the ale-house, shoving aside the drinkers near the door. One was a bulky young farmer, come up to Eoforwic to buy horses. Small eyes and wide nostrils in a broad face gave him the look of a self-important pig. He was followed by his stableman, whom he called his reeve and who flattered him for drink, and by the horse-coper. He had sold all his stock but was keeping close to a customer who still had silver to throw about. The farmer ploughed his way towards Alchflaed.

'Hey, Lightskirts, give us another dance! I didn't get enough of you last time. Hitch your kirtle higher, so I can see if you've got legs to your feet. And get up on the table, so I don't have to crick my neck!'

He leaned forward and jabbed his finger into Meilyr's shoulder. 'You! Welshman! Strike up and don't keep me waiting or I'll shift you!'

Meilyr was about to strike up at once, with his dagger. He was in a hopeless trap, penned in by the alehouse wall. The three new-comers had knives; they were in that stage when drunken merriment quickly turns to drunken fury. Likely the others in the ale-house would side with them. The farmer had the price of drinks all round and Meilyr was a foreigner.

Alchflaed grabbed Meilyr's dagger-hand by the wrist with an upward jerk as if she was hauling him to his feet.

'Didn't you hear what the lord said, you idle good-for-nothing? It's a fine life for you—sitting and swilling away what I earn, while there's thanes and ealdormen here waiting for their wishes!'

Her voice shrilled up into a raucous screech—the righteous wrath of a Northumbrian fisher's wife when her man has let the tide slip for laziness and missed the catch of the season. Meantime her eyes signalled Meilyr a different message.

'Give me something lively—something to get the feet moving—'Follow my leader' or 'Catch me if you can'. Get your harp and see you're ready when I want you.'

Meilyr nodded, smiling. He took his harp bag and made play of untying the cord as if having some difficulty with the knot, while he waited, poised to follow Alchflaed's lead. She changed her shrew's tone to a huckster's fawning as she turned to her admirer.

'I'm ready lord. What would you like me to show you?'

'Everything.' He leered at her. 'I'll have a rousing gallop over the hills and down to the little well among the bushes. But that's just for you and me. You can give us all a dance first.'

He straddled, puffing out his chest and grinned at his hearers. He was proud of himself, a man of wit and wealth, able to have any woman he fancied. Alchflaed looked up at him spellbound, nestling close. Hidden by her skirt, her foot slid between his legs; her toe found a stool behind him where a group of drovers had put their ale mugs. She shoved hard and tipped the stool, spilling the drink and sousing one of the drovers. He yelled and jumped up.

'You clumsy tyke! Get your bitch out of here and go to rut in the gutter where you belong. Just pay me for my ale before you go.'

'I'll pay you!'

The farmer smashed his fist into the drover's face. The alehouse was packed; he fell across a crowded bench, bringing two men to the floor with him and scattering more mugs. The drover's friends hurled themselves at the farmer. Alchflaed screamed, 'Save me!'

Shouting, 'Hands off my woman!' Meilyr caught her round the waist and twisted through the crowd like a fox making off from a hen-coop.

Coming up to help his master, the stableman trod on the tail of the drover's dog; it yelped then sank its teeth into his calf. He swung round howling and crashed against the ale-wife who had turned from her brazier still clutching a frying pan. The pan jerked upwards; scalding sausages rained down. Drops of fat splattered on to the charcoal, there was a gush of flame. Someone yelled, 'Fire!' and there was a clawing scramble to get to the narrow door over the threshing heap of fighters on the ground.

Meilyr had dodged round the ale-house and behind a row of booths. He paused at the mouth of a narrow alley, looking down the road that led to the bridge, wondering if there was time to bolt across the river and get lost among the crowds in the township on the other side.

His arm was still around Alchflaed. She was shaking, he could feel her breasts quivering. He turned to her, meaning to tell her not to spoil their chances at the last moment by a fit of fear and saw she was laughing, as she had laughed on the sands at Bebbanburh when he put the knife to her throat. He grinned and drew her closer.

'Got your breath back? Right. One more dance of 'Follow my leader' or 'Catch me if you can' over the bridge and we're away!'

He was too late. Out of the gate of the royal city came a dozen Cumbrian horsemen with a few spearmen of the palace guard. Prince Alchfrid was coming to see for himself where Eanfled would disembark next morning and to check that the town was orderly. The smoke and screams made the riders swing round to the ale-house at a brisk trot. The spearmen, wise in the ways of Eoforwic rioters, headed straight for the bridge to catch anybody on the run.

Meilyr pulled Alchflaed back into the alley. She was white and trembling; it was the first time he had seen her scared.

'Mother of God, it's my brother! He's angry with me already — he'll want to kill me for this!'

'He'll certainly kill me.'

Meilyr unpinned his cloak and wrapped it round Alchflaed, drawing the hood up. They watched until the warriors had got well past, then slipped inside the walls and up the street towards the palace. The sun had set now, though the west was still rosy. A few yards from the palace gate, he stopped to make sure that her gaudy dress and painted face were well hidden in the folds of her cloak.

'No hurrying now, remember — and no sign of fear. Keep your head down and turned to me, you're shy, not scared — a harper's wife from the Forest of Elmet, come to a city for the first time. And you only speak British. I'll do the talking.'

She did as he told her and they strolled through the gateway. Meilyr had his harp well in view; he nodded and smiled to the gate-guards with a word or two about the great day tomorrow. As they crossed the courtyard he muttered, 'Which way?' She guided him by pressing his arm, thankful that she knew the right colonnades and corners when she saw them again.

They reached the door of the Queen's rooms; she went in warily but they were deserted. She found her travelling chests in one of the inner rooms, a bed made up, a basin and ewer of water with a towel beside it, even a plate of cakes and a flask of wine. Nest had prepared a show of her own innocence and goodwill by getting the room ready, as if she had expected Alchflaed to come back safe and sound.

Meilyr was standing in the shadow of one of the columns when she came out.

'All's well. There's nobody about.'

'Now listen. Change your clothes at once and pack them away. Don't wear them again while you're in Eoforwic. And wash that paint off your face—it's not for maidens. I must be going now; it's dusk, they'll be closing the gate. When you're ready, come out and call for the servants—complain about being left alone without proper—'

He broke off at the sound of footsteps. The night-watch had started their rounds, lighting the cressets that burned in the colonnades all night. There was no time to separate; he pushed her against the wall and hid her face by covering it with his own in a lingering kiss. There was the scent of mead-honey on his breath; his body was hard and warm against hers. She felt the same light-hearted happiness that had come into her when she danced to his music, with an extra stir of her senses that over-mastered her. She opened her mouth, her arms slid round his body to draw him closer, her hands tightened on his back.

The watchmen grinned as they passed the pair, noting that the girl's hands were soft and delicate, wondering which fine lady of the court was getting her evening's pastime from a strolling harper. One of them called cheerfully, 'Thirsty, darling? Take a good long pull at the spout!' and they tramped off laughing.

Meilyr brushed his fingers lightly down Alchflaed's cheek, said, 'Sleep well, sweetheart, I'll be with you tomorrow,' then raced light-foot to the far side of the courtyard before the night-watch came round to the other colonnade. It was a pity to leave her just then, with a bed made up beyond that door, but he hadn't got long to wait. She couldn't get away from him. He had her on a leash.

Next morning was misty; the sun was as pale as a full moon and gave as little warmth. There was a thin frosting of damp on the hair and cloaks of the crowds who were early astir. Willibrord and the palace officials were waiting in the courtyard; their womenfolk clustered in the colonnade. Nest was not among them; Willibrord had ordered her to stay out of sight in his quarters. He could not believe that Eanfled would welcome the presence of a Welshwoman. The war-host that had slaughtered Edwin and the army of Deira had been led by Cadwallon of Gwynedd. Even after twenty years his name could chill the blood; and if Eanfled had inherited anything of her father's temper, twenty years was too short a time for a grudge to go to sleep.

Nest had taken the order, and the bracelet he gave with it as a sweetener, with charming good humour. She had learned from the servants that Alchflaed had spent the night in her room and was not known to have ever left it — the girl must have had the Devil's help to manage that. All Nest wanted now was for the episode to be forgotten; likely it would, if she kept well away, in the bustle of the new Queen's arrival.

The Deiran nobles had all gone to the riverside. Alchfrid and his war-band rode with them, escorting a travelling cart to bring the Queen up the street to the palace. Alchflaed went down in it; old Lady Hildelith insisted on coming with her. Her head was pecking more sharply than ever; Alchflaed saw, with some guilt for having laughed at her, that her blinking eyes were full of tears and her withered cheeks were wet.

Eanfled was being brought by sea — Penda was overlord of all the kingdoms between Kent and Deira. There had been fears for her safety in the terrible storm that followed Oswine's death, but riders had brought word that her ship had made the Humbre and was coming upriver.

The folk were crowded on both banks and across the bridge. Shouts from downstream told that the boat had been sighted and at last it came round a bend, a grey shape in the mist, heading for the jetty where Alchfrid's riders and the palace spearmen were holding the crowds back to keep a space.

Alchflaed got out of the cart, helping Hildelith to walk to the jetty, though she too felt weak and breathless. She was afraid for herself — what power would a stepmother who was also her queen have over her? She had to fight down a stupid feeling that her own mother had been betrayed; she knew this marriage was needed to save Northumbria.

Her mind went out to Eanfled. The exiled princess was bringing the fate of three kingdoms as her dowry. In what spirit was she coming? In bitter vengefulness for her murdered kin? In terror at being handed over to her hereditary foes? In grief and loneliness at being torn away from her mother's family down in Kent, the friends she had grown up with? Perhaps there was someone she loved — a landless warrior — or a minstrel — that she would have chosen to live with if she had been lucky enough to be lowly-born and free?

She remembered the pitiless truth of her father's warning: 'It can be worse for a princess sent away to bedding and childbirth in a strange land where the womenfolk maybe hate her for old feuds' sake and wish her harm.'

Her own fears and resentments melted in a gush of pity for her stepmother.

It's worse for her than for me. I'm in my own land and I've still got some freedom of choice. I'll help her—I'll comfort her—we must work together for peace.

While the ship was mooring she gazed eagerly at the group waiting to land: warriors of the escort, a couple of priests, a small, almost dwarfish, elderly woman and one tall figure that brightened the dank morning.

She was rather startled at the rainbow brilliance of Eanfled's clothes. Her robe was saffron yellow, her tunic green with red borders, her cloak bright blue. Each garment was heavily embroidered but no two patterns were the same. Her arms and bosom were agleam with trinkets but none of them made up a set. Alchflaed supposed this was the Kentish fashion; it reminded her of her own first dreadful efforts at illuminating manuscripts, when she had been drunk with the joys of coloured ink.

But if Eanfled's dress looked the handiwork of an over-eager pupil, she herself was like the masterpiece of some great artist in Constantinople. Her hair was the bright gold of embroidery thread, her eyes were sapphires, her skin had the clarity of enamelling.

Alchflaed was a craftswoman, she loved the colour and texture of precious materials. These were the terms of her highest praise. She did not ask herself, then or later, why she never thought of Eanfled as flesh and blood.

There was a shout to crack the ear-drums; the illumination stepped ashore, smiling at her dazzled audience.

'How wonderful it is to be home! Why, Dunstan! You used to carry me, remember?—when I got tired of playing in the palace courtyard—and now you're captain of the guard! Oh, my dearest Hildelith! How often through the years I've thought of you, sitting with my mother at your embroidery and teaching me my stitches. Whenever they were praising my work down in Kent, I used to tell them I had the kindest and best of teachers! Prince Alchfrid—of *Cumbria*? It's very courteous of you to honour my homecoming. And your little sister, come all the way from the far north! Eoforwic must seem very strange to you, my dear. The travelling cart? Oh no, I've just set foot again in my own dear kingdom. It's only a little way to the palace and I know every inch of it. How often my dear father, King Edwin, used to walk along this street with his standard carried before him! Let poor Grimhild ride with you, Lady Hildelith,' bringing forward the little old woman, who had a face as sour as a crab-apple. 'She's tired after our long journey. Prince Alchfrid, will you take my arm? Don't let the crowds frighten you, Alchflaed, my people would never hurt you. You can hold my hand. You're both truly welcome to my home.'

Having made it politely clear that Deira was her kingdom and that Cumbrians and Bernicians were her guests in her city, Queen Eanfled took command of her step-children and went smiling up the street towards her palace with her people's shouts of joy ringing in her ears.

The sun was defeated by the mists; as the day passed, Eoforwic was shrouded in fog that crept up the river. It could not blot out the revelry in the city; folk clapped fast their doors and shutters, making their own suns inside with their hearth fires and the mulled ale in their bellies.

The palace was aglow with blazing logs, torches and costly wax candles that woke the colours in brightly-dyed wall-hangings and garments. The reflected flames danced among jewels and table silver at the Queen's feast in the great hall and even gave a touch of golden splendour to the lesser feasts that were being enjoyed in the spearmen's hall, the gate-towers, the kitchens and the stables.

Meilyr was standing in the street outside the palace gate. He had been there several times that day, then turned down to the river, wandering in the thickening fog along the banks and among the broken tombs of the Roman graveyard like a restless ghost, but always coming back to the same spot. The gate had been left open so that beggars could come in freely to feed on the leavings of the feast. He could see the palace across the courtyard, the cressets in the colonnades fuzzy through the mist, the line of glazed lattices shining above them. The gatewardens were bellowing a chorus in their guard-room, along with a fiddler. During the pauses Meilyr could hear the fainter sounds of laughter and applause from the hall.

He walked slowly inside the gate and took a few steps across the courtyard. Nobody stopped him. He could have gone straight on into the hall, his birth and musicianship gave him the right to a place at the high table. Yet he came to a standstill again.

Alchflaed was there. Remembering how her body had stirred in his arms, how she had pulled him close, he knew it would not take much effort to charm her away. He had seen where she slept, could find his way there, have her in her own bed if he chose, everyone in the palace would be too drunk to notice. Afterwards it would be her turn to kneel, begging him to take her away with him and save her from the wrath to come. Then he would tell her that she had only done what she wanted, that she had no claim on him, he could take her or leave her as he chose. So his boast to Morfran would be triumphantly fulfilled.

But the cracks in his will and spirit had opened again, burst apart by a flood of rage that he, a prince of the old British blood, should have to come into the hall with gleemen and tumblers while the heirs of German mercenaries and North Sea pirates were lords of the feast.

He wished that he could open the graves and call up Peredur, the last British king of Efrog, with his war-band to come back to their palace like the mists that were swirling up from the river. Then the noise of alien revelry would die, and the songs in the hall would be in the ancient tongue once more.

Even Morfran's magic could not do that, yet. He would need other warriors than mist-wraiths to take the city. It could be done. Not twenty years ago, that woman, for whose return they were now bawling their lungs out, had been carried away in headlong flight before Cadwallon of Gwynedd arrived. Cadwallon had held all Northumbria under British rule for a year. It had been a year of massacre; such unspeakable hell that the Northumbrians had blotted it from their annals and even the Deirans had welcomed St Oswald of Bernicia as a deliverer.

Cadwallon was slain, but the Mercian warrior who had been his ally was now the most powerful king of all the English. Penda had not forgotten Cadwallon, the only king and fighter he had ever thought of as his equal. He had said as much to Meilyr, when praising him after he had fought his way single-handed to the walls of Bebbanburh and cut down the gate-guard. Penda would still welcome a British alliance to destroy Oswy. It was common talk through the island that this was his main aim, the more so now that Oswy had reunited Northumbria.

Meilyr had heard the Deirans drinking death and hell to Oswy and all Bernicians. He had also listened, which few English could do, to what the folk of Elmet said among themselves in their own tongue about their forced and bitter union with Deira. Oswy's Northumbria would fall apart at one blow, if the British kingdoms threw in their troops beside Penda in his next attack.

Getting the British kings to drop their endless feuding and act together for once would be a greater feat than smashing Oswy. Surely, though, he and Morfran, uniting their magic, could bind the kings in a peace-spell strong enough to hold their minds under one will—at least for a time?

Meilyr saw himself riding into the palace at the head of the Powys war-host. The fog became the smoke of the burning city behind him; the cressets and the lights in the hall were the torches of looters, firing whatever they did not choose to take. He saw Alchflaed dragged out and thrown at his feet—he would have named her as his price when he settled terms with Penda. He tried to keep her image grovelling in front him, her clothes half torn from her body, her flesh grimed or reddened where her captors had gripped her—but try as he would, he could only see her kicking over the stool in the ale-house to get him out of a corner, or laughing when he put the knife to her throat on the sands at Bebbanburh.

He struggled against the thought that she was too good for such handling. There would be no pleasure to be had from her when her spirit was crushed—she would be no more use to him than a spoiled hawk or a badly-broken horse.

His anger veered like a flame blown in the wind—why should he, a prince of Powys, have to ask Penda's leave to take her, as if he were one of Penda's churls cadging a gift? And what terrible danger might he be bringing on Powys, and the other surviving British kingdoms, when Penda had nobody left in England to fight and could call the war-hosts of all England to march behind him. Yet how could he win Alchflaed nobly, as a warrior-prince, and not reckon with Penda?

Every riddle has its answer; bards and magicians are trained to find them. He would use Penda as his weapon to destroy Oswy and so avenge the old insult that Riemmelth had given to his father. Then, moved by pity and their shared British blood, he would rescue Alchflaed from slavery and send envoys to her brother, calling on him to bring Cumbria into a holy war against the heathen. He would offer to marry Alchflaed to bind the alliance; the offer could hardly be refused since she would already be in his possession and only a marriage could save her honour.

Penda would be destroyed, weakened by his fight to death

with Oswy, taken unawares by the desertion of his British allies and the onslaught from Cumbria. Meilyr and Alchfrid would be left to part the island between them. Alchfrid could take the north; Meilyr would rule in Llundain as High King of Britain—or as Imperator of Britannia, if he chose to follow Maxen and Arthur by reviving the old title. Alchflaed would reign beside him—but she would still be his war-captive, his slave-woman. There would be no need to spell it out for her in crude insults. She had keen wits; she would carry the knowledge every moment of her life like a brand and chain. Meanwhile, he would make every other man who came into her presence bend the knee to her. What a rich pleasure it would be to own the High Queen of Britain!

Standing alone in the mist and gathering darkness, Meilyr built the old governor's palace of Londinium around him in his mind. He made it ten times as large as the building in front of him, setting it ablaze with golden candlesticks and tableware, brilliant with rainbow tapestries. He enthroned Alchflaed on a dais, dressing her like a Roman empress in a brocaded purple tunic and a coronet cascading with pearls. Taking her hand, he led her from the hall into his secret room, warm and scented. There he made her shed her splendour, jewel by jewel, one silken layer after another until she stood before him as he had first seen her between the sand and the waves. Then he made her dance to his tune and play every tumbler's trick his mind could devise for her body to perform.

Meilyr's hair and skin were drenched by now and his lips had a bluish tinge from the cold but he did not feel it.

'They only hear and see what they want and never know that they're using their own wishes to build the trap that will catch them.'

Alchflaed was still dancing for him in the warm and scented room behind his eyes as he turned away downhill and was swallowed up in the thick fog by the river.

The army of mist-wraiths came pouring through the gateway. They occupied the courtyard and the colonnades, pressed against the walls of the palace. But there was no power in their arms; the torchlight and firelight kept them at bay. Inside the great hall, the heirs of German mercenaries and North Sea pirates enjoyed their feast, unheeding.

CHAPTER
11

The new Queen rested against her duck-feather cushions. She watched Grimhild stooped over her baggage bundles, unpacking. She had a costly but random collection of jewels and robes, grudgingly put together by her Kentish kinswomen when it was known that she was to be Queen of Northumbria. Eanfled was the only one of her family who had not been taken by surprise at her new-found luck and title.

King Edwin had died with his army in the marshy wilds of Haethfeld. His body had been hacked to pieces, his kingdom wrecked on a tide of blood, his widow fled as a beggar to her kinsfolk's charity in Kent. He had still passed two priceless treasures on to his last heiress: the grip of a mastiff's jaws on whatever she saw as her rights, and a rock-like faith that God would do His duty in the end and see that all her claims were granted in full.

She stretched and sank back, pleasantly tired after the river journey and the feast.

'What a beautiful day! How the people cheered me—I've never seen folk so happy! Oh Grimhild, when you snatched me up in this very room, and carried me after my mother to the boat, I never dreamed how long it would be before I came home again!'

Grimhild's sour face curdled even more.

'Too long. And to my mind, those who kept you from your rights are more to blame than those who stole them in the first place. At least Cadwallon and Penda never called themselves your cousins. How any men calling themselves atheling-born could be willing to live soft, making free with your halls and lands, while you were an outcast! It was a crime against God.'

It had also been a crime against Grimhild. When she was young she had devoted herself to Queen Ethelburg, hoping that royal favour would gain her some rich gifts and a little reflected importance to make up for her plain looks and small dowry. Instead, it had gained her nineteen years of dreary exile. The King of Kent thought he had done all he needed for his sister when he founded a convent and made her Abbess.

Ethelburg was a grave, pious woman; she was contented ruling her nuns and praying for her husband's soul. Grimhild had found

115

no better use for her time than going over and over the vanished glories of the palace in the north. The little princess loved to hear her; this was how she got her uncanny memory for the people and places of her youth, which so touched and delighted the Deirans.

Eanfled had picked up a silver mirror and was gazing tenderly at her reflected face. 'Will you comb my hair now, Grimhild, if you're not too tired?'

Grimhild was not in the least tired, nor did she think the act beneath her. Though she was not rich, she was a noblewoman; one branch or other of her widespread family had great estates in every part of Deira. Now that the good times had come back, she could have had high-born bower-maidens with maidservants of their own to carry out these tasks. But no one was going to budge her from her place of power close to Eanfled's ears and lips. Her rich kin had already shown a flattering interest in what she could tell them about the Queen's wishes and plans. Eanfled loved to have her hair combed; this was when she talked most freely.

'If only King Edwin could see you now, my lady, back where you belong.'

Eanfled took her eyes from her image to give a pious glance at the ceiling.

'He does, Grimhild, he does.' She sighed, then looked at herself again. It always saddened her to think of her fate — so beautiful, so nobly-born, so cruelly wronged.

'My troubles aren't over yet, Grimhild, dear. Of course, I had to come back and take my father's kingdom — it's my duty. I'm glad it makes my people happy. But there's not much happiness in store for me, married off to a cruel barbarian like King Oswy. Everybody says he planned my poor cousin's death — though that was very likely a judgement on Oswine for taking my kingdom and never even offering to share it with me.'

Eanfled had a nine-year-old grievance against Oswine. It had been his clear duty to marry her when the Deirans offered him the kingdom but he had not done so.

'Besides, Oswy's an old man, nearly forty. And he's a lecher. I dare say I shall be forced to endure shameful insults — drunken riots with vile women, threats, blows perhaps —'

Apart from her own loveliness, Eanfled's greatest pleasure during her exile had been listening to the scops at the Kentish court. She was deeply touched by any tale about wronged and suffering princesses, having a fellow-feeling for such victims. At last the two pleasures had flowed together. When she dreamed or mused about the tragic heroines, she saw them with her face; when she looked at her face in the mirror, it held all the sorrow and dignity of the old legends.

'I never heard tell of Oswy rioting with drunken whores.' Grimhild was rather unwilling to admit this, but she saw tears in Eanfled's eyes. 'Not in the last Queen's time at any rate. But then, she was a Welshwoman, likely she'd have put a knife through Oswy or poisoned his drink if he'd wronged her. And he wouldn't want to offend the Cumbrians—they wouldn't stand by and see their queen slighted.'

'My people wouldn't stand any slight to me,' said Eanfled, jealously. 'Those two—the Prince of Cumbria and his sister— they're her children, aren't they? They don't look or speak like barbarians.'

'*Welsh.*' Grimhild's tone was baleful. 'The Welsh are just as blood-thirsty as the Bernicians, and cunning with it. Take good care, my lady. You need to watch them both, the girl as well as the man.'

Grimhild's spirit was not as poetic as her queen's. She told her eager kinsfolk that Eanfled felt sick at the thought of marrying Oswy but was forcing herself to do it, to rescue Deira from the Bernicians' bloody claws. She added for good measure that Eanfled believed Oswy had killed her cousin and had some fears that she would meet her own end at the same hands. In this form, the tale was soon on its way across Deira.

Eanfled took Grimhild's advice and watched her step-children. She could not see anything but the reflection of her own image in their dazzled eyes. She was very gracious to them both. If quarrels and bloodshed were to come, there must be no doubt in anyone's mind who was guilty. Also, she wanted to make clear that she was at home in great cities like Eoforwic and Cantwaraburh by right of birth and breeding, unlike the alien savages from the north. She became so overpoweringly Roman one would have thought she descended from Constantine the Great rather than Hengist the Jute.

Alchfrid was bespelled. He saw his dreams of the lost Empire alive and smiling at him in her face and form. Here was Britannia, here was Roma herself, incarnate on earth in beauty and majesty.

For his sister, Eanfled's kindness brought the only warmth in a cold world. Meilyr had not come to the feast, nor did he visit the palace at any time during their stay in Eoforwic. At first, remembering the riot in the ale-house, she had feared for his life. She made discreet enquiries; she told Willibrord she was worried about a Cumbrian harper, one of her mother's minstrels, who had promised to attend her at the palace. Willibrord had a search made in the city and along the quayside. He got no reports of a brawl; no one of that description had taken ship; no body was found in an alley or floating in the river with its throat cut. Meilyr had simply gone away because he chose to go.

'Where will you go?'

'Wherever I want. A minstrel's at home anywhere. There's no border can keep us in, and no locked gates to keep us out.'

The palace gate would have been open to him; he had just not wanted to step through and meet her again. After the adventures and laughter they had shared, after the kiss and the promise to meet that had passed between them, she felt betrayed. Also, there was a ceaseless nagging ache in her senses that she had never known before. It robbed her of most of her joy in music and colours and poetry.

Even that was not the worst. She had asked after Nest as well. This time she got plenty of news. The women told her so much, in such spiteful detail, about who Nest was and exactly how she served under the Dish-Thane, that she never needed to mention the name again.

Alchflaed would not have troubled herself unduly for that. Mary Magdalen, with her warm heart and her courage to stand by Our Lord when the men had fled, was one of her favourite saints. But though she had as yet little knowledge of the world outside her convent and its moorside farm, she was neither blind nor stupid. One day in the palace had been enough to teach her that no well-born lady, no decent woman, ever acted as Nest had encouraged her to behave. The brawl in the ale-house had shown her some of the dangers Nest had deliberately sent her to meet; she could imagine the rest.

The pointless malice of it bewildered and sickened her. She did not want to sour Eanfled's homecoming by hunting out Nest to punish her. It was lucky that Willibrord was keeping her out of the Queen's way. She hoped that she would never have to see or speak to the British girl again. The fact that Meilyr and Nest were both of her mother's race was an added pain. She had been drawn to them because of the blood they shared, had liked them, could have loved them, had thought they felt the same bond to her.

If they had only told me they disliked me—hated me, perhaps—because I'm Bernician, because I'm English, because our forefathers were at war, I could understand that. But they smiled at me—Meilyr took my help twice; Nest sought me out and made a show of kindness—and yet neither of them cares what becomes of me! Nest could have ruined me—why? To give herself an evening's sport with me, like Meilyr?

She was glad when they left the city and set out for the north, where Eanfled was to meet Oswy for their nuptial mass and the consummation of their marriage. Her step-mother was so lovely and sweet-tempered, surely she would join her husband and his children into a happy family.

The sunshine of the journey was only clouded once. Eanfled had found that Alchfrid was very pious and took care to display her own strict virtue. She also wanted to pass judgement on her Kentish cousins and spoke of her mother's horror and her own that King Eadbald had once been excommunicated.

'He separated himself from Christ?' Alchfrid could hardly believe it. 'How could he let himself fall so terribly from grace?'

'He made an unholy union with my grandfather's widow.' Eanfled put it more simply in case they had missed the disgusting fact. 'He married his stepmother.'

For a moment, Alchflaed felt bodily sick with horror; Alchfrid was shocked out of his usual courtesy.

'The filthy German barbarian! This is what comes of letting savages into a Christian empire! It was casting pearls before swine!'

Eanfled's face was as hard as mosaic; her sapphire eyes were wide with outrage. She could judge her kinsfolk but it was an insult to herself if anyone else decried them. Her chaplain, Romanus, interposed smoothly.

'We must not be harsh on those of our brothers who have not yet been shown the true Light. Holy Scripture tells us that righteous men lived before Christ came into the world.'

'*Righteous!* How could you ever call such vileness—'

'Consider, prince. We know that queens are married to keep the peace between peoples. Your English poets call them 'peace-weavers', a lovely name for a lovely and blessed vocation.'

He bowed to Eanfled. 'Well now, it may be that an old king has married a young wife to heal a long and bloody feud between two tribes. He dies and the link is broken. What should his heir do—let the war break out again, with all the death and maiming,

119

the slavery and grief that war brings, whoever wins? He would surely see it as his duty to take the queen and keep the peace. "Blessed are the peacemakers", as Our Lord said Himself.'

He smiled kindly at Alchfrid. 'We who are Christians know better, of course. Christian kings are lucky, they can ask learned priests to draw up treaties in Latin for them and have them sworn at the altar on holy relics. But let us not sit in judgement on the poor heathen, who do their best according to their lights.'

Alchfrid had recovered his control; he listened gravely to the priest and said earnestly,' I spoke without thinking, Father. Thank you for your instruction.'

Romanus had stopped smiling. 'King Eadbald's sin was that having received the Light from holy Augustine, he turned his back on it and returned of his own will to heathen darkness. He was punished for it, like Nebuchadnezzar, with the darkening of his wits, till he repented and broke the unhallowed wedlock. I am sure he was saved by the prayers of that blessed lady, his sister, Queen Ethelburg.'

Alchfrid bowed to Ethelburg's daughter who looked at him kindly. She was pleased with the picture of herself as a peace-weaver, blessed daughter of a saintly mother. Her stepchildren soon forgot the incident. It was an odd little fact about the Kentish royal family, but not important.

. Eanfled dwelt on it longer, especially in the restful evenings when Grimhild was combing out her hair. The idea had crossed her mind, looking at Alchfrid's fair handsome face, flattered by his courtesy, that the old heathen German customs had a great deal to be said in their favour. It was a pity that Oswy had not had her married to his heir. If he died soon, an old man of forty worn out by constant debauchery, what would become of the holy alliance between Deira and Bernicia? Marriage with Alchfrid was out of the question now, of course. She had seen the sick disgust on his face at the idea of marrying a stepmother. Besides, Father Romanus had said it was evil and therefore Eanfled could not think about it, because it was impossible for her to think or to do evil.

If only she were not married to Oswy—but was she really married? She tried to recall things she had heard in Cantwaraburh, doubts that Father Romanus had shown, grave-faced and shaking his head, about the sins of the British and Irish Christians among whom Oswy had been brought up. They had refused to obey St Augustine, there was some heresy about the time of the Resurrection, whispers of evil customs. She had not paid much heed at the time, being full of her new queenship. She must ask Romanus to make everything clear to her, for if Oswy did not follow the Catholic faith then marriage to him was unhallowed and she was not his wife. In which case, she was not Alchfrid's stepmother and could think of him without sin.

She spoke some of her doubts aloud, talking half to herself as was her habit while Grimhild combed her hair. She named no names, only wondered about the plight of a queen, virtuous and holy, sent to marry an enemy king who had usurped her land, then finding to her horror that the man was a misbeliever. Would she not be sinning against her own Christian faith to live with such a man and call herself his wife?

Grimhild reported to her kin that Eanfled believed her marriage to Oswy was unlawful and that she would be leaving him as soon as she was sure.

Oswy was waiting to greet his queen at one of his estates near the bridge over the Tina. The travellers spent the last night of their journey in the guest halls of the monastery at Gatesheafod on the south bank before riding in procession over the bridge to their royal welcome in the morning.

Eanfled had been trothplight to Oswy by her oath in front of his messengers. They were lawful man and wife, but as devout Christians they would hear mass before they bedded. After all she had told him on the road of her doubts about British and Irish priests, Romanus was taken aback when she said she meant to let Oswy's bishop, Finan, say her nuptial mass alone.

'I'm a foreigner,' she said wistfully. 'The folk here likely hate me as a Deiran. They'll hate me still more if the first thing I do is find fault with their churchmen.'

Romanus still looked grave. Her lovely eyes filled with tears.

'And what about my stepchildren? You know the trouble I've taken to overcome their coldness and suspicion, to make them trust and love me. I think they're beginning to—just a little. How will they take it if I start casting doubt on the sacraments of their church? They might think I was attacking their mother's marriage, hinting they were bastards to clear the way for children of my own, like the wicked stepmothers in the old stories!'

'That would be very painful; but still, when your real intention is innocent—'

'That's just what I say!' Eanfled smiled radiantly. 'I'm not afraid

121

of doing harm when I've got you to take care of me, Father. Perhaps I'm wrong about the priests up here. Stories do get garbled when they've come a long way. I'm trusting you to watch everything very carefully and tell me at once if you see the slightest flaw. Then we can send to Cantwaraburh or even to Rome, and get it put to rights.'

Romanus was touched. He signed her with the cross, then kissed her on the brow.

'God keep you, my daughter, and bring your pure soul the blessings it deserves.'

'Amen,' said Eanfled, devoutly.

Though the royal estate, At-Wall, was near a large Roman fort, Oswy was not living in a refurbished ruin. He had held court in both Caer Luel and Eoforwic. He knew that no other township in the north could equal them and had no taste for feeble imitations. His halls and bowers were in the English style: roomy, high-gabled, timber buildings, heavily carved and gilded. He had passed the time waiting for his queen's arrival in seeing that they were well furnished with a lavish display of his treasures.

As fitted the couple's age, the wedding-feast was a dignified ceremony rather than a riotous drinking bout. There was no shortage of ale and mead but the usual crudely-shouted advice for a callow groom, and bawdy hints to make the bride blush or titter, would have been out of place. Still, it was a very pleasant celebration. Everyone had a good time. Oswy was witty and hospitable; he knew how to make folk enjoy themselves and he was delighted at the sight of his consort. He would have taken Eanfled and made the best of it if she had been bow-legged, toothless and her breath stank, because Eanfled was Deira. When Deira took shape in a body like Eanfled's he was eager to make the united kingdom.

Eanfled was good-humoured to be the centre of attention and to be wearing the splendid jewels that Oswy had left ready for her at Gatesheafod. The Bernicians were pleased to have such a beautiful queen and to see how well she got on with her stepchildren. The Deirans in her company could find no fault with the courtesy and warm-heartedness of their welcome.

When the guests were floating happily towards drunkenness but still had some way to go, Eanfled rose and went out of the hall followed by the other women in procession. They crossed the courtyard to the Queen's hall and went straight to the private chamber at the far end. It was glowing: rich hangings on the walls, bearskins on the floor, the hearth blazing with applewood and scented nard. Warming by the hearthstone was a flagon of mead if the couple should want more fire inside their bellies. Under the embroidered coverlet the wide bed was piled with feather mattresses and bolsters. No October chill could get in to make the bride cold to her husband.

Undressing the Queen was a solemn affair with Grimhild in charge; besides, Eanfled was in a strange mood. It was neither the anger nor the fear of an unwilling bride, but it killed jokes and giggles before they could be uttered. As they unpinned brooches and lifted off layer after layer of embroidered wool and fine linen, Alchflaed found herself thinking — to her own horror — of that moment when the altar is stripped of its trappings on Holy Thursday after the Mass of the Last Supper. Did Eanfled see her marriage as a sacrifice to peace, would she have rather lived as a nun in her mother's convent? Certainly she was as lovely as any virgin martyr in the legends of the saints, going naked to her death in a Roman arena.

Unlike Alchflaed, the Queen had not been suckled by a ploughman's wife in a farmhouse where foster-brothers and sisters slept together like a litter of puppies and a new baby came every year. Queen Ethelburg had spoken to her sombrely at times about duty and the need for a wife to submit in all things to her husband, as St Paul commanded. Her Kentish cousins had gone into more detail. When King Oswy's offer of marriage had been taken up, Eanfled had told them — not boasting but as a simple truth — that if Kent were set down in reunited Northumbria, it would be the size of a nobleman's estate. Her kinswomen had paid her back by reciting Oswy's life-story; in their saga he made a good third with Eormanric Wife-slayer and Attila the Hun.

Eanfled was ready to believe anything about Bernicians; it now crossed her mind that Attila had died on his wedding night. The scops said he had worn himself out; none of the tales told what had happened to Queen Ildico. These were only heathens, though; Father Romanus had promised that God would take care of His pure daughter Eanfled. She sank into her mattresses and pillows to wait for her martyrdom.

They could hear steps in the hall, scuffling, the sound of men's voices, laughter. Oswy had arrived. There was a knock; the door opened to Godric's grinning face.

123

'The King of Bernicia asks leave to enter Deira. He comes in peace.'

A voice further from the door made some remark. The women caught the word 'bloodshed'; this was greeted by a guffaw outside and some furtive sniggers behind Grimhild's back. She said impassively, 'I wish you goodnight, my lady,' moved to go, then waited for Alchflaed, who stooped to kiss the Queen's hand and hurried away, not looking for Oswy among the crowd of men by the door.

Grimhild went out after her, followed by the other women, who were thankful to get back to the feast, where the drinking, songs and jokes would go on unchecked as long as Alchfrid saw fit. The men cheered their king through the bedroom doorway. Then they left in their turn, apart from the bodyguard who were to spend the night at the far end of the hall.

Oswy had stripped outside the bedroom to the jesting and laughter of his nobles and warriors, letting them have a good helping of the time-honoured wedding-night ribaldry that Eanfled had been spared. He had his cloak round him as he came in, but threw it off before sitting on the side of the bed. Eanfled studied him under modestly lowered lashes. His tall figure was lean, with hard muscles and smooth, taut skin. It was golden in the firelight with a sheen of silvery body hair. She found it easy to imagine that he was Alchfrid.

'This has been a happy day for our people, my dear. I'm sorry you had such a long and stormy journey to bring us the happiness.'

Eanfled opened her eyes.

'It was a long way, and a very long time, before I could come home to my kingdom.'

There was a note of reproach in her voice.

'Better late than never. Luckily, it's not too late for either of us. And now you're Queen of Bernicia as well, remember.'

He smiled and swung his legs up on to the bed.' I hope you're not too tired to let me take you on one more little ride across your new kingdom. I promise you the going won't be too rough.'

Oswy liked women and preferred them good-humoured. He did not find tears or lumpish submission amusing; all Eanfled's surprises that night were pleasant ones. Towards dawn, after they had been resting for a while, he got up and poured mead for them both. While Eanfled was sipping, propped up on her pillows, he put an ivory casket on her knees.

124

'Your morning gift, my dear, with my thanks and good wishes.'

Eanfled opened it eagerly and found a parchment, also a very costly girdle with a golden buckle. Hanging from jewelled chains were every tool and trinket that women liked for their daily use: scissors, knife, herb-strainer, needle and thread box, all delicately made of gold. On the parchment was a list of all the royal estates in Deira, which Oswy had made over to her. Watching her, he saw her run over the names hastily, then go back to the beginning, reading slowly as if searching for something.

'Is anything lacking, my lady?'

'I don't see Getlingas listed.'

'Getlingas?' Oswy looked at her sharply. 'That's not a royal estate.'

'Hunwald was a traitor. His lands are forfeit to the royal House—to me. By the way, what happened to Hunwald?'

'He died.'

'He should have been accused before the witan.'

'He was Oswine's trusted friend. His treachery was a foul disgrace on every other thane in Deira. It would only have added to the bitterness if I'd let the vile details be shouted to the four winds. Least said, soonest mended. I promise you he didn't enjoy dying, if that's what's worrying you.'

Eanfled shivered. She was not blood-thirsty; she preferred killing to happen out of her sight.

'No, it's not pleasant to think about, is it? Neither is Getlingas. The whole place was burned; whatever would you want with it?'

'I'd like to found a monastery there. The monks could pray for Oswine's soul. It would be an act of great charity—besides it would look so well to the people that I—that we were taking thought for my poor cousin.'

This was reasonable; Oswy was ready to please her.

'Very well, my dear, if that's your wish. And now, as your women won't come in for some time yet, suppose we thank each other again.'

When they lay back drowsing in each other's arms, both husband and wife felt well satisfied with their bargain.

Eanfled thought, without the slightest sense of blasphemy, that just as God was said to have spared Our Lady the pangs of childbirth, so He had spared her the pains of deflowering, as a mark of His special grace. Also, that it would be very pleasant to found a house of religion, and draw up rules for it, and visit it with costly gifts, instead of having to live in one on charity. And every year, on the anniversary of Oswine's death, the people of Deira would be reminded of their queen's piety and her care for her cousin's soul.

They would also be reminded every year that her husband was believed to have arranged the murder, which would do no good to Oswy's power in Deira. His power was now her own; as Oswy's wife she had no other. But all Eanfled's ideas about state-craft had been gathered from songs and old stories through which a beautiful princess, with her face, walked unscathed so she never thought of that.

Oswy thought that he was very lucky in his second wife. She did not cause him either passion or ecstasy, thank God. He had known both with Riemmelth and had learned how they could strip him of his armour, leave him naked and helpless under the blows of grief. He wished he could forget a happiness that he had lost for ever; but he was forced to remember her every time a gull's wing flashed white in the sunlight; whenever the summer lightning flickered over the western hills; whenever the heather bloomed. Oswy bore her death smiling, as he would have borne the loss of a hand in battle, or the dragging pain of a badly healed belly wound, knowing that the harm could never be made good. His cousin Eanfled was beautiful, well-mannered and good-humoured. She seemed to have a healthy regard for her own interests, but as these were now his own as well, that was all to the good. It promised to be the best kind of state marriage: profit-able, friendly and bringing affection in the end, given time and children.

He had seen almost from the moment of meeting that his new wife was very vain, but told himself with tolerant amusement that such a lovely woman had every right to be.

CHAPTER
12

Alchflaed soon found that life in Eanfled's court was as mild as life in Ebbe's convent but had much less meaning. The Queen thought that charity meant sending a maid to give some silver to a beggar; she did not tend the common folk with her own hands. She liked well-painted books in costly covers as she liked any other costly trinket; she did not talk much about what was inside them unless Alchfrid was present.

Eanfled asked the prince to stay on after her wedding. 'I want him to know me before he goes,' she told Oswy. 'Sons are often afraid that a second wife will rob them of their rights, or turn their fathers against them. Cumbria's so far away and I daresay there are mischief-makers all ready to carry tales. If he's learned to like and trust me, they can't do any harm.'

Long ago, Eanfled had scaled the highest and most blessed peak of hypocrisy. She devoutly believed in herself and so gave off no whiff of treachery even to Oswy, whose senses were as keen as a hunting wolf for any threat or trap.

Talking to her stepdaughter, she had found that Alchfrid ruled in a great city, far to the west. He had a proper city-based bishop, whose diocese had been founded in Roman times, not one of those wild Irish monks that Oswy favoured. This was a good omen; it also reminded her of something that her family had tried to forget. One of the Welsh kings of Cumbria, a man called Rhun, had gone into the church. When her father had become a Christian, Bishop Rhun had officiated at his baptism beside Paulinus, Augustine's envoy.

'God's ways are wonderful,' she told her stepchildren. 'We were meant to be one family. You're Bishop Rhun's descendants after the flesh and I am the daughter of his spirit!'

Alchfrid was deeply struck by this and looked at her worshipfully; his sister found the idea amusing. She did a quick calculation: Rhun had been their mother's grandfather, so—

'Of course! That makes you our spiritual great-aunt!'

Oswy chuckled; for a moment they looked at each other as if they were old friends who had suddenly met in an alien land. This happened from time to time when she made him laugh.

Eanfled's face hardened; then she said plaintively,' It's so simple to bring down the highest thoughts with mockery.'

'Only for those whose tongues act quicker than their minds!' snapped Alchfrid, glaring at his sister.

'You must forgive Alchflaed, my boy. It's so easy to be mistaken. I myself get the feeling you could be old Bishop Rhun's spiritual son—which would make you my spiritual uncle-by-marriage. Sometimes you talk as if you were.'

Alchfrid went back to Cumbria at last; Oswy was often away, busy with the cares of his kingdom. Eanfled was deep in her plans for her monastery at Getlingas, talking for hours with Father Romanus and her chosen abbot, a nobleman called Trumhere who was related to the Deiran royal family. She was busy and important over drawings and lists and letters to Cantwaraburh.

Alchflaed would have liked to help but her offers were sweetly refused. 'Dear child, you're too young to be burdened with such cares. Enjoy your girlhood while you can.' She was thrown back on the company of the highly-born bower-maidens, who gossiped and giggled and squabbled about clothes and the charms of the bodyguard, just like Edyth, Osburg and Leoba at Bebbanburh.

Oswy had said no more about making her choose between the convent and Cadman's son. She might have thought he had forgotten, absorbed in his own marriage and statecraft; watching Oswy taught her that he forgot nothing. She guessed, with bitter amusement, that he was leaving her alone. If he did nothing to rouse her into defiance, she would go back to Ebbe in sheer hunger for something to fill her mind.

'Gifts like yours would be wasted outside the Church. Where else could you use them?'

She got no answer to that from dreams or visions. She had never seen the enchanted hill of her vision again since Meilyr evoked it for her as the Land of Youth. She could hardly remember what it looked like. No sign came from her mother, though she went to sleep every night holding the moon-necklace. She touched the robes that her mother had worn, but since she now wore them herself the sense of her mother's body had been driven out of them.

At last, desperate for something to do, she began to embroider a silk border for the green robe her mother had worn in the herb garden. She chose a strip of deep blue, the colour of a clear

128

evening sky, and wove an elaborate interlace pattern of branches across it, with leaves of many trees in their own shapes and shades of green. As it grew under her hands, the design took on a life and meaning of its own. She began to set flowers, seeds and berries among the leaves, always white couched with silver. She chose plants for each month of the year and set the thirteen full moons among the branches, flanked by their crescents as on her necklace.

Fairy-flax, knot-weed, thorn-apple, old man's beard. The year of Our Lord 651 drew to its end. Mistletoe.

The girls, watching her always bending over her stitches and seeing the gleam of silver thread, thought she was at work on an altar cloth. Eanfled told Oswy that Alchflaed was well-meaning but had little spirit or aptness for court life; she would be happier in a convent.

Eanfled's own piece of embroidery, her silent story of the beautiful wronged queen, had met with a set-back. Sharing Oswy's bed, she could no longer tell herself that he would likely die soon, worn out with old age and debauchery. He seemed to grow more vigorous as the months passed; his Christmas revels went beyond anything she had seen in Kent.

Snowdrop, barren-strawberry, blackthorn, daisy.

Spring, longer days, roads drying out would bring the raiding season again, and Penda. It was hardly possible that Oswy could hold out much longer. Apart from Kent, protected for the time being by the Thames and by its Frankish allies, every other English kingdom was subject to Mercia. Oswy was to blame for the Mercian raids by his stubborn refusal to pay tribute and take Penda as his overlord. He would surely be killed in battle, likely this year. She told her fears to Grimhild at hair-combing time: if Oswy in his folly led the army of Northumbria to destruction, what would happen to her own Deiran people? Wouldn't it be her duty to make an alliance with Cumbria, to save the Christian north? She could see that Prince Alchfrid was worried too, and often displeased by his father's handling of affairs.

Grimhild informed her kin that Eanfled wanted to separate her kingdom from Bernicia and believed that Cumbria was ready to secede as well. This news caused a stir of interest in Deira; some of the southern nobles made visits across the Mercian border.

If anyone had told Eanfled that she was doing more to destroy Northumbria than even Penda could manage, she would have known that the speaker was a demon, sent to tempt her from her

129

duty. Wasn't she striving her hardest to save the country?

Cuckoo-flower and mouse-ear. Hawthorn, whitebeam.

As one full moon followed another and the embroidery grew under her hands, so Alchflaed's decision became fixed. When the year ended and the embroidery was finished, she would go back to Ebbe and take the veil. She thought about marriage; but she hadn't seen the man her father had picked out for her and had no sense of loss. She had discovered nothing about married life during her time out in the world that made her want a repetition of gossip, embroidery, decking herself out and meals in the hall for the rest of her days. She was eager to get back to her studies, to craftsmanship, to useful work.

Meadowsweet, hoarworthy, enchanter's nightshade.

While Alchflaed's embroidery was coming to full circle, so Eanfled's monastery was nearing completion. Oswine had died on the 20th of August. The royal family went to Getlingas for his anniversary mass; Alchfrid rode over the Stony Moor to join them. Alchflaed had resolved that this was the last gathering she would attend as a laywoman. She would make it a feast for her own dedication as well as that of the monastery; it would mark the end of her life in the world as well as Oswine's.

Travellers' joy.

They followed the same road south that she had taken a year ago. What high hopes had led her on — and what a barren wilderness she had found. Another night at Perscbrig; she wondered if Oswy recalled their clash of wills. He had won in his usual style, by avoiding battle and letting her defeat herself.

Next day they left the Roman road and took a track to the south-west skirting the moors. In the early afternoon the track breasted a rise then ran down to a ford across a stream. She looked down at the monastery buildings on rising ground at the other side of the water. The little valley, sheltered by gentle hills, was brimming with sunlight that gilded the ripples of the stream and the rich grass of the water-meadows where sleek cattle were grazing. There was no sign of the fire; the ashes were under the foundations of the new buildings, the paved courtyard, the newly-laid-out herb garden.

She could not imagine a more peaceful scene; and when they arrived at the guest halls she could not have asked for more comfortable quarters. Eanfled planned to make frequent visits of inspection and had taken care that she would lack none of her usual luxuries.

Yet the air of Getlingas breathed neither peace nor comfort. Many Deiran nobles had arrived with bands of followers; those who could not pack into the monastery guest halls were in nearby farm steadings or camping out, as the weather was warm and dry. The time and place had revived their bitterness and suspicion about what had happened there last year, and Oswy's part in it. They were simmering with resentment against the Bernicians, who were edgy and ready to take offence. There were too many thoughts that had better not be spoken.

But beyond this, there was some deeper, darker trouble in the gentle little valley. The pain and horror of those who had been penned in it and burned to death, the ugly rage of those who had no mercy even for children and innocent animals, swirled through the place like muddy flood-water. And a current of cold evil seemed to be flowing down from the low wooded hills that sheltered it.

Abbot Trumhere, a good man, felt the nearness of devilry and was disturbed by it. He had already vowed many vigils and masses for the repose of the souls of the unhappy dead; though it would take years of prayer and devotion before Getlingas won back the peace that belonged to it.

Most of the folk who were there on that 20th of August were fortified in some way against assault from the world of darkness. The Deirans were taken up with their loathing for Oswy. Alchfrid was full of plans for restoring the Roman Empire in Britain; Eanfled was full of herself. Oswy was counting up allies and planning defensive moves in the everlasting board-game of his mind. It was Alchflaed—lonely, adrift in life with no very strong aim or hope, the Welsh side of her nature wounded and starving—who met the full force of the attack.

The Deiran thanes had put on black cloaks to show their grief for their last king and as a silent reproach to Oswy. He and Alchfrid were dressed sombrely but richly, as a mark of respect to the ceremony and as a sign that they were not guilty penitents; while Eanfled was so smothered in mourning robes and veils that she might have been Oswine's widow.

Alchflaed had been taught in Ebbe's convent that the entry of a good man into heaven was a cause of rejoicing. Also, this day was her own farewell to the world of kingship and high adventure. She wanted to go proudly and make a brave outward show because in her heart she felt she had been defeated. So she put on her mother's green robe, now glittering with its embroidered border, set the moon-necklace openly at her throat and bound her veil with a silver head-band. She came into the church last, looking like the Queen of the Wood appearing to her votaries at a full moon festival.

There was an indignant stir among the Deirans at the sight of her. Alchfrid glared; Eanfled looked insulted. Oswy's face was impassive but he compressed his lips. As they were in a holy place and mass was about to begin, no one dared to make an outcry but Alchflaed could feel that she had made some mistake and that the others had withdrawn from her in spirit.

Perhaps it was shame and confusion that made her break out into a sweat and then the stone building chilled her. She felt a clammy coldness that seemed to be trailing slime across her skin; her guts were empty and shrivelling in sick hunger. Water-brash rose in her throat; she longed to vomit but had nothing to void. All the while waves of hatred washed through her, hatred of her family, the folk in the church, Meilyr and Nest who had betrayed and deserted her, all mankind. Her mind worded curses, obscenities she had not believed she knew; she had to fight not to scream them aloud.

She struggled to ward off the evil with the holy words of the mass, to fix her thoughts on them alone so that no foulness could come inside her, but the chant faded into a meaningless bleating; the robed, cowled monks were no more than a huddled flock of sheep. Her eyes blurred, the world grew dim—or the surface of life as she knew it thinned to a veil so that she could see the death underneath. Alchfrid was a crumbling Roman statue, cold and blank-eyed. There was nothing of Eanfled but a bit of whittled and painted stick trimmed with gold wire and snippets of rag, the sweepings of a craftsman's shop cobbled up to make a child's doll. She swayed; Oswy glanced round to her; she saw he was a lean grey wolf with yellowing fangs.

Still, she forced herself to stay on her feet, shaped her mouth to whisper the right responses, walked her fainting body to the altar to receive the Host, clinging to the faith that she would be healed as it entered her body. The Abbot turned towards her, holding the paten. The bread in it had indeed become flesh for her, suppurating and acrawl with maggots. She looked in horror at the Abbot; there was nothing but bones under the vestments. The finger-bones took a stinking gobbet from the paten and held it to her mouth; she shrieked 'No!' and threw herself backwards, falling into a gulf of icy darkness.

CHAPTER
13

When Alchflaed came back to herself, sick and shivering, she was lying on her bed in the hospice. Oswy was sitting at one side of her, Abbot Trumhere at the other; both looked stern.

The Abbot leaned towards her; she remembered how he had done so at the altar and shuddered, closing her eyes.

'Why did you cry out and disrupt the mass?'

'I was taken violently sick—it came on me without any warning signs.'

'Why did you refuse the Host?'

'I dreaded I'd spew on the paten.'

The Abbot nodded slightly, his grim look softened.

'Daughter, you made your confession last night. Have you any sin on your soul that you have not admitted?'

'Not that I know, Father. But if I've ever done wrong without knowing it, or forgotten anything, I pray God to pardon me.'

He held out a crucifix towards her; she kissed it devoutly without any sign of fear or hate. He blessed her but he had not done with her yet.

'Why did you deck yourself out like that?'

She felt tears of weakness coming.

'I wanted to honour King Oswine. Nobody told me it was to be a mourning. He was a good man, Bishop Aidan's friend. I've heard folk saying he's a saint. My aunt told me that when saints went to heaven, even if they went through a lion's mouth, Christians sang *Te Deum* for them.'

The tears began to roll down her cheeks, her lips were trembling. 'I could feel as soon as I went into the church that you were all angry with me, but I meant no harm, believe me.'

'I believe you.' The Abbot sighed and looked across her at Oswy. 'I've told you before, my lord. There has been very great evil done in this place—mostly by Deirans, I'm sorry to say. It's all too likely that the most innocent should feel its presence most keenly and be sickened by it.'

Oswy smiled bitterly. 'I won't try explaining that to Deirans. Say she had a fit, made herself sick by too much fasting and vigils.'

This was the story that was told. From courtesy and fear the Deiran thanes pretended to believe it in front of Oswy. It made no difference to the rumours that ran from one band to another of their retainers, who had been following the mass outside the church porch. They carried the tales across Deira on their way home.

Alchflaed had tried to flout God and his ministers by coming openly into church as a priestess of Frea. She was Oswy's witch; she had taken the place of her Welsh mother who had trained her in magic. Alchflaed had carved the hel-runes that had maddened Hunwald into slaying his lord—how else could a Deiran nobleman ever act so shamefully? Then she had spirited Hunwald out of the world of humankind so that he might not reveal her sorcery. Bishop Aidan had found out about the crimes she and Oswy had committed—hadn't he died in the open air rather than go under Oswy's roof? Alchflaed had come down to Holy Island and Bebbanburh to destroy Aidan before he could denounce her; he had died just after she arrived. Her guilt was proved by the fact that she could not take communion; the Host itself had struck her down at the altar before she could profane it. And so on.

However widely and wildly the stories diverged in the telling, they all agreed in one point. It was clear that those of Oswy's blood were accursed; none of them would be allowed to enjoy their ill-gotten gains for long. Nor were they.

While the royal party was still at Getlingas, a messenger brought bad news. The thanes of southern Deira had rebelled. Eoforwic was in their hands. Either they despaired of getting Eanfled out of Oswy's power or they did not choose to put themselves under the rule of a woman. They had offered the kingship to St Oswald's son, Athelwold, who had been brought up by monks close to a convent at Heruteu where his widowed mother was living. Athelwold had accepted the offer—and had put himself under Penda's protection.

With Mercia at their back and Eoforwic in their power, the rebels could easily tempt other Deiran nobles to join them. There was little or nothing that Oswy could do to check this without risking all-out war. He had seen the masked resentment at the consecration of the new monastery and knew he would be lucky if he could keep even a foothold in northern Deira along the Tese. He showed no outward anger when told of his nephew's new kingship.

'They said,' reported the messenger, studying Oswy's face with

134

wary insolence, 'that not even Oswy would murder his own brother's son.'

'They were quite right,' said Oswy calmly. 'I won't.'

He gave the messenger a gold ring and sent him away pleased at the gift but cheated of any display of rage or fear. Eanfled had enough regard for her dignity to keep her recriminations till the royal family was alone.

'I thought your brother was supposed to be a saint. His son does little credit to his birth and upbringing.'

'That's his mother.' Oswy spoke tolerantly. 'She was one of the prettiest women I've ever seen and quite the silliest. Kingship meant no more to her than wearing richer jewels than anyone else and sitting at the head of the table. But she clung to it, for all that. I'm sure she took Oswald's martyrdom as a personal slight because she had to give all that up.' He laughed. 'She'll have filled the boy's head with idiot's tales about his rights. I should have had him brought up under my eyes and kept the nonsense out of him, but I felt sure he'd be a monk.'

'What's the good of saying what you should have done? What are you going to do now?'

Eanfled made the demand as if she expected Oswy to rush off and call Athelwold to single combat. She was furious at the loss of her city; it was a slight to herself. She wanted to fix the blame on her husband but she did not really believe he would act at once. His answer startled her.

'It's time you were married.' He looked at Alchfrid. 'You need an heir in these troubled times and we both need an alliance.'

Alchfrid thought that this was good sense. 'Whom do you suggest, Father? There's Strathclyde on our northwestern border. I've always kept on good terms with them, another British kingdom and Christian. They're natural allies for Cumbria. Or the Picts—they're heathen, but they'd be strong at your back and they've stood by you in the past.'

'And they'll stand by us now against a threat from the south, so we don't need to win them over. I'm glad you don't object to working with the heathen in a good cause—you're going to ask Penda to give you his eldest daughter. She's about your age, perhaps a year or two older but that's all to the good. Her body will be stronger for child-bearing.'

'Penda's daughter!'

'Who better? Penda's a stickler for honour, he'd never attack a would-be son-in-law during the haggling or at the wedding feast.

I just need to hold off trouble and give our queen time and peace to win over the Deiran rebels. They'd choose her before Athelwold given the chance.'

'Penda will know you're only buying time. You couldn't trick him into thinking otherwise. He'll never accept.'

'He'll accept, to make me think I have tricked him, to lull me off my guard while he gets the final blow ready. He needs a bit of time, too. He's had trouble with the East Anglians. He wouldn't want me coming in at his back while he's settling with them. And above all, he'll want to frighten Athelwold and those who are using him. He's thrashed all the other kings into submission but Athelwold might be seeing himself as an equal ally. Making friends with me behind Athelwold's back will scare the Deiran rebels into crawling to him on their knees. A marriage treaty could win me a year if you handle it properly.'

Eanfled had got her breath back. 'How could you sacrifice your own son to buy time from an enemy?'

This was a mistake; sacrificing oneself to duty was a Roman virtue.

'Don't grieve for me, my lady. I'm happy to obey my father.'

'But a filthy, coarse heathen!'

'That's no trouble,' said Oswy cheerfully. 'I'm sure Alchfrid can convert her — if not, it'll be all the easier to break the marriage when it's no more use to us.'

Eanfled silently digested this and found it not unpleasant. Alchfrid was the age to marry. An only son's duty was to get children as soon as possible. As the first year of her marriage had passed with no sign of Oswy dying, she had begun to dread the news that he had pledged his son to some Christian princess from Wales or Ireland. But if he had to take a wife before she herself was free to marry him, who better than some heathen savage he could discard at will and who would disgust him every moment they spent at bed and board together? How much brighter she would shine in his eyes by contrast!

Thinking of this, she was ready to lap Alchfrid in tender sympathy at his cruel fate: she knew just how much he would suffer; she herself had been sold into wedlock for the peace of kingdoms.

'I'll get messengers on the way to Mercia at once. You'd better go back over Stony Moor and then move down to Lonceaster. If Penda takes up the offer, you'll be ready to move south and meet him before he has time to change his mind. If he refuses, it'll mean he's going to strike now, before the winter, so you'll need

136

to check the southwestern defences.'

'He'll think it odd — a reigning prince coming to seek a bride himself. We're not living in a scop's tale — I'm not a wandering outlaw like Prince Sigemund.'

'All the better if he does think it odd — I want him taken aback. The Mercians will try to make this marriage look like submission. After all, we're the ones who are doing the asking. Penda wouldn't insult a guest at his court — he's too great a king for that — and he'd punish any of his own folk who did so, if anyone dared. But there are all sorts of ways short of open insult that can be used to make a stranger feel small or look ridiculous — covert taunts, sneering praise. Bernicians would find that very difficult to handle without either letting themselves be put down or goaded into losing their tempers.'

'So you're sending Alchfrid to be baited instead!' In her motherly concern, Eanfled put her arm round Alchfrid's shoulders.

'There'll be no baiting. The Prince of Cumbria, a great Welsh kingdom, comes to honour Penda by asking for his daughter's hand. He won't be expecting that.' He chuckled. 'Penda's never had a war with Cumbria but the only time he and his men got within sight of Cumbrian troops, last year at Bebbanburh, it was the Mercians who ran away. I don't suppose it's their favourite memory.'

'You don't expect me to bandy vulgar boasts —'

'Far from it, even if you knew how. You're to be as Roman as you like. The Mercians won't know what to make of you.'

Suddenly he turned to Alchflaed. She had been listening to the talk with no other feeling than grief for her brother and a pity that she would never show, since he seemed not to want any, that his young body was to be mated with a creature no better than an animal, by all accounts. This was wordly statecraft; but it was no longer any concern of hers. Soon she would be shut away from the sight and sound of it.

'I want you to go with your brother. You've been sick and some fools have been making a story about it. A ride'll do you good and give a chance for stupid talk to die down. Out of sight, out of mind.'

Alchflaed knew then, once and for all, by the joy that rose up in her like sap in springtime, that she had no vocation for the religious life. Her vision at Bebbanburh had been a true Sending; she should have trusted it and not fallen into childish impatience that great events did not happen so quickly in the world as they do in a minstrel's tale.

She was to ride out at her brother's side, just as she had dreamed last year. Not for a quick gallop over the moors after fugitives; not for a stately journey to a Christian city to welcome its returning queen. They were going together into the heart of the danger that had threatened their land and their faith since the day that Penda and Cadwallon slew Eanfled's father in the wastes of Haethfeld. She realised that she had not felt so happy for a year—not since she danced for Meilyr.

Eanfled had been shocked out of her selfishness for a while at the idea of sending a girl on such a quest. She was even more horrified at the girl's high spirits as she got ready to go.

Standing at the gate of the monastery by Oswy's side, she watched the Cumbrians ford the little stream and take the track to the north, as Hunwald's wife had watched him go a year before, following Oswine's body to the lingering death that had been chosen for him. When the riders turned the corner round the hill-slope she spoke her mind.

'There are times when I wonder if your daughter is quite maidenly. I don't want to say a word against Ebbe's up-bringing of her—but what high-born lady could be willing—more than willing, *relishing* the thought of riding headlong into danger and defying a monster in his own lair?'

'Her mother,' said Oswy.

CHAPTER
14

The sands and marshes at the mouth of the Dee give fine hawking. A man can be so rapt, watching the feats of his falcon, that he forgets time and tide. Then he can be in deadly danger. This is specially true when the days shorten in October and the water creeps in silently with the dusk.

The sun was still quite high over the Welsh hills when a woman began to keep her watch from the northern wall of Legaceaster. She had been there beyond an hour, sometimes pacing to and fro, more often standing by the north gate, tense as a look-out in war time, gripping the edges of her cloak tight to her body though the air was warm and still.

At last, she must have seen what she was waiting for; she

turned so sharply that her hood fell back from her face as she hurried towards the steps of the gate tower. She was a handsome woman, tall and slender, with pale brown hair neatly braided under her veil and large grey eyes. She could have been beautiful, might have been so once. But though she was not old—her skin was smooth, she moved briskly—and her rich clothes showed that she could not be suffering from want, she was not far from looking worn and haggard. Her skull was too close under her skin; her eyes stared from hollowed sockets.

The gatewardens knew her; they stood aside respectfully as she passed through the guard-room but did not speak to her. Still hurrying, she crossed the north gate and went towards a large hall at the northeastern angle of the walls; with its surrounding barns and stables it was like a thane's homestead picked up from the fields and set down inside the old City of the Legions.

She passed swiftly through the hall and into the chamber behind, said, 'He's coming!' to the girl lounging on a bench near the hearth, then went out again through a side door. A lean-to shed had been built against the wall here; it too had a raised stone hearth where a cauldron of water was on the boil watched by a slave-woman. There were several buckets of cold water near the hearth, and a large wooden tub. Some towels and body-linen were laid ready on a bench by the wall. Seeing that all was in order, the mistress said, 'You can start filling the bath now, don't forget the herbs,' and returned to the chamber. The girl watched her idly as she picked up an embroidered shirt that was airing across the end of the bench, shook and turned it, then spread it out again.

'I'll call when he's had his bath and got his breeches back. Then you can bring the shirt and help him put it on. I'll tell him you embroidered it.'

The girl pouted and laughed. 'You always keep the best bits for yourself, sister. No wonder the scops call you Wulfrun the Wise.'

She was very like her sister, softened into bewitching prettiness. Shining tendrils of hair escaped from her smooth plaits and waved about her brows and cheeks; her full lips were red and smiling; when she laughed, which was often, her cheeks dimpled.

'It's not fitting for you to handle the body of a naked man.'

'It fits you well enough, so I see.'

'I'm a married woman, Winefride.'

'And I wish you joy of it, with old Eadbert.'

139

Winefride had lost interest in the dispute, which she was bound to lose anyway. A late butterfly floated in through the door from the hall; it settled on the table where some scraps of marjoram and mint were lying. Winefride watched it for a second, then unfastened one of her brooches and stabbed the pin through the insect's body. It twisted frantically, fluttering its wings. Winefride smiled; Wulfrun said sharply, 'Don't do that!' snatched out the pin, swept up insect and herbs together and threw them in the fire.

'Why ever not?'

'It's a stupid waste of time. And men don't like to see it.'

'I know what men like to see.'

'Well, don't let anyone hear you say so. If the word gets round, men'll ask you to let them see it, but they won't ask for you in marriage.'

Winefride laughed. 'You'll fret yourself into your grave soon, if you don't take life more lightly. Men are so blind drunk on their wedding nights they don't know what they've got. You could bed them with their grandmothers and they wouldn't notice.'

'They're not so blind drunk afterwards they can't count up to nine or notice a family likeness. Stop talking nonsense. A prince's bride mustn't be touched by loose talk. Even you couldn't be such a fool as to throw away the queenship of Mercia for the sake of a moment's pleasure. You could be the most powerful woman in England when Penda dies.'

Winefride showed very little interest in the prospect; Wulfrun put the point again in her sister's terms.

'You could have finer robes and jewels than any other woman in the country. And you could buy slave-girls to do what you liked with.'

She gripped Winefride's arm and gave her a hard shake.

'Behave yourself in front of Peada, do you hear me?'

She went back through her hall, walking slowly like the great Mercian lady that she was, coming out by chance just in time to see and greet a group of riders who had entered by the north gate. They had been hawking; the first-comer had a falcon on his wrist; two others had poles laden with dead birds.

The falconer hailed her with a shout, jumped down from his horse, gave its bridle to one of his servants, his falcon to another and hurried to embrace Wulfrun. Though she was tall, he overtopped her; he was broad and strong as well, and very good to look at, with clear brown skin and curly gold-brown hair and beard. There was a faint likeness between him and Wulfrun: they had the same grey eyes and large, well-shaped features though hers looked so worn and strained while his were glowing with life.

Wulfrun stepped back from the hug, laughing and scolding playfully.

'Oh, my dear—have you left any mud on the shore or brought it all back with you? If you were still living with me I'd give you a bath this minute—I've just got a pan on the boil.'

'Wulfrun—would you? Then I could get myself to rights without Father seeing me. He told me to get out beyond the east gate and see those ill-begotten Northumbrians safely into the palace. But I was having good sport and the time went by. Anyway, I didn't see why I should put myself out for that rabble.'

As he talked, they were heading for the outer door of the lean-to, Peada still with his arm across her shoulders. She gave her cloak to the maidservant and sent her away with a jerk of her head. While Peada stripped, she took off her embroidered tunic, rolled up the sleeves of her gown, ladled the boiling water, fragrant with herbs, into the tub and then cooled it, testing the heat with her forearm. Peada stepped in, folded his huge limbs, then sat back with a comfortable sigh.

Wulfrun crouched behind him, splashing the water over his body and rubbing him down with a soft woollen cloth, across his shoulders and arms, down his spine and the cleft of his buttocks, round his loins to the strong young prick in its bush of curly hair. Peada enjoyed the handling, grinning at the thought that Wulfrun, the most virtuous wife in Mercia, was as skilful with her hands as any portqueen from the waterfront brothels. It wasn't a joke he could share with her, of course; such ideas never crossed a decent woman's mind and he respected Wulfrun as much as he loved her.

'Ah, that's good. Nobody cares for me like you, Wulfrun.'

'I've had plenty of practice over the years. Do you remember the first time I bathed you?'

'Dear Wulfrun, you've always been a kind sister to me.'

Wulfrun made herself laugh and kept her hands steady. If Peada had seen her face he would have thought she had been struck by an elf-bolt, her lips were so twisted with agony. When she moved round to the front of the tub to wash his legs, she kept her head bent over the task.

141

I was too young and too old, she was thinking in sick despair, as she always did when she touched Peada. *If I'd been older I could have loved him like the child I can't bear in my own body. No shame, no pain. And if I'd been Winefride's age I could have made him turn to me as a woman. I know him better than that stupid, empty-headed little bitch; I'd have been such a wife, such a queen as Mercia's never known.*

Penda's first wife had died in childbirth when Peada was three. The king had not re-married at once; he had sent his son and his new-born daughter to Wulfrun's mother who was his kinswoman. She had just given birth to Winefride and took the little princess to her breast with her own baby. Wulfrun, at eight years old, was already, in her proud mother's words, 'the best and cleverest little housewife, as good as another right hand'. She took the bewildered and unhappy little boy as her charge, her plaything, her baby, her dearest love — comforted him, tended him, told him stories and taught him games, slept with him cradled in her arms until the time when her childhood and her happiness ended together.

Five years make an impassable gulf between a woman and a boy when the boy is seven and the woman is twelve. At twelve years old Wulfrun had been married to Eadbert, Penda's most powerful ealdorman and greatest warrior, a Fenlander who guarded the East Anglian border. He was a tough old widower with a large family, most of whom were older than herself.

Wulfrun took a bitter pride in the name she had won as a wife for her faithfulness, her prudence and her housekeeping skills. Though an early miscarriage had left her barren, her husband thought no less of her. He had enough children and had married Wulfrun merely to get another link with the royal kin and a mistress for his household. As such, she was beyond price. She managed the farms so that Eadbert's hospitality was famous yet his stores were always full. She used the gratitude that Penda felt towards her mother and herself to get estates for her stepsons; decked the stepdaughters' looks with fine robes and jewels, found them rich husbands. The dead wife's family trusted her as if she were a kinswoman of their own.

And in all the years of her marriage, with its endless planning and working, its unfailing chorus of praise, these brief times she spent with Peada were the only life she had.

Peada stepped out of the tub; she wrapped him in warmed towels and helped him to dry, gave him a fine linen body shirt, called servants to empty the tub and take his cloak and boots for brushing. When Peada had his breeches on again, she called Winefride, who came in smiling with the embroidered woollen tunic. Wulfrun heroically let the girl help him on with it and take the credit for its making. This was not an utter lie; Winefride had stitched the pattern that her sister had marked out for her.

Wulfrun meant to bind Peada to her for life by a marriage to Winefride. It was quite possible: they were mother's kin to the royal family as well as foster-sisters to the eldest prince and princess. The Mercian House was so ancient and powerful that it did not need to take brides to gain either ancestors or allies. Its kings often married inside the folk; Penda's present wife, Cynwise, was a Mercian. Apart from her clothes and her pastimes, Winefride did not have an idea that Wulfrun did not put into her head and left the ordering of her life to her sister, who did it so much better. She would make a perfect tool.

I'll be his real wife, just as I've been his real mother and sister. I'll rule his household; he'll turn to me for counsel, share all his plans with me. His children will look to me as a mother—Winefride can breed them for me but they'll be mine.

The three went back to the chamber. Mulled ale had been brought in. Wulfrun poured it, Winefride served it, Peada sat on the bench and stretched his feet towards the fire.

'Nobody keeps such a comfortable house as yours, Wulfrun. I wonder that Eadbert can bear to part with you.'

'We wanted to be with poor Cyneburg before they hand her over to the Northumbrians. Winefride and I can never forget that she drank from our mother's breast—we're her sisters too. Eadbert would never keep me from her at a time like this.'

Eadbert would never keep his wife from her royal kin at any time. Penda was ageing; the day would not be soon but it would come, when Peada had the rule. He would never turn on his father's old councillors but he would have friends of his own age who would have a greater say in his affairs. It pleased Eadbert very well that the prince should look on Wulfrun as his eldest and dearest sister. She could always have an escort of Eadbert's warriors to see her to the court wherever Penda was holding it.

'She puts a brave face on, even with us. How did she take the news when they first told her she was going to Oswy's son?'

'She couldn't pretend to be happy. But we gave her our word it wouldn't last long. That twisting weasel Oswy won't be able to dodge or bolt much longer. He believes he's bought himself time with this marriage—he must think we're fools. We're going to settle the Northumbrians once and for all, as soon as the fighting season starts next year. Prince Meilyr arrived today—the Welsh are coming in with us. We're keeping that quiet, of course, till the wedding party leaves. As far as they're to know, Meilyr's just making a chance visit of courtesy and staying on to see the hand-fasting. If he can make the Northumbrians think the Welsh are friendly to them, so much the better.'

Peada finished his ale and wiped his hand across his mouth.

'Will you eat something?'

'No, thanks. There's a party of spearmen waiting for me at the east gate. I'd better go and join them; it's not far off sunset. Oswy's lot will come crawling in any time now.'

'You said your father told you to see them safely in. Is he expecting trouble?'

'Nobody's going to attack them, though I dare say they're shaking in their boots. But some of the jokes might be a bit rough. Father doesn't want anything to happen that they'd have to take offence at for very shame. He doesn't want this marriage broken till he says so.'

He kissed his foster-sisters and went off refreshed and pleased with himself, as he always was after time with Wulfrun. She watched him wistfully till he turned out of sight.

Peada joined his spearmen, lounging outside the east gate, and spent the last half hour of waiting happily enough, exchanging descriptions of Northumbrians, their ancestors human and otherwise, their wedding-night customs and their strange inability to find their way towards enemy warriors. A few churls hung about gaping but most folk were getting stock in or cooking supper.

There was a shout and pointing eastwards. Peada looked up, ready to be scornful, to where the road came out of the forest into the cleared land. He blinked; then stared.

The newcomers were mounted; that was to be expected, a royal embassy would not walk from Bernicia. But instead of the jostling gaudy jumble that a group of horseback nobles usually showed, each trying to outdo the other in bright cloaks, showy jewels and even more showy horsemanship, these riders were mounted alike on greys; their cloaks were the same crimson; their shields had the same device, a strange-looking rune; they rode in equal-numbered ranks keeping the same pace. It could be the same man, one body looking like many, through wizardry.

Apart from colour and life—if they were alive—they could be a troop of the Stone-Giants, the ones who had built the paved streets and the walled chesters, come down from their carvings.

As his skin prickled at the thought, one of the riders galloped up to him.

'Alchfrid Oswysson, Prince of Cumbria, greets King Penda. He comes in peace to bring his bride home.'

Peada was taken aback. For a moment he was at a loss how to greet the newcomers. It was not usual for a reigning prince to fetch his bride himself. He would have to offer a stately welcome. All his jests, kept just this side of insult, about meeting Bernician warriors face to face at last after being disappointed so often, would be out of place, and meaningless as well, to Cumbrians.

Cumbria: that was a Welsh kingdom; his father was friendly to the Welsh. There had never been a war with Cumbria. His father said you couldn't get at them, hidden in their mountains; that there was nothing worth taking in their barren land; that Cumbrians were a tribe of elf-blooded witches and ill to meddle with. His face would darken at the rare moments he spoke of them; other folk wisely kept off the subject.

None of this helped Peada to choose his welcome. He was neither stupid nor feeble but he liked life to follow neat, simple patterns chosen by himself. Usually it did. He saw, with growing anger, that the riders had not quickened their mounts' slow walk. Either they were going to keep him standing till they chose to arrive, or they were waiting for him to walk forwards and greet them. Here was another problem: if they did not dismount he would have to walk at the prince's bridle as if he were the prince's man, looking small in every sense.

He decided to walk forward, as this would be an action of his own choice. Coming closer, he saw that as well as holding their horses to a walk they kept glancing behind them, back towards the forest. Surely, no one was hunting them—neither Deira nor Elmet would dare in the face of Penda's anger and they looked dangerous enough to keep outlaws and cattle thieves at bay.

Then one of the rear-guard, escorting their pack-horses, called out something. The Cumbrians halted as three riders burst out from under the trees, going full pelt. Two of them pulled up among the pack-train; one came galloping up to the leader, a tall man with a coldly handsome face, reaching him almost at the same time as Peada. The wild rider was a girl in horseman's leathers; her cloak and hood were blown backwards, she had lost her cap, a cascade of rich brown hair tumbled across her shoulders, her lovely face was in a glow. Peada was now beyond being startled, even by the thought that his new brother-in-law had brought his fancy-woman on his bridal journey.

'Oh, Alchfrid, I'm so sorry—have I made you late? I didn't mean to be so long, but the poor child had inflammation of the lungs—'water-elf-sickness' they call it here—and I had to make a decoction of elder and show them how to use it, and then—'

She saw Peada and stopped. Prince Alchfrid said quietly, 'I hope our delay has not been wearisome to King Penda's household. My sister Alchflaed stayed to treat a sick child at our last halting-place.'

Peada raised his eyebrows; he just stopped himself from whistling. If it was rare for a reigning prince to bring his bride home, it was unheard of for a princess to come and welcome a sister-in-law. Royal ladies only crossed their borders on their own wedding journeys. He liked the girl for it; she was brave and high-spirited as well as kind. Also, he was pleased to see that under his frosty calm, the Cumbrian prince had just been upset by his sister. This made him more human, less like a Stone-Giant. And the girl had solved his own problem: it was no shame to walk at the bridle of a princess who had come so far to honour his sister—and he'd be well-placed to lift her down from her horse and feel what was under her leather jerkin. He beamed at Alchflaed.

'It's never wearisome to me to welcome my father's guests. Let me lead you to his palace, you'll be tired after your long road.'

He took Alchflaed's bridle rein and led her ahead of everyone into what Eanfled called the monster's lair.

CHAPTER
15

Legaceaster was now a frontier town. The Maersea, the river that bordered the Cumbrian March, was a few miles to the north; the Welsh kingdoms were a few miles to the west and south. The city was in the hands of the Mercians though the Welsh made free use of its port and market. It suited them to have Penda as a fearsome watch-dog at their northern gate; their kings each preferred that he should hold it rather than a rival of their own race.

The Mercians had little use for cities as such and knew nothing of the Stone-Giants who had built them. They had been great but they were gone, leaving their mighty works to wonder at, carved with strange runes that no one could read—which was a pity since they told about buried treasure. Sometimes it was found by chance, bags of coin or vessels of gold and silver wrought with the forms of goat-legged monsters and beautiful elf-women.

King Penda found Legaceaster useful enough. Its huge walls made a good stronghold where he could meet his Welsh allies. It blocked the Northumbrians' road to the southwest; they had twice come ravaging down that way. Oswy's pagan father had defeated the king of Powys in battle outside its walls, massacring the monks of Bangor-ys-y-Coed who were praying against him, on the grounds that a prayer is a weapon like any other and they had earned the warriors' death. King Edwin had gone even farther; though he had been fostered at the court of Gwynedd he had attacked that kingdom and swept through to Môn and Manau.

That was a mistake: he had earned the relentless vengeance of their warrior king Cadwallon, who had destroyed him and nearly destroyed Northumbria too for good measure. Penda had won his first fame on that campaign; he admired Cadwallon more than any man he had ever met and kept up his liking for the Welsh long after Cadwallon's death.

Beyond its usefulness as a fort and a meeting-place, Legaceaster was the greatest port on the western sea-board. Ships came in from Ireland and the northern kingdoms; ships sailed up from Little Britain and Spain; packmen travelled from the east to exchange goods with the merchant captains. Penda took his share of the outland luxuries that passed through the place and also claimed port-dues and tolls that added to his wealth and power. He built a palace there, with a grand feasting-hall and royal lodging for his guests. Many of his nobles had their own halls as well, fine timber buildings that stood on Roman foundations but owed little to Roman style.

The palace took up most of the north-western quarter of the city, the great hall towering over the other roofs. Alchflaed thought of Heorot when she saw it; she nearly began to recite aloud the lines describing its splendour:

> *The hall towered high*
> *lofty and wide-gabled—*

Then she checked herself with a shudder, remembering what came next, trying to stop hearing the words that sounded remorselessly in her mind:

> *—fierce tongues of loathsome fire*
> *had not yet attacked it; nor was the time yet near*
> *when a mortal feud should flare between the father-*
> *and son-in-law, sparked off by deadly enmity.*

A bridal should be a time of hope and merriment but surely Alchfrid's wedding was doomed from the beginning. Eanfled's disgusted voice had dismissed the bride: 'a filthy coarse heathen', Oswy's sneer had made nothing of the bridal vows: 'all the easier to break the marriage when it's no more use to us.' But even a monster can love its offspring, as the *Tale of Beowulf* also told in blood-spattered detail. What deed of 'deadly enmity' was more likely to madden Penda than insulting and betraying his daughter?

It must not happen, she told herself. *I've got to stop it somehow. Surely that's why I was sent here?*

The palace officials were waiting to welcome the newcomers. Peada named them, ordered the Cumbrian horsemen to be attended to their quarters by his own spearmen and saw Alchfrid ceremoniously received and conducted to his guest hall by the Thyle, the court orator, and the Dish-Thane. He took it on himself to escort Alchflaed to the women's bower to be given into the care of the Queen. So, as the King had called in to speak with his wife before the evening's feast, she was the first of the visitors to meet their terrifying host.

Her mind had been running on *Beowulf*; she could not help making a picture of the king as a monster like Grendel. Her distant glimpse of him at Bebbanburh had shown a giant, a mountain of a man. He had come like Grendel, out of the high moors, the *'wolf-slopes and windswept headlands'*, bringing slaughter and destruction; then vanished like Grendel into the wasteland again. It was easy, though childish, to add other details from the poem, to see him ripping open iron-bound doors with his bare hands and

> *'seize a sleeping warrior, slit him,*
> *bite his body, drain the blood-streams*
> *gulp huge gobbets—'*

So when she saw a well-dressed nobleman doing nothing more violent than giving a small boy a lively gallop on his knee, at first she could not believe who it was.

He was sitting down, surrounded by his family like a mountain among its foothills; the Queen, a handsome woman with a kindly sensible face, sitting beside him with a baby in her lap, a cluster of little boys and girls jumping up and down beside their galloping brother and a young woman very like Peada, who was standing at the King's shoulder clapping her hands and singing a riding song. They were all tall and long-limbed, with brown hair and brownish skins, the same strong comely features and large wide-set eyes.

Peada's voice rang out cheerfully over the hubbub.

'This is our new sister-in-law, Princess Alchflaed. She's come to bear Cyneburg company on her way.'

They looked across at her, surprised but friendly. Cyneburg murmured, 'That's kind!' and smiled at her shyly. The Queen said, 'You must be very weary, my dear. Cyneburg, take some of the maids with you and see that a bower is made comfortable for our guest. Wait on her yourself.'

Penda got up; then indeed she felt she was standing at the foot of a cliff. He came towards her; he limped slightly, dragging his left leg but this did not lessen the dignity of his presence or his gait. He put his hands on her shoulders and stared down at her face; she looked back at him without flinching. He was gigantic, monstrous, seen so close; there was something more than human about him but nothing evil. She felt none of the foulness that had touched her at Getlingas. He was more akin to the huge logs burning on the hearth, both the oak tree and the flame at once. Of course he was dangerous, as fire is dangerous, as an oak forest in a thunderstorm is dangerous, and yet he was the heart of strength and warmth.

At last he nodded, as if satisfied. 'Rode all the way from Northumbria so that my little girl wouldn't lack a sister's company when she goes among strangers? Then you're as stout-hearted as you're fair to look at. Make yourself at home, lass.'

Cyneburg took her hand and led her away, signing to some of the maids to follow. They went to one of the smaller buildings that clustered round the Queen's hall. Her orders to make the bower comfortable had been more polite than needful; at the Mercian court the guest halls were always ready and as comfortable as the weariest visitor could ask. The girls were willing and cheerful, her baggage was brought in, Cyneburg herself served her with cakes and ale as she sat by the fire. When she was ready to wash and change her dress, Cyneburg took her leave, promising to come for her when they went to the feast. Then she hesitated, glanced round to see that the maids were out of earshot and said in a hurried whisper, 'It was truly kind of you to come for me. I've never been away from home before and—and—this marriage seems—strange to me.'

She went away before Alchflaed could reply either to the words or to the questions in her eyes: *Is he like you? Will he be kind to me? Will he find me pleasing?*

This was a relief, as the answers were mostly No. Alchfrid was not in the least like her; it was not probable that he would find Cyneburg pleasing; and though he would never be cruel—that would be beneath his dignity—she would find him lacking in tenderness.

Alchflaed felt guilty, too, that Cyneburg and all her family took it for granted that kindness to a new sister-in-law had brought her to Legaceaster. But that, at least, she could make true; she vowed that she would be Cyneburg's friend and use all her power to bring bride and groom together.

To do that, she needed to have Alchfrid well-disposed towards herself. She had angered him that very day; her pity for a sick child was well enough in his eyes, but her wish to treat it before going on with their journey had led to a quarrel, ending in outright defying him. He had been furious at the defiance and the delay; the manner of her arrival under the eyes of Peada and his men would have set the seal on her iniquity. Though he would never rebuke her in public she knew she was not forgiven.

She felt a moment's regret that Peada was not her brother in blood, rather than her brother-in-law; he was so much easier to get on with. She had felt at home with him at once, without any need to be always watching her words or checking her actions. But now she must atone for her crimes by being especially

dignified at the feast; she recalled Oswy's advice: 'You're to be as Roman as you like.'

This, at last, was the time for wearing one of her mother's royal robes, the heavy silks and brocades from Constantinople, some of which had been brought to Caer Luel nearly a century ago when Urien the Great was king. She chose a long gown of rose-coloured silk with its hem embroidered in gold and pearls, its full sleeves ending in tight jewelled cuffs. Over this went a purple tunic, so stiffly brocaded with gold palm leaves that it hung straight and ungirdled to her knees, clasped round the neck by a great collar of amethysts with a rim of gold medallions. Her head-dress gave her some trouble: it was a coronet trimmed at each side with ropes of pearls that hung on her shoulders. She had never seen her mother in full state but she knew from the painted queens in Ebbe's Bible that her hair should be elaborately plaited under a golden net. Neither she nor the Mercian maids were skilled enough tirewomen to do this, so she pinned most of her hair on the crown of her head and fixed the coronet round the coil. The loose curls waved around her neck, twining among the pearl lappets.

The maids were wide-eyed with wonder; they were used to splendid clothes but had never seen garments like these in real life. Some shadows of them could be seen faintly on the walls in the ruined palaces of the Stone-Giants. If Alchflaed had not been so simple and friendly in her manners the Mercian girls might have been scared of her, she looked uncanny.

Alchfrid was pleased with her when he saw her come walking behind Queen Cynwise along the mead-path to the great hall. He also had dressed in a long brocaded robe of Roman style; he could see the value of his father's advice. The Mercians did not know what to make of him; it gave him the advantage that a civilised man should always hold over barbarians.

There was another guest for Alchfrid to meet; the Thyle named them to each other before they took their places by Penda at the high table. He was a prince of the Britons of Powys, a darkly splendid figure. His cloak of chequered crimson was clasped by a great ring brooch, worked in the swirling curves that grew as naturally from British craftsmen's fingers as from honeysuckle stems, set with studs of amber and malachite. There was a gold torc with dragons' heads at his throat; his black hair was bound by a golden circlet.

Alchflaed, watching from her place among the women, did not

need him to be named, though he looked as different as she now did from the minstrel and dancing-girl who had brawled their way out of the ale-house in Eoforwic. After the first surprise, she was no more amazed to find him in Penda's hall than that she should be there herself. His secret visit to Eoforwic had been an adventure, the sort of dare-devil quest that she would have enjoyed herself if she had a man's freedom. Knowing his rank, she now knew why he had not come openly to the palace at Eoforwic —there might well have been some of Alchfrid's Cumbrians or the Elmet folk who could have named him. The thought that he had not just walked away from her friendship lifted her spirits; she smiled at him with the slightest lowering of her eyelids, trying to let him see that she would keep her mouth shut on his secrets.

Meilyr smiled back politely, taking the glance as a woman's furtive signal to her partner in a love-game that she is ready for another round. He also was not truly surprised to see her, though he took no heed of the story that she had come out of tenderness for Cyneburg's feelings. No princess ever acted as bridesmaid to her brother's wife. Alchflaed had been drawn to her master by the leash he had at his wrist; she could not keep away from him even though he had not summoned her.

The feast was outwardly friendly and cheerful. The Mercian lords knew that Prince Meilyr had come to offer the alliance of the Welsh kings for the breaking of Northumbria. Though Alchfrid never babbled about his plans or his feelings, most of his high-born companions were well aware that their prince had come to marry a few months of peace while he prepared for war. He cared nothing for the flesh-and-blood bride who went with the bargain.

The man who found the meal time most burdensome was Hereberht, the royal scop, who was having to entertain all these feasters and keep them in a good mood. He had a rich wordhoard of hero-tales and had himself composed the great *Lay of Offa of Angeln* that was Penda's favourite hearing. But tales of war could rouse too many evil memories—of Penda's savage raids into Northumbria, of the bitter struggles between Anglians and Britons. Many a feast had ended in bloodshed when songs set fire to tempers.

He would have liked to pay tribute to Cyneburg by reciting the story of one of the heroines, some princess who had gone like her to be a peace-weaver between peoples. But as he told over their names to himself—Hildeburh, Freawaru, Ealhhild—he could not think of one whose wedding had not brought grief and death. The peace that they had woven out of their heart-strings had been torn apart when the old feuds broke out again, as the feud with Bernicia was due to break out next spring. What would be done to Cyneburg when her father's war-host came over the border? And that fair young princess from the north, sitting by Cyneburg's side—where would she be by the next harvest? Burned in her hall or carried off to slavery?

Every poet and minstrel must have woman in his spirit as well as man. The scop's heart ached for the fates of helpless girls destroyed by men's hatred. He determined to give his art that night to them alone. Let them believe for a while that it was possible, by the power of magic and music, to win back happiness from the gates of death.

He stepped out to the hearth; the hall fell silent. The notes of his harp wove the words of his tale into living pictures for his hearers as he told it:

'Golden the sun, golden the harvest corn, when Geat the minstrel rode south to bring home his bride.'

The harp rang out the jingling of bit and bridle; the listeners smiled at Alchfrid and Cyneburg.

'Fair and bright was the feasting hall, fair and bright the mirth—fair and sad the face of Maethhild as she sat by her bridegroom. When the songs were sung and the feast was done, Geat and Maethhild were bedded together. He took her in his arms; her cheek was salt to his kiss, bitter to his lips as the words he spoke:

"Are you weeping for lands and an earl to your lord?
Are you weeping for gold as your morning gift?
Are you weeping because you have married a minstrel?"

' "I'm weeping for the land that I must leave for ever. I'm weeping for my golden hair that must rot under the water. I'm weeping because I will never live to be your wife. Alas for the day when I walked by the riverside gathering garlands for my bridal! The water-elf, the river-lord, set his love on me; he offered me all the jewels in his cold kingdom. When I refused, he told me he would take me, no mortal man could keep me from him. Night after night he comes to me; whenever I close my eyes I feel his cold arms clasp me, the river runs over my head. His terrible longing robs me of my rest." '

The harp rippled, soft and menacing. The listeners shuddered, for all the logs blazing in the hearth, thinking of the sands of Dee and the tide creeping through the river mist, that had taken many a fisher and fowler and herd-girl bringing her cattle home too late in the dusk.

'Geat laughed and caught her close. "Fear nothing, Maethhild, now you're mine. Warm arms of flesh and blood are stronger than any water-wraith. I have you and I'll hold you."

'Next day the bridal procession set out to bring her to her new home. But when they came to the water-meadows a white hart sprang up before them. All the young men hallooed and hurtled off in a wild chase, forgetting the bride in their wish to hunt the hart. They tracked it to the wild moors—and it melted before their eyes in a whirl of mist. Then they remembered the bride and turned back; the bridesmaids came riding to meet them. But where is Maethhild?

' "Is she not with you? We saw her last in the water-meadows."

'Too late they went looking for her. They found her horse's hoof prints going down to the water but horse and rider had vanished like the hart. Then they wept for their heedless hunting, the bride drowned on the day of her home-coming. They had set out singing; they went home weeping.'

The harp gave out a melody of unappeasable sorrow and longing. The listeners were quiet; the women, and some of the men, had tears in their eyes thinking of dear young lives that had ended too soon.

'Only Geat lingered, looking down into the water, thinking of his lost love in the crystal hall under the waves, her tears flowing salt into the stream, her white body wrapped in the water-elf's cold arms. He took out his harp, wrought by Wayland and strung with the swan-maiden's hair.

Geat played over the hill, the bird was forced off the bough;
He played over the forest, the bear was forced out of its lair;
He played over the dale, the child was forced out of the womb;

He played by the ford: the river stirred, the crystal hall was shaken, it rose and burst like a bubble, Maethhild floated in the water. Her golden hair gleamed in the sunlight; she laughed in her lover's arms: "Happy is the mother who has such a son, happier the girl who gains such a husband!"

'Long ago, Geat led his bride home; the river still sounds with the water-wraith's weeping.'

154

There was silence in the hall for a moment while the listeners came back out of the story. Then Cyneburg murmured, '*Happy is the mother who has such a son, happier the girl who gains such a husband,*' with a shy look at Alchfrid. There was a burst of laughter and clapping. Only Alchflaed said nothing, lost in thought. Peada, who had been watching her most of the meal, asked what was on her mind.

'I was thinking of the water-wraith. He loved Maethhild too; he wouldn't stop wanting her even though he'd lost her. And she—how could she ever forget the time she'd spent with him?'

Her words sounded odd in her own ears. She looked at Meilyr, smiling, sure that he at least would understand what she felt. She had never forgotten how he had talked to her at Eoforwic; he too knew what it was to long for a lost enchantment.

'I wonder if he ever came seeking her, when the mists were rising from the river and creeping across the meadows towards her hall—and did she ever look out to watch for him?'

Peada guffawed. 'A girl who waits up for water-elves is likely to get the ague for her morning gift!'

Alchfrid had taken off one of his rings to give to the scop. 'It makes a pleasant change to hear a happy ending to that story. Greek Orpheus was not so lucky—English minstrels are more skilful.'

Meilyr managed to smile at both the joke and the compliment; he kept himself smiling and talking till the feast dragged to its end. Alchflaed's words had smashed into him like a blow suddenly struck at an unarmed envoy during a peace meeting. He nearly vomited from shock and rage, as he had seen men spewing in battle when a spear went through them.

She knew.

She had seen him standing outcast in the river-mist at Caer Efrog, like a beggar at the gates of the palace where his own people had once ruled. She must have been watching from some lattice, in the light and warmth and revelry of her halls, and had never sent to invite him in, though there had been a welcome for every fairground juggler in the island. And she had laughed to see him, as she was laughing now and tossing the insult in his face in front of Penda's court and her brother's war-band, knowing there was no way he could defend himself or strike back without giving away his own secrets.

She'd mocked him and made light of him from their first meeting, throwing one of Britain's priceless treasures away as a gift to a tramping gleeman. *'You can say you had it as a reward for amusing the King's daughter.'* The little jeering slut in her second-hand Roman finery, wherever she got it—whether it was English pirates' loot from a British city or some of her mother's hand-downs. She was aping her mother's manners as well as her dress, that treacherous Cumbrian whore who had beguiled his father and then laughed at him from the safety of Oswy's bed. Blodeuedd the traitress had been born again in both of them.

Anger is slavery. Meilyr turned round and round on these thoughts all night like a slave grinding at a quern. He was haggard and heavy-eyed when he met Alchflaed next morning coming from the guest halls. She looked fresh and lively, dressed in her riding clothes, and gave him a cheerful greeting.

'You're up early, princess. Better to lie soft and warm, out of the cold river mists.'

'Prince Peada is going to show us some hawking down by the Dee.'

He already knew this; the sport had been fixed so that he and Penda could confer about breaking her people, without pointedly excluding Alchfrid or rousing his suspicions. Still, her use of the English name goaded him.

'Do you mean the Dyfrdwy? Mind where you go—it can be risky down by a riverside, as you of all people ought to know—and our Dyfrdwy isn't kind to trespassers.'

The mongrel bitch dared to laugh at him. 'You think I might meet some wandering water-sprite? I'm not afraid.'

He was in such a black fury that he could hardly see her; he grinned like an angry cat.

'Don't be too sure of yourself, girl. Our Britain can spell death to pirates—and to light-footed pirates' daughters who walk where they like over other folk's lands and think they're queens.'

It was Alchflaed's turn to feel the spear go through her. She was so startled at the sudden vicious attack that for a second she gaped at him open-mouthed, looking as stupid as he liked to imagine the English. Then her own pride of birth and race struck back.

'And it can spell death to Welsh who don't learn to keep their insolent tongues in check, as my grandfather King Ethelfrith taught you, not so far from here.'

They each had knives at their belts and were ready to use them. Only their inbred sense of what was fit for princely guests at a king's court held their hands for a second while their minds threw hate at each other.

156

Meilyr knew exactly why he loathed her. Her sneers that had stabbed home into the wounds of his nature. Her mother's shameful betrayal of his father and her own people. And behind that, two hundred years of strife, defeat and revenge that had made the two races ever ready to go for each other's throats like wolf-hound and wolf, their very closeness giving them the power and skill to wound each other to death.

Alchflaed was bewildered by the strength of her own fury. True, it was painful to get good-humour and kindliness thrown back in her face; bitter to be tricked three times by a show of friendship from a Briton into letting herself be a butt for scorn. Yet she had suffered no real harm; no one but Meilyr or Nest knew that she had been humiliated. There was no reason why she should feel so hungry to sink a knife-blade into Meilyr's flesh. It was too like the craving hatred that had overcome her during Oswine's mass. Part of her loathing turned against herself.

In the moment of silence, the hush before the storm broke, they heard Peada's voice calling, 'Hey, Bernicia! Aren't you awake yet? I can hear you snoring!'

He came round the corner of the guest hall and beamed at them.

'Oh, good morning to you, Prince Meilyr. My father would be glad if you'd give him some of your advice at his council this morning. There's a border landmark he'd like to ask you about.' He took Alchflaed's arm. 'Come along, sister-in-law, I'm going to teach you how to handle a hawk.'

Alchflaed was glad to get away to the mews and fill her mind with hawking. Though she had learned to be a good rider on moorland ponies she knew nothing about lordly sports except by reading and hearsay. Peada enjoyed showing off his birds and his knowledge to a beautiful girl who asked sensible questions and listened intently to his answers. He was specially proud of a peregrine falcon that he had caught wild when she was already adult and trained himself. He explained how he had named her Striker and stayed with her day and night for a week, talking to her and stroking her with a feather on her breast and legs. He told Alchflaed, grinning, that there was nothing like it for soothing a wild female. He had got Striker to fly to the lure by now and decided that she was ready to be entered at live quarry. Edgar, the head falconer, disagreed.

'She's not half-trained yet, my lord.'

'She's had more time from me than you've given to any other bird in the mews.'

'Remember she wasn't bred up in the mews from an eyas. She's had a year in the wild. If you take her out too soon, she'll go back to the wild, mark me.'

'She won't leave me now. I'll have her out today.'

'You'll lose that bird, my lord,' prophesied the falconer with gloomy relish.

'I never lose a bird once I've handled her.' Peada winked at Alchflaed and the party set off.

They rode northwest, towards the wide sands that bordered the Wirheale. The autumn visitors had arrived in flocks, feeding among the natives on the mud and sand below the red cliffs: teal, mallard, widgeon, geese of every kind, here and there a heron standing like a watchman on one of the tide channels.

The last taint of sick anger was scoured out of Alchflaed by the sea wind, the tang of the salt marsh, the clear air alive with wings and bird cries, the great hawks soaring and stooping in a glory of fleetness and strength. She laughed for joy when Peada loosed Striker from his wrist—and even more heartily when the peregrine ignored the prey along the shore-line and headed straight for the ridge of wood and heath inland.

Peada headed after her, cursing. He had poor pleasure in losing his falcon and even less in the prospect of telling Edgar. Alchflaed rode after him. The hawk was headed north; even when they lost her they kept to the same line with dogged stubbornness. As the ground grew steeper they had to slow down to a walk. Alchflaed had given up hope of the truant when Peada pointed to a clump of birch trees where rooks were in commotion.

'She's there.'

He took a dead bird from his saddle-bag, fixed it to the lure and swung it, whistling her call. To their joy, she rose, circled and stooped, striking at the bait. Peada let her fix on it to plume and gorge, then quietly drew near to take hold of her jesses. She settled quite contentedly and let him hood her, then place her on a tree stump. He stretched out his arms with a gusty sigh.

'That's a relief. Edgar would still be laughing this time next year if I'd lost her. I hate being laughed at for a fool.'

He rummaged in his saddle bag. 'I don't suppose you thought to bring anything to eat or drink? I did; we'll share. The others will be miles away, down on the shore. We'll eat, then get back to Legaceaster.'

She sat down on the springy turf, hugging her knees and

158

looking out over the estuary. Heath, bilberries and birch-trees made her feel at home.

'Are you cold? I can soon get a fire going.'

She shook her head. 'It's as warm as summer while the sun's up.' She had loosened the thongs of her jerkin and opened the neck of her shirt to let the air touch her throat. Peada stretched himself beside her.

'It's clear on the other side. I can see Moel Famau. Prince Meilyr's court is only a few miles to the south of it—he says it means "Mothers' Hill".'

She winced at both names. She was sick of the sound of British; she was nearly ready to deny her mother's part in her. She'd had more than enough of the British—the Welsh, the *foreigners*—with their smiles and their shows of friendship that were only ambushes for some vicious sneer or attack. Foreigners, foreigners. She silently jabbed the word over the gleaming estuary towards the alien land on the far side. Then she had the feeling, that comes in evil dreams, that she was stabbing herself with her own dagger while trying to ward off an enemy.

Too many voices all around were speaking to her about her first meeting with Meilyr—the crying of the sea-birds, the distant murmur of the tide, the moorland breeze. The times they had shared sparkled in her memory like the waves, brighter than common daylight with danger and laughter and strangeness, like the adventures in her mother's Welsh tales.

She could hear Meilyr in the tavern, describing the minstrel's life till she had felt she was living it—'and then, over the ale, you'd spin your tales of adventure and enchantment till the folk would swear they saw the wizards and elf-women you told about, floating out of the peat-smoke.'

And all the while there would be nothing really there, her mind added bitterly. *Nothing but smoke, and a spell of beguiling words. The Welsh were good at that, master-craftsmen. But, oh Meilyr, why did you—*

She turned her shoulder abruptly away from the question, from the memories, from the sight of the Welsh lands beyond the Dee. Peada had been busy sharing out his food between them he had a hunk of bread and cheese ready for her and reached it to her with a friendly grin as if she were Cyneburg. Peada now—he was as simple and as good as bread. He'd never lure folk to trust in his goodwill, like Meilyr and Nest, then mock them or play spiteful tricks on them. An annoying little voice inside her mind muttered that he wouldn't have the wit to do it, but she smothered that. She couldn't think of Peada as an enemy—anyway, she'd rather have Peada as an enemy than the Welsh as friends.

She smiled at him with a sense of relief, leaning towards him to take the food. He saw the gleam of silver at her throat.

'Hey, I didn't know you served Frea. I thought you were a Christian.'

'I am. What do you mean?'

'You've got her sign on your neck.'

'My necklace? It's only the moon in her three phases. It was my mother's and she was a Christian.'

'Well, I've only seen necklaces like that on Frea's women. Don't let my father see it.'

'Why? Doesn't he worship Frea? I thought she was one of your greatest—' Ebbe's training nearly made her say 'devils' but she checked in time—'goddesses.'

'Oh, he worships her all right, honours her, gives her splendid offerings. But he's scared of her for all that. He thinks she's his enemy.'

Alchflaed looked as startled as she felt at the thought of Penda being afraid of anything.

'He doesn't like to talk about it—and when my father dislikes anything folk keep their mouths shut.' Peada hesitated, but only for a second; he liked telling things to Alchflaed and watching her admire his knowledge.

'Old Saebald—he taught me my weapon-drill, he's dead now—he knew about it. He told me, to stop me asking questions, in case I brought Father's rage down on my head.'

He lowered his voice and leaned his head closer to her, though they were alone in open country.

'He had a woman once, a long time ago. It was over in the east, by Doneceaster, that it happened. He didn't ask "by your leave" when he took her but then he saw her necklace and knew she was Frea's woman, so he was scared. My mother was dead, so he told the woman he'd marry her. He thought she was willing but she stabbed herself before they were handfast. The priestesses came and took her body back to Frea's great shrine at the Buckstones in Peaclond. My father thinks Frea's had a grudge against him ever since.'

'Whatever makes him think that? He's never lost a battle, he's got a great kingdom, a healthy family—'

'Wait, I haven't told you all of it. You've seen he limps. You

160

must never speak about it or even show you've noticed. Well, soon after the woman died, he made a big raid into the north along with the Welsh, and somewhere on the way he fought a single combat with a Northumbrian warrior. Father had the best of it, of course, and got the other man down but he was only shamming dead and struck upwards as Father stood over him.'

Peada's mouth twisted a little; there was a chuckle in his voice. He loved his father, almost worshipped him, like all Mercians; but he also felt overshadowed by him, a feeling that grew as he got older. Mingled with the love and worship was some of the resentment of a young bull towards the king of the herd.

'The Northumbrian nearly took his balls off. He didn't quite get there—father married Cynwise and sired five more children. But he was lamed for life. And as Frea's the Lady of the womb, he thinks she guided that sword to set her mark inside his thigh and one day she'll destroy him. You can see why he doesn't love Northumbrians.'

Alchflaed was silent. She was at a loss what to say. Peada's story opened a way of life and thought strange and alien to her, that had nothing to do with Ebbe's convent or Oswy's court. He seemed to be speaking from some older world, that ancient Germania of Offa and Sigemund and Beowulf, that her people had shipped from two hundred years and more ago.

She fingered her necklace doubtfully. It was clearly a talisman of stronger power than simple moonlight. *My mother was a Christian*, she told herself but could not stop the words *Was she?* from forming in her mind. She remembered the scowls that had been thrown at her when she entered the church at Getlingas for Oswine's mass; Abbot Trumhere's stern questions about the designs on her robe. The necklace had put the images into her mind and driven them through her fingers.

And there was another mystery in Peada's tale. That warrior, as clever as he was reckless, who had dared to face Penda single-handed and nearly destroyed him. Surely, any Northumbrian who had succeeded in crippling his king's greatest enemy would have deafened the land with his boasting, as he hurried to claim his reward of jewels and fine armour from Oswy. Yet there was no whisper of such an exploit to be heard in Bernicia, though it was just the sort of story the northern folk would have relished and embroidered in bawdy detail at Penda's expense.

So far as she knew, the only one in the whole north who had tackled Penda single-handed and lived was her mother, when she fought her way out of the blazing ruins of Gefrin. Riemmelth had been the only survivor of the massacre and she had never cared to boast of her own courage or what she had suffered during the months she had spent as an outlaw before she could win back to Oswy.

As her fingers touched the silver moons on her necklace, remembering how Riemmelth had always worn it—she could not picture her mother without it—she became quite sure that it was her mother, bearing Frea's sign, who had set Frea's mark on Penda.

'What's come over you? What are you staring at?'

'I was just thinking about what you told me.'

'You think too much. That's the way to go strange in the head, especially for a woman. You looked just like that last night, when you were listening to the scop.'

Peada got up and stretched. 'Come along or we won't be back in Legaceaster before sundown. Folk will think I've carried you off—and then Oswy will come and conquer Mercia to take vengeance on us all!'

He laughed at the idea but not unkindly and reached a hand to pull her to her feet. The sun was so low now that the Welsh hills were in shadow but the Wirheale heath was still bright and warm. In all the bitterness and horror that were to come, this was how she always remembered him: birch leaves and bracken, furze still golden with blossom and Peada, brown and golden like the autumn woods, laughing in the sunlight.

CHAPTER
16

'*Anger is slavery.*' Meilyr remembered his uncle's warning more than once that day, while his smiling mouth named allies to Penda, exchanged numbers of warriors, suggested meeting-places for war-hosts. He cursed himself for the outburst of temper that risked the hold he had gained on Alchflaed. He'd soon coax her back, of course, a few smiles and beguiling words would do it but he was uneasy till it was safely done.

He had no chance at the evening meal; that was mostly taken

up by Peada telling them about his day's hawking, calling on Alchflaed every so often to agree with what he said. When she wasn't looking at Peada, smiling and nodding, she was watching Cyneburg watching Alchfrid.

It was clear that the Mercian princess had fallen in love with her chosen husband. She dragged his name into every moment of talk she had with Alchflaed, giving herself away at each word.

'He's not very like you to look at, is he?' Then blushing, avoiding Alchflaed's eyes, 'When I saw him first, I thought he was like Bealdor, the young lord coming back from Hel's kingdom in the spring.'

Alchflaed was sorry for her. Her brother's quiet manners and flawless courtesy made him seem gentler than he really was and hid the contempt he felt for his wife and his new marriage kin. She liked Cyneburg more with every hour they spent together; she was drawn to the whole Mercian family by the warmth they showed for each other. She found it good to hear Penda calling the Queen 'Wife' rather than 'My lady'; or speaking of tall Cyneburg as 'my little girl' with an arm round her shoulder. It did not lessen his dignity in the least; in spite of her brother and her own Latin education she could not see the Mercians as barbarians.

They lived in a simpler world, the word of the old hero-tales— the world of her own ancestors. Their own line was Woden-born, too, though Alchfrid would hate to be reminded of it. People weren't savages just because they weren't Romans.

Alchfrid couldn't be made to see it; he was blind and deaf to the strength and nobility of the old Germanic life, just as the Mercians understood nothing of the richness and complexity of Roman civilisation. When they did look across the boundaries of their separate worlds, Alchfrid saw savages and the Mercians saw loot.

The only man she knew in Britain who could live at home in both worlds with equal pleasure was Oswy. She recalled that he had also shown some feeling and pity for what it was like to be a woman married outside her own people; he was broad-minded and intelligent. Surely Oswy could bring the two worlds together if he could only meet Penda and talk to him in peace. That was just what he could not do; he had not even been able to send his own people on his heir's wedding journey in case it looked like submission.

Why should peace be a matter of submission? Why couldn't the

163

two worlds join, each giving what the other lacked? She wondered if Cyneburg could be their peace-weaver but knew the task was beyond her power. The girl was kind and sincere, she had wisdom of the heart—but she could not fight evils that she did not see or guess.

Since she lost her mother, most of all during this last year, Alchflaed had come to think that mixed blood was a curse. She never felt quite at home with either her father's or her mother's people. With Meilyr, even for a brief while with Nest, she had felt as if a gate had opened and she could step back into her mother's lost world. The gate had been slammed in her face, leaving her lonely and homeless wherever she stayed. At least, her solitude gave her the power to stand aside from Alchfrid and the Mercians, to see their strengths and weaknesses without hate or favour.

If only this marriage link had been the other way round. I could have held the balance between both sides because I don't belong to either!

This idea came more than once. At first it only brought regret for a lost chance; then came the thought *Why not?* The answer was easy: Penda had not asked for her as a daughter-in-law; her father had not offered her. Women did not choose their husbands; princesses did not make their own alliances. *Why not?* The question nagged at her. A woman was half a marriage; she had a mind as well as a body, skills to use, a soul to lose or save by the choices she made.

Alchflaed had grown up under a woman's rule. She was as free of the world of Latin learning as her brother. The great heroes and martyrs of her faith were as many women as men. Christian princesses—Clothilda, Bertha, Ethelburg—had changed history. None of them had chosen a husband, though. Then she remembered her mother's stories of magic queens like Rhiannon and Blodeuedd who had taken husbands—and changed them too—at their own choice.

If she could love Peada and weave peace for two kingdoms out of that love, why shouldn't she choose him and tell him so? It would not be hard to love Peada, she was happy and at ease with him, felt closer to him and more at home than she did with Alchfrid. She told herself that this light-hearted happiness was love. This was the easier to believe because it gave her none of the pain that Meilyr had been able to make her suffer. She was not altogether deceiving herself. She had truly fallen in love; but was too young to know that what she had fallen in love with was

Peada's world, the world of her father's ancestors. She was as much in love with Cyneburg, and with the great Mercian king himself in whom Offa of Angeln seemed born again, as she was with the prince. She enjoyed them all, grateful to warm her loneliness at their cheerful hearth.

Then, lying awake at night, she would be heartsick, foreseeing the ruin that would come when Northumbria and Mercia went into the final battle. Everyone else in both the royal Houses seemed to be pledged to war in one way or another: by alliance, by feud, by betrothal or by the demands of kingly pride. Her solitude—half-alien wherever she went, overlooked and unvalued by her father—gave her some freedom of thought and action.

She took every chance to be with Peada—and Peada gave her many chances during the days he led the visitors riding and hunting, while his father talked war with Meilyr.

'If all Bernicians were like you it would be easy to live on good terms with them.'

'Is it so hard to live on good terms with folk who live a hundred miles and more away?'

Peada was at a loss to answer this. If another kingdom wasn't an ally and didn't pay tribute, of course you raided it. What else would you do?

'Is it going to be hard to keep on good terms with Alchfrid? Do you hate him so much?'

'No, of course I don't!'

Peada was almost as dazzled by Alchfrid as Cyneburg. He admired his manners, his war-band, his mastery of the Stone-Giants' runes. If Alchfrid had boasted and swaggered like most young princes, Peada would have resented his insolence and tried to put him down. However, Alchfrid knew, as one of the eternal truths, that he was superior to all barbarians. He did not need to stress the fact. He treated his hosts kindly, aware that savages are childishly touchy about slights. Only Alchflaed and Meilyr guessed what he was really thinking.

As well as admiring, Peada was envious of the freedom Alchfrid seemed to have over his own affairs, though he was several years younger than his new brother-in-law. Whenever he heard Alchfrid saying casually, 'So I decided to rebuild Caer Ehedydd—' or, 'I told my bishop—' or, 'I wrote to the King of Strathclyde—' Peada thought rather bitterly that his own father had never let him take such decisions. He forgot that Alchfrid had inherited Cumbria from his mother; he thought it was the Stone-Giants' knowledge that gave him such powers.

'Oh yes, you cry out at the idea of hating Alchfrid!' She kept up her attack. 'But you'd be at sword's point with him tomorrow if war broke out. Wouldn't you? Be frank.'

'My sister's marriage will keep the peace—'

'Oh, Peada! How often has a princess been given in marriage to keep the peace and then the slaughtering starts again! A scop can hardly open his mouth to tell a story but we hear of some woman's wedding drowned in blood! Freawaru, Hildeburh, the Waelsings—they all end the same way. Why?'

Before the bemused young man could grope for an answer she swept on: 'Because the old men who make these marriages don't really expect them to bring peace. They're waiting for war to break out again; I believe they want it. And the women are traded over like cattle, without a word to ask them what they feel about it, frightened, loathing even! Was Cyneburg happy when she was told about her betrothal?'

She saw the answer in his face. 'How could there be any peace in a marriage made like that? But if a prince and princess came together in love—made a free choice—gave themselves willingly—then true peace could be born!'

'Well, I'm willing to have you.' Peada had got her drift now and liked the idea. 'I'll tell my father and we'll have a word with your brother. You've got a wedding party here already so we can settle everything before they go back north.'

'But if they made difficulties we'd be forbidden—and then we'd be watched. We must act first and then tell them when it's too late to stop us.'

'Good idea.' Peada beamed approval, then glanced round. 'The beach is too open, some of the others might ride round the headland before we've finished. We'll find a smooth patch back among the furze.'

'Not like that! Folk would say you'd raped me and then there would be a war.'

'And we'd win it.' Still, Peada was ready to please her, though it was hard to see how. 'If I mustn't ask for you openly and you don't want to go behind the bushes—'

'We'll follow the old custom, with a handfasting and a feast, but secretly. It's still a true wedlock—once we've slept together we'll be man and wife. The priests of my faith don't deny that, though they wouldn't regard the marriage as hallowed unless one

166

of them blessed us. So our fathers won't be able to part us without more trouble than it's worth to them.'

Peada was excited and amused at the prospect of sleeping with Alchflaed, of winning a bride from the enchanted world of the Stone-Giants. She could teach him their magic and make him as powerful as Alchfrid. Also, it was pleasant to be making a choice of his own, outside his father's knowledge or consent. It made him more of a man, more his father's equal.

'Find a place where we can keep our wedding night without anyone seeing or knowing. I'll come to you there.'

'Right.' Peada drew his dagger. 'Do your people swear faith on iron?'

'I'll swear on the hilt, that's a holy sign to us.'

Peada put the dagger blade across his left palm and laid his right hand on it. Alchflaed took the cross-shaped hilt between her two hands. They spoke the ancient words with the sun to witness.

'Alchflaed, I plight you my troth to be your true man so long as my life lasts.'

'Peada, I plight you my troth to be your true wife till death parts us.'

They were only just in time. Hoof beats and cheerful shouts behind the headland told that the rest of the party had found their tracks. Peada sheathed his dagger, caught Alchflaed in his arms and gave her a hard kiss. When their companions came within sight and earshot they were having a lively quarrel over whether Peada's horse had really beaten Alchflaed's pony. As he swung her to the saddle she was able to whisper, 'Don't let anyone guess!'

The last days the wedding party spent in Legaceaster were golden days for Alchflaed. Her happiness was as unclouded as the autumn weather, even though she did not spend so much time as before with Peada. He was hunting for a good place to celebrate their hidden marriage; besides, they were keeping up the play of a half-joking quarrel over their horse-race, to hide their secret.

They could not hide it from Meilyr. He had been watching for a chance to speak with Alchflaed and saw how they looked at each other while their mouths kept up a flow of cheerful abuse. He found it impossible to win a glance of meaning from her. If she had still been furious over his insult, or had turned from him in hurt pride, it would have been easy to win her round, even if she had stormed at him first, and got her back docile to his hand. But she only smiled at him with the same sweet, regardless goodwill she seemed to be feeling for the whole Mercian court, from Penda to the slave-girls.

It surprised Meilyr that though Peada and Alchflaed couldn't keep their eyes off each other when they were together, they avoided each other's company. Cyneburg was getting her gear together for her wedding-journey; Alchflaed spent most of her time helping. Peada had given up his hunting parties but rode out every day by himself. Meilyr noted the odd fact that when he went out his game bags seemed to be full; when he came back they were empty. He took to shadowing Peada. It was child's play.

Cyneburg, turning out her chests, unfolded a large green blanket with a border and stripes of blue that she had woven herself. She asked Alchflaed if it would be fit for her new household. She looked to her sister-in-law for counsel about everything to do with Alchfrid, as if she feared that none of the treasures in her father's palace would be good enough for her bridegroom.

'It's beautiful. May I have it?'

'Gladly. Were you cold on your journey here? I can give you more.'

'No. I want to stitch it.'

Alchflaed had been brooding over the thought of peace-weaving. She had a sudden picture of a gift she could make to her brother and his wife that would hold all her love and care for them, her prayers that they should be happy together.

'I'm going to put our lands on it—Cumbria and Northumbria and Mercia. Look—I'll show you. The green stripes will be the land. I'll put farms with their stock, forests and marshes with all their animals and birds, and the hills with their crests coming up into the sky—that's the blue. I'll put clouds there and more birds, with the moon, sun and stars in the top border. And I'll set the cities from north to south, Bebbanburh, Caer Luel, Eoforwic and Legaceaster—and the Roman wall going right across one of the stripes. And some of the blue bands can be the rivers, with fish and otters and herons. When it's finished I'll give it back to you for your marriage bed, so that you and Alchfrid can lie snug at the heart of your kingdom. It should take me a year; maybe there'll be three of you to keep warm by then.'

Cyneburg was greatly touched by the idea. So were the rest of her family, who were also struck by Alchflaed's skill with her hands. They came to hear her explain her plan and to see her first stitches taking shape. Wulfrun came, she looked at Alchflaed while Cyneburg and Peada described the design. She said quietly, 'It will be very fine'; she was not a chatty woman.

Peada was proud of his bride and pleased with himself for having won her. She was hardy and venturesome. She was a rune-mistress of the Stone-Giants' magic, she had read him some of the writings they had left carved on their stones. She was also mistress of the womanly crafts, embroidery and herb-lore. All Britain would envy him for having such a queen.

Under cover of asking her more about the embroidery, he was able to give her his news.

'I've found just the place for our wedding feast. It's a little round Roman house not far from here.' He was beaming with pride at having made such a fitting choice for his lady, and also at having remembered to say 'Roman' instead of 'Stone-Giant', a word Alchfrid never used.

'It's not ruined, just dusty, and it had some broken pots lying around but I'm clearing it out and getting some things for us, blankets, pillows and a few candles. I've laid a fire—don't forget to take a strike-a-light with you. I'll bring the food and drink with me on the night. We'd better not go together, make sure you find a way to slip out without anyone seeing you. Wait till dusk.'

'How will I find it?'

'That's easy, it's just a little way up from the north gate, west of the road out to Wirheale. There are all those carvings of the Stone—Romans just outside the walls and then this round house on its own. It's set back from the road in a clump of trees but you can't miss it, there's no other house. It's not two furlongs from the gate but nobody goes that way at night.'

Peada did not think to add that nobody went there because it was believed to be haunted. He was not afraid of spectres; he wore the sign of Thunor's hammer at his neck. Besides, he was confident that, like Beowulf, he was strong enough to master any flesh-eating ogre he might meet with his bare hands. As for Alchflaed, she was a rune-mistress, so she could control any Stone-Giant ghost and just tell it to go away.

'You'll like it when I've got it ready for you. There's a picture carved on the wall that's just right for a wedding feast!' He grinned and winked at her. 'Don't worry, you'll easily find your way there.'

Meilyr had already easily found his way there, looked at Peada's gear and seen that he was getting ready to spend a night—he could guess with whom. In spite of his rage he felt a bitter amusement when he saw the place they had picked. It must be Alchflaed's idea, Peada wouldn't have the wit. What a shelter for a night's whoring—Messalina couldn't have chosen a better!

Roman law had forbidden the placing of corpses inside a city, so their cemeteries were always outside the walls. So were English burial grounds but they did not look in the least alike. To Peada, Stone-Giant ruins were just Stone-Giant ruins. No one knew how they had lived or what they had done among their stone-works. Judging by their pictures, many of them had been monsters with goat legs or snakes for hair. Peada's 'little round Roman house' was a very large Roman mausoleum with room for the kin to bring offerings and share the Feast of the Dead.

Knowledge is power. Meilyr lingered thoughtfully over exactly how he would use the power he now held over Alchflaed's and Peada's lives. He had been obsessed so long by the belief that he owned her, that she was roped to him by the hair he had bound on his wrist, that he felt her choice of Peada like a wife's adultery. She had betrayed him and he had to punish her.

At first, he thought simply of cutting her throat when she was on her way to her secret bed. She'd surely come alone; they wouldn't walk out of the city arm in arm. Then he could leave her body in the tomb for Peada to find and watch the Mercians trying to find an explanation for her brother next day. Likely there'd be a war at once; let the English destroy each other and good riddance.

There was little pleasure for him in this. He couldn't make a picture of himself killing Alchflaed. He told himself that killing would be too quick. She would be free and he would have lost the power of tormenting her. What he would really like to do was take her himself; find her alone there before Peada arrived. She could hardly cry rape—what was she doing, waiting with a bed made up?

He played with the idea of coming in on her, seeing the shock and terror on her face, putting his dagger to her throat and ordering her to get down while he did what he wanted. Or, better still, coming in cloaked and hooded, quickly blowing out the light and then letting her give herself to her lover. He felt her body in his arms, the thrust and release of entering her while her arms and legs twined round him, the touch of her mouth and tongue on his flesh. Then he withdrew, lit the candle, watched her while she took in the knowledge of what had happened to her, and then—

And then what? Thank her for her hospitality and walk out,

leaving her in that state to wait for Peada? She could not accuse Meilyr and make a public outcry without soiling her own name. What quarrel could Peada fasten on him? He could say, with a laugh and a shrug, that he'd thought she was anybody's game by the way she was behaving and offer to buy the Mercian prince a slave-girl to make up for spoiled sport.

However, he'd twice seen Alchflaed lie and trick her way out of trouble; he had a high respect for her gifts in that line. She'd spin some tale for Peada, blaming him that she'd come to such an ill-omened spot to be raped by some outlaw. He'd be bound to shield her name and offer to marry her.

Carry her off? The Powys border was only a few miles away. He could force her to come with him, they could be at Dinas Brân tomorrow. But their vanishing on the same night would tell their hunters where to come looking for them. He felt cold at the thought of what Northumbria and Mercia, united for once by a common hate, could do to his people.

Then he smiled. There was no need to carry her off. He could make the court think she wanted him to be her man. After he'd lain with her he'd order her to get back to the palace without being seen. He'd leave the bed for Peada to find, with every sign that folk had enjoyed themselves there. He'd threaten her that if she wanted to keep her name clean, all her looks and smiles were to be for him from now on. She must show herself to be besotted with him, abject for his favour, worse smitten than poor Cyneburg. He would be publicly amused, scornful of the way she was humbling herself, the fool she was making of herself but then—making it clear he was only interested in her family descent and her dowry— he would offer for her to her brother. He could tell Penda that this would blind Oswy to the Welsh alliance that was being formed against him. His own plan, to destroy Penda after Oswy's death and take the High Kingship, would be helped by having Alchfrid already as his brother-in-law.

Meilyr knew that there were far too many flaws in these hasty schemes. He should be putting his mind to working out all the details and strengthening all the weak spots. Instead he indulged himself by living over and over again the night in the tomb when he would have her at his will. This sent a pleasant warmth through him at first but left him exhausted and craving, with a hot ache in his loins. He was wildly angry at being so trapped by his desire. It was almost as if that plait of hair round his arm were his fetter instead of being hers.

The tress seemed to be alive and growing; it burst out of the arm-ring, he felt it spreading over his body, twisting its tendrils round his limbs. In a moment of panic he saw himself trapped in some dark place, bound by living ropes of her hair, starving to death for her.

CHAPTER
17

Alchflaed was working at the problem of leaving the city unseen and staying out all night without being caught or suspected. Though she was a girl and staying in the palace as an honoured guest, this proved easier than she had feared.

As a princess, she had been given a bower to herself. It stood behind the Queen's hall, nearer to the city walls. Her maids were Mercians, very much in awe of her magic powers when they saw her reading and writing. They would not dare to spy on her. There was no need for a woman to come to the King's hall every day unless she chose or unless he was holding a great feast. She would simply tell Alchfrid that she wanted to pass a quiet evening with her embroidery and her Psalter.

She told Cyneburg that the Feast of St Justina was at hand. This was true, in case Cyneburg mentioned it to Alchfrid. She said she needed to spend a night alone at her prayers, hinting darkly at certain sacred rituals which only Christian eyes might see. The maids must not come near her till she called them next morning. Cyneburg knew that Alchflaed had been brought up in a temple of virgin priestesses and was aware what fearful things happened if holy rites were profaned. Watching the dread in her eyes, Alchflaed felt sure that whips and swords could not drive a Mercian near her bower on the chosen night.

Meanwhile she and Peada kept up their war of words, insulting each other at every chance. One evening in the King's hall they started to ask riddles. Alchfrid was playing a board game with Meilyr as an excuse to ignore them.

'I know a good one!' Peada's ringing voice was not easy to ignore. 'It might be too hard for Bernicians, though, your wits get frozen up there in the far north.' He glared a challenge at Alchflaed.

'I caught a couple coupling—
an odd pair, they did it in the open.
If the work went well, one flaxen female
got a good bellyful under her flounces.
Can you read my riddle? Unravel two answers
said in one spell?
There were two needs, one bright ash tree
among two oaks; hail fell twice.
What shall we call this shameless couple?'

Everybody laughed, looking at Alchflaed to see how she would take it. It was not a riddle to ask a maiden—not in public at least—as she could hardly show she understood it. Alchflaed had sorted the runes quickly enough and was ready with her answer.

'If I were at home in Bernicia I'd say "Cock and Hen".' She added impudently, 'Though here in Mercia "Man and Wife" might do as well!' while her eyes gave another message to Peada across the listeners.

'I knew you'd think that. You women are just like hens, whenever you lay, you go cackling to give away your nesting-place.'

'And you men are like cocks—whenever you do succeed in making love, you clap your wings and crow when you've finished!'

Their audience guffawed. Penda beat his thigh, roaring, 'Keep at him, girl! Give it to him with your sword!'

'I'll give it her back with my spear.'

'Mind how you use it,' jeered Alchflaed. 'If you're careless, your spear could lost its point then you couldn't even prick with it.'

Alchfrid managed a tight smile. Meilyr's face was expressionless, he hardly spared a glance from studying his pieces on the board.

You foolish, clumsy children—who do you think you're cheating? Alchflaed, look at me, look at me! You pair of idiots, don't you know you're giving yourselves away every minute? If the English weren't as stupid as their own cattle, they'd see what you're doing!

One of them at least had seen it and was not content just to watch. Early next afternoon, Meilyr came to the courtyard in front of the King's hall. He was tracking the lovers' every move. It would not be long now to the night in the tomb. Peada was chatting to his foster-sister; Alchflaed rode in and he turned to

173

help her dismount, with jeering advice to let herself fall on her back if she slipped. For a moment Meilyr saw Wulfrun's face.

Hatred knows its own kin. Meilyr stepped behind a porch-pillar, as shocked as if he had come upon her naked. He was sure that if she noticed him she would see the knowledge in his face and kill him.

It was startling to know what lay under Wulfrun's calm dignity. In spite of his obsession with Alchflaed and Peada, he was interested enough to study her next time he saw her. He was strolling towards the north gate; Peada had ridden out some time before but Meilyr knew where he had gone and was in no hurry to follow him. Nearly everything was ready at the meeting-place; Alchflaed would be there tonight.

Wulfrun was standing outside her hall. At her shoulder was Berhtwald, the leader of her bodyguard. He was wearing a richly embroidered cloak and so many brooches and arm-rings he looked as if he was going to his wedding feast. Two other warriors were standing by; between them was a man of the sort that Meilyr, who knew Legaceaster's waterfront, called a 'port-rat'. They made an odd group; when they went into Wulfrun's hall together, he wondered what they would all find to talk about.

The two spearmen were on guard outside the chamber door. Berhtwald was inside by the hearth, looking at the flames. Wulfrun was seated by the table, her hand resting on a leather bag that chinked softly when her fingers moved. The port-rat stood in front of her, his eyes fixed on her face with a look of uneasy greed.

He was a Frank called Dagaric, a good seaman with a vile temper. A few days before, he had knifed another crewman over a game of dice. He'd had right on his side; the other man was cheating. His captain had agreed on that; he wanted no trouble with the port-reeve so the body had been put over the side. But neither captain or crew had liked it; the ship sailed without him. Word had got around, as usual, along the waterfront; nobody else would take him on. He was aground in a strange land, getting hungrier and more desperate until two men had come along and asked if he needed a job.

'There's no shadow of doubt,' the lady was saying. 'My sister-in-law is an adultress. My brother,' she looked at the richly-dressed lord by the fire, 'has the right to take blood-payment. But her lover is one of the highest in the kingdom. We will not lift a hand against him, for our love and loyalty.'

174

And fear, thought Dagaric. He guessed what was coming.

'The harlot's going to him again tonight. They meet outside the city walls. She mustn't live to dishonour my brother's bed again.' Her brother said nothing, just went on staring into the fire, unwilling to speak about his wife.

'We're not perjurors. When we take oath we had no hand in her death, we'll be speaking the truth. Our men will show you where she is — you can give her what she's waiting for, if you like, but be quick about it, then cut her throat and leave her as she is. Those two will be keeping watch, you'll be quite safe.'

'Are you sure I won't have any trouble afterwards?'

'None at all. You'll slip away down river or stay in this land for good — whichever seems best.'

The lord was smiling now. The lady opened the bag and took out two silver pieces. 'Have a meal in one of the taverns to get yourself into good heart. I'll keep the rest till I know the job is done.'

He was torn between two fears: fear of being cheated and fear of crossing them. If they'd murder a kinswoman, they'd think nothing of ridding themselves of a stranger — who would ask after him?

'If there was an alarm — if I had to get away fast and couldn't —'

'I never pay in advance.'

'Let's put his mind at rest.' The lord spoke for the first time. He took the bag and went to the door. 'Look after this,' he said to one of the spearmen. 'It's only to be paid when it's been earned.' He smiled at Dagaric again. 'There. These good fellows will see you get your wages.'

Berhtwald watched Dagaric go off with them, heading for the water-gate, then came back into Wulfrun's chamber. She looked up.

'They know what to do?'

'Yes. They'll wait till he's on top of her, then kill them both and leave the corpses as they lie.'

'They can share the silver between them.'

'They'd do it without that for you, my lady.'

'I always reward faithful service.' She stood up, putting her hand on his shoulder. 'There are rich water-meadows at the edge of the Fens and sleek cattle to graze on them. And when you look on your lands with pride, you can be prouder yet that you helped to save the king's son from that murdering northern witch who's eating his soul.' Her lips were so tight she could hardly speak. 'He

175

scorned the Bernicians as much as any of us before she came—
and now she's got him bound like a war-captive by her spells.
We've got to break him free of her.'

The autumn dusk came earlier every day; the sun was behind the
Welsh hills when Alchflaed bolted the main door of her bower
from the inside, pushed the rear door ajar warily, then slipped
out into the twilight. She had her riding clothes under a heavy
cloak and hood of grey hodden, so that no chance glimpse of
brightly-dyed cloth or gold embroidery might draw curious eyes.
The guards at the north gate hardly noticed her—a farm woman
going home before dark from some errand to the palace.

Peada was to follow later. If there was any delay and the gates
were locked, he could order them to be opened for him, whereas
she would have been trapped. His story would be that he was
going to spend a night at a fisher's house on Wirheale to start
hawking at first light among the flocks of migrant geese in the
estuary. He often did so on impulse without taking any train of
servants; it would cause no remark in the palace, nor the fact that
he had filled a saddle-bag with better food and drink than his
simple hosts could offer.

Alchflaed's hardest task was to keep her feet to the slow, steady
plod of a countrywoman, when she was longing to dance and
sing or break into a run. The days of delay and shamming had
made her wild to reach the little house where she would hold her
wedding feast with Peada, the bed where she would lie in his
arms.

Meilyr watched her go, standing quietly in the shadows, a
shadow himself in his plaid of chequered blue, green and grey.
Then he turned away and walked openly towards the water-gate.
He was not going to risk following her. There were few folk
abroad at that hour and no cover on the road. She might look
back and see him—or he might be overtaken by Peada on horseback, who would certainly hail anyone going the same way, to
find out what he was doing. Though Meilyr had not been boasting when he told Ashferth he could find cover in the shadow
thrown by every rock, he was not taking the slightest chance of
startling his quarry now she was so near the trap. There was a
safer way to come at her.

The Dyfrdwy flowed close by the west wall of the fort. The
Romans had built up the waterfront, with quays for the ships that

had supplied the Twentieth Legion. It was a lively place, with its ship-wrights, rope walks and sail-makers, merchants' stalls and ale-houses; much more like the old days than the palace inside the walls. The main buildings were close by the water-gate and the road that ran through it down to the quayside. The port-reeve had a house there and a body of spearmen to take the tolls and keep order. The merchants stacked their wares in the old granary; part of the bath-house was still in business as the largest and costliest of the brothels.

Lights were beginning to gleam in the dusk; folk were still abroad, doors were still open, there was loud-voiced talk, bursts of singing, the notes of a pipe half drowned by clapping and stamping in jig-time. The lights and noise would go on through the night, as the ships were waiting for an early tide and though many of the folk would be in bed by nightfall they would not be asleep.

Meilyr walked along the quayside looking at the ships. He knew some of them and their owners from visits in the past. If he needed a reason for being outside the walls all night, he could find a friend to back his story with no questions asked.

Towards the north the buildings petered out, the waterfront ended. There was a stretch of sandy foreshore changing with the tide; behind it lay a tract of wasteland, part marshy part wooded, where he could cut across to the cemetery.

Near the end of the waterfront, by the door of a small dingy ale-house, he saw three of the men who had been with Wulfrun that afternoon, the two warriors and the port-rat. They spoke together in a huddle, then turned away from the city walls towards the wild country.

Nothing odd in that. There was always more to do between the lively port and the lonely wasteland than folk talked about. If Meilyr had not seen them with Wulfrun he would have supposed they were just going to see a witch, or settle a fight, or share out stolen goods. He recalled Wulfrun's face as she watched Peada taking Alchflaed into his arms. It could not be chance that was leading these three towards the tombs by the north road. Wulfrun could have had Peada followed in these last days; that was easy enough. Peada seemed to think an act was secret if the scop didn't sing about it in the royal hall. Wulfrun wanted Peada; she wouldn't kill him, at least while there was any other way of keeping him from Alchflaed.

Noiseless and dark as a patch of shadow, he began to stalk them.

*   *   *

177

There were no more broken slabs, ivy-grown pillars or crumbling statues. The road ran out ahead into a desolate land. Alchflaed stopped and looked around, suddenly aware how lonely she was. The evening was mild and clear but there would be no moon tonight. Soon the dark would be upon her.

Away to her left was a clump of alders, the only trees that could be called near the road. She set off towards them. If there had ever been a path she could not see it; she stumbled over tussocks of grass and clumps of thistle; the hem of her cloak was caught by brambles. She was glad to make out the solid blackness of a building among the trees; this was the right place.

The little Roman house was like no building she had ever seen before. It was round and had a porch in front like a peasant's hut but was made of stone with a domed roof. The door creaked when she pushed it; the noise made her start. Inside it was almost pitch-black except for a circle of grey sky at the centre of the dome.

She suddenly felt afraid to go in and had a mind to wait in the porch till Peada arrived. Then she saw that he had left a torch by the door. She had brought a strike-a-light and soon got a spark to catch. Now she could see her bridal chamber.

Peada had taken trouble. He had made a rough hearth with broken stones, laid kindling and piled a stack of dry branches. She soon had a fire going; the little room had solid walls and warmed up quickly. The heat and golden light made her feel better; the flames were company.

There was a sconce in the wall; she fixed the torch there, noting that the stonework was blackened by smoke. Many lights had burned in the same place; she wondered about the folk who had lived in the little house and how many other brides had come there.

Beyond the hearth was a bed, a deep pile of dry bracken with a sheepskin and blankets; there was no other furniture, so she sat down on it. The wall was carved into a row of shelves with niches hollowed out at intervals. Peada had put a lamp in one, and a flask of oil. She saw with tender amusement that Peada's 'clearing out' had not been done with a housewife's skill. There were still fragments of broken pots under the ledges, with some dust and withered leaves that had drifted in through many autumns.

The heat of the fire was making her cloak and horseman's leathers uncomfortably hot. She took them off and laid them folded beside the bed, hesitated a moment then took off her shirt as well. She lay back naked on the blankets, enjoying the warmth now, shaking out her hair and running her fingers through its curls watching the play of light bringing out its colours, gilding her skin. She remembered the solemn dignity of Eanfled's procession from board to bed, chuckling to think that she would be saved such a walk. Her feast and bedding would take place on the same couch.

Opposite her, beyond the hearth, there was a panel of carving against the wall. The shapes seemed to move with the flames. This must be Peada's picture 'that's just right for a wedding feast'. She jumped up to look at it, clutching the cloak round her.

A young woman was reclining among pillows on a richly-carved couch. She was beautiful; her face smiled at Alchflaed under woven wreaths of curled and plaited hair. Her robe and mantle that had fallen to her hips were so fine that every line and curve of her lovely body showed as clearly as if she were naked. She leaned back on her left elbow, holding a large goblet in her right hand. Garlands hung across the arch over her couch; a dove perched on each loop.

It was clear why Peada thought she was the right guest for their wedding feast. Alchflaed supposed she was some nymph or goddess—Hebe, perhaps, or one of the Graces. There was a faint inscription under the carving; she read it slowly, tracing the letters with her finger. In spite of the fire, it chilled her to the bone.

D.M.
FESONIE SEVERIANE
VIXIT ANN. XXV

'To the shades of the departed—Fesonia Severiana—she lived twenty-five years.'

She had never seen a Roman mausoleum before but she recognised the Latin formula. Peada had brought her to celebrate her wedding in a heathen tomb.

She stared in horror at the scraps of broken pottery; she knew now what they had been and what they had held. That dust, on the soles of her feet, stirred up into the air she breathed.

There's a curse coming on us. Our marriage will be blighted. What good can ever grow from a love that roots in such a place?

She had an urge to bolt; then called up her courage and her sense. Fesonia Severiana, whenever she had lived her twenty-five years, however they had ended, had nothing to do with this present moment and could not hurt her. Hadn't her faith taught her that life rises again from death? It was that faith, as well as her affection for Peada, that had brought her to his bed—that they should bring life to their peoples after years of killing.

'Nisi gramen frumenti—unless the grain of wheat falling into the ground, die, itself remaineth alone. But if it die it bringeth forth much fruit.'

She should look on the place as a good omen—a seed bed. She told herself so; she could not believe it. The shape crouched behind her did not seem to be her shadow. She did not think the whispering outside came from the alder trees.

When his quarry turned inland from the river and the undergrowth grew thicker, Meilyr closed up on them. By the time they were among the crumbling Roman tombstones he was almost at their heels, had caught snatches of their talk, gathered that Dagaric was a foreigner and frightened, that neither he nor Wulfrun's men trusted each other. He knew where they were going and what they meant to do to Alchflaed.

He was angry and reckless enough to hurl himself on them, though they were three to one, trusting in his speed and skill, his almost animal sure-footedness and the shock of an attack in the dark. If it had just been a matter of a fight with them, he would have pounced at once and enjoyed himself. But these were paid killers, working for a reward. Outside four walls, he couldn't hold the three at once. There would be the danger that one of them would go on to kill her and claim the full payment, cheerfully leaving Meilyr to wipe out the other sharers. Somehow he had to get them away from the tomb using himself as bait, both hunter and hunted.

He was wild with fury that his girl—his quarry that he had marked out for his own and stalked so patiently—should be crudely defiled and butchered at someone else's pleasure. He needed to kill soon. All the while he raged, his body trod noiselessly in the shadows and his mind worked on the movements of the three men as if they were pieces on a gaming-board. He had a better idea of the ground than they did, thanks to the hours he had spent there, shadowing Peada. He decided to begin by startling them, getting them so jumpy they couldn't think clearly.

He gave an owl's hoot, close in on their left.

'What's that?'

'Only an owl at her hunting.'

'It seemed to come out of the ground.'

180

Meilyr had moved behind them over to their right and laughed softly.

'There's something over there—behind that grave!'

'Leave it, then. It'll be some witch getting bones for hel-runing. They don't meddle if they're not meddled with.'

Meilyr glided further away, crouched behind the statue of some legionary officer with an arm raised in salute. He slipped off his cloak and hung it over the arm. The folds stirred gently in the evening breeze.

'Look over there! A man's watching us from behind that stone —I saw his cloak move.'

As they turned, Meilyr threw a pebble over their heads to fall in the way they were going to the mausoleum. They swung round again.

'They're waiting on the path ahead of us! It's a trap!'

One of the Mercian spearmen took command. 'I know why you went to sea, Dagaric. You're scared to walk on land in case you meet a fox on his way to a duck's nest, or see an ivy trail waving in the wind. Just step along to that stone, Dunn, and check there's nothing. I'll scout around to the left. You keep watch here, Dagaric, and mind you don't trip over your skirts.'

The man called Dunn advanced cautiously towards the shadows where Meilyr's cloak was hanging. The other Mercian moved over to the left, knife in hand, looking behind gravestones, stirring ivy clumps and parting bramble trails with his blade. Dagaric, his own hot temper goaded by the Mercian's insult, ignored his orders and went on ahead to the clump of alder trees. He could see the shape of a hut; the door was slightly ajar, a gleam of firelight showed in the porch.

'You can give her what she's waiting for if you like but be quick about it—'

He grinned and drew his knife.

The Mercian was making so much stir among the undergrowth that it was easy for Meilyr to crawl close. Lying nearly flat, he said in a hoarse whisper, 'That you, Dagaric? Why are you being so long about it? Get them up into the alder trees, the others are waiting to take them there. Which one's got the silver?' If the Mercian had time to think, he would have remembered that Dagaric had had no chance to fix up a treacherous ambush with some of the waterfront riff-raff. But he was on edge and things happened too fast.

Dunn had got near enough to the statue to see that a cloaked man was standing behind it, his back luckily turned. Dunn came up quietly, clutched for the throat and put his knife into the intruder's back. As he did so the creature melted back into the tomb, leaving nothing but the empty cloak. Dunn screamed with terror.

The other Mercian swung round, just as Dagaric came charging back from the alder trees straight at him, knife in hand.

'You filthy scum!'

Dagaric took the Mercian's blade full in the chest, choked, spewed blood and was dead. The Mercian glanced beyond him to see if anyone else was coming, then raced to help Dunn.

'That stinking Frank tried to cheat us. He's got his friends up there waiting—they'll make off with the woman and the silver once they've killed us.'

They were warriors and Wulfrun's men; they didn't give up easily. Dunn was steadied by the news that he just had flesh-and-blood enemies to deal with, not ghosts. He turned towards the clump of alders.

'D'you know how many?'

It was time for them to see the bait. Meilyr suddenly sprang at them; slashed Dunn's leg with a force that would cripple him or leave him bleeding to death; twisted aside from the other man's blade, parried the blow with his own dagger but then had it knocked out of his hand by an unexpectedly quick and powerful recovery. Unarmed now, he fled for his life in a wild game of hide and seek, turning and doubling this way and that round the graves but always drawing his hunter further from Alchflaed's marriage tomb.

The door creaked again. Alchflaed jumped up screaming as a big thickset figure stooped under the lintel. She backed against the wall.

Peada straightened up, grinning, and threw his bag of provisions on the bed. 'I've scared you. You've worked yourself up into a fine fright, haven't you, jumping every time your shadow moved! Now stop looking as if you could see a ghost. You haven't bid me welcome yet.'

She ran into his arms, sobbing with relief. Peada fondled her, running his hands down her back, pulling her haunches close to his body. It was the first time he had seen her terrified. He liked it; she was less awesome and more docile.

'Never mind. It's easy to think things at night. Sorry I took so long, but I had to see to my horse and find a good perch for my falcon. I'm supposed to be hawking at first light, if I don't sleep too heavily—or stuff too heartily beforehand!' He slapped her rump. 'I thought for a minute there was a man lurking among the trees but when I went after him it was only the boughs moving and hunting creatures scuffling. So you see, even a warrior like me can make mistakes—there's no need to feel ashamed of yourself.'

Peada's broad shoulders could block out all the horrors of the dark, better than a city wall; his arms were like a rampart. She clutched him tight for the joy of his strength and his living flesh. She needed to feel him inside her, part of her; then she'd never be afraid again. He laughed.

'You've had time to work up an appetite for your wedding feast. All right, we'll have the sweetmeats first. Let go of me for a minute while I get my belt unbuckled.'

The tide came creeping up river towards the waterfront. It lapped the body of a young man lying on the sands with his throat cut. The rats had already found Dagaric, sprawled among the bramble-grown tombs. Dunn toiled along the road back towards the north gate; the strips of shirt he had pulled tight round his leg were wet and sticky. He was going over and over in his mind the story that he would tell Wulfrun and Berhtwald, so that he would not slip among the details. He thought of hiding the bag of silver somewhere under a wayside gravestone, where he could find it later; but decided to hand it back as a proof of his courage and honesty. She might still pay him something; anyway, there would be other jobs.

In Mother Godelif's house by the watergate an Irish merchant and a Viscayan shipmaster were drinking with Meilyr. They were laughing uproariously at a version of 'The Two Wives and the Widow', done with actions so that clients from overseas could enjoy the story. Meilyr showed no trace of the wild hunt he had led Wulfrun's spearman towards the foreshore. He had turned on his hunter at last in the darkness and cut his throat with his own dagger. The body would be well down river with the tide by dawn. Meilyr seemed to be in high spirits; Mother Godelif and her girls wished that all their customers were so good-humoured and easy to please. He was trying to fill his mind with mead and the lewd antics in front of him, to leave no place there for a picture of Alchflaed on the makeshift bed in the tomb.

Alchflaed and Peada were lying in each other's arms, half-drowsing then waking to fondle each other with kisses and love-names. The wind sighed in the alder trees; it came under the door and stirred the withered leaves by the wall. The dust of Fesonia Severiana, who had lived twenty-five years, whispered, '*You too will come to this.*'

CHAPTER
18

It was now the second week of October. Alchfrid wished to set out for the north before winter came. He would be going more slowly than he came, with his bride, her maids and all her gear. Peada had promised his sister when she was first betrothed that he would go to the border with her. When Alchfrid said politely that he wished his brother-in-law might come the whole road and see her in Caer Luel, Peada took up the invitation at once. His father was willing. The fighting season was over for the year. Peada could see something of Cumbria's strength, including the strength of its ties with Oswy. He had heard from Deira that Alchfrid might break with his father; it was a chance worth watching.

The four young people enjoyed their journey, long and hard though it was through the forests and marshes and over the high moors. Alchflaed and Peada had little chance to lie together. Hunger put extra zest to the meaning looks and smiles they gave each other, chance touches, quick furtive couplings among the bushes or behind the stables in homesteads where they lodged for the night. Once, she whispered the first lines of his 'Cock and Hen' riddle in his ear and he nearly gave them away by guffawing.

She would never have believed that she could travel the length of her mother's country and come to stay in her mother's child-hood home with so little heed. Her eyes and thoughts were mostly on Peada. He was far more struck by Caer Luel than she was—the first living Stone-Giant city he had ever seen.

Even Caer Luel was not quite as splendid as it had been under the Empire but it had never been sacked or suffered a violent change of masters. Its palace, its bishopric and its monastery were several centuries old. The grandparents of some of the older folk living there had spoken with grandparents who had seen Arthur ride out to his last battle at Camlann.

The Mercians were awe-stricken, almost stunned. When Cyneburg saw the palace where she was to be both wife and princess she was terrified, though she did not show it. Alchflaed could not help. She knew no more of life in Roman palaces than her one brief stay in Eoforwic and that had not been pleasant. Remembering her own helpless bewilderment and how the women had received her, she watched Cyneburg with anxious pity.

Cyneburg was lucky; the woman who received her was Mildred, Earl Cadman's wife. Mildred ran the great household with quiet skill. She gently and tactfully guided the nervous bride through the first days, covering mistakes and screening hesitations so that others hardly noticed, helping her to talk and make friends, teaching her all the time but not making a show of it.

Alchflaed would have liked to talk more with Mildred, drawn by the charm of her manner and the kindness in her grey eyes. She remembered how Oswy had said this woman was her mother's dearest friend—she could have been her own mother-in-law by now. She had to admit that Oswy would have made a good marriage for her, if she had not found a better for herself.

She often saw the grey eyes gazing thoughtfully at her; at the first meeting they had a look she knew only too well, of someone who hopes yet fears to meet a long-lost friend, then sees a stranger. It would have been good to hear Mildred talking about Riemmelth, to meet her mother as a girl at home before her marriage. But all Mildred's time was taken up by Cyneburg and the feasts in honour of the bride; most of her own hours were given to the wedding-guests, Cumbrian and Mercian, and watching for the chance to steal a meeting with Peada.

I've got plenty of time, she told herself. *When my marriage is made known—when there's a sure peace—when the only folk crossing our borders are merchants, minstrels and guests—then I'll come back to Mother's home and talk my heart out with Mildred.*

The Cumbrians approved of their new princess. She did not have Eanfled's overpowering beauty, but she was comely and carried herself with effortless royalty. Her father was the greatest warrior and most powerful king in England; her House was descended from Offa of Angeln. But Cyneburg's dignity was not just an heirloom; she had a clear integrity of spirit that could neither think evil of others nor see evil in them, so she could never lose her self-respect or attract contempt.

Alchfrid was pleased with her. He was enjoying marriage more than he expected. He'd had women, of course, ever since he started his warrior's life at thirteen; it was part of a man's knowledge and also needful to keep the respect of his war-band. The healthy, cheerful country girls—first picked out for him by Cadman, later chosen by himself—were very agreeable, like a well-cooked dinner or a glass of good wine. But he was not a man whose life centred on bodily comfort. His girls could not win his interest or respect, though he treated them well and when they got married they boasted about him to their husbands.

It was impossible not to respect Cyneburg and he found her warm, long-limbed body very pleasant in bed. His chaplain was instructing her in the faith; he liked to talk over what she had learned and answer her questions. When he saw her walking through his halls, or listening to Mildred, or sitting with her spindle, he found himself quoting the proud words that Propertius had written for Cornelia:

'My life was spotless always,
pure from the wedding torch to the torch of death.
Nature gave me a code of laws drawn from my blood,
terror of justice could not better them.
However harsh the standard, I could meet its test.
No woman could be sullied by my touch.'

It had crossed his mind that Cyneburg was more like the ideal Roman matron than anyone he had ever seen in Britain.

Some time after the bride's arrival, one evening as Cadman was getting into bed, Mildred said, 'I think it will work. There need not be a war.'

Cadman looked at her with grave respect, but she knew her husband.

'You're laughing at me.'

'I never laugh when people tell their dreams. It's unlucky.'

'You think peace is just a dream? But folk don't have to hate each other for ever just because their forebears went to war. Think of Oswy and—' her voice trembled—'my dear lady.'

'Don't base any plans or prophecies on Oswy and Riemmelth. Yes, they loved, as men and women of different races have done

186

before and since. But they were also highly intelligent and they each had the rule of a powerful kingdom to strengthen them. It's not usual for love, power and wisdom to be united—except in the Holy Trinity, of course. Those who love generally lack wisdom; those with knowledge have no power; and those with power generally have neither. You won't find Oswy and Riemmelth again in Alchfrid and Cyneburg; even less,' he gave her a meaning glance, 'in Alchflaed and Peada.'

Mildred chose not to answer this last remark. 'I still believe there needn't be a war.'

'Pray that there won't be, my dear. You'll do as much good praying as prophesying. Because when—oh, very well, *if*—there's a war, we're going to lose it.'

Peada was not very good at hiding his feelings. Alchfrid had seen, like Mildred and Cadman, which way his eyes were turned. Thinking it over, weighing Peada's obvious admiration—close to hero-worship—of himself he decided on a piece of statecraft that could lift the dark cloud of war and let the lights of religion and Roman culture shine on the benighted midlands.

Penda was ageing; his heir looked up to Alchfrid as guide, teacher and model—at the moment. Alchfrid had no doubt he could hold his power over the Mercian while they were together. It was all too likely that once he was back home he would fall under his father's sway again, unless he had some living reminder of the higher life.

Alchflaed was very much better at hiding her feelings. When her brother spoke to her gravely about her duty as a princess of their House and a sacrifice she could make for the safety of her father's and mother's lands, she listened quietly with downcast eyes and promised to do her best to carry out his wishes. He kissed her; then she rushed away to tell Peada that her brother was going to help them secure their marriage—he must be sure to ask Alchfrid's advice in everything. Peada cheerfully did so.

One thing he learned that surprised him. Coming back to Caer Luel one early winter's evening from a lively hunt in Englawud, Peada had spoken about the carved stones by the high road. Alchfrid, amused at his ignorance, but politely hiding it, explained what the 'little round houses' really were. Rather alarmed, Peada asked Alchflaed if she had known and why she had not told him. She laughed and kissed him, saying that to

Christians love was stronger than death. He was glad to know she was mistress of such powerful magic.

In early spring when the roads were passable, they went east to meet Oswy and Eanfled. After the first looks and words had passed between them, Oswy treated his daughter-in-law with an affectionate courtesy that was never broken as long as her marriage lasted.

The Mercians were dazzled by Eanfled; beside her, Cyneburg looked like a taper in the sunlight. Alchfrid returned at once to his worship at her shrine. She was pregnant and not very pleased about it, though she looked as lovely as Our Lady at the Visitation. She was quite convinced now that her marriage to Oswy had not been sanctified by the true rites of the church as taught by Rome. Still, the arrival of a half-brother or sister for Alchfrid would make her seem uncomfortably like his stepmother. She might, of course, miscarry of the fruit of an unhallowed union.

She was very interested in Cyneburg's instruction and kindly took a lot of trouble herself to help. She would start theological discussions on nice points of doctrine with Romanus and Alchfrid, referring to Latin texts but always trying to bring Cyneburg into the talk. She would ask her smiling questions that left the Mercian girl looking dull and confused.

One night, after a long and lively session that had brought Cyneburg near to tears, Eanfled and Oswy were alone in their chamber. A maid brought in cakes and a posset for the night. Oswy helped himself but Eanfled waved the dishes away. He looked at her.

'A virtuous lady never falls into the sins of the flesh. Least of all, gluttony.'

Eanfled smiled her agreement.

'So perhaps you won't completely devour my son's admiration? Leave something on the side of your plate for poor Cyneburg.'

Alchfrid saw Oswy alone and described his plan to keep the peace with Mercia in a double bond by a marriage between Peada and Alchflaed. His father listened in silence. At the end, he merely said, 'Have you spoken to him about this?'

'He spoke about it to me, just before we set out to come here. I told him that everything depended on your consent but I gave him my word I'd back him.'

'And Alchflaed? Has he spoken to her?'

188

'He's never had a moment alone with her—I wouldn't permit anything so immodest. But I've explained to her why she ought to take him and she says she's willing. She behaved much better than I expected.'

Oswy said nothing. After a tense pause Alchfrid remarked, 'Perhaps I shouldn't have spoken. But after my first campaign you said we were to work together. I won't be much use to you if I never use my own judgement.'

He spoke with careful respect but Oswy had quick eyes and ears; he knew that his son was on the edge of taking offence. He was well aware how Alchfrid saw him: an ageing German barbarian, given some polish of learning by the monks of Iona, married to the heiress of an ancient Roman House to guard her lands for her till her son was old enough to do it. Oswy needed Cumbria and he loved his son, with knowledge but without illusions.

He smiled. 'You've used your judgement excellently. If it had been anyone but Penda's son I couldn't ask for a better—'

'I know how you feel, Father, but you still made me marry Penda's daughter. I find her perfectly satisfactory. Besides, Penda's active life is coming to an end and I can make Peada do whatever I tell him.'

'That's useful. Thank you, my son. I'll speak to Alchflaed.'

The messenger called her out of the Queen's bower to the chamber behind the great hall. Oswy was waiting for her; he had the door shut on them with orders that no one else was to come in.

'It seems that Penda's son has asked for you. Your brother says he told you he wanted the marriage and you gave him to understand you were willing.'

She nodded, looking anxious.

'I can see you'd find it hard to hold out against your brother's wishes while you were in his palace—perhaps you thought you'd no right to. But no words between Alchfrid and this man can bind you without my knowledge and consent.'

'Of course, Father. Alchfrid wouldn't—'

'The main problem will be how to send the Mercian away, now that your brother has come out so strongly in his favour. I don't want either of them to take it as a personal slight from me—but if we go carefully we can manage it without ill-feeling.'

'Send him away?' Her eyes widened in amazement. 'But you're mistaken, Father. Alchfrid didn't force this on me. I didn't like to

189

seem too eager—you know what Alchfrid's like, he'd think I was unmaidenly—but I'll take Peada as my husband with all my heart.'

'No, you won't, because I forbid you.' He spoke calmly, without anger.

'But why?' Her voice was high with bewilderment. 'I can go to live in Mercia, working to keep peace for us. I want our lands to be safe from this endless looting and slaughter that starts again every year with the spring. You said you needed an alliance with Mercia—'

'I've already got one. I don't need another.'

'Well, you've already got another. We're handfast.'

Oswy sat quite still for a heart-beat. Then he said very quietly, 'Were there any witnesses?'

'No, and it doesn't matter. We took an oath—he swore on his dagger, I swore on a cross. I've given my solemn word to him.'

'To a heathen—and without your father's consent. Your word has no force.'

'I've given him more than my word. We've lain together. I'm his wife.'

If Oswy had shouted curses, hit her, drawn his sword on her, she would not have been so scared as she was by his stony face and the icy rage in his eyes. She forced herself to feel Peada's body pressed close into hers, to help her keep her courage.

'I'm sorry, Father, what's done is done. If I'm not Peada's wife I'm his whore and I'm ready to say so before the world. Nobody else would take me after that, even if he'd let anyone else have his woman. He'll never give me up.'

'He'll have no choice when his father tells him to.'

'King Penda? He likes me—why should he?'

'I'm not so small-minded as to think that only Christians keep faith. Penda won't stand by and see his son forswear his gods.'

'I'd never ask Peada to do that against his mind and his soul.'

'Yes you will. That's the answer I'll give him and Alchfrid from you, now you've had time to think things over; and that's the message my envoys will take to Mercia. Either he becomes a Christian, with all the people he's brought here, or you renounce him and take the veil.'

'Penda will never agree.'

'I know. But for once the Mercians won't blame me. They know a man mustn't stop a woman who's called to be a priestess—that's what they think nuns are. And Alchfrid can hardly quarrel with such a holy resolution in a convent-bred girl. So you'll write a letter setting out your feelings—some Welsh priest can read it to Penda.'

'You can't make me hold a pen. I'd have my fingers broken first.'

'No need to put you to such trouble. I got good schooling in Iona. I'll write you a letter that will make Penda and his council weep to hear it; so noble, so generous, so tender with regret. I'll write it now to save delay. You'll have a copy before you go back to Ebbe.'

She clutched his hand; she was desperate.

'But why—why are you so against me? Is it just to punish me because I followed my own judgement without asking your leave first? But if what I did was useful, why undo it out of pride and spite? Will you give me one good reason why I shouldn't have married Peada?'

'No, I will not give you a reason. I'll give you an order—get into the Queen's house and stay there.'

She stared at him, dumbfounded. If there was one thing she had believed about Oswy, it was that he was reasonable. She felt furious—and completely helpless. He took her arm and steered her to the door.

'Remember, I see more than Alchfrid does and I'll be watching you.' At last he smiled at her and it was not pleasant. 'Don't try anything stupid. If I must have all-out war with Penda some time, it might suit me if it started while I've got his eldest son.'

CHAPTER
19

Oswy had miscalculated. When his envoys first gave the message, Penda had roared with fury. 'Are you telling me that after getting my little Cyneburg for his own heir, he thinks my son isn't good enough to bed his girl?'

Watching the length of his arm, the spokesman said warily that the terms had been set by the Lady Alchflaed, who had been brought up in a household of sacred virgins.

'It's some whim of the girl's?' Penda's temper eased. 'Well, she's a fine girl with a good spirit in her. You'd never think she was Oswy's daughter.' He smiled at the envoys. 'I'm sure you're weary after your long road. The Thyle will take you to the guest halls. We'll talk about this again when you're refreshed.'

Alone with his councillors he spoke his mind. 'I'm well enough pleased that Peada should have her. She's healthy and good-humoured and she doesn't scare easily. She'll do well to breed from. And it could be useful to have an heir of her blood when I've destroyed the rest of Oswy's line. When Peada has a son by her I won't need that rat Athelwold.'

'But what about turning Christian?' asked one of the councillors with a look of disgust.

'He can say so if that's what's needed to make her open her legs with a good will.' He chuckled. 'I can remember when I was his age, I'd have taken an oath I believed hares got into packs and hunted wolves, if it'd have made the girl I fancied pull her skirt up. He'll soon get tired of being a Christian, it's no worship for a warrior. And she's only a girl; when he's got her he can always turn back again.'

Suitably reworded by the Thyle, Penda's answer was that his son could do as he liked. Oswy saw Alchflaed by herself to tell her the news. He gave no sign of anger or disappointment. She did her best to hide her joy; she did not want to embitter him by celebrating a triumph. She made one last effort to reach him.

'Father, I'm truly sorry if I've seemed to be going against you. I only want to make peace, for all our sakes.'

'Don't fret. I never fight for a lost cause. Enjoy your victory. You wanted this marriage, you've got what you wanted. You've made your choice. Whatever happens to you now, you'll have done it to yourself.'

Peada had been following his sister's instruction and made quick progress with his own. He agreed with everything the priest told him and dutifully echoed all Alchfrid's comments. His own chief idea about Christianity was that its priests had the keys to the Roman learning and power he admired so much in Alchfrid. The same skills and power would come to him by magic after he had gone through certain rituals and he was in a hurry to get them over. He told Alchfrid that he would gladly turn Christian even if Oswy refused to give him his daughter.

He was baptised by Bishop Finan that Resurrectiontide, with his bodyguard and servants, in the royal estate At-Wall. After his

chrism-loosing, a nuptial mass was celebrated for him and
Alchflaed. It was a pity that King Oswy could not be at any of
these ceremonies. He had been called north by reports that the
Scots of Dalriada were raiding deep into Pictland and getting
close to his border. Alchfrid acted as Peada's sponsor and
Alchflaed's kinsman, with Eanfled presiding graciously over the
feasts, so the Mercians had nothing to complain about the dignity
and splendour of the occasion.

After that, it was time for both young couples to go home.
Alchfrid set off westwards along the Wall; Peada headed south.
His father had given him a kingdom of his own to rule, the land of
the Middle Anglians that bordered the Fens. Penda needed to
keep a strong Mercian power there to hold East Anglia, which
had been defeated by him several times but refused to stay
defeated.

Alchflaed was taken aback. She had thought she would be
living at the Mercian court close to Penda, winning his trust,
pleading the cause of peace. Peada was overjoyed. The magic
Roman spells of the Christian priests had worked quicker than he
hoped. He was a king, he had a kingdom where he could give his
orders like Alchfrid '—and I've got a Roman city,' he boasted to
Alchflaed. 'It's called Leirceaster, it's got stone walls all round it.
I'll live in the palace there and make it my capital.' He was proud
of himself for remembering to use the Roman terms.

Their way south would take them through Deira. She foresaw
unpleasantness. Athelwold was her cousin. Oswy had kept the
peace with him, as there was no way he could dislodge him
without bloodshed. But he had taken the kingdom from Oswy
and Eanfled with the help of Deiran rebels who said openly that
her father was a murderer. What would she do if they said it
to her face, publicly, on her way through their country?
Athelwold's father, St Oswald, had been slaughtered and muti-
lated by Penda but Athelwold had put himself under Penda's
protection; everybody knew he couldn't stand against Oswy
without it. What would she do if Peada said that to Athelwold's
face, publicly?

Athelwold solved that problem by going to visit his mother in
her convent. He left fulsome greetings for his overlord's son and
his dear cousin Alchflaed; he bade them welcome to his palace in
Eoforwic for as long as they chose to honour him by staying
there.

Her mind was as much on her first visit there as on the present

193

moment, while she walked along the colonnades and through the courtyards. How quickly life changes; how little we can foresee what will become of us and what time will do to our plans! She and Peada were going to sleep in the fine room that had been prepared for Eanfled. Oswy had married Eanfled to hold Deira and now he had lost it. She herself had come to Eoforwic as a nervous girl to welcome her new queen; now she was a queen herself and married to the arch-enemy's heir.

Other folk had also met unexpected changes. There was a new Dish-Thane; Willibrord was lately dead. She recalled his red pouchy face, his fussy, self-important courtesy. Who would have thought he had so little time left? Nest was nowhere to be seen; she must have taken herself off when her keeper died. Likely she'd already found herself another. And Hildelith—how had she taken the change of kings? Was she still pecking and clucking about 'Queen Ethelburg's time'?

But the one she thought about most was the one she wouldn't hear about in Eoforwic. Likely she'd never see or hear of him again when she was living far away on the edge of the Fens. Meilyr's wraith seemed to be everywhere in the palace that evening, haunting her steps and her memories: in the colonnade where he had kissed her to hide her face—she touched the wall there as she passed—among the shadows of the pillars where he had dodged the guards, under the arch of the gate-house where he had smuggled her back to safety.

She stood there for a while, looking down the hill to the bridge-end. The sun was still rosy-warm on the quayside where she had danced to his playing but gleams of firelight were beginning to show at the ale-house door. She saw his dark face laughing at her and was surprised to find she was laughing aloud all by herself. Her spirits lifted; for a moment she felt it would be good to run off again down the hill to find adventure, to follow a strain of music and, perhaps, meet him again.

'Wouldn't you like to come away with me and look for that lost island floating in the sunset clouds?'

That would be a stupid thing to do, stupid even to dream about. You didn't find a lost island floating in the sunset clouds. You found a brawl in a quayside tavern, or a gang of bloodthirsty churls hunting you along a beach while you hid in the bottom of a boat and hoped their lurcher wouldn't smell you out. None of that had any place in the lives of a sober married woman and a dignified prince of—where was it?—Iâl. Whatever unforeseen changes that fortune could bring them, those days would never come again. *We were young then*, she thought; *but*, with a sudden cold shock, *it was only eighteen months ago!*

Behind her in the palace folk were shrill and busy about the work of real life. Voices were raised in high words somewhere in one of the courtyards. She turned away from the gate, determined to turn away from memories and regrets, scolding herself: *Don't get lost in dreams, don't—*

'Don't! Oh don't! For God's sake! *No!*'

The voice lifted to a shriek, then choked away, drowned in a burst of shrill laughter. Alchflaed froze, then raced round a corner towards the noise.

The maid-servants had got Nest down among their feet. They had dragged her some way from where her cloak was lying. Her dress had been torn away from her shoulders, there were claw-marks over her cheeks and breasts, her lips were bruised, her ears were bleeding where her ear-rings had been torn out. She had been carrying a small chest; it had fallen and the lid had burst open scattering trinkets of all kinds: brooches, necklaces, rings and bracelets. Nest had tried to crawl towards them to pick them up; one of the maids had grabbed her hair and pulled her back on to her knees, jerking her neck cruelly.

To Alchflaed's disgust, this vicious scene was being watched by an outer ring of noblewomen, one of whom was Hildelith. They were egging the maids on like farm churls round a dog-fight.

Nest's hands still clawed towards her trinkets.

'He gave them to me! He gave them to me!'

'You lying slut!'

'Strip her and turn her out of doors. See how soon she can collect another hoard of other folk's goods.'

'Slit her nose and lips,' suggested one of the well-dressed onlookers, a red-haired woman whose narrow eyes and long nose made her as much a vixen in looks as in temper. 'Then no decent woman's husband will touch her. She'll have to hire out her backside in the gutter.'

'Take her thief's hand off first. Then she won't be able to open jewel-boxes!'

This was no empty threat. A brawny harridan, who looked and stank as if she had come from the kitchen, was brandishing a meat-chopper. One of the other maids grabbed Nest's right hand and pulled her arm across the low parapet at the courtyard's edge, so that her wrist was underneath the blade. Nest screamed like a hare in a wolf's jaws and tried to struggle. The servant-girls held her down, their mistresses closed in to watch.

'Stop that at once!'

They turned to look at Alchflaed. Some of them had a blind, drunken look; they were so far gone in the lust of cruelty that they might have clawed and slashed at her as well as Nest, just because she had come across their way. Several of the noble-women knew her from her last visit, she saw hatred of Bernicians in their faces. They would not do much to control their servants. She did not fear for her life but she might well be shamefully beaten or harried through the palace till the guards came to her help, and she was not sure that she could save Nest.

'Who are you to give me orders?' The harridan underlined the question with the chopper. 'One of this whore's workmates?'

'Or her bawd, come to claim your cut?'

The women were starting to bunch round her. The kitchen-maid picked up the last word with a screech of laughter at her own wit.

'I'll give you your cut all right!'

Alchflaed sensed a movement towards her. Another second and they would pounce. She stood firm.

'I'm King Peada's wife. Daughter-in-law to the King of Mercia.'

They recoiled. She knew she would have no more trouble for herself. It was the first time she had failed to claim respect as due to her own name and race. Even while she sheltered behind Mercian power she felt belittled.

'Lady Hildelith, when we were waiting on Queen Eanfled, I never thought I'd meet you again at a scene like this. You disgrace yourself.'

Hildelith's head was jerking so violently she seemed to be smitten with the palsy.

'This harlot took shameless advantage of my kinsman Willibrord's widowed state. She battened on him like a leech, plundering his goods that belong by right to his heirs.'

'To his daughter,' said a grim-faced bejewelled woman.

'To his son's wife!' snapped the vixen.

'When he died the family turned her out at once and quite right. But the thieving whore sneaked back to help herself to his treasure and got caught in the act. Just look what she was carrying off.'

'He gave them to me!' Nest was shaking with terror, her tears smearing the blood and dirt on her face, but she kept stubbornly to her claim.

'You can't prove it,' said the daughter triumphantly. 'There's enough stolen goods here to get you hanged or sold as a slave if it came to lawing. You've got no one to vouch for you.'

'I'll vouch for her. When I was here last, while Willibrord was alive, I saw her wearing some of those jewels openly—in your company, Lady Hildelith—and yours, Goldburh. There was ample time to accuse her if you thought she'd been stealing.'

They looked at her resentfully. A queen's word, though unsupported, would carry more weight in a law-suit than theirs. Also, Hildelith at least was too proud to be forsworn.

'I'm surprised to hear a royal lady speaking up for a harlot.' She pecked spitefully at Alchflaed. 'Especially one who was brought up in a convent by King Oswy's sister. Did she never teach you the text "Thou shalt not commit adultery"?'

'Could Nest do that with a widower?' In spite of the danger of provoking them, she could not resist adding, 'And did you never learn the text "The labourer is worthy of his hire"?'

'Grant that he let her wear the jewels while he lived,' persisted the vixen, 'they come back to his family now he's dead. No need to charge her, as we've got them again. Put her out of the gate.'

'She can hardly stand! Look what you've done to her. She needs tending. Get her into a room and put her to bed.'

Hildelith looked outraged. 'She's not staying in the palace—a creature like that. She's got no business to be here.'

'She's staying in the palace as long as King Peada and I are here as guests. And she will have business here because I'm taking her as my bower-woman.'

She half-lifted, half-dragged Nest to her feet and supported her on the way back to her own apartments, as nobody made a move to help her. There was whispering behind her back that she was meant to hear.

'Bernician!'

'Oswy's daughter.'

'One thief helps another.'

She ignored it.

Peada was not minded to welcome his wife's new attendant. She told him that night what she had done. Nest was now asleep in a little storeroom near the royal apartments where two Mercian maids could watch over her. These girls had come north on Cyneburg's wedding journey and Peada was seeing them home. They wouldn't take trouble from Deirans.

'You don't want to meddle with a woman like that,' he grumbled. 'What are people going to think about me if my wife's seen in the company of a Welsh whore?'

'I should be worrying about that, not you. They'll think I'm a trusting fool to let her near you. And I thought the Welsh were your friends.'

Peada was surprised; he had not thought she could be so stupid.

'The ones in the west — they've got armies, they're useful allies. But Elmet folk count for nothing, they were conquered long ago.'

'Nest was of enough account to bring me food and drink when I first came to the palace. None of those Deiran hags gave me even a word of welcome.'

'That's because you're a Bernician and they hate Oswy's guts. Don't worry they'll try it on while you're with me. Father's got Deira in harness, they just need to feel a touch of the reins or the whip from time to time. But if this woman did you a good turn, give her a piece of gold in the morning when you put her out.'

'Oh Peada! It would be cruel to put her out. She's got no one to help her.'

'I'm not having her in my household.'

They had not long been married. She said coaxingly, 'But it would please me so much,' and loosened the neck strings of her shift. He grinned.

'Would it? Oh, very well then. But I know something that will please you better.'

He pulled the shift down to her feet, picked her up and put her on the bed with himself on top. It did please her; she delighted in him and loved him dearly. Yet that Deiran woman's ugly sneer kept muttering inside her head: *'She'll have to hire out her backside in the gutter.'* The words made no sense in her own life. She was an honest wife; husbands and wives had been using the same persuasion since the world began. Yet she still felt that a matter of justice and mercy should not have been settled on such terms. For the second time that day it seemed her marriage had belittled her.

Eoforwic marked the southern rim of the world in Alchflaed's life; she had never been beyond. The Roman road went on through southern Deira and Mercia towards Lundenburh, the Saxon kingdoms and the Narrow Seas.

One thing she did know about the mysterious lands to the south. For the first day or two the road would pass through the marches of Elmet, Nest's country. She must find out about Nest's home and family, take full advantage of Peada's good humour to get the girl safely and happily settled before she went on to her own kingdom.

When Nest came to her next morning, she set her to work hanging out her robes to air so that they would not get creased from lying too long in the travelling chests. This kept Nest away from the sight and clutches of the Deiran women and gave her the chance for private talk.

At the first mention of her family, Nest's face went hard and blank.

'They wouldn't have me back.'

Alchflaed was afraid of touching some wound; she said uncertainly, 'Did—did Willibrord—carry you off?'

Nest suddenly screamed with laughter. Alchflaed took her firmly by the arm and made her sit down on one of the chests. She sat down beside her and took her hand.

'Gently now. I don't want to upset you; but if I'm to help you, you must tell me how to do it. What happened to you? How did you lose your home?'

Nest gave her an odd look: nervous, yet insolent and curious to see how far she could go.

'Folk here laugh at your father,' was her strange answer. 'They call Oswy "the tireless leader"—he'll lead his army five times round Bernicia before they get to the battlefield and find the enemy's got tired of waiting and gone home.'

Shocked and furious, Alchflaed drew her hand away; Nest gripped it.

'You be proud of him, girl, he's the best king your country ever had. He hasn't let you be beaten. We weren't so lucky. We had a hero ruling us, too proud and stupid to do anything but hurl himself straight into battle and get wiped out with all his fighting men. Your stepmother's father, King Edwin, destroyed him and drove his heir into exile. Elmet was beaten and we've stayed beaten.'

She laughed bitterly. 'Edwin wasn't a savage. He didn't slaughter us all—what good is a kingdom with no one to work in it? He was a just man too. He didn't take all our lands. When he'd rewarded his thanes and warriors with our best estates, we could keep what was left. We have our rights under his law—our honour-price is one third of a Deiran's. So we live. A peasant-farmer needn't starve except in a bad year, if he works all the hours God sends and he's got a wife to work beside him till her skin turns to leather and her back's bent and she's a withered hag by the time she's twenty!'

Though she was glaring at Alchflaed, her eyes were blank to her new mistress and everything in the room. She seemed to be carrying on a furious quarrel somewhere else with other people, hurling arguments she had used many times before.

'And then, in the long winter nights when the year's work is done, we can crouch over our hearth-smoke eating greasy stew, drinking sour ale and recite our pedigrees and tell tales about our ancient heroes in their crimson cloaks with their fine steeds and our queens in silken dresses!'

She went into fits of laughter; then suddenly became her usual quietly respectful self. 'Willibrord saw me when he came to oversee the payment of food-rent on his estates beyond Caer Galch. My ancestors had a villa there. His wife had just died; he wanted a bed-warmer. He wouldn't marry me — a dowerless foreigner from a beaten race — but he offered to take me to the palace at Eoforwic. He promised to treat me as if I were a lady.'

For a second her anger glittered in her eyes again.' As if I were a lady! My people were lords of this land before the Romans came! But I had the choice between taking Willibrord's offer or marrying some high-born dirt-farmer like my father — and I chose Willibrord. My family called me a traitress but then,' she glanced at Alchflaed with sly defiance, 'I've heard folk say the same about your mother.'

Alchflaed's thoughts were so filled with pity for Nest and how she could help her escape from the trap that life had sprung on her, that she missed this last muttered remark.

'Life's been hurtful to you, Nest. But it'll heal, like these scratches.' She stroked Nest's cheek. 'Come with me into my new kingdom, make a new start. You'll have a high place in my household. I'll dower you — you can make a noble marriage.'

Nest shook her head in disbelief. 'Coming from Deira? I've told you what Deirans think about Elmet folk. Well, Mercians think the same about Deirans — they count for nothing.'

Alchflaed brushed this aside confidently. 'But I'm not a Deiran.' She smiled. 'As you said yourself, they haven't beaten my father.'

Nest looked at her. 'No, your father's still undefeated.' *For how long?* she asked herself. Most folk gave him a year, if his luck held.

*   *   *

The road went on, day after day, high on its causeway over the heavy wet soil. The oak woods pressed close to either side of it, the great forest that covered the whole midland plain. From time to time the road bridged or forded one of the great rivers making their way to Humbre mouth: Weorf, Yr, Caldre, Wenet, Don. If it had not been for the changing river names, Alchflaed might have thought a witch had cast runes over them to keep them toiling along the same few miles till the end of the world. Even Peada's Mercians were low-voiced and ill-tempered as if they felt the road was evil-omened, though they had gone up and down it in triumph often enough with Penda. She wondered if they were remembering, as she was against her will, how Penda had taken one of Frea's women in the forest here. It had been by the River Don, that bore the old British name of the Great Goddess, that she had killed herself and left the King under the shadow of Frea's curse.

To the west the forest ran up into the moors of Elmet, where some of its chiefs still held out as cattle-raiding outlaws. Eastwards the land got lower and more marshy in the wastes of Haethfeld. King Edwin had died there under Cadwallon's sword; she recalled it to Peada for something to say that might rouse his interest.

'Cadwallon was a very great warrior, my father's sword-friend. He made one big mistake though and it cost him his life. He should have gone on into the north to hunt out your father's family where they were hiding and killed the lot before they had time to strike back at him. My father says it was a good lesson — we won't make the same mistake twice.'

He saw Alchflaed's face and laughed. 'Don't look like that. You're my wife — I wasn't talking about you!'

Prince Alchfrid's influence had quickly vanished as soon as Peada was out of his company. Besides, he now had all the things he had admired and envied in Alchfrid. He was a king: he had a kingdom and a Roman city all of his own with stone walls round it. He had Christian priests of his own too — four of them were coming down from Holy Island, led by Diuma, a pupil of Aidan famous for his learning and holy life. Soon, he also would be able to say 'I told my bishop —' They could read the Romans' books and write letters for him, so that he wouldn't have to keep asking Alchflaed what they meant. A wife shouldn't know better than her husband, she made him look a fool. He remembered one of Alchfrid's remarks, taken from a holy rune-book, 'I forbid a woman to teach or to bear rule over a man'—a truly wise saying.

Alchflaed felt that the forests were casting a shadow over her spirits. She was longing for her new home, for rest, warmth and laughter but she began to feel that she and Peada were really trapped by evil spells on an endless journey. At last, however, the road climbed a ridge of heathy upland. Peada drew rein and pointed.

'Look! There's Leirceaster—my capital!'

She looked. It was indeed, as Peada said, a Roman city with stone walls all round it. When they arrived and she saw what was inside them, her heart sank.

CHAPTER 20

This was not the first time Leirceaster had been a capital. When it was Ratae Coritanorum it had been one of the loveliest of the tribal cities, with splendid public buildings, bustling shops and houses with jewel-bright mosaic floors. But its trade had died with the Empire; it had no port to keep it alive and bring folk into it with goods and news from the wide world. When a disastrous fire swept through its centre, destroying the forum and basilica, the heart went out of the forlorn little city.

The Mercians neither knew nor cared about its past. The stone walls made it a useful strong point. Landowners collected their food rent here and had barns and cattlepens to hold it, with huts for the men who kept guard. Wulfrun's husband, Eadbert, would come from time to time to hear difficult law suits and check the readiness of the menfolk to muster for war service. He had a fine homestead in the southeastern quarter of the city, with every comfort—Wulfrun saw to that. When there was a weapon-showing, the warriors mustered in a great hall that had been built over the foundations of the basilica. Under Eadbert's stern eyes they tested their fighting skills in the empty space that had once been a forum.

For the rest, a smith had his forge here; a potter had a kiln. Packmen came through on their way north and west from the ports on the eastern sea-board. Folk farmed outside the walls and even inside the walls. Pigs rooted, chickens scratched, goats were tethered among crumbling weed-grown ruins. Sometimes the dwellers patched up a shelter in the corner of a house or temple; sometimes they robbed the stones and heavier timbers to put up their huts wherever they chose to clear a space.

Coming through the north gate where most of this squatting had taken place, Alchflaed met Leirceaster at its desolate and sluttish worst. She had seen nothing like it since her first night in the ruined fort on the Wall. She remembered her brother's fury. *'This is what comes of heathen barbarism. Dozens of petty thieves calling themselves kings—'*

She had been startled at Alchfrid's rage, even repelled by his dream of rebuilding the shattered province under *'one Church, one Law, one Emperor'*. Now she began to understand the pure cold rage that might drive him to fight, to rebel not for selfish greed but for the sake of order and beauty.

She could not give much time, though, to her brother's plans for the ruins of Roman Britain. The problem had suddenly become her own.

They had reached the central cross-roads, or rather cross-tracks, and turned to the right alongside the warriors' hall. Beyond lay what remained of a large Roman building. She had seen enough of Eoforwic and Caer Luel to know that it had been the bath house. The exercise hall had lost its roof, but its colonnades were still standing to make a great open courtyard. At the far side, a lofty doorway with two portals made an entrance of some splendour to the bath. Peada led the way through.

The front halls had gone; where they had stood was now a roughly-cobbled court. Straw and dung round the patched-up changing rooms showed that these were doing duty as stalls. In front of her she saw the hot bath, a sturdy building with three big rooms side by side. Wisps of smoke were coming out of the centre lattice which had lost its glass.

'This is my palace,' said Peada. 'I sent word for them to get it ready for us.'

They went in. It was a warm May; though the sun was near setting, the air was still mild outside. Inside it was chill and slightly dank, though a dispirited fire was trying to burn on a small hearth in the middle of the floor. Some of the smoke had found the unglazed lattice high under the roof. Most of it was still in the hall, drifting round the walls which had no other hangings. At the far end a table and benches had been set up. A group of men and women waited near the door. They had the sullen, righteous look of folk who have been given impossible orders, getting ready to defend themselves against blame. It was not like Caer Luel and Eoforwic.

Winefride came towards them, carrying the guest cup. She was the only one in the hall who was smiling.

'Welcome to King Peada and his bride.'

'Welcome! What sort of a welcome do you call this?'

Winefride's smile vanished. She looked surprised and reproachful, as if someone who had asked for water suddenly asked angrily why he hadn't been given mulled ale.

'You said you wanted to eat and sleep here.'

'So why didn't you put up any wall-hangings?'

'There aren't any hooks in the walls.'

'Why haven't you lit the torches?'

'There aren't any torch-brackets.'

'Couldn't you even get a decent fire going?'

'There isn't a decent hearth. There wasn't any hearth at all — we had to make one in a hurry when we got your message.'

Peada turned scowling to Alchflaed. 'See to it, will you? Tell them what to do and see they do it quickly. I'm not used to be kept waiting when I come to a hall, least of all my own.'

'But what do you expect me to do?'

'Order my hall to be got ready for me. You're the Queen, it's for you to rule my household decently. You know all about Stone-Giant palaces. I'm going to see what they've done with my horses.'

He went out. She stared hopelessly at her new subjects, who stared back sulkily, resenting her as the cause of their trouble. She had not the least idea what to do. Life at Ebbe's convent, except for devotions and studies, was exactly like life on the northern farms around it. In Eoforwic and Caer Luel she had been a guest, staying in a well-run palace not the remains of a bath.

Nest murmured at her ear, 'Braziers.'

'What?'

'Braziers. Fire-baskets with charcoal. There must be some in the place.'

Alchflaed turned smiling to her household. 'Could you get some charcoal burning as soon as possible? If we have braziers all around the rooms, we'll soon warm the air without all this smoke.'

Nobody budged or smiled back.

'There aren't any here,' said Winefride sullenly.

'Then look for some. Ask around the city. Surely folk will be glad to lend to their king?'

'I don't think I can—'

Alchflaed stopped trying to be gracious to her subjects. Her eyes flashed wide. 'You can do what you're told!'

The tone of her voice startled everybody including herself. There were no more protests. In the end, enough fire-baskets and candlesticks were mustered to get the hall, and the room to the left which was to be their bed-chamber, quite pleasantly warm and bright. Nothing could be done that evening about wall-hangings, but she got some fresh herbs strewn on the rushes, garlands on the table and embroidered coverlets on their bed. It was not splendour but it was comfort. Peada was still out of humour, complaining that their food was tepid and tasted of smoke, that he felt cold even in bed. To her surprise, he seemed to hold her at fault for every shortcoming.

'I'd never have come here if it hadn't been for you. I can't think why you want to live in such places.'

She held herself back from retorting that she had never felt the slightest wish to live in such a place.

'Let's move into the warriors' hall. I know just how to make that bright and splendid for you.'

'And what happens when the men are summoned here for a weapon-showing?'

'We'll have had time to build a new royal hall. Let's build our own hall, Peada—our own palace where no one else has lived before! We'll plan it together, just as we want it. You can order the greatest oak timbers and choose the carvings, I'll design the most wonderful hangings. We'll make it lovelier than Heorot. We can live in the warriors' hall for the time being.'

'Folk will laugh at me, moving out of my palace at once after giving orders to get it ready for me. You'll make me look a fool. I've given you a Roman palace; you'll live in it and stop complaining.'

Wulfrun arrived from Eadbert's stronghold at Ceastertun at the edge of the Fens and settled into his well-provided hall. Peada went to greet her and found her looking through a pile of men's shirts to see which needed darning. She asked his pardon for going on with her task.

'It's not a fitting sight for the eyes of a king, I know. I love fine embroidery as much as any lady. I wish I had more time to sit at my ease over my coloured silks, planning designs, but my first duty is to see my household well-stocked with clean clothes. Summer's coming.'

'Your household's lucky. At least you don't think simple womanly tasks are below your understanding.'

'You're vexed with Winefride. It's hard for the poor child. I've never seen her cry so bitterly as when she told me about your home-coming. She thinks she's failed you. She was so proud—we all were—to think of her being chief bower-maiden in your queen's court. We never guessed—' She stopped.

We never guessed that your queen would be too stupid and feckless to order the palace you brought her to.

'I'm not blaming Winefride, it wasn't her fault. Whoever gave her that idea?'

Peada shifted impatiently. Wulfrun asked anxiously if the fire was too hot.

'Not for me, I'm enjoying it. It makes a pleasant change.' He added bitterly, 'I can't think how the Romans kept warm. I've asked Alchflaed but she doesn't seem to know—at any rate she doesn't tell me.'

'Perhaps they didn't. Perhaps they had no need to.'

Peada looked startled. Wulfrun went on in the same quiet tone, her large eyes fixed on his face.

'They were strange folk, the Stone-Giants. I've been into some of their houses here—I like to see and know things. I've gone into rooms where there were windows opening on to gardens with roses blooming and coloured birds flying in the blue sky, though it was winter outside. And then I've stretched out my hand and there was nothing—nothing but a little film of colour spread over cold stone.'

In spite of the fire, Peada felt as chilled as when he first entered his palace. Wulfrun went on.

'Perhaps they didn't have warm flesh and blood like us. Who knows what they really were? In their pictures some of them are monsters—perhaps they all were in their true forms. I know they were shape-shifters.'

She leaned towards Peada, her eyes wide in their hollowed sockets. 'Our ploughman turned up one of their golden dishes in the Fens. My lord gave it to me, he's very generous. I got our jewel-smith to melt it down to make brooches for me—it had a very evil picture worked into the gold. There was a young man, very fair to look at; he was naked, ready to make love to a woman. He'd got her in his arms and she was changing into a tree —her toes were taking root, her fingers had turned into twigs and her hair was leaves!'

Peada shuddered to listen to her. He almost believed he had the girl in his arms and could feel the horror happening against his naked flesh.

'Perhaps that's how their women really were, like those alder-wives who haunt the Fens, lovely and elf-sheen in the moonlight but when a man embraces them, they're hollow behind, just empty rotting tree-stumps.'

She laughed. 'I'm wasting your time with my chatter, I'm just an unlearned woman. You must ask Queen Alchflaed to teach you about the Stone-Giants. Her mother was one of them.'

'Her mother was a Welshwoman.' Peada's lips felt stiff and dry.

'The Welsh lived with the Stone-Giants for four hundred years, so they say. They must have learned a lot of the magic.'

Nest was a tower of strength. She had served a good apprenticeship as mistress to the Dish-Thane of Eoforwic; she had learned a good deal about keeping Roman palaces light and warm and serving hot meals in them. She also had wonderful skill in putting her hand on what was needful; it seemed like enchantment. Again and again Winefride would claim that some object had never been seen in Mercia; or that those goods could not be got at that time of year. Soon afterwards, some man of the household would approach Nest and say that he thought he'd found what the Queen wanted but would Nest come and look to make sure. The woodwright had made Nest a new trinket box; it was already filling up.

If Wulfrun had been in the Queen's household there would have been war, ending fairly soon in Nest's murder. But Winefride was as lazy as she was stupid. She had no mind to bother herself with the running of the palace; if she did little to help, she did as little to hinder. She did a fair day's work, though, in passing on the hints Wulfrun gave her about Alchflaed to the other women of the court. She liked that, so she did it well. There was never anything insulting or outrageous enough to cause an outburst; just a faint mist of poison in the air, that made Alchflaed seem alien or dangerous and stopped her from making any friends among her new people.

She could feel that she was disliked. As she could not understand

why, and she was never given any open defiance, she was helpless to cure the ill. It made her very unhappy, tainting even her
successes with grief and failure.

There was a house standing just south of the baths; she had
taken it for her bower. One room had a mosaic floor with a
peacock in pride at the centre, a beautiful bird with a grey-blue
body framed in a fan of red, yellow and brown feathers with
'eyes' at each tip made of shining blue glass. When it was cleaned
it shone like one of her own illuminations. She should have been
glad to have such a room to read and embroider in and exchange
pleasant talk.

There had once been a garden in the courtyard. It was wild
now but there were still straggling rose-bushes to be pruned into
shape and coaxed to fuller blossom; also some surviving herbs,
grown rank. She made cuttings and hunted for wild roots along
the bank of the Soar, which flowed close under the west wall of
the city. She began to make some of the simple infusions and
ointments she had learned from the convent herbalist. She would
have liked to compare cures and chat about their ailments with
the other women. It would be a good way of learning about them
and being drawn into their lives. But she earned little thanks,
except from some of the cottars. Most of the women avoided the
topic when she mentioned it, listening to her in cold politeness,
sometimes with a look of fear.

Though it was a hard struggle she was making the bath house
more like a palace. The day after she arrived, she had gone over
every inch of the site, from the roofs to the huge drains which had
once filled the baths from the aqueduct and discharged under the
city walls into the Soar. They were dry now; underground tunnels that branched to run along the north and south sides of the
building. She found a way down in one of the out-buildings near
her bower; she had no idea it had once been a latrine.

After exploring the bath house she set about furnishing and
stocking it. Some life and grace began to creep back into
Leirceaster. More packmen came with richer wares, once the
word went round that there was a lavish patroness. The potter
added to his range of styles; the forge made handsomer metal-
work; a jewel-smith arrived. The thanes who made up Peada's
witan brought their wives to meet the Queen, so they had to see
to the comforts of their own halls inside the city. Gleemen and
jugglers began to visit the place even when there was no weapon-
showing. More houses were patched up to lodge the visitors;

some householders began to serve food and ale to passers-by.

She got little help from Peada. He was angry with her for taking salves and draughts to churls, even thralls, and tending their sick with her own hands. He lost his temper violently when he saw her hurrying or stepping lightly, telling her to 'stop jigging like a tumbler's whore'. He called her Roman robes of state 'flaunting' and ordered her to look like a decent Christian wife instead of trying to snare every man's eyes.

He spent more and more time in the warriors' hall. He liked the idea of himself as a warrior-king among his fighting-men, as befitted Penda's son. In spite of his objections to leaving his palace, the warriors' hall became, in effect, the King's hall except that there was no queen in it. Alchflaed seemed to have lost every charm for him. He still came to her bed but took little notice of her while he was in it, except as a woman's body to be ridden as long as he chose.

Sometimes her loneliness and bewilderment flared up into anger, as she asked herself why she should be treated so, and what point was there in going on enduring it. She had the idea of telling Father Diuma that she had decided to take the veil. This would leave Peada free to marry again and she could go home to Ebbe.

Then she told herself sternly that peace-weaving, like any other weaving, could not be done well and finished in a day or two. She was a stranger; she had no right to demand that folk should love and trust her at sight. So she struggled on, month after month till the year dragged round to spring again. Time seemed to stop. She won nothing but some useless gratitude from the thralls, whose lives were so desperate they would take help from anyone, even a northern witch, and also—though she did not know this till later—the grudging admiration of Peada's warband who knew courage whenever they saw it.

The time came when she was quite sure that an ally was on the way, the one who could help her most. She counted from her last monthly flow, glad that the waiting had been so long. Her child would not have been conceived in a tomb or in furtive couplings as if she had been committing adultery. It would not have been conceived in much joy either, but surely joy would come back now. The new life had started in March; she might well have a son for Christmas.

Peada was pleased and boasted to his men. Folk began to smile when they saw her. There was warmth and laughter and kissing in bed again, for a time, until Wulfrun spoke a sisterly word to Peada.

'It was my duty to warn you—I know too well what may happen. How I would have loved to bear children but you know what befell me.' She sighed.

Wulfrun was getting ready to go home. Eadbert was soon to try an ugly case of murder. She wanted to be by his side to help keep him from danger.

'Danger?' Peada frowned. 'Who's being charged? Are his kin likely to make trouble? I'll come myself—'

Wulfrun shook her head. 'Not that sort of danger. My lord's well able to deal with armed men. This is a case of sorcery—a woman and her brother. She married a rich man who had no family and no close kin. It seems she destroyed the children he got on her before they could be born. Then she murdered him too, by death-runes and killing herbs, and gave his lands to her brother.'

Peada was appalled. 'Would any woman destroy the fruit of her own body even for a great estate?'

'For her brother. Blood kin are closer than marriage kin—that's why it can be dangerous to marry outside one's own folk. And this woman is a very evil creature with a bad name. There's no doubt she was hel-runing. She used to visit old burial grounds to collect dust and bones—and she was a harlot too. She had men coming to her, even among the graves.'

Of course Peada looked shocked, even white with disgust; it was a loathsome story. Wulfrun modestly changed the subject.

It was late summer, drawing towards autumn. The dews were drenching thick in the mornings, the leaves were fading, gossamers glinted on the twigs and bracken fronds.

Wulfrun, careful housewife, took her younger sister out to gather mushrooms and tell her how to cook them, before she left. They went on ponyback, in case they strayed some distance and got weary in the midday heat. They set off through the north gate into the oak woods.

They went northwest through the dappled shade and sunshine, their ponies brushing through the yellowing fern. Sometimes Wulfrun stopped when she saw a cluster of mushrooms or puff-balls; she had come out to gather them and would need to return with some after being out so long. She did not linger, though, or leave her path to search for them but kept on mile after mile, making for Charnwood. They forded several streams; the last one was flowing fast and dashing among huge boulders.

Beyond it the ground rose steeply, the trees did not press so close, rocks broke through the earth, pointed and slanting like fangs. At last they reached the crest of a ridge. Below them the tree-tops spread like a green-gold ocean over the Mercian plain. The women dismounted and tethered their ponies to the last tree, then followed a rough track along the ridge till it turned downhill so sharply, among such great slabs of rock, that they had to scramble using their hands. At the end of the ridge an oak tree was leaning from a crevice; stunted and deformed it looked like an etin crouching to snatch an unwary traveller. The women went on round the edge. Facing them was an opening, framed by two slabs and a heavy capstone. The oak hung over it; except from the front there seemed to be nothing but a fold in the rocks.

No cave mouth was ever so even; it was the door of an earth-house, an ancient home of the dead. It made a strange house for the living but then, it had a strange housewife.

Aino had been carried off from East Anglia in a Mercian raid when she was a girl. That did not worry her overmuch. It was said of the women in her family that they only went where they chose, whatever means they used to get there, including war. Her captor had married her, though she was not beautiful as the English saw it, being short and squat, with a flat nose, yellowish skin and coarse black hair. Her man never took another woman, though, as long as he lived; he got steadily richer as his land and stock flourished.

Aino had inherited her looks, along with her name, from a Finnwife who had come to East Anglia with fugitives from Geatland. When Beowulf was killed, and the Swedes came south in force over the great lakes to take the country, King Wiglaf with the last of his warband had fought a way to the coast. They were shepherding as many women and children as they could rescue and carrying some of their treasure; they took ship and fled westwards. The Finnwife had shipped with them, though no one knew how she had come on board or who had brought her. They were glad enough to have her: when the rowers had struggled in vain for days against a head wind and folk began to sicken, she undid a knot among the coloured braids in her hair and whistled up a brisk following breeze for them. They made landfall among the East Anglians, where they were welcomed kindly for their noble birth, their misfortunes and their treasure. The king gave Wiglaf his daughter. The Finnwife also married; her descendants

211

for the most part took after their father's people but every so often the strange northern strain would crop out, always in a girl.

When she had seen her children and grandchildren richly married and her husband die peacefully at a good age, Aino had suddenly moved to the earth-house, taking what goods she chose from her household. Nobody knew how she lived there or what she did far inside it. No visitor ever went beyond the first chamber just beyond the door, and nothing untoward was to be seen there. The room looked so much like a well-to-do churl's hut, one might wonder why Aino had troubled to move there from her lordly hall. She never gave an account of herself to anyone, but did not seem uncomfortable or unhappy.

She was sitting on the ground outside the entrance to her house, basking in the sunshine. She did not move or speak as the two women came up to her. Wulfrun stooped and laid a gold buckle in her lap, then sat down on one side of her. Winefride added a ring and sat down also.

The silence went on. Winefride began to fidget; Wulfrun frowned and shook her head. At last, Aino spoke.

'What do you want?'

'There's a woman carrying a child. I want her to lose it.'

'And her life?'

'Yes!' said Winefride eagerly. When her sister said 'No!' at almost the same moment she began to sulk.

'How much longer have I got to wait? You can see he's tired of her—'

'What a fool you are, sister. They've not been married long—it's little more than a year since he was besotted over her. When a young wife dies with her first baby, a man always feels tenderly for her. I've even known some who blamed themselves. And I pity any woman he marries after that. Even if she's as lovely as Eostre or Frea herself, there'll always be one who was lovelier and wiser and sweeter-tempered. You can't outshine the dead.'

Winefride pouted. She was sure she could outshine anyone.

'She's not to die till he wants her dead—till he orders her death. Then her ghost won't walk in your bower or come to lie in your marriage bed.'

Aino chuckled. 'You're a wise woman, Lady Wulfrun.'

She got up and went into her house, taking her gifts. When she came out again she brought a little bone phial with a carved stopper.

'No more than five drops. You can put it in ale. Mead is too sickly, she might void it at once.'

Wulfrun took the phial, kissing Aino's hand. The old woman sat down again in the sun and took no further notice of them. The sisters went back the way they had come. Two days later, Wulfrun set off for her home, to shield her husband with her faithful care from possible attacks by a murdering sorceress.

The weather was hot and close. Roman buildings with stone walls and mosaic floors became pleasant. Alchflaed was in her peacock room, busy with her great embroidery. She had got on well with it in her many hours of loneliness, putting into it all the love and care she felt for the peace of Northumbria and Mercia, for the safety and happiness of their families, that she had not been allowed to give to the folk around her.

She had stitched a good deal of her own life across the green and blue stripes: Bebbanburh, where she first met Meilyr; Eoforwic, where she had danced and laughed with Meilyr; Legaceaster, where she had quarrelled with Meilyr—and joined her life to Peada's for the sake of their two lands. She had worked her way down to Mercia now; she wanted to make it just as beautiful, with its wide forests and mighty river Treanta; little Leirceaster, waking up again to life and pride; Tomeworthig, Penda's chief court at the heartland of the country; the hills of Peaclond where Frea had her shrine.

Nest was singing to her, to while away the time. Winefride was partly stitching gold braid to the wrists of a gown and mostly yawning. Alchflaed yawned too, and eased her back with a sigh; she was beginning to find stooping a strain.

'You're weary, so am I.' Winefride jumped up. 'I'll get us some ale, we could all do with a drink.'

She hurried off, coming back with a jug of ale, followed by a maid with three beakers. Winefride found fault with the girl, saying that they had not been washed fully clean. She bustled away to do it herself.

'This hot weather, the least little thing can turn you queasy.'

She smiled at Alchflaed with that new kindness folk were showing since it had become known she was with child. The beakers were cool and shining when she brought them back, with a few water-drops still gleaming in them. Winefride poured ale for them all and handed it round.

Winefride had been interested enough in what she was doing to take trouble over it. She had managed quite cleverly. What happened next was a piece of unearned good luck for her—or some evil fate that was working against Alchflaed.

She got a plea to bring help for a sick woman in one of the huts by the north gate. She had been feeling sick herself all morning; she had vomited once and hoped that had cleared her but she thought she would lie down when she got back to her bower. Perhaps she was still dizzy from the earlier qualm and made herself worse by stooping over the sick woman in her smoky hovel. Perhaps she stumbled in her hurry to get to her room before another bout of sickness took her. She twisted her foot and fell heavily on the broken pavement; when they picked her up she had already started to bleed from her womb.

It was all her own fault. She had gone to wait on a slave-woman when she knew Peada disliked it; she had been running in public after he had forbidden it; and so she had killed Peada's heir. One might almost have thought she had wanted to.

CHAPTER
21

It is hard for a husband and wife to rejoice at the birth of the Christ Child when they have lost a child of their own, with bitter anger on one side and grief on the other. Pride alone helped Peada and Alchflaed to make a decent show when Father Diuma arrived for the Feast of the Nativity.

If Diuma had been living in Leirceaster he might have saved them; but with only three other priests in the whole of heathen Mercia he could not afford its rulers the luxury of a private chaplain. The King was a Christian who had got good instruction; the Queen was convent-bred and could read her Psalter and Gospel. They must do their own work; they were the sound folk who had no need of a doctor. Diuma's task was to save souls in danger of eternal death. So he tramped the country in all weathers, like his teacher and fellow-countryman Aidan, and only came to the court for the high feasts.

He found a king who was eager to talk to him about building churches and monasteries; a queen who was gentle and gracious but kept silence before her husband as St Paul directed and dressed with sober modesty. She was still weak and melancholy from the loss of her unborn child. Diuma blessed and comforted her but reminded her that queens must bear their crosses as bravely as farm-women did.

Peada wanted to found a monastery. It was a kingly act, displaying his power and wisdom as well as his wealth for coming ages to wonder at. He thought of giving a royal estate at Medeshamsted and went there in early spring to look at the ground. Eadbert's stronghold was near at hand, where he was gladly welcomed. Eadbert was away, making a show of strength to awe the Fenlanders but Wulfrun was ready to help her king with her advice. Her husband said proudly that she was better than any reeve.

One day, when they were riding homewards, she asked him about Christianity.

'My lord is like King Penda. He keeps to the faith of his fathers. I'm not a woman to go against my husband, much less try to turn him against his people's gods. But I'm sure you have good reason for everything you do. Tell me, may a woman be a Christian and a priestess of Frea as well?'

Peada chuckled at her simplicity. 'Oh no, Wulfrun dear, that could never be. Our priests wouldn't have it.'

'Wouldn't they? That's strange—I thought Queen Alchflaed— but I must have heard wrong, or muddled it in my mind. I'm not a learned woman.'

'What have you heard?'

'Earl Immin came down from Northworthig to marry my step-daughter Edgifu. He spent Giuli with us. He had a strange story out of Deira; he was asking me about it but I couldn't explain. I'm not a Christian.'

'What story?'

'Well, it seems King Oswy built a temple where his cousin Oswine was killed, to pay for his blood-guilt and to keep Oswine's ghost quiet. Everybody in Deira knows Oswy brought about the murder though nobody can say just how he did it. Oswine's dearest friend suddenly turned against him, then vanished like the morning mist. Oswy called all the Deiran thanes to come and be witness how much he'd spent on the place—this was just before they rebelled. They say Queen Alchflaed came into the temple in Frea's robes with the power of all the thirteen moons on her.'

Peada opened his mouth to object that a Christian maiden

would never dress like that. Then he thought of Alchflaed's necklace and her claim that she didn't know what it meant. '*My necklace? It's only the moon in her three phases.*'

Still, he tried to deny the Deiran story. 'She couldn't. She wouldn't be let come near the altar.'

'It seems she wasn't let. She tried; but when she reached to take that holy bread you eat, they say she cried out 'No!' and put up her hands to save herself but some unseen hand struck her down. She was carried out of the temple like one dead.'

Peada was white and sweating slightly. He said nothing. Wulfrun laughed gently at her own ignorance.

'I'm sorry. I shouldn't be wasting your time asking you to explain idle tales when your mind's full of high affairs. What do you think of Medeshamsted? Will it serve your purpose?'

When they got back to Ceastertun there were messages for Peada from his brother-in-law with news from the north. Queen Eanfled had borne a son to Oswy last harvest; he had been named Ecgfrid. And Cyneburg was with child.

Peada was bitter.

'At least some of that race are fertile. But then, they've got better stock to breed from than a white-faced mute who does nothing but sit over an embroidery frame.'

Looking at him, Wulfrun knew that she could stop hinting.

'That embroidery—all Mercia, our fields and forests, our rivers and our strongholds, stitched on to the borders of Northumbria. A fine present to lay over her brother's marriage-bed, to keep him warm while he gets sons of Penda's blood.'

Peada stared at her.

'Your father's ageing. Your half-brothers are children. When Penda dies, if anything should happen to you, they won't be old enough to take the kingdom. But Alchfrid will, with Penda's daughter as his queen and Penda's grandson as his heir.'

'Happen to me?'

'She came down out of the north and Oswine died. Then she came to Legaceaster—why? No king's daughter ever leaves her father's kingdom to act as bridesmaid for her brother—and precious few ruling princes go to fetch their brides home themselves. He came so that she could come. What did she come for? To snare you, to cast runes over you to make you ask for her.'

Wulfrun had spied on Alchflaed and Peada at Legaceaster and guessed much of what had happened between them. She did not know that Alchflaed had been the one to offer marriage; she

216

could not think of any woman doing such a thing.

Peada could think of it; he was thinking of it now. He remembered how she had ridden out with him as bold and shameless as a man. How clever she was at secret words and signs. How she had bespelled his mind to make him lie with her in a tomb, just as she had made Hunwald betray his lord.

'Now she's come to your city and your heir is dead. And you'll die too—unless it suits Oswy to keep you alive, childless, as good as gelded, while she makes you do everything he tells her.'

'I'll kill her. I'll shave her head and tie her to a hurdle and drown her like that other murdering whore Eadbert caught.'

Peada moved towards the door as if he was minded to take horse and set out for Leirceaster at once. Then he stopped, looking deathly.

'They've got Cyneburg. Anything I do to that hel-runa they can avenge on my sister. And Oswy will be warned to get ready for war—Father meant to take him unawares.'

Wulfrun put her arms round him. 'Don't trouble your heart, my dearest. Most of her power's broken now that you know her and can name her as she is. She won't cast any more spells over you. You've only got to hold your hand for a few months. When our war-host goes north, we'll rescue Cyneburg then you can bring that creature to the end she deserves.'

Alchflaed was nearly at the end of her embroidery. She had made herself go on, though sometimes she could hardly see her hands for weeping. She prayed that she might make some happiness for Cyneburg and Alchfrid, though she could do nothing for herself.

A door slammed. Feet trod loudly on the stone floor. She lifted her head to see Peada staring at her. He only came to the palace now on days of state and had not been in the bower since last autumn, before she lost the child.

He smiled. Perhaps the wounds were healing. New life might come with the spring. She smiled back and he crossed the room to look at her work.

'So you've just about finished. Good. When you're not giving every moment to making presents for your brother, perhaps you'll have time for some wifely duties—making cheer for my guests, say, or making me a living child.'

She still thought she might reach him. She put her hand on his arm.

'Try not to be bitter, my dear. What happened is past. Father

217

Diuma says we must not question the judgements of God.'

'There's nothing to question. A woman who mates in a tomb—what else could she bear but a corpse?'

The injustice of the attack took Alchflaed by surprise. While she stared, he gripped her hand, driving his nails in viciously.

'Can you make a living child?'

He pushed her hand backwards over her wrist.

'When are you going to make me a living child?'

The pain and the stupid, meaningless insult coming after months of starved loneliness, rasped her patience.

'How can I make a child all by myself, you fool? Do you think I'm—'

The sheer loathing in his face stopped her short.

'*A witch.*'

He drew his sword. She shut her eyes, trying to word a prayer in her mind before she died. The blow did not fall on her; there were sounds of tearing. She opened her eyes again and stood watching while Peada slashed the great embroidery of the united kingdoms into rags.

'Now you'll have to find another wedding present. You won't be able to roll Mercia up into a bundle with Northumbria and send it to your brother. He'll have to use something else to keep the frost from his seedlings after he's put in his dibble.'

He went out. During the little time that was left he never came to her bed but she kept the name and place of a queen.

Alchflaed picked up a few tatters, moving like a sleepwalker. Then she sat down, staring at the pieces. She did not move when Nest came in, gasped, then set to tidying away every thread. She must have burned the rags; Alchflaed never saw another trace of her work. When Nest came back she was carrying a wine-cup and put it to her lady's lips. Alchflaed had not stirred; she looked so white and forlorn that even Nest felt a touch of pity. She had no particular fondness for the Queen but she detested the Mercian women as much as the Deirans at Eoforwic.

'You need a change from this place. Why don't you come away with me for a few days? You haven't been out riding for months. It'll do you good.'

'Away? Where?'

'I was going to ask your leave to go up into Peaclond for the festival. They hold games there every—Resurrectiontide—racing and wrestling and hurling boulders to find the champion.

It's the finest sport of the year! There's feasting and dancing and a great procession to Annis's holy well—' she shut her mouth quickly on her slip of the tongue.

Alchflaed had not been listening carefully, now she began to take some notice. 'A holy well—dedicated to St Anne—Our Lady's mother? Does it do cures? Does it—' her voice shook— 'can it help women conceive and carry their children to full term?'

'Indeed it can. It's power's never been known to fail. Every woman who goes there asking for help comes home with her womb quickened.'

Nest was not being malicious. She wished Alchflaed no harm; she thought the jaunt would give her lady some much-needed pleasure. If she wanted a baby she'd be given every help. And if the miracle child had the look of the ancient British race, with hair flaming red or black as a raven's wing, that would only make the event more amusing for Nest. Peada could hardly complain. Alchflaed's mother had been a Cumbrian princess, so her children could well take after the Cumbrian royal family.

Alchflaed was looking more alive than she had for months.

'How would we get there? Is it far?'

'Only two nights on the Roman roads—up the Fos Way to Weligtun, ferry over the Treanta to Northworthig, then northwest over the hills. Most of the folk who go for the games sleep out if the weather's fine, but there's a farm in an old fort on the River Noue, only three miles down the road, where I've stayed sometimes.'

'But would the King let us go? We wouldn't travel that far alone, we'd have to ask for an escort.'

'He's away to Medeshamsted again. Either he's thinking of turning monk when it's ready or he's got a woman there, he can't keep away from the place. He'll never trouble himself to ask where you are, if you don't make a big stir over it.'

Nest gave her a shrewd look; she knew, like every other woman in the court, that the King could hardly bear to hear his wife's name.

'As for an escort, let me alone for that. I know a couple of men who'll gladly come with us to get to the sports. There's nothing to stop you riding out where and when you choose—he hasn't forbidden it and you're not a prisoner.'

Alchflaed looked rather doubtful. Nest grew more urgent.

'Don't let the chance go by. It's worth the journey just to see the last race for the champions—to stand on the summit of Mam Tor

219

at sunrise and watch the young men coming along the ridge—'

She broke off, startled at the change in Alchflaed's face. She looked once again like the eager girl who had cried, 'Oh is there a fair? I love fairs!' when they first met in Eoforwic.

'What did you call it? Mam Tor? Mother Hill or The Hill of the Mother? It doesn't matter! Will you speak to those men you mentioned? Tell them to make ready to ride with us!'

She found that she was singing under her breath as she packed her saddle-bags. Joy of life had begun to flow in her again, like a frozen stream at the spring thaw. She knew whose festival she was going to honour. Christians did not hold games to celebrate the Resurrection. Folk were going to Peaclond in springtime to bid farewell to Hreda, the wild virgin of the cold winds, and to welcome Eostre the flower-bride—or rather, to rejoice as the one turned into the other.

These were hardly thoughts for a decorous convent-bred wife. But Peada now stood between her and the loving faith of her childhood, learned from Ebbe. He seemed to have taken all that was stern in the Christian discipline and turned it into a rod to beat her, without justice or mercy. During his last crude and vicious outburst he had shrunk to a spiteful child in her eyes and her respect for his commands and beliefs shrank with him.

Yet she did not feel that she was a rebel, rather that she was obeying a summons from one who had a right to command her. She touched her silver necklace, fingering the three pendants. The new moon, the full moon, the old moon: the Virgin, the Queen, the Hag. Peada had told her it was Frea's sign and that only Frea's women wore it. But for her, it was her mother's sign; she could never picture Riemmelth without it. The Mother Goddess and her mother.

Frea's great shrine was in the wild hills of Peaclond and one of those hills—the very one where Nest was taking her—was called Mam Tor. 'Mam' was 'Mother' in her mother's own tongue, it was the first word that Alchflaed had ever spoken. She smiled, stroking the full moon on her necklace, whispering 'Mam Tor— Mam —' She was going to Mam Tor to meet her mother.

That night, she dreamed she had already set out. She had lost her companions and was wandering over a waste land. Mist was rising from the rivers and patches of marshy ground, flowing towards her, reaching out wraithlike arms to clutch her, drawing veils across her eyes. Then far ahead, it thinned into a hazy light.

220

She caught a glimpse of the hill-top of her vision that day at Bebbanburh golden under the morning sun. But then the mist closed in, wrapping her in a shroud.

Meilyr came to the Lady's Bower from the southwest, riding over the moors with the spring wind and feeling as free. Since he had left Legaceaster after his visit to Penda, he had made a great circuit of the courts and strongholds in the British kingdoms of the west. He came to their lords when the summer wars were over, when they were sitting feasting with their warriors enjoying the spoils of their own hunting and raiding. Then they had long hours to listen to their bards praising their great deeds. They made boasts of what they would do when the fighting season started again.

Meilyr's task was to bind the kings by their sworn promises to join Penda in a great alliance to destroy Northumbria in the coming year. He spun a web of words and music round them. He gave them passionate speeches to fire their blood, haunting melodies to snare their souls, mysterious prophecies, memories of past greatness, hopes of vast loot. While they were listening to him, he could have led them to storm Constantinople. He knew that when he left each court, the kings would forget his words and their own vows as soon as they remembered their feud with the neighbours in the next valley.

Morfran's task was to keep the web from breaking, sending his own mind out along the threads that Meilyr had spun. In his tower in Dinas Brân, alone except for the invisible powers who came at his call, he gathered the whole strength of his will to keep the alliance together.

For the first time since his maiming he felt like a king. It was good to force princes and their warbands to do what he chose; he felt as if he had come at last into his lost inheritance. It was even better to be able to travel again himself, unseen by pitying or curious eyes, after his long years of confinement and seclusion. He rode out wherever Meilyr's strong lithe body would take him. Morfran was beginning to command the skill needed to do this, though he could not keep it up for long, as yet. The joy of his success made him feel very close to Meilyr in more senses than one. He was willing to help the boy get Riemmelth's daughter to play with, or make himself High King of Britain, if that was what he wanted.

When Meilyr was tired after a winter journey across the hills to one of the courts, and even wearier of listening to petty squabbles when he got there, his mind would sometimes go blank when it was his turn to speak. Then he could feel his uncle standing behind him, with an arm round his shoulders, whispering what to say. Sometimes it seemed that his uncle was inside him, thinking for him, moving his lips and hands into eloquence. This gave Meilyr a great sense of power at the time, but left him wearier than before and a shade resentful.

This springtime ride was a sudden idea of his own. He needed to find out for himself what was happening in the east. Above all, he wanted a chance to talk to the Elmet folk. They were British; surely they would join with their fellow-countrymen from the west when war came. But they had been conquered by Deira and the Deiran king was Penda's ally. They were just as likely to take the chance of striking at their hated overlords. Whichever side they took, their land lay across the best road north out of Mercia. They could be useful or deadly dangerous. Someone should speak to them in their own language and find out what they were thinking.

Meilyr went to Arnemeton first, the Goddess's great shrine at the hot springs. It was on his way to the east and a shrine was one of the best places to gather news and gossip. Folk came there from all ends of Britain. The Goddess loved poets and harpers, so he was sure of a welcome. Everybody would be ready to talk to him.

He found the town on the ridge above the sacred grove strangely quiet. He went down to the Nine Springs, to make his offering to Annis and hear the news. An elderly priestess took his gold brooch and filled a silver goblet with the holy blue water for him. She noticed his accent and chatted to him in British. She told him that the young folk had all gone to the Hafod, the Lady's summer bower, northeast among the hills. Olwen—Eostre, the English called her—was coming early that year. A week of sunny days and mild nights had got the earth ready for her bridal.

The priestess advised Meilyr to go there. The young goddess would be glad to see a harper come to honour her wedding feast. She would surely reward him and tell her maidens to be generous to him. Not that they would need much bidding, she added wistfully, stroking his cheek. Meilyr kissed her as if she had been a young girl and they parted kindly.

The sun was gaining strength; it gleamed on his gold and garnet arm-ring. The plait of hair underneath felt warm against his skin. He suddenly felt quite sure he would find Alchflaed at the Lady's

Bower. This was not unreasonable. Many Christians did go to the seasonal festivals. Either they still secretly followed the Old Religion or, like himself, moved lightly between the two faiths; or they told themselves that the holy wells belonged to St Anne, the mother of Our Lady. But Meilyr's belief was beyond reason. He knew that he would find her there because he had bound her to him. Her plait seemed to tighten on his wrist as if he were giving a gentle tug to her leash.

He felt laughter bubbling up inside him, warm as the water from the holy springs. He could ask nothing better than to meet Alchflaed under the trees when all the land was dancing to welcome Eostre.

The terrible anger, that had made him turn on her for a heedless word spoken at Penda's court, had soon left him. He cursed himself for the folly that had thrown away her friendship—thrown her into Peada's bed as a result—just to ease a fit of temper. This was so unlike his usual huntsman's control that he had been startled and alarmed at himself. It was almost as if some wandering demon had been using his mind and body to vent its own hate.

He shook his head and took a deep breath of moorland air to clean out the thought of hate. The fresh wind, the swaying branches of rowan trees, made him see Alchflaed as she had danced on the sands at Bebbanburh. He played with a story in which he won all the contests for the championship—the wrestling, the stone-casting, the race at dawn over the hills. He saw himself crowned King of the Wood and led in triumph to meet his bride. He saw the earth-house, the hollow hill of the dead, with its doors open, the darkness inside pricked by torchlight. He heard the singing as the spring goddess came out of the earth, crowned with flowers—and she was Alchflaed.

It was only a story to shorten his road. Nothing like that could ever happen. The Eostre-bride would be a chosen priestess from Arnemeton. He was too late for the games; he'd be lucky if he saw the final contest. Anyway, though he would have backed himself against all Britain for a race over wild country in the half-light, he had no mind to sweat and grunt in public, wrestling with Mercian louts. Still, it made a good story. He worked over it, adding details, during his twelve-mile ride across the hills.

He came down at last into a valley walled by two ridges that met at a narrow pass. In the lower lands the springtime was making a greater show than on the moors. Leaves had opened, the grass was starred with flowers.

He let his horse amble slowly down the valley along a faint track. He was taking the feel of the place in the touch of air on his skin, the scents in his nostrils. He began to hear a rushing sound that was stronger than the wind in the branches, then found his way barred by a fast-flowing stream that came swirling round under a wall of sheer cliff. Upstream the track seemed to be heading straight for the rocks. It was overhung by trees and vanished into the darkness. For the first time that bright day he felt menaced.

He turned downstream, where the track grew wider and more level and the trees did not crowd so closely. He came out into pastures and saw the track going up to a farm stockade. A man was leaning over the gate. He greeted Meilyr, glancing at his gold arm-ring and the harp-bag he carried; then asked if he would like a night's stabling for his horse and supper before his vigil. It would be an honour to his house.

Meilyr gladly took the offer and the chance it gave him to learn how they kept the festival in this valley. All poets honour the Goddess; he'd welcomed the spring every year, but each place has its own customs.

The farmer, Brid, told him that the small band of champions who had come through the vicious wrestling bouts and made the furthest casts with heavy stones had already set out for Eadale End for the last test. This was a three-mile race along the crest of the ridge back to the citadel on Mam Tor, where the victor would be crowned.

'They get their start at first light and the choice they make then is part of the test. Some set off at once and risk a crippling fall in the dusk before dawn or drowning in a clough. The ones who fancy their speed wait till the light strengthens. Sometimes they leave it too late and never make up the distance. Or they tread carelessly trying to go too fast and break their legs or their necks. No one will turn aside to help them or come looking for them later. The Goddess does what she likes with her men. Then, if they do catch up, the leaders don't give the path without a struggle. There aren't any rules—the Lady likes her king to be ruthless and yield to no man. There's wild work up on the ridge, I can tell you, before the winner comes in.'

Brid chuckled. He was a softly-spoken man; Meilyr looked at his heavy arms resting quietly on his knees. He saw the farmer as a young man, breaking a rival's back among the high rocks in the dawn twilight.

'Most of the folk will be up on Mam Tor, waiting to see the king crowned and bring him down to his wedding. I'll come with you, if you like, when you're rested after supper. I was going that way myself. Or you might like to go up to the Lady's well, round behind the crag. It's lucky to drink the water at sunrise. Sick folk stay there all night, and women who want children. It's a good place to wait if you want to watch Eostre coming. The girls are all out in the grove beyond the meadow now, making her bower — all the ones who've kept their maidenheads for tomorrow.' He grinned.

'Where will she come?'

'She's inside the Mother now, waiting.' Brid's voice sank, he stopped smiling. 'You'd have seen the passage into her womb opening in the rock if you'd gone the other way towards the cliff. Only Frea's women go inside. That's her water running by the track.'

Meilyr tried to guess where he would meet Alchflaed. He did not worry about it, because he was sure he was meant to meet her in this place. The Goddess would make it happen where and how she chose.

When he had eaten and rested, he set out in the dusk with Brid, back up the valley towards Mam Tor.

Alchflaed was feeling better just with the ride, as Nest had promised. Her spirits lifted with the road as it left the forest and climbed on to the moors. The land was like enough to her own Northumbria for her to feel at home, though there was something eerie about the strange rock edges that topped so many of the hills. They looked like misshapen giants squatting behind the crests to watch her.

The farmstead in the old fort at a loop of the river Noue was comfortable; the folk were well-to-do. All strangers were welcome at such times. They were guests of the Goddess, it was an honour to serve them. Alchflaed passed as a friend of Nest, who had clearly stayed there several times and was quite at home. The two spearmen from Leirceaster went on up the valley after a meal; they were eager to see the last day of the sports. Alchflaed did not ask what terms Nest had made with them for their protection to and from the city but they were in high good humour.

The long journey, after months of illness and keeping still, had tired her more than she knew. Nest told her to spend the rest of the day quietly if she meant to keep the vigil and offered to stay with her.

'Tomorrow's the great day. It starts at dawn when they crown the champion as King of the Wood on Mam Tor, then bring him down to meet the Goddess.'

During their journey, Nest had stopped pretending that they were going to drink the water at one of St Anne's holy wells. She could see that Alchflaed knew what she was doing, but was too wise to probe her feelings if she did not want to talk about them.

'There'll be a big crowd up there tonight, waiting for the racers to come in. The winner belongs to the Goddess, of course, but the rest are all champions of the other sports—well worth meeting!'

Nest's eyes were shining at the thought.

'Is Mam Tor where we're going?'

'If you want. Most of the women like to wait at the Lady's well. The waters are specially powerful at sunrise on the morning that Eostre comes—and it's nearer, so you can get a good place to see her. Lie down now and get some sleep. I'll wake you when it's time to set out.'

It was far in the night when Nest gently shook her shoulder. The farm folk were all astir; they had lit candles in horn lanterns but these were hardly needed. Eostre's moon was bright; it glinted on Alchflaed's necklace. She would have liked to wear her silver-embroidered dress, but that would have marked her out as alien to the country festival. She put on a plain woollen robe, green for the new spring leaves. She wanted to be a woman, not a queen, to sing and dance, to win back her joy in life that seemed to have died—in a tomb outside Legaceaster.

'A woman who mates in a tomb—what else could she bear but a corpse?'

She shuddered and pushed the memory away. She held her necklace up to the moon, making the silver shine, flooding her mind with moonlight to wash away the evil darkness.

Nest glanced at her sidelong but said nothing. She had unpacked thick hooded cloaks for the two of them. They muffled themselves up and set off with the rest of the party.

Their path went beside the river. About half a mile along, it was joined by another stream coming in from the west and they turned along this for another mile or so. Though it was dark under the trees except for the glow of the lanterns, there was nothing evil in this darkness. When the trees parted, their branches were tipped with moon-silver, the river water sparkled with it. Sometimes a pair of eyes glinted in the undergrowth; there was a chatter and flurry from a startled bird; a water-fowl called out from the rushes. Alchflaed sensed that not only mankind was ready to welcome Eostre. She could feel happiness rising all round her, like the tide that the full moon would be drawing up the coast; it was rising in herself. Her companions chatted in whispers with sudden outbreaks of laughter.

'If you want to drink from the well, the farm-wife's going up there, she'll take you,' murmured Nest who was walking by her side.

'And you?'

'I'm for Mam Tor. If I don't see you sooner, I'll meet you at the farm the day after tomorrow.'

She saw Alchflaed's eyes widen under the shadow of her hood.

'You won't lack for anything. Every farm and hut in the valley is open to all—you'll have a bite and a sup and welcome from anybody you ask. And don't fear for yourself. There's never any harm done. It's death and the curse of the Goddess for bloodshed— except maidenheads, and that's not our worry!' She laughed.

They came to a parting of the ways. Nest went on with the menfolk. The farmer's wife took Alchflaed's hand and set off with her daughters and maids up a steep track to the left. The ground was very rocky, they had to watch their steps. Suddenly Alchflaed stopped with a gasp; the path in front of her had turned into a stream, shining in the moonlight. It ran almost to her feet, then vanished as if by magic. The farmer's wife drew her aside.

'That's the stream from the Lady's well. It's just beyond us, up there on the slope.'

They climbed the hill among the birch trees and rowans. Soon they began to see groups of women sitting huddled in their cloaks. There were no lights. The farmwoman blew out their own lantern, the moon was enough. The crowd grew thicker close to the well; she could hear the spring bubbling up somewhere near. They found a clear patch of grass; her companions spread sheepskins for them to sit on. She wrapped herself tighter in her cloak and rested her back against a smooth birch stem. She lifted her face to the moon, listening to the rustling leaves and the clear song of the water, waiting for the dawn. Tomorrow, Eostre would come with the sunrise. She was going to give herself to the springtime and take whatever the Goddess chose to send her.

Brid and Meilyr climbed the steep slope to the ancient fortress on the summit of Mam Tor. Unlike the Lady's well, the hill crest was ablaze with fires and torches. Most of the crowd up here were men.

Some bold and determined girls like Nest had come up to pick their partners and keep track of them before they were all too drunk to know what they were doing. There were priestesses in a large roundhouse, getting ready to deck the champion for his crowning. They had heated a bath to wash the mire and sweat off him and infused herbs in his drink to get his strength up.

The watchers did not keep silence like the women at the well. They were passing their flasks round with ribald good wishes for the coming day. Meilyr, like everyone else, was already in a festival mood when the sky grew grey, then pale, then bright towards the northeast. There was a surge towards the eastern rampart. A loud cheer went up as the leading runner came in view—plodding, heavy-legged, bespattered and scratched but still going strongly and well ahead of his nearest rival. He was greeted by the priestesses and disappeared into the roundhouse.

There were more drinks to celebrate. The other runners staggered in one by one to back-slapping sympathy and a helping from as many flasks as they chose. By the time the King came out, his court was boisterous. He had been crowned with oak twigs bound into a wreath of rushes. From the crown hung streamers of green cloth on which sprays of leaves had been tied. He looked like a walking bush; his head was hidden but as he marched the fronds swung aside to show his naked limbs.

The priestesses escorted him, the other champions marched behind, then everyone else followed in a singing, shouting procession. When they came down among the trees, they began to pull young branches that they waved over their heads like banners. By the time they reached the track that led to the Mother's Womb, it looked as if the woods themselves were marching down the valley.

Alchflaed was standing among the trees, where the stream ran out into the meadow. She was as still as a young birch tree herself. Among the shadows in her green gown she could hardly be seen. If she could have felt anything, it would have been despair.

She had risen as soon as it was dawn and helped the other women to find more flowers: bluebells, primroses, windflowers, daisies, to deck the well. It was hung with fresh garlands every day of the sports. She had taken some of the blossoms to crown herself and put a posy in her bosom, wondering whose hands would pick those flowers. At sunrise, she had drunk the holy

228

water, pure and cold as ice, that had left her body glowing.

With the other women she had gone down from the well and followed a track leading to a great cleft in the sheer rock wall that towered over the trees. She had heard the singing and saw Eostre come out into the sunlight, crowned with spring flowers, masked and veiled with flower-decked green streamers that parted with the breeze to show a slender white body and tresses of fair hair.

She had joined the procession that formed behind the young goddess and the green-clad priestesses. She watched the Oak King come marching down the valley at the head of his army of waving branches. The bride was joined to the groom, spring came to the woodlands. The couple went together into the summer house that had been built for them overnight out of willow wands and birch twigs, hung with garlands.

Alchflaed had joined hands and danced in one of the circles that went round and round the bower, as light-footed as anyone there. When the circles linked into a chain and headed for the woods, when the chain broke up and its links scattered, she glided away alone into the silence. She was no more alone then than she had been all during the Lady's wedding.

She had watched but she had not become part of the rejoicing. The blessing had not touched her, though she had seen nothing that was not lovely and innocent in her eyes. She envied the girls she heard laughing under the trees, giving themselves to the springtime in the arms of the first man who caught them. She could not take a step to join them; she was outside the paradise garden and could not find the way back. Joy was dead; desire was dead. If a man took her now he would be mating with a corpse.

'All alone, sweetheart?'

A big young man with a thatch of wiry reddish hair had come up to her. He grinned at her, slapping his arm across her shoulders to swing her round. Then he saw the track of tears on her face and touched her cheek with rough kindness.

'Eh, lass! It's not as bad as that! I'm here to help you.' He began to unfasten the top of her gown to pull it off her shoulders and saw her necklace. 'One of the Lady's bower-women all by herself on Eostre's day! We can't have that!'

He tugged at the gown. Alchflaed's hands came up to push him away; her body said *No* to a cold mating without wish or pleasure. The man chuckled good-humouredly.

'Want a bit of a wrestle first to work up a heat? Well, I didn't have much luck yesterday but I think I can win this bout.'

He pushed his right leg forward, flung his arm round her and tossed her over his hip in a neat cross-buttock but caught her again before she landed on her head. He threw her on the soft turf and flung himself on top of her, pushing with his knee to get her legs apart and thrusting his tongue into her gasping mouth. She bit it hard; as he jerked away she scrambled up, kicking him viciously in the groin.

She turned to run and would have got away while he was twisting in pain but she rushed into a group of revellers. They caught her, laughing, thinking she was running away in play and swung her round to push her back on to her lover; then stopped in amazement when they saw the state he was in. He had put his hand to his mouth; he could hardly speak but he jabbed his blood-stained fingers towards her.

'Get her! She's hel-runing—she's cursed the spring!'

For a moment they recoiled, staring from the blood to Alchflaed; then turned on her like farm dogs on a cornered vixen. They clutched her hair and dragged her head back, she felt her breasts being clawed, her arms were pulled wide as they tried to tear her body apart. There were howls of 'Hel-runa! Kill! Kill!' but her own voice went up over them in scream after scream of mindless terror. Then the tearing agony and the howling stopped; she screamed again once and fell silent.

A minstrel is at home anywhere. Meilyr was sitting on the sunlit grass with a cluster of pretty girls round him, wheedling him for a song. It wasn't the time or the place for great bardic poetry; he made dancing little scraps of melody for them with words as light as spring leaves. His listeners caught them up and sang along with him. Centuries later, after all the changes that time and war can bring, they were still being sung:

> 'Blow, northern wind,
> Send thou me my sweeting,
> Blow northern wind,
> Blow, blow, blow.'

A few of the girls linked hands and began to dance. Meilyr was still half-expecting to see Alchflaed's figure stepping lightly among them. The spring was getting into his blood, though. Any girl with primroses in her breast was Olwen or Blodeuedd now.

Other folk came to join in, drawn by the harp music and singing. Soon there were two lines, men facing women, advancing

230

to breast each other, stepping back, crossing and swinging as they sang against each other:

> 'Maiden in the moor lay—
> In the moor lay,
> Seven nights full—
> Seven nights full.
> Maiden in the moor lay
> In the moor lay
> Seven nights full and a day.
>
> Well was her bower.
> What was her bower?
> The red rose and the—
> The red rose and the—
> Well was her bower.
> What was her bower?
> The red rose and the lily flower.'

Someone picked up the tune with a pipe and tabor so Meilyr joined in the dance. The steps got faster, the swinging wilder. The piper's breath gave out; the dance went on for a while then broke up and became catch as catch can among the bushes.

After some lively turns and changing partners, Meilyr found himself with a young woman who had hair like black silk and a plump supple body. She was well-bred, for her hands were soft and she knew what to do with them; she had more tricks than a churl's daughter could learn in a farmstead. She was one of his own people, too, which was pleasant; when they were resting, he could whisper his finest love-talk to her while her mouth and fingers were gently teasing him back to more delight.

You cannot do better than the best. Meilyr cheerfully cast anchor in her bay and stayed with her for the rest of the festival. Once, he lifted his head at an outburst of wild screaming deeper in the woods. Churls got rough when they played. He was glad when it stopped; he settled back happily on his girl's smooth breasts.

A priestess had pushed her way through the riot and was standing over Alchflaed's body.

'How dare you!' She looked round at their furious, terrified faces. 'Who started this? You'll bring the Goddess's curse down on you.'

231

'She's already brought it down.'

The red-haired man had risen to his knees. 'She refused—and she a priestess of the Goddess! She's drunk my blood and—oh, Frea!' he pressed his hands to his crotch, 'she's crippled me!'

The crowd surged towards Alchflaed; the priestess said, 'Stand back!' and they stopped. She stared down at Alchflaed with cold loathing, noting the silver moons at the torn neck of her gown. Then she looked at Alchflaed's victim.

'Don't worry. You meant no ill and you'll take no ill. I'll tend you myself. But first we'll get this,' she touched Alchflaed with her foot, 'out of the light of the sun.'

'Shouldn't she die, lady?'

'Of course. But Eostre's day must not be polluted with blood. She'll go to the Mother.'

A cloak was bundled over Alchflaed's head and shoulders, trussed round her with a couple of leather belts. Hands avoided touching her flesh. Blind and unable to protect herself, she was half-dragged, half-carried along a steep rocky path, stumbling, stubbing her toes, wrenching her ankles. She was picked up, then thrown down on to planks that rocked under her; they had put her in a boat. She heard splashing as it moved over the water. A hand was pressed hard on the back of her skull, keeping her from raising her head. She had a sense that she was passing under the earth.

Now she was tormented by a dread that was worse even than the savagery she had seen on the faces of the crowd who mobbed her. She was being taken living into Hel's kingdom. She would not meet her death at human hands—would she even be able to die fully in all eternity?

She began to hear a dry hoarse voice whispering to her, but it did not seem to be any of her captors'; she could hear it muttering inside her skull and it would not be quiet:

'May they be trapped into living death. May they die alone in terror. May their names be blotted out from memory and may their souls be eaten—'

The dark nightmare went on. She was dragged out of the boat again. She was brushed by rain, yet she was not in the open air. Sometimes she seemed to be in vast echoing spaces, sometimes rocks pressed close. Now the river seemed to run beside her path; now it sounded far below. Once she fell over a rock; one of her feet went down into empty space. She was pulled back; a woman's cold voice said, 'Watch her. Lady Freawynn wants her alive.'

At last the track became steps that went round and round until she was dizzy; then the ground levelled, she was thrown down and the cloak was pulled off, but for a few moments she was afraid to see where she was.

Women's voices spoke against her without anger or pity.

'She's a sorceress, come to cast hel-runes to blight the spring.'

'She took our shape but she refused to give a man the gift of the Goddess.'

'She tore his flesh and drank his blood.'

Alchflaed opened her eyes and almost cried out with the pain of light after long darkness. She was in a hall of amber and jewels. Strange misshapen pillars of amber were all around her, some hanging from the roof, some rising from the floor to meet them, all glowing with the light of many candles and braziers that gilded and warmed the air. Behind them the walls glittered in hues of blue, green and purple. Set on the floor and on ledges of rock were pitchers full of flowers and branches. The source of sunlight and springtime seemed to be here, in the heart of the cold rocks.

Her accusers were standing round her, girls in green robes and silver necklaces. There seemed to be at least a dozen of them, more than enough to kill her in any way they chose. They were not looking at her; perhaps they felt that her sight was as much a pollution as her touch. She looked to where their gaze was fixed, at a woman sitting on a couch covered with sheepskins. The Lady Freawynn, who wanted her alive. She too wore a plain green robe; she was crowned with a silver circlet bearing the same full moon between horned crescents that hung from Alchflaed's necklace. She was neither old nor young but very beautiful with pale gold hair and golden-brown eyes that shone in the candlelight. The eyes were fixed on Alchflaed's with a look of scorn and disgust.

'So, you're one of the servants of untimely death. You feed your masters on blighted crops and diseased cattle. You glut your lust with sterile marriages, on young wives dead in childbirth, on babes miscarried before their time—'

Alchflaed cried out at that, in the words of her childhood's faith.

'No, by the Mother of Christ! That's not true!'

Freawynn raised her eyebrows; her scorn seemed to deepen.

'A Christian. Then why did you come here? To insult us? To have a free helping of the pleasure your own priests call sin—and enjoy it all the more because you think it's sin? To spite a husband? Or have a wider pick of lovers? And where did you steal that?' She pointed to Alchflaed's necklace.

Alchfaed got to her feet. She looked steadily at Freawynn.

'I didn't come here to mock or spoil your rites. If I've broken your law you can kill me but I meant no evil to you.'

'We don't kill anybody. The Mother gives life, the Mother takes it away when she chooses. Turn round and go to the other side of the cave.'

She obeyed. The circle of priestesses parted to let her through. She came to the edge of a sheer drop. Far below she heard the river rushing in the darkness. From the edge where she stood, a narrow spine of rock, sharp and jagged, arched over the abyss to the other side which she could just dimly make out. The arch did not reach the opposite edge; it sloped down and joined the rock face some feet below it, about the height of a man. Anyone trying to get from the arch would have to stand, balance, try to grip the rock and pull himself up by the strength of his arms and such holds as he could find.

'The Sword-Bridge.' Freawynn had come to her shoulder. 'Everyone given to the Mother's judgement sets out to cross it. If she judges life, she takes them to the other side and they go down the main passage and out through the Arch of Birth. If she judges death they fall, and she pisses them out with her water.'

'Very well. I'm ready.'

Freawynn looked into her eyes to see if this was bravado.

'You're so sure of your life?'

'I'm dead. I died months ago.'

Freawynn looked at her again. Then she signed to her attendants to withdraw. They seemed to vanish into the rocks. She took Alchflaed's hand and led her back to the couch.

'Sit down. Now tell me where you got that necklace and why you came here.'

'It was my mother's. She worshipped the Goddess.'

Freawynn looked at her suspiciously. 'Your mother was a priestess—had you reared as a Christian and then gave you that? Her name?'

'Riemmelth of Cumbria. She always wore it while she lived, that's how I knew what faith she held. My father had me brought up in a convent. I found her necklace among her jewels after her death and so I wear it for her sake. That's why I came here—I hoped—I must have been mad but I wanted to ask her help—I hoped I'd get some message from her.'

234

Freawynn shook her head; her eyes were sad though she was smiling.

'Your mother was never one of us—except so far as every woman is, whether she knows it or not. She was a Christian but we helped her. That necklace belonged to a kinswoman of hers, Arianrhod, who was a priestess at Arnemeton. I knew her when I was a girl; she was a very great woman, full of the Goddess. Your mother was fleeing from Penda, after a terrible raid in the north. We hid her and helped her to get away and Arianrhod offered—a sacrifice, for her safe return to her husband. The necklace was a token between them.'

Alchflaed bowed her head. She unclasped the necklace and held it out to Freawynn without looking at her.

'You don't have to do that. It was a love-token.'

'To my mother. Take it back where it belongs. It doesn't belong to me, any more than I belong here. I don't belong anywhere.'

'You came to find your mother. The Mother of all of us is here. What help were you looking for?'

'I married against my father's will. I'd meant to be a peace-weaver, to stop the war that's coming between Northumbria and Mercia. But I lost my baby and my husband's turned against me. My father's given me up. Soon my people will be put to the sword. I came here to get new life from the spring, to get power from Eostre to save other lives. I wanted to be part of the worship. I would have given myself to that man but I couldn't. Then I knew I was dead.'

'My poor child. Do you believe that roses are dead at Midwinter, because they have no leaves and last year's flowers are withered on their stems? Spring never comes back at quite the same time every year or every life.'

Freawynn stood up, gently pushing her back on to the sheepskins.

'You're in the Mother's Womb. Lie and rest for a while before you go back to life.'

She brought mead spiced with herbs, and honey cakes. She served Alchflaed then sat quietly beside her, looking into the darkness that lay beyond the lights. Time paused. Alchflaed could feel her pain going to sleep; it was still there inside her but it would not trouble her for some time.

At last Freawynn looked at her and smiled. 'Everyone who comes to visit the Mother gets a gift. You couldn't take what we offer on Eostre's day; you're not ready for it yet. So I'm going to give you something else. Stand up and look at the Sword-Bridge.'

Wondering, she did as she was told.

'Now, take a line from it to the cave wall behind us.'

She looked between the gleaming amber pillars to the glittering walls beyond. There were many patches of shadow; some were thrown by the pillars, some were crevices in the rock. When she followed her line, she found that what seemed to be a crevice was really a large opening hidden by an outcrop of rock. It led into a tunnel.

Freawynn had put on a green cloak and picked a flowering twig of blackthorn from one of the pitchers. She came to stand facing Alchflaed.

'Look at me. I'm going to give you a number—nine. Three is the number of the Goddess—Maiden, Harlot and Hag. Nine is three times three.'

She tapped Alchflaed's right shoulder. 'Remember:

> 'Thrice to thine and thrice to mine
> 'And thrice again to make up nine.'

Now say it back to me.'

'Thrice to thine and—'

'No. Say it *back* to me.'

She was puzzled for a second. 'Oh I see.

> 'Thrice to mine and thrice to thine
> And thrice again to make up nine.'

'That's right.' Freawynn picked up a lantern. She stood at Alchflaed's left shoulder and pointed her into the tunnel with the blackthorn sprig.

'Now I want you to count the third opening on your right.'

Alchflaed did so and they turned into another tunnel.

'Now the third right again. No, the third, that's the fourth. If you went down there you'd never be seen again. Come back and look more closely. Yes, that little crack—only it isn't little when you look behind it. Now the third right again and take care this time. That's right.'

The path was rising steeply now. Freawynn said, 'Next time, it's the third to the left—'Thrice to mine'—and then three more on your side. Don't lose count and don't let your eyes or your mind wander for a second or you'll be lost.'

In spite of all her care, she needed two more checks and warnings or she would have passed openings that seemed to be no more than shadows or marks on the rock. Sometimes the openings were only a few steps apart in deeply scored and jutting slabs; sometimes there were long passages between them. Light began to filter down from cracks in the rock above them. At the ninth turn, Freawynn blew out her lantern and showed her a dry niche in the rock where another lantern and some candles were laid ready. They were now in a cave with a narrow mouth; stooping, they came out into the open air. It was late afternoon; the grass was golden in the sunlight. In front of them a long ridge lifted to a hill that was scarred with a landslip and crowned with ramparts.

'Mam Tor. Look back where we've come from.'

The slope behind them was pocked with dips and holes. The one leading to their cave looked just like the others; after turning and taking a few steps away it would be hard to remember which it was.

'Take a line from Mam Tor and draw it on your memory. I've trusted you with a secret that only the priestesses know. Everyone else thinks that the Arch of Birth is the only way in and out. If you should need shelter and all else has failed you, come back here. Don't do it except as a last resort. It's not a path to be taken lightly and you'll be on your own. Remember, it's the other way round going in.'

She tapped Alchflaed's left shoulder. 'Think of me at your side and say "*Thrice to thine*" —'

She wrapped her green cloak round Alchflaed and handed her the sprig of blackthorn.

'No one will stop you or question you while you're carrying that. Fare you well; may you always find light on your path.'

Alchflaed flung her arms round the priestess and kissed her. 'May the Mother of Christ bless you for your kindness to me.'

Freawynn bowed her head in grave acceptance of the prayer.

'Thank you, daughter.'

CHAPTER
22

Alchflaed and Nest asked each other no questions how they had passed their time at the Lady's Bower. For all the shock and terror she had suffered there, Alchflaed was the better for it, as Nest had promised. This was just as well, as her fate looked to be stormy.

In early summer Penda suddenly accused Oswy of plotting war against Mercia and demanded that he should clear himself by sending his son as a hostage. This caught Oswy in a trap. If he refused, Penda would attack him at once and he was not ready yet to face the huge forces that Penda could bring against him when he called on all his allies and under-kings to join him.

If he sent Alchfrid, Cumbria would be out of the war. Penda would have the right to kill him if Cumbrian troops fought. Yet without Cumbria, Oswy could not hope to hold his own borders. In any case, Alchfrid was a prince ruling in his own right and in the right of his mother's kin. Even if Oswy had wanted to, he could not send his son to Mercia without his own consent, unless he seized him and sent him as a captive. If he did that, Penda would set him free at once and Cumbria would be Mercia's newest ally.

Alchfrid had already come east to discuss their plans in Oswy's estate At-Wall, when the Mercian demand arrived. Oswy heard it in silence, then gave orders for the envoys to be entertained courteously after their long journey. He and his son withdrew to the Queen's bower to talk in secret. Alchfrid's face was as still as a statue's.

Eanfled listened wide-eyed as Oswy told her what had happened.

'Is that all Penda asked?'

Oswy raised his eyebrows.

'Yes, my lady. Just that I should send my son as a hostage. He didn't ask for you as well.'

'He didn't give his name or title? Prince Alchfrid? Prince of Cumbria? Atheling of Bernicia?'

'He doesn't have to remind me, I know who Alchfrid is.'

'But if Penda didn't name him—you have another son.'

Eanfled rose and stood over Ecgfrid's cradle. When he had been washed and freshly swaddled and well-fed at his wet-nurse's ample breasts, she liked to have him with her in her bower till he woke up again. She looked very beautiful, seated over her embroidery or her Psalter, smiling down from time to time at her sleeping child's face.

Alchfrid cried out in horror. 'I could never let you do that for me.'

'And yet you expect me to let you go and die for me.'

Eanfled gave him a proud yet tender smile, the look of a heroic Roman matron about to sacrifice herself for her land and her duty.

'I am the Queen of Deira. I cannot stand beside you and the King when you go out to battle against the heathen. At least let me give my flesh and blood for you—my dearest flesh and my heart's blood.'

She put her hand on the bosom of her blue gown and looked soulfully at the roof-beams. So must St Perpetua have looked when they came to take her to the arena.

'I do it gladly.'

She spoke the truth. Time had stood still for her during her quiet exile in her mother's convent. She had been as lovely at twenty-five as at fifteen. Time had not stood still in Bernicia. She was twenty-eight, with a lusty son. She had not suckled him and now she was with child again, conceived at the Christmas revels. When she looked in her mirror now she was worried. If Oswy managed to stave off trouble for a year or two more, what would become of the beautiful wronged princess when she was an old woman of thirty with a pack of little half-brothers and sisters for Alchfrid?

But if her son died now, slaughtered by the evil heathen king in his fury at the trick Oswy had played on him—if he then went on to slaughter Oswy—if she miscarried from shock and grief—then she and Alchfrid could come together to save their kingdoms and the Christian faith. There was, unluckily, Cyneburg; but Alchfrid would surely repudiate her in disgust at her father's brutalities—or perhaps the Cumbrian people would rise and kill her—

Eanfled looked at these pleasing visions while Alchfrid looked at her as if she were a vision herself.

Oswy said, 'What a good idea!'

Alchfrid turned on him. 'You'd send a babe still at the breast to be slaughtered—'

'Penda won't lay a finger on him.'

'You think he couldn't be so cruel?'

'He could perfectly well be so cruel. But he'd never willingly be

239

such a laughing-stock. It'll be hard enough for him not to look a fool when the prince arrives with his escort. The child'll need plenty of wet-nurses in case some of them go dry, and they'll all need attendants, as they mustn't have any toil or worry that could upset their milk. And a large bodyguard to keep him safe on the way — sturdy old men, well beyond the age of war-service. And Penda will have to keep them all in comfort. He will too — he's not a mean man. I wish I could be there to see it.'

He kissed Eanfled's cheek. 'Thank you, my lady. You're better than a witan to me.'

Alchfrid kissed Eanfled's hand, kneeling as if he were at a shrine.

The Mercian envoys were told that Oswy would meet Penda's demands and send his son as a hostage. Prince Alchfrid set off at once for Cumbria to settle his affairs.

Oswy won a little more time. When his son's escort crawled into Tomeworthig at last, it was July. Spring had come early that year; folk were harvesting in the south.

Penda kept silence as his red-faced, yelling hostage was presented to him. He looked at the escort of strapping big-breasted nurses and aged spearmen. Then he said, 'Take him to Queen Cynwise. Tell her to deal with him and see his folk are fed and housed.'

He waited till his hall was quiet again and cleared of all except his councillors.

'Oswy is a clever man. I'm glad I've never had to play against him at a board game. But his time for playing is over. The next time I send, it will be to tell him to come here and lay his hands and head on my knee and take me for his overlord. If I don't have his oath, I'll take his lands and his life.'

When the news came to Leirceaster, Peada came to the peacock room just for once so that he could tell his wife himself and watch her face.

'My mother wondered that Oswy could set so little store on his own flesh and blood.' He laughed unpleasantly. 'I could have told her Oswy's ready to use his spawn in every foul way that suits him — it's not the first time, is it?'

'If using a man's son as a hostage is foul, what about the one who demands it?'

Peada had come to insult his wife not to argue with her. He was still rather scared of her when she was in the same room with him—anyway, a witch could twist words to mean anything.

'Your father thinks he can wriggle out of trouble again by putting a sucking child in his place, but we're going to make an end. He'll be punished for this.'

'Punished for what?'

Alchflaed put the question to Peada's retreating back; she went on trying to answer it herself. Punished for keeping his people free and using all the quickness of his mind to do so?

Every time she saw Nest, so lovely and gifted, not ill-disposed, she thought how the girl had coldly prostituted herself to an old man she neither liked nor respected. How helpless she had been as soon as her keeper died. How Peada would have had her put out like an unwanted cat.

'*Elmet folk count for nothing, they were conquered long ago.*'

She remembered Nest's look while she described the bleak prison that life became for the folk of a defeated kingdom. It wasn't the hardness of life; it was the loss of hope and self-respect, being treated as lower till you came to believe you were lower; then tried to make up for it by smiles and fawning or by empty boasts. Why should people want to beat down their fellow-men, children of one Father, brothers in Christ whether they knew it or not?

She thought of King Penda and tried to feel the joy that came to him when he looked down at an enemy crouching at his feet. She could not imagine it. She could only think of him as she had known him in Legaceaster galloping his little son Wulfhere on his knee; roaring with laughter when she baited Peada, calling, 'Keep at him, girl! Give it to him with your sword!' offering the hospitality of his court with blazing generosity.

She had been expecting to meet a monster like Grendel. That was how folk in the north still saw Penda. From what Peada said, Mercians saw Oswy as a vicious cowardly traitor ready for any foulness. *No one has ever put our case to them*, she thought. *There was only one person who could do so.*

This is why I came to Mercia. It's no good trying to speak to Peada. He won't listen to me, I can't reach him any more. Anyway, he isn't the war-leader. Penda is the only one who can stop this war, I'll go and face him. He may kill me. Likely he will. But at least I'll have spoken—for all the nameless folk, for Cyneburg and her unborn child, for myself. That's better than waiting to be destroyed like a blind puppy taken out for drowning.

Peada was riding far and wide, making sure that his kingdom

was ready for war. No one tried to stop her leaving Leirceaster and she was not hindered or threatened on her way to Tomeworthig. It was unthinkable to Mercians that she would go there without being sent for. Her eager, almost light-hearted manner showed that she was not afraid of what might happen when she got there. Penda must be in a good humour with her, whatever he felt towards her father. When she got to Tomeworthig she simply told the gate-warden, 'King Penda's daughter-in-law has come to see him.'

Penda was in his hall in council with his ealdormen. He was surprised to hear the name of his visitor but nodded his consent for her to come in.

It was high summer; the light was golden on Alchflaed as she came through the high doorway. She knew she might be turning her back on the sun for the last time and lifted her head to welcome her fate like a king's daughter. There was silence in the hall; the stern warriors grouped round the high seat turned their heads to watch her coming.

Looking at her, slight as a boy in her horseman's leathers, walking calmly up to her enemies, Penda suddenly thought of his own great ancestor. Angeln had been in deadly danger, threatened by the powerful Swabians, its war-host out-numbered and leaderless, its king old and blind. Prince Offa, a boy untried in battle, had called on the Swabian king to meet him at the River Eider to fight for Angeln's freedom. With proud generosity, because the last Swabian king had been unfairly killed by two Anglians, he had told his enemy to bring another champion with him, vowing to fight both at once.

Offa must have looked like this girl to the eyes of the hardened fighters waiting for him on the banks of the Eider. He'd always said she was a fine girl; he wondered how Oswy had managed to get her.

'Well, daughter-in-law, have you got anything to say to me from Oswy?' If Oswy could send his baby son as a hostage, he could send his daughter to be his mouthpiece and take the brunt of any anger that his message might rouse.

'No. I've got several things to say to you from myself.'

'Indeed? Then I'll hear them.' He turned to his witan. 'These are family matters. Give us leave, lords.'

She followed him into the chamber behind the hall. He sat down and pointed to a stool but she remained standing.

'If you've come to ask for a favour just for yourself, I'll grant—'

242

'I've come to ask you why you want to destroy me and my family.'

'I'm not going to destroy you. And your father can have peace and my protection the moment he admits my overlordship. He only has to take the oath to be my man and pay me tribute.'

'What right have you to claim overlordship? My father's Woden-born, like you.'

'I claim overlordship because I'm his overlord. I'm descended from Offa of Angeln. I rule the Saxons by conquest; the Welsh are my allies but I claim the heart's loyalty and obedience of every man of English blood. Offa won that on the banks of the Eider.'

'And is that how you show your pride in your English blood — by wanting to make other Englishmen grovel to you? Offa fought for our freedom.'

Penda scowled at her, clenching his fist.

'Be careful what you say.'

'What have I got to be careful of? I know I'm standing on the edge of death. But while I'm standing here I can still ask you why a man of your power should be afraid to think he's got equals?'

She thought that would be the last word she ever said to Penda, but he looked at her with a gleam of kindly amusement.

'By Woden, you've got courage! My answer is that there can only be one Bretwalda. What sort of kingdom would you have when the king was afraid to use his power and couldn't make his orders obeyed? It wouldn't be the end of war, as you seem to think. You'd have a bloodbath every day.'

'What sort of kingdom will you have when the bravest are dead?' She stepped close to him and clasped his hand. 'I'm not just pleading for my father, or for myself, though my marriage has been wrecked by your quarrel. What about Cyneburg — what will happen to her child when you've killed its father? What about the folk whose hearts' loyalty you claim? The fine young men turned to dead flesh, their families burned in their huts, or starving because their farms are untended, or breaking their hearts in slavery? Is that what you mean by *overlordship*?'

'No, that isn't what I mean.'

Her eyes shone. 'Then you'll make peace with my father?'

'No. There can only be one Bretwalda. But I'll give him the same choice that Offa gave the king of the Swabians. Let him find a champion — I'll give him time, he can send to the Picts, the Irish, the Franks, wherever he likes. Let them come down to the marches of Deira. I'll meet them at one of the river crossings there to fight the pair of them for the Bretwaldaship. Nobody else need lose a single drop of blood. The nobles must swear beforehand to take the winner as king, whichever he is.'

Ten years ago, even five, there would have been no doubt which he would be, even if the odds had been five to one. But Penda was ageing; his old leg wound was slowing him more as time passed; he had put on flesh. Oswy was a skilled swordsman and there was no chance that he would imitate Penda's heroic generosity when the safety of his kingdom was at stake. Oswy would hire the most powerful champion in the world, if he had to send to Constantinople to get him.

Looking distressfully at Penda's face, she could see he knew all this as well as she did. The old warrior was challenging death, and defeat which would wound his spirit worse than death. She felt a great surge of admiration for him, almost love. She wanted to tell him so, to say that even defeated he would still be the greatest man in England. She knew that she must not say this. To speak of his defeat to his face would make it real, would sound as if she were already looking at him struck down and lying shamed at his victor's feet.

Penda patted her cheek. 'You've done all you can, lass. Go to the Queen now and let her tend you, you'll be tired. You're a good little warrior; you can tell your sons you fought Penda to a draw.'

She wanted to give him something, to meet his generosity with generosity of her own. Now his last words told her what to say. She could give him the admission of her own family's defeat at his hands and use it to show him that defeat and shame could never touch him, whatever happened in battle.

'Let my father know your offer. He must take his chance or be disgraced before all England. But honourable defeat is no disgrace. It's honour to both sides, so the wounds don't fester. When you sacked our palace at Gefrin, my mother couldn't save it for all her courage but she fought her way out and won her freedom. Defeat comes and goes but our hearts stay the same.'

She kissed his hand and went out smiling. Penda heard her running lightly down the hall. He made no move to follow her or to call his councillors to hear what had passed.

He was wrestling to make sense of what she had just said. The struggle was painful; he had to face memories that made him fearful and ashamed. Shame and fear were deadly enemies to Penda.

He had taken the Bernician palace at Gefrin and burned it with

244

all its folk. A woman had fought him, a waelcyrige in warrior's armour, but she had not fought her way out. He had taken her body; then see that she belonged to Frea by the silver token she wore. That scared him; also her courage and beauty had drawn him more than any woman he had ever known. He had offered to marry her and make her his queen, but she had killed herself on the way back to Mercia, in the forest beyond the River Don. He had found her dead, her white face smiling from its cloud of black hair. He still saw it, whenever the full moon was bright enough to cast a shadow.

A year later he had cornered Oswy when he was in flight, as usual. It was the only time he had ever come within sword's reach of that wary fox. His queen had been with him, a white-faced, black-haired woman so like the lost priestess that he had thought she was the walking dead. Perhaps that had shaken him, so that he fell victim to Oswy's trick that had left him lame for life. Queen Riemmelth had called the priestess her kinswoman and accused him of raping her cousin. She had watched, while Oswy shammed dead then struck the blow which nearly gelded him and set Frea's mark on him. He'd heard her laughing like a witch when the blade went into his flesh. She must have put a curse on him—or the priestess had come back and used her body to do it.

There had certainly been two women; the priestess had been truly dead. He'd found the body and kept watch over it for four days till her sisters came and carried her back to Frea's shrine. Riemmelth had lived for years after that. But if Riemmelth had been the woman he fought at Gefrin—if the priestess had taken her place on the road back to Mercia and offered herself as a sacrifice for her kinwoman's escape—then Riemmelth was the woman he had lain with.

And if that was so, the girl who had just faced him could be his own get.

You could see it if you knew what you were looking for: the brown hair, the frank eyes and smile, something of Cyneburg. The idea warmed him at first; she was a fine girl, he'd always wondered how Oswy could have got her. And it was a deep, sweet satisfaction to know that he'd had Oswy's proud woman down and got into her. How the pair of them must have writhed at the memory all these years, while they were bringing up his bastard and having to keep it secret!

He was not troubled by the thought that Alchflaed had mated with her half-brother. They were both Woden-born. It had happened more than once in the royal lines that a brother had come to a sister to get an heir who would have the god-power twice over. The greatest hero of all, Sigemund the Waelsing, had lain with his sister to make the son who would avenge his slaughtered kin. It would be just like Oswy to try to get Offa's blood into his House twice over. If ever a man needed Woden's help at this moment—

Penda chuckled, then stopped. That made no sense. For Oswy to win the prize of a Sacred Marriage, the brother and sister would have to be Alchfrid and Cyneburg. Alchflaed's children would belong to Mercia—why would Oswy make him such a priceless gift?

And anyway, Oswy was a Christian, he wouldn't think it a priceless gift. Christians had to ask leave of their High Priest before they could even marry a cousin. They had been forbidden the honourable and sensible custom of marrying a stepmother on pain of a terrible curse. A brother lying with his sister was the vilest sin in their eyes. Yet Oswy had sent the girl to her father's court to rouse her brother's lust. Oswy had insisted that the boy turned Christian and married by Christian rites.

Penda was not stupid. In war and statecraft he was quick-minded and not easily deceived. But he had always been so strong, both in body and in the power of his kingdom, that he had never been forced to scheme and dodge his way out of traps. He had the deepest scorn for those who were forced to, like Oswy. When Penda did stoop to notice the activities of such vermin, he gave them credit for more cunning and ill-will than they truly had. Instead of desperate juggling to stave off dangers as they came, he saw plots of unspeakable complexity and long-thought-out betrayals.

He was getting old; he would die soon, in battle he hoped. Peada was his heir. He loved the boy and was proud of him. He was brave, a skilled fighter, generous and good humoured with his war-band, liked by men and women. But he was not great. Penda knew that. Perhaps the sapling had been too much over-shadowed by the huge oak tree. It had not seemed to matter; Mercia was the most powerful kingdom in England; Peada was quite capable of holding what his father left him.

But if Oswy managed to stave off defeat till he died and then revealed that Peada's marriage was accursed—that any children he had by Alchflaed were worse than bastards because they were under a curse also and all their seed—if they hounded him into a monastery, very likely, as he seemed to be under the will of those priests Oswy sent him—who would take Mercia then? His other sons were children.

Alchfrid would take Mercia. He would kill the other boys and give the kingdom to the children he got on Cyneburg. So the blood of Oswy and Riemmelth would rule in his land and the House of Offa of Angeln would be no more. What a revenge for the wrong he had done, all unknowing, to Oswy's woman!

Oswy had planned it, of course, with the same board-gaming skill as he had removed his cousin Oswine. He had sent the girl to bewitch her brother, as she had just bewitched him into promising single combat against impossible odds—

Penda smashed his fist against the table top and roared for a servant.

'Bring that girl back here!'

'She's gone, lord. She asked if her horse was baited and when she found he was, she mounted and rode off the way she came.'

The man looked anxious. 'There didn't seem any reason to stop her but we can go after her, or have her sent back from Leirceaster.'

'No matter.'

Penda had second thoughts. Let her believe she had bewitched him; it would keep her quiet. He'd rather she lived until she had seen what he did to the rest of her kin.

'If any of my lords have left the hall, send for them to come back. The council was broken off before I'd finished.'

When the witan had gathered again he took his place on the high seat.

'Summon the war-host. Send my orders to all my subject kings to come to me with their armed men. And take my greetings to my allies in Wales. Tell them I'm marching to Northumbria and I'd welcome their company if they'd like to enjoy my hospitality. We'll meet at Doneceaster.'

The councillors glanced at each other. The oldest thane put their thoughts into words.

'It will take some time to gather the war-host, lord. It's Lammas, the folk are all well into the harvest.'

'Let them finish it. I'll need a lot of corn to feed my armies.'

'But then it will be Haligmonath.'

'Good. We can thank the gods for the harvest and ask their help to clean up this Christian filth.'

His councillors were looking worried.

'But then it will be Winterfylleth.'

247

'Good. I'll need the first full moon of winter to light my armies to the trysting place. Some of them have a long way to come.'

The spokesman licked his lips.

'But then it will be—' He stopped.

'Blotmonath. What better time than the month of Blood Sacrifice?' Penda smiled. 'I'm giving that land to Woden. It's going under the spear. I'll not leave one of that blood alive.'

CHAPTER
23

More warriors came to Leirceaster for weapon-showing. They stayed on afterwards. The weapon-smith was busy all day and far into the night. Cartloads of weapons were brought in from other forges. The carts went away full of the corn and fodder that had been piled in the barns after harvest, they took the road to the north. The city was like an armed camp.

Alchflaed was rather surprised after her return to see that the preparations for war went on and got busier. There was no word yet of Penda's challenge to Oswy. She supposed that Penda wanted to leave her father no doubt what would happen if he did not take the dare. She had utter faith in Penda's word, so the threat of war against her people did not scare her. She was so joyful that her women looked at her askance; this was yet another sign of her uncanny nature.

Peada had been away among the East Anglians, making sure their king would bring his warriors to march behind Penda. She was eager to tell him that there was now no need for killing. Hatred and suspicion between them could end; they were still young, they could live usefully and find a sober happiness together.

She waited near the door of her bower to watch him ride through the arch into the palace courtyard. She saw him look at her; she raised her hand to greet him, smiling. When he dismounted and began to walk towards the bower, she called urgently to her maid to bring her a goblet of mead so that she could offer him a guest cup.

'What's this all about?' He took the cup. 'Are you in a hurry to say farewell? Wish me luck when I go to kill your father?'

He poured the mead on to the ground. 'Because if you're trying to witch me back to you, you've got as much chance as making me drink that mead.'

Suddenly he caught her wrist and dragged her inside the doorway out of sight from the courtyard.

'"Thou shalt not suffer a witch to live"!' He sounded triumphant. 'I asked Diuma the Christian teaching on witches and he taught me that saying out of the Holy Book.'

'You put that name on me before. Why?'

'Why indeed? And why do you wear that necklace all the time? It's a pretty trinket for a Christian woman!'

He dragged at the neck of her gown, so that the brooch pin tore the embroidered edge.

'Where is it?'

He pulled her trinket box open and hurled the contents across the room, threw up the lids of her chests and tossed her robes about, then turned on her again.

'I said, where is it?'

'I haven't got it any more.'

'I suppose you offered it to an idol. I know where you went to, after Resurrectiontide. Practising heathen filth up in the hills. I'll send my men to smash the whole place and cut those whores' throats on their own altars.'

He waited to see if she would show fear or try to plead with him. He was disappointed.

'Are you with child, like that Welsh slut you brought to be your bawd? If you are, don't give yourself the trouble of voiding it like the first one. You won't live to give it birth. As soon as I've killed your father and brother, I'm bringing you to trial for the witch that you are.'

'You're not going to kill my father and brother. I saw King Penda. He promised me that there would be peace not slaughter.'

'Yes, you tried to witch him too, didn't you? But he's generous, he's going to give you both—slaughter first and peace afterwards.' He grinned at her and went away.

After this, Alchflaed found that there were no horses for her to ride. The grooms were perfectly civil: King Peada wanted every mount for his warriors. Also, wherever she went in the city, some of Peada's spearmen would be going the same way. If she went out of the gates to look for herbs down by the Soar, a bodyguard formed up around her at the gate-house. They showed her all the respect due to a queen; it was war-time, she should not walk out unguarded. She knew she was a prisoner and wondered why Peada did not keep her chained in a cellar; he hated her enough.

Peada was still very proud of himself as a Christian king. If his father were killed in the coming war—which was likely, as he was getting old and slow but always placed himself in the forefront of battle—then Peada would be Bretwalda. Most of his subject kingdoms would be Christian. He did not want to show as a bloodboltered lout to his own subject kings. He had founded a monastery; he was having a church built in Leirceaster opposite his palace; he had learned priests who could write his laws on parchment. Alchflaed would be tried in open court where all her evil would be shown to the world. Meanwhile, everyone could see that he had treated her fairly with mercy as well as justice.

Most of his subjects in Leirceaster still followed the Old Religion. They knew that Penda was going to give the Bernician House to Woden. They showed Alchflaed the reverence due to a gift for the god. Woden would not like his present damaged and they all wanted to be there when he got it; it was interesting to watch. They were going to take good care of Alchflaed till Peada came back from the war.

Unable to move without being spied on, she could not warn Freawynn of the danger to the shrine or the priestesses. Nest might have wheedled her way out of the city but Nest was with child. This had caused careworn hours to some of the spearmen, especially those who were getting betrothed, but Nest made no effort to father her baby on any of them. She said the father was a bard of British race from the household of a great queen in the hill-country, who would be her baby's foster-mother. Her listeners set this down as Welsh talk and guessed that the lover was some Welsh cattle-herder or a fair-ground harper. Whoever he was, Nest looked very content and handsomer than ever.

Alchflaed found her sitting by a brazier, warming herself and singing under her breath.

'Is there any way I can send word to the Lady's Bower?'

'Word's already gone. Peada's got a loud voice. The message was on its way from mouth to mouth before he walked out of the house.'

'What will happen?'

'His men won't find anything.'

'Where will the priestesses go?'

'Melt into the country and come back when times change. Most

of them will be in Arnemeton now, anyway. The Lady's gone back
to the hot springs for the winter, so they'll be under Penda's shield.
He won't like this attack on the shrine, but the bull-calf's starting to
butt against the king bull.' Nest laughed.

'What about next spring?'

'There are other places. Peada can't watch every inch of the
country. Eostre always comes back.'

Nest started singing again.

> *'Maiden in the moor lay —*
> *In the moor lay —*
> *Seven nights full —*
> *Seven nights full'* —

The words brought back the springtime, the moorland air, the
sound of running water, the scent of crushed grass. Alchflaed
joined in, singing the echo:

> *'Maiden in the moor lay —*
> *In the moor lay —*
> *Seven nights full and a day.'*

The tune had a dancing lilt. Suddenly, for no reason, she remembered Meilyr by the bridge at Eoforwic. She lifted the hem of her
skirt and began to dance with the singing; her shadow danced with
her. Nest raised her voice and began to clap out the beat.

> *'Well was her meat.*
> *What was her meat?*
> *The primrose and the —*
> *The primrose and the —*
> *Well was her meat.*
> *What was her meat?*
> *The primrose and the violet.'*

Outside the door, her bower-women clustered and stared wide-
eyed as the Bernician witch-queen danced under the shadow of
Woden's spear, singing of the springtime.

Eanfled's child, a girl, had been born at the beginning of October
and named Elfflaed. Oswy ordered a litter to be got ready, with an
escort of spearmen to take the mother and child to Ebbe's convent
in the north. He came to say farewell to them.

'You'll have plenty of warning to get away if you have to. The
Picts will take you in, I've got marriage-kin there. Remember,
Elfflaed is to be a nun. I promised a daughter to God, it's time I paid
my debt.'

'And Alchfrid?'

251

'He's holding Cumbria. He should be able to do so without too much trouble.'

'Are you going to join him?'

'No. I'm going to take Eoforwic. It'll be almost undefended. Our dear Athelwold will have trotted off to Doneceaster with all his men when he heard his master's whistle. Then I'll go south and hold the river crossings. At this time of year the clay down there will be so heavy, Penda can only come up by the Roman road. I'll make him fight for every ford and bridge on the way. A small force is as good as a large one for that and it can move quicker.'

He laughed. 'We'll have a long, fighting retreat—I'm good at that, had lots of practice. By the time we get back to Bernicia, Penda's great army is going to be somewhat smaller—and if we have to take to the hills, they're my hills.'

He touched Eanfled's cheek. 'Keep up your heart, my lady. There's hope for us yet.'

Eanfled kept up her heart gallantly as she watched him ride south. This was the moment when she took her fate into her own hands. The epic tale of the beautiful exiled princess, which she had been composing so long, was sweeping to its triumphant close.

Oswy would be killed with his small army in the south, fighting nobly for the Cross against the heathen like his brother St Oswald. She would pay all honour to his memory, have churches built and masses said—she tried to imagine a St Oswy but the picture blurred at this point.

She herself would take refuge with Alchfrid. She would be quite safe in Cumbria, Oswy had said Alchfrid could easily hold it. Then, next spring, he would sweep back over the Long Hills and—Cyneburg having been disposed of—she would ride into Eoforwic at his side.

When Oswy was well ahead of her, she sent baby Elfflaed north with Grimhild in the litter and went south herself. Romanus was with her. He had made up his mind to go on alone into Deira. Like Eanfled, he thought that Oswy would be killed and the kingdom would fall to the heathen. Priests would be slaughtered; the poor flock would need every shepherd who could get to them. He went on while Eanfled waited at Perscbrig, by the road to Cumbria, for the news of Oswy's death. When horsemen rode through the southern gate carrying the Cumbrian banner and Alchfrid came into the guest hall, it was part of a story she had always known. She threw herself into his arms.

'You've come to me!'

252

'Of course I came. I rode over the hills from Gretabrig this morning. I was making for Cetreht but when I heard you were here I came back at once.' He glanced round the chamber. 'Where's little Elffaed?'

'I've sent her north to Ebbe. The King said she was to go.'

'That's all right then.' He looked relieved. 'She'll be quite safe there and we can make good time to Eoforwic without her.'

'Eoforwic?' She stared at him in horror. 'Aren't you going back to Cumbria? Oswy said you could hold it,' she licked her lips that had suddenly gone dry and stiff, 'without too much trouble.'

'Cadman's holding it. I haven't brought the war-host, just my own band of cavalry. My place is at my father's side.'

'But the danger—he's only got a little army—there are so few of you—you'll be slaughtered—'

Alchfrid looked at her with tender admiration. 'Always so much loving care for others, while you sacrifice yourself. Did you think I'd skulk behind my mountains in safety while my father was battling for his kingdom and my queen was alone in Eoforwic, waiting to hold it against Penda's hordes?'

He kissed her hands. 'Are you rested, my lady? Good. I'll give you my finest horse. We'll ride at once.'

Eanfled had played the heroic queen so often in her mind that her body went on making the right moves and her mouth said the right words like a well-trained scop. But her story made no sense and she could no longer listen to it instead of facing the real world and what it was bringing to her. All down the road to the south— even while she was getting her wish of riding into Eoforwic at Alchfrid's side—then as she stood at the palace gate and watched him going away from her down the hill and over the bridge—her thoughts scuttled round and round her various fates, like rats trapped in the last standing corn.

He would be killed, throwing his life away in some reckless charge. Penda would take Eoforwic; she would be raped, passed on from one to another of his grinning brutes, kept as a drudge, sold into slavery or sacrificed to idols in some cruel and long-drawn-out ritual. Worse than all these, there was one fate so unspeakably hideous that slavery or death would be a welcome refuge from it.

Kent was rich. Her Kentish kin would unwillingly pay out the gold to buy her back from Penda. She would be sent to face them, shamed and poverty-stricken, to swallow their pity and pass the rest of her days in her mother's convent.

Only Oswy stood between her and this horror, holding the river-crossings with his little army of Bernicians. She tottered into the church, threw herself down before the altar and prayed for Oswy's life and victory with all her heart and soul.

Meilyr stared at the waters of the River Don, grey as a sword, bleak as his thoughts. He had been walking outside the walls of Doneceaster for more than an hour since the cold dawn. The sound of the east wind in the withered rushes was restful; the leafless trees made pleasant company. Inside the walls, the memory of old feuds and resentment at new quarrels seethed endlessly as the war-bands of Penda's allies gathered there.

The Powys warriors had not arrived yet, apart from Meilyr's own small band of retainers. Meilyr was the only one who knew that they were never going to arrive. The King had flatly refused to throw his troops into battle on the other side of Britain for a war that would leave Mercia and Gwynedd all-powerful, with Powys trapped between them. He sent friendly words to Penda: when he had made sure that his borders were strongly guarded, he would march.

In itself, this would not have troubled Meilyr, pleased him rather. He liked better to find adventure as a lone hunter or warrior than to ride as one of many chiefs—and not the most powerful—behind the banners of the King of Powys.

The King's refusal, though, was a bad omen for the hope of restoring British rule in the island as it had been under Arthur. As the British war-bands arrived in Doneceaster, Meilyr had to go between them, quietening suspicions, soothing hurt pride, whipping up failing zeal, keeping them from each other's throats and from brawling with the English, promising glorious victory while his own hope faded. He wondered if it had ever been a living hope or only a restless ghost haunting the ruins of a lost empire.

The net he had woven to bind the British princes in unity was already fraying and breaking. Perhaps Morfran's power could not reach so far into England to rule their wills. Perhaps he was exhausted after holding them for more than a year. As Meilyr struggled to keep the alliance together, he could no longer feel his uncle standing behind him, pouring his own strength into him. He would have been glad of it now; he could feel his own will cracking. His evil demon was coming upon him again; soon he would be shattered into fragments, unable to plan or act.

The future was as dreary as the river-bank. Last night had been

Calan gaeaf, the Night of the Dead, which was not a time to cheer the heart. Today was the beginning of what Penda called Blot-monath, which was a time to daunt the boldest spirit.

A terrible change had come upon Penda since Meilyr had last seen him. Then he had only been interested in statecraft; he had wanted to conquer Bernicia so that he could call himself Bretwalda and make it pay tribute to him like every other English kingdom. Now he only spoke of giving the land to Woden and making a blood offering of the whole House of Ida and the Bernician nobility. This morning he was going to throw the spear over the Northumbrian bank of the Don and sacrifice some Bernician captives as a foretaste of what was to come.

Meilyr surprised himself by thanking God that Alchflaed had a Christian husband. It would keep her alive long enough to give him a chance of rescuing her. He thought of it now as rescue, not as taking her for his war-captive. Peada had been free and ugly in his talk to fellow-Christians about what he was going to do to her when the war was over. He seemed to see his heathen father as God's scourge on the Bernician royal house for its treachery and witchcraft. Meilyr thought this was an odd sort of Christianity; then asked himself bitterly if it was any worse than his own.

He wondered if he should make a sudden dash to Leirceaster now and carry her off while most of the Mercian troops were away up here. He could move fast with his little group of mounted spearmen and everybody would be taken unawares. But this would be to show himself as an open deserter and traitor. He would have to get her across Mercia with the hue and cry after him and Penda's riders ahead of him on the way to the Powys border to put everyone on the look-out. He doubted if even he could evade capture in such a case; he had lost most of his faith in himself.

It would be better to wait until the march north had started and the first battles had been fought. He could make Penda's whole war-host witness his bravery and recklessness in battle. Then he would disappear with his men, lost in some ambush among the forests and marshes, and double back to Leirceaster. He could get Alchflaed away on the pretext that Peada had sent for her to meet her fate in the north with the rest of her family. It would be easy to escape over the Long Hills with her to join Alchfrid in Cumbria.

He felt some of his pride in his hunter's craft come back to him. He lifted his head and looked around. There was a movement among the bushes that was not the wind rattling their dry twigs. He strolled past, thumbs tucked in his belt, eyes turned to the river as if still deep in thought—then pounced. There was a shrill cry. He dragged out his capture and found that the prize was Athelwold, the puppet King of Deira. Meilyr hardly bothered to pretend he respected him; none of the Deirans did.

'Lost your way? The gate's back there.' He gripped the King's arm and turned him round. Athelwold was shaking. He was a tall, slender young man, almost girlishly beautiful. He showed none of St Oswald's courage and shining integrity; some of his troops said that Oswald's queen had lied to her husband about the sex of his heir.

'I can't stay and watch that foul, bloodthirsty heathen—he's going to—'

'Penda is an honest and honourable man. He worships his god and does what he thinks is pleasing to him. It's not all of us can say the same, is it?'

'I never dreamed—I didn't know it would be like this—'

'Didn't you?' Meilyr sneered. 'Penda's never made any secret of his religion. You must have led a secluded life in your nunnery.'

This was going too far, even with Athelwold, so he added, '—where your mother took you as a baby.'

All the while, Meilyr was walking firmly along the riverside track towards the north gate of the fort that commanded the crossing. Athelwold pulled back.

'Where are you going?'

'There's a religious rite about to take place. Look, the folk are already gathering. We want to get a good view, don't we?'

'You're going to *watch* it?'

'And so are you. Some of our fellow-Christians are about to be sacrificed to Woden for our success in battle. And we can't do a thing to save them, any more than if they were being thrown to the lions in a Roman arena. We'd just get killed ourselves and lose any chance of saving other victims. But we can do what those Christians did who went to watch the martyrs die at the games— we can pray *Requiem aeternam* to their souls.'

He dug his fingers into Athelwold's arm and dragged him mercilessly towards the gate.

Penda had not got many Bernician victims for his first sacrifice. Oswy's folk rarely came south now. But last autumn an elderly merchant who had been converted by St Paulinus in Edwin's reign had gone to pass the season of Advent and keep the

Nativity at the saint's shrine in Kent. He took his young wife, who had suffered several miscarriages, to pray for another child that would not be lost untimely from her womb. Their prayers seemed to be granted; the wife had conceived in the spring. They had waited to be quite sure, then set off home through Christian East Anglia, travelling slowly because of the woman's precious burden. They had left it too late; Eadbert had taken them and sent them as a gift for the King's Blotmonath sacrifice.

They were being taken out through the fort now, a forlorn little group, stripped naked for the offering, their skins greyish-white, blotched with blue and pimpled in the biting east wind. The old merchant and his men had their nooses round their necks. Their wrists were bound behind their backs; they wore leather caps that had been pulled down over their eyes. The women were blindfold and bound to hurdles for their drowning. The wife was silent and motionless; Meilyr hoped she had fainted; but the mound of her belly shook slightly. The babe was alive and kicking. Her maid-servant was screaming obscenities, tearing against the thongs that held her wrists and ankles, arching her back and pushing out her knees in a way that froze lust and made a man ready to take monk's vows.

The Welsh told themselves that the victims were only English; it was not their concern what Penda did to his fellow-countrymen. That thought did not give them much joy. They were free allies, so they did not have to watch a heathen rite. They kept to their own camps and busied themselves with their weapons and horses, unusually silent.

Penda had ordered his subjects, Anglian or Saxon, to attend him whatever their religion. Refusal would be taken as open rebellion. The slope above the River Don was crowded with willing and unwilling watchers as the sacrifices were brought out of the north gate. Athelwold moaned; he kept shutting his eyes, then opening them again in horrified fascination. Meilyr made himself look steadily.

I did this, he told himself brutally. *Not by myself, of course, I'm not great or powerful enough. But I added my will and my strength to bring it about. Let me look at my handiwork and remember it. God, have mercy on their souls. Holy Mary, Mother of God, pray for them. God forgive me. And if I ever help to bring this on another fellow-creature may I starve in Hell for all eternity.*

Woden's tree, a fine ash with wide-spreading branches, grew

on a knoll above the river. The east wind had dropped, the tree was still. Some of Penda's warriors climbed up and bent the branches downwards. The ropes were flung over; the branches were released and the men strung up. Penda was standing by with a spear; as each victim was jerked into the air he gashed him so that the blood ran, crying, 'Now I give you to Woden!' The nooses had been carefully knotted to tighten slowly so that the victims should dance for Woden as long as possible.

The maidservant was hurled into the river; she screeched to score the listeners' brains; there was a splash, then a circle of wavelets with bubbles at the centre. Then the wife—she was heavier and they did not throw her far enough. The hurdle landed among shallows and she was slowly sucked down into the mud. The belly with the quickened womb went last from sight. The watching Christians thought of Mary and shuddered; some of Woden's men remembered Frea and felt their loins go chill.

Penda had watched it all, even the final horror, with grim pleasure. Now he stepped forward carrying his blood-stained spear. He had left off his shirt, his huge chest and shoulders were bare except for a golden collar; his breeches were held by a jew-elled belt. He strode out across the bridge, raised his arm to threaten the land to the north, cried out in a loud voice, 'Woden has you all!' swung the spear and hurled it in a mighty cast.

There was a gust of air from the west, wind-flaws on the water, a few drops of rain. The spear was dashed aside in its flight; it fell short and was caught by the Don, the Mother's river, who carried it off and swallowed it.

Penda paused for a moment, staring; then he turned to his war-riors with a yell of laughter.

'Look! Woden has given the spear to Frea and she has taken the gift. Both the All-Father and his Lady are with us!'

He strode back into the fort, leading the way to the ritual cattle-slaughter that would be followed by a feast and a carousal. The warriors streamed after him, eager for fires and beer. There was a hideous retching sound not far from Meilyr's feet; Athel-wold was heaving his guts out under a bush. A voice with a Deiran accent said, 'There's someone who won't want roast beef for supper.'

The drops of rain turned to a steady drizzle. The ash-tree's heavy fruit swayed in the west wind. Even Athelwold had stumbled back inside the fort.

Meilyr lingered by the river, trying to see the path he should take. His one aim now was to get Alchflaed out of Mercian power; his blood and nerves told him to go to her at once, in spite of the strong reasons against doing so. If he waited till later as he had planned, he could be killed before he could help her. But if he moved too soon, he would make her death certain and immediate. Time might be on her side. Peada's priests might shield her. She could appeal to Archbishop Deusdedit. A Christian queen in a Christian land could not be huddled out of life as easily as Penda had destroyed a trader's woman.

Still the terrible fear remained. Peada could stop her appeals being heard; anyway, if he liked to kill his Bernician wife, as he clearly wanted to, would his father let anyone stop him?

Meilyr's mind was torn into arguing shreds; he prayed to God for a sign.

Someone tapped him on the shoulder; it was one of the spearmen who had come with him from his brother's court at the promise of adventure and loot.

'There's a man here looking for you, lord. He says he's got a message for your ears only.'

He went back down the path to get out of earshot; the man who had followed him stepped forward. It was Morfran's chattel, Asyn.

Meilyr got his sign. The beast of burden spoke, looking at him with intelligent eyes.

'Your uncle is ill. I think he is dying. He is in great agony and calling for you.'

Meilyr's years of hunting and hairbreadth escapes kept him steady and alert against the shock.

'What's happened?'

'I found him in his room, where he—studies. He seems to be choking, he has to fight for every breath. The Abbot is with him, he says it's lung disease. I should say so myself, except there are no other signs—no sweats or heat or bloody phlegm.'

His dark intelligent eyes fixed on Meilyr who could see that Asyn knew what studies his uncle had followed in the upper room.

'I think the disease is not in this world. His suffering is killing him but he cannot die until he sees you.'

Meilyr thought, *God has sent me a sign and He hates me. He's cast me out. He won't let me help Alchflaed. If I tried I should only destroy her. I was only fit to wreck her country and her people, not to do her good. But my poor uncle—he's been wrecked as well by this evil business. I felt him lose his hold over a week ago; I should have known. I must go to him. I'm the only one who knows enough to find out what's attacking him and track it down to fight it for him. Likely it will destroy me. If I live, I'll have Penda as my enemy for deserting him and I'll lose my honour in the eyes of the world. What odds? In God's eyes and mine, I've none left to lose.*

He beckoned to the spearman. 'We're going. Order the men to get ready as quietly as possible. Leave word with anyone who isn't already too drunk and gorged to understand what you're saying, to tell Penda there's been an urgent message from Powys.' He turned to Asyn. 'Go with him, he'll get you a fresh horse and give you some food and drink before we set out.'

They went back into the fort. Meilyr had one thing more to do before he followed them. He knelt on the river bank among the dead Bernicians, the men in the ash tree, the women lying close by in the Don, and commended Alchflaed to the protection of Mary the Mother of God.

Athelwold was not the only Deiran to be sickened by the morning's work. Three of his thanes were sitting gloomily over their mead, listening to the rain drumming on their leather tent. Between emptying his cup and filling it again one of them said, 'I don't like it.'

'Like it! As soon as that horde sobers up enough to cross the Don, they'll be on the loose in Deira.'

'We're their allies.' The speaker did not sound too happy.

'To a Mercian, everyone from north of the Humbre is a Northumbrian. They won't stop to sort out Deirans and Bernicians.'

'D'you think we could get away now—while they're all drunk? My hall's at Aldeburh, the other side of Eoforwic, right in their path, my wife's there—'

He stopped, while they all thought of the wife who had gone into the Don.

'You can't get up the road now, Oswy's at Ceasterford. Think of coming up to him with Penda's war-host at your heels and trying to tell him you've had a change of heart.'

'Oswy at Ceasterford? Who told you that?'

'Elmet folk, of course. If anyone coughs in their forest they hear about it. One of their cattle-thieves rode in yesterday with his gang of cut-throats. They say they're scouting—spying I'd call it.'

'Elmet folk hate Deirans. Give them the chance, you can guess whose throats they'll cut.'

'Oh God!' The man from Aldeburh beat his fist against his brow.' If I could only get home! I'd take my folk up into the Long Hills.'

'Go east through Haethfeld and across the Humbre.'

'Across the Humbre at this time of year? The ferry stopped last month.'

'You can always get across by daylight if you've got a stout boat and a man who knows the tides. Listen, I've got lands over at Heafoden. I was going there to gather my men and bring them to meet Penda. As it is, I'm going to keep on gathering them till I see what happens. If there's bad trouble, I can get up into the wolds and stay there. You can come with me, if you like. I'll put you on your way the other side.'

He was as good as his word. They were far out over the Haethfeld wastes by nightfall, sheltering with a cottar. Next day they were over the Humbre. The thane of Heafoden gave the other two fresh horses and a guide. They set out through pouring rain for Eoforwic.

They found it getting ready for a siege. The King's reeve told them that Prince Alchfrid and his Cumbrians had passed south the day before but Queen Eanfled had come back to her city. They had better come and speak to her, though she was at her prayers.

As soon as they saw her, they knew they had made the right choice in coming. There in King Edwin's old church they found King Edwin's daughter on her knees at the altar, her golden hair flowing loose and dishevelled, her lovely eyes raised to Heaven, a Queen of Sorrows.

They wept and kissed her hands, swearing deathless loyalty. Romanus shrived and blessed them and gave them the Host. Then they set out to raise Deira for Christ and Eanfled.

The settlement inside the Roman walls at Ceasterford boasted an ale-house for the traders who went up and down the great north road. Oswy had taken it for his headquarters; he was sitting by the hearth playing a board-game one hand against the other, when Alchfrid walked in. He looked up.

'Is all well in Cumbria?'

'Very well. The harvest in, the war-host assembled, the borders guarded.'

'And the prince absent. Why?'

'To fight by his father's side.'

Oswy smiled and stretched out his hand. 'Welcome.' He poured ale for his son. 'What sort of ride did you have?'

'Wet.'

'Good. The rivers will run high and the ground will stay water-logged.' He chuckled. 'Penda's mighty army is sinking into the mud. They tried to march at the beginning of November but the rain held them at Doneceaster for a week. Then, when they did set out, they couldn't move except on the road. The men who tried to march at the side of the causeway went in nearly to their knees. So they had to wait another day or two till the land dried out a bit.'

'How do you know all this?'

'From Elmet, of course. They hate the Deirans, and Penda is Deira's ally. I feasted Bledri ap Iddon when I stopped at Calcaceaster, he came down from the hills with his war-band to meet me. His mother was cousin to Ceredig, their last king, the one Edwin drove out. He's the nearest thing to a high chief in Elmet now. We had a very pleasant talk—he loves Taliesin's poetry as much as your mother did. You and your Cumbrians should get on well with him.'

'Is he here? Do you want me to join forces with him—our style of fighting will be very different.'

'He's gone on ahead to join forces with Penda. He's offered his services as a scout. Elmet folk know every path over the Long Hills and through the forest. They can find every dry track across the marshes of Loidis. And, of course, they can talk to all your men without an interpreter, instead of having to come to me. That's why I'm going to leave you to hold the road. As things are, you could do it with thirty men, let alone your three hundred.'

Alchfrid took this news calmly. He drank his ale in silence, then asked quietly, 'And you?'

'I'm going to do something I've been wanting to but hadn't the men till you arrived.' His finger sketched moves on the table top. 'Even if we have some dry weather the ground will still be heavy. Most of Penda's men will keep to the causeway, they'll be strung out in a long line. The next river down from us is the Weneta, the crossing's seven or eight miles south. There's a steep ridge to the east of the road, the Weneta's cut a gorge through it. I'm going to move my men up on that ridge and take Penda's flank or rear.'

262

'It's a terrible gamble.'

'No, just a gamble, like everything we do. I've been in retreat long enough, it's time I made a forward move.' He smiled. 'And at least I'll have all the advantage of surprise. The last thing everyone in Britain expects to see is me coming to meet my enemies.'

CHAPTER
24

The rain beat steadily into the faces of Meilyr's party for seven days as if it was trying to drive them back from Powys. Nevertheless, his men were in good spirits. Their sheepskin cloaks and leather breeches kept out the rain and they were thankful to be going home. They thought Meilyr had pulled out in disgust at the human sacrifice. They heartily agreed with him. If ever they'd seen a war-host under a curse it was Penda's; they didn't want to be there when the curse struck.

Meilyr's body was as well-clad as his spearmen's and it was at home in wild weather. His spirit was in chill agony. The English had always said Hell was cold; now he knew they were right.

Asyn the slave rode beside him; he had taken up the duties of Meilyr's body-servant without being ordered. Without interest, as a man dying in pain might call for a harper or a storyteller to take his mind off the suffering for a little while, Meilyr said, 'Who are you?'

'Your uncle's slave, Asyn. Once I was Stephanos Maleinos, Eparch of Constantinople.'

Meilyr was startled into real interest.

'How did you—come to be here—like this?'

'Through the piety of my son-in-law. He led the palace revolution that destroyed me. But it was on St John's day, you see, and St John is his patron saint. He thought the saint would be displeased with him if he murdered his wife's father during the feast day. He had me gelded, so I can never get a son to avenge me; sold as a slave, so that I should be helpless without legal rights; and taken overseas in a Visigothic ship to barbarian lands where I would be as good as speechless.'

'But when you came to Llangollen—they know some Greek in

263

the monastery, my uncle reads it — and you must know some Latin. You could have spoken then — you needn't —'

'I'm quite willing to work for your uncle. He's injured, like me. I know how he suffers. And he's a learned man, it's honourable to serve him.'

'As a scribe or reader, not as a beast of burden!'

'I chose Ioannes Phokas as my son-in-law. I was stupider than a beast. I asked for this.'

Meilyr blinked the rain out of his eyes, trying to read Asyn's face.

'Do you mean you've been punishing yourself all these years for that? You couldn't have guessed what he was.'

'I knew perfectly well what he was. I just believed I was too powerful for him to attack me. And knowing his nature I put my daughter Theophano in his bed. She was terrified and I saw it, but she obeyed her father. A man who does that to a helpless girl deserves to be helpless himself, and gelded and treated like a beast.'

Meilyr winced, remembering the helpless girl at Doneceaster, thrown naked and screaming into the river.

'You've paid for it. I'd buy you from my uncle but he'll surely give you your freedom as a gift if he lives. If not, I'm his heir. I'll find a ship for you in Caer Legion, give you money —'

'For what, lord? If Ioannes is still in power, I'll be killed. If not, I shall have the pain of looking for old friends and watching them try to remember me. Would we want to see our loved ones after they'd been twenty years in the grave, however much we loved them?'

'But your daughter? You could write a letter. Abbot Sulien could send it by a pilgrim. There's always some Irish monk going —'

'Either she is dead or she is living as Ioannes' wife. He may have killed her; but I think he will have kept her for her wealth and high blood. She was very beautiful, too. She may have borne him children. Habit is stronger than love, in the end. They may even be fond of each other. Any message from me would only come as a ghost to haunt her and destroy her peace. One of the best ways of loving people is to keep out of their lives.'

This was another bitter pill for Meilyr to swallow but it was good medicine. The Greek's clear-eyed view of life, without rage or self-pity, braced him.

He had no trouble from the Mercians on his journey. Everyone took it for granted that he was taking a message from Penda to his Welsh allies. His party got willing hospitality and guides on their way. But the week of rain slowed them. Even when it stopped, the going was hellish. Hill streams, and paths too, had become waterfalls; rivers were floods; earth was bog. It was the 14th of November before Meilyr and Stephanos came into the tower at Dinas Brân.

Morfran was lying on his couch in the lower room. Abbot Sulien was at his side. Meilyr wondered if he had been into the room above, and if so, what he had found. He glanced towards the trap-door; Stephanos caught his eye and touched a string round his neck. There was a key on it. Meilyr went to his uncle's bedside.

Morfran was lying on his back; his arms were outside the blankets. He seemed to be trying to raise himself, not by pressing on the couch but by clutching at the air and making faint beating movements with the palms of his hands. All the while he was putting up a horrible fight for breath, lifting his head, swallowing mouthfuls of air, his lips gaping like the jaws of a fish. His flesh was wasted; Meilyr saw the bones of his rib cage going in and out like a bellows over his struggling lungs. He was choking but as Meilyr bent over him he could just make out words among the gurgling and the moans.

'The water . . . the water . . . Meilyr . . . the water . . .'

Meilyr filled a cupful from a jug on the table and put it to his uncle's mouth. As soon as his lips touched the water, Morfran writhed his head back and clutched the air more desperately.

'Meilyr . . . go away . . . the water . . . over my head, over my head . . .'

Meilyr touched his uncle's forehead; it was quite cool.

'Does he want his head bathed?'

Stephanos shook his head. 'He cannot bear the touch of water.'

Meilyr looked round helplessly. 'Then what does he mean—water over his head?'

'He is making an act of contrition,' said Abbot Sulien, much moved. 'He is trying to say the Sixty-Ninth Psalm—let us join our voices to his and strengthen him with our prayers.'

He got down on his knees and began to recite. '*Salvum me fac Deus—Save me, O God, for the waters are come in even unto my soul. I stick fast in the mire of the deep and there is no sure standing—*'

'Meilyr . . . Meilyr . . .'

Meilyr took his uncle's hand and pressed it gently.

'I'm here, Uncle.'

Morfan tried to push him back. 'Go away . . . the water . . . you'll be trapped . . . leave me . . .'

'*Infixus sum in limo profundi—I am come into the depths of the sea—*'

The words of the Psalm flowed over the mutterings of the figure on the bed and carried their message for him. Meilyr stared at his uncle. If he had not known about the secret studies, partly shared them, he would have thought he was going mad.

In Dinas Brân, on a hill-top hundreds of feet above the Dyfrdwy, Morfran was drowning.

Meilyr forced himself to empty his mind of every thought and feeling, to stop being Meilyr and let his uncle's terror and suffering flow into him. As he stooped over the couch, he seemed to catch the swirl and dull gleam of brownish water, to feel the whip of moist wind on his cheek, his feet sinking in cold mud.

'Don't worry, Uncle. I'm holding on to this tree.' He put his arm on the head of the couch. 'Keep fast to my hand, I'll draw you up.'

'The bank's giving way . . . the water . . . uprooting the trees . . . Meilyr . . . leave me . . .' He pulled away.

Meilyr, leaning over him, was jerked forward; his face went under the water. It was flowing fast and strong, sweeping trees and the corpses of men and horses along with it. Though it was thick with mud, he caught a glimpse of fishes gleaming pale in the depths. They floated up towards him; they were the women who had drowned at Doneceaster. The maid's eyes glittered; she darted in and tried to bite his throat but the wife drifted between them. Her eyelids were closed and she was smiling. She lifted one of her heavy breasts and put the nipple to his mouth. Meilyr screamed; his mouth was filled with muddy water, he felt it going down to his lungs and heaved to retch it out. He nearly lost consciousness but struggled to get his head above the surface. Stephanos was thumping his back.

'*Eripe me de luto—Draw me out of the mire that I may not stick fast; deliver me from them that hate me and out of the deep waters—*'

Stephanos said, 'I've got you by the belt. Use both your hands to lift him—take a deep breath.'

Meilyr filled his lungs and plunged forward into the invisible waters. As soon as he gripped his uncle's hands he shut his eyes so that he might not see anything that came at him. A tide of hate swirled against him, trying to pull Morfran away from his hold, trying to drag him, too, out of the life of this world. His lungs seemed to be bursting, the river roared in his ears yet he could still hear the Abbot's voice.

'*Non me demergat tempestas aquae*—*let not the tempest of water drown me nor the deep swallow me up: and let not the pit shut her mouth on me*—'

Suddenly whatever was attacking him lost its force and let him go. He opened his eyes. Stephanos was leaning across him to raise Morfran on his pillows. He was weak and breathless, barely conscious, but he was no longer struggling to breathe. Stephanos poured some liquid from a pan that had been warming near the brazier; it was wine smelling of herbs. He managed to make Morfran swallow a few mouthfuls, then settled his head back on the pillows.

'He'll sleep now.'

Abbot Sulien finished his psalm and got to his feet. He looked thoughtfully at Morfran then took off his crucifix and put it round the sleeping man's neck.

'Keep candles burning here all night even while he's sleeping. I'll see that one of the brothers is here watching all the time; they can take it in turns. Then you won't have to worry about interrupting your prayers while you attend to his bodily needs.'

He looked kindly at Meilyr and Stephanos as he blessed them. He might not know what Morfran did in the upper room but Meilyr could see that he was well aware of what had just happened on the couch in front of him.

Penda's great army was crawling north. It was strung out in a long column down the Roman road because the embankment lifted men's feet above the heavy clay. The streams that ran down from the western hills were swollen to rivers; by the time the men at the rear came to the fords the mud was so trampled they could hardly get across. The few dry days after the week of rain had not done much to drain the land. It was only seventeen miles to Ceasterford but as the short mid-November daylight faded towards dusk, Penda knew that they were not going to get there.

They had barely covered ten miles by nightfall. The moon was full; it had been in the eastern sky before sunset, pale as the face of a dead priestess. It was brightening now, but the mists were rising; no night for a moonlight march. There was a stretch of higher, firmer ground to the side of the road; Penda gave the order to make camp for the night. There was no danger on the road ahead. Bledri of Elmet had heard no firm news of Oswy on his ride down from the Long Hills; he said the word went that the Bernicians had retreated north.

Bledri's men were a little way ahead of the army, followed by the war-band from Gwynedd, who were leading the march. They were hardy and tireless, well-used to bearing cold and facing wild weather but their spirits were sunk by the flat miles of water-logged earth and the dank woods crowding in on them. They did not seem to be getting anywhere; for all they knew they might be under some evil enchantment that would keep them riding the same mile of mud for centuries. The human sacrifice at Doneceaster would surely have brought the demons of the air flocking to them like carrion crows. They felt they were under a curse; every man of them was longing to be back in the mountains with rock under his feet and sweet air in his lungs.

A shadow moved beside the road. It was Bledri; he had dismounted and was leading his pony on the grass. He made a sign for silence. King Cadafel of Gwynedd halted his men and came forward.

'What is it?'

'Horsemen about a mile ahead, coming from the north. Get your men off the road, then I'll show you.'

Cadafel gave the word to his war-band to get out of sight among the trees and to muffle their horses' heads if they heard anyone on the road. He took two of his men with him; on Bledri's advice they dismounted and left their horses with the rest of the troop.

'They could give us away. If we're sighted we can escape faster without them under the trees—but if you do as I do we won't be sighted.'

Cadafel followed the Elmet chieftain, deeply uneasy. He had joined Penda's expedition because he wanted a victory to bring him fame like Cadwallon's. Now, every moment seemed to be taking him nearer to disaster.

Bledri led them unhesitatingly along a track that wound among the trees about a hundred yards west of the road, following the same northwesterly direction. At last, signing to the other three to move as silently as possible, he led the way back towards the road, keeping to the shadow of the trees. Then he stopped.

The road ran down to a ford across a river flowing east.

'The Weneta,' whispered Bledri. 'Look.'

He pointed to the other side, where the land rose again. A group of armed horsemen waited there, looking towards the south. The river mist was lying close to the ground; the strange riders were partly veiled by it as it drifted round their mounts' legs. Their heads and shoulders rose into the moonlight that silvered their grey horses, turned their red cloaks purplish-black and made full moons of their lime-washed shields each marked with a Chi-Rho. They did not look like English troops; they did not look like any warriors the Gwynedd men had ever seen, except on carvings in the Emperor Maxen's old city of Caer Seiont.

Bledri touched Cadafel's arm and they went back to the hidden path. Cadafel paused, glancing over his shoulder.

'Who—what do you think they are?'

Bledri was ready with his answer. 'It will be Peredur of Efrog and his war-band, come from their graves to fight the heathen English again. And this time he will win. You can't kill the dead.'

The Gwynedd men shuddered and crossed themselves. Cadafel exclaimed bitterly, 'I said this war was cursed, ever since Penda fed Christians to his demons. I would have left him then— only the Powys men would say I was a cowardly deserter if I'm gone when they arrive.'

'The Powys men aren't coming. Their king sent word to Penda that he needed to see his borders were guarded before he marched.'

'God! I know whose borders he'll be marching over, while we're being slaughtered on the other side of England.'

'Go home. Why should you die fighting for English heathen?'

'How can we? With Penda on the road behind us and—them— on the road ahead?'

'There are plenty of tracks over the Long Hills. Then you can pick up the road to Manceinion and Caer Legion. We're leaving tonight. We're your fellow-countrymen, we'll put you on your way.'

Looking at his spearmen's faces, Cadafel saw their hearty approval of this offer. He rejoined his waiting troops. Guided by Bledri's men, who had come silently through the forest, they set off westwards in the moonlight.

Alchfrid had taken a small escort and ridden with Oswy as far as the Weneta, partly as a dutiful son, partly to look at the road he might be fighting on next day. Oswy's troops had long since vanished over the crest of the ridge to the east. They had taken leather tents and a good supply of cold meat, oatcakes and beer to keep their spirits up, but they would not be lighting many fires that might betray their camp. The moon would be their torch.

Everything was quiet. Alchfrid turned his horse; the Cumbrians rode back the seven miles to Ceasterford. Much later that night Bledri came in to tell him where Penda's forces were halted, and that Cadafel had left him.

Athelwold also left that night. He dressed in plain dark clothes like a churl and fled on foot towards the east. He was lucky. After wandering over the wastes all night, cold and frightened, he came to a forge at Smithatun. He told the folk that his brother, a monk at Lastingaeu was dangerously sick and likely to die. He was trying to make his way there but had been driven off the north road by fear of Penda's war-host. He said a little about the horror at Doneceaster but could not go on for crying; he was not shamming his fear. The smith and his wife pitied the gentle, comely young man. They set him on his way and he was passed on from farm to farm. A week later he was in Lastingaeu, grovelling at the Abbot's feet and sobbing, 'Father, I have sinned . . . I have sinned . . .'

The night had been bitterly cold; towards the late dawn the air grew milder. This brought no relief, it brought clouds from the west. Most of the subject kings would have turned home days ago if they had been waging war on their own account. They were being driven on by Penda's will. Not that he showed it by anger or threats. Ever since he had made the Blotmonath offering he had been filled with a blazing joy that rain and mud could not quench. It seemed to flame higher as the march went on; nothing tired him, his eyes seemed to be fixed on that place in the far north where he would run Oswy to ground at last. Most of the time he was smiling; he smiled when they told him that Athelwold had fled.

'Deira will need a new king,' was all he said. Then he looked at the miserable faces of the Deiran thanes and roared with laughter.

'I think I'll give it to Bledri of Elmet, he lives next door. Now, let's be stirring. The men of Gwynedd will be well ahead of us.'

His own Mercian thanes and spearmen had caught and shared his high spirits. Penda had set a troop of them under Eadbert, along with Peada's men, to keep the rear. Some of his allies would have turned tail without them blocking the way. Slowly and unwillingly the allies broke camp and got ready to move north. Before they could start the rain began to fall again, a sudden vicious downpour that only lasted half an hour but left men and horses soaked and miserable.

Even Penda might not have been able to make the subject kings go forward, if one of the Elmet men, whom no weather seemed to hinder or daunt, had not ridden in on a light-footed hill pony.

'Have you seen the men of Gwynedd? How far ahead have they got? You'd better ride back and tell them to halt on the road and wait for us.'

'Oh, they went on last night, lord, under the moonlight.' The Elmet man looked fresh and cheerful. 'There was a good feast in Ceasterford last night—it's a fine place, there's an ale-house, plenty of cattle to roast, dry roofs and blazing fires to eat them by.'

'You hear that!' shouted Penda. 'Let's be on our way or they'll have cleared the beef and the ale before we get there.'

The Elmet man turned his pony and headed back north. With better spirits the allies hurried to follow the impatient Mercians. Peada and Eadbert waited to see they were all on the move, and going in the right direction, then fell in behind.

A few miles further they should have come to the ford where Cadafel had watched Alchfrid's horsemen. The ford was no longer there; the Weneta had risen and covered both ends of the road. It was impossible to guess how deep it was now in the centre, where the river was running fast and strong, carrying a litter of branches, and even some uprooted bushes. Crossing would be dangerous if it could be managed at all. The long column halted from its head, with the men at the rear asking impatiently what the trouble was now.

'No trouble!' Penda laughed at the dismay on their faces. 'I know this road. I've travelled along it often enough on the way to victory over the Bernicians and back home in triumph. There's a ridge of high ground only a few hundred yards to the right. You can get up there and keep your feet dry till the water goes down again. This is just from that rainstorm, but the sky's clear now. It's only a few more miles to Ceasterford. We'll all be under cover by nightfall.'

Wearily, the men began to turn right, off the line of the road, to make their way downstream. The going was very muddy; they

271

had to keep well away from the river but at least the trees had been cleared to make rich water-meadows. They could see the rocky ground they were making for, blocking their path and reaching towards the water's edge. Another ridge rose opposite, with the Weneta cutting a gorge between.

The winter sunlight brightened the rocky crests and glinted on the armour of the warriors waiting there. They held both sides of the gorge; Oswy had sent part of his troops across the day before while the ford was still passable.

The Mercians thought at first that the strangers were Deiran war-bands coming to join them, who had made for the high ground while the waters were out. But they neither waved nor called any greeting. Then they saw the banners on the hill-tops: The Cross, and the Head and Hands of St Oswald, which Oswy had taken as his own personal standard.

Penda gave a great cry of joy. 'Woden must be pleased with us! He wants his sacrifice—he's saved us the trouble of hunting it, he's brought it to our spears' points.'

He got down from his horse and told his servant to lead it away.

'I'll not sit in his saddle again till I've stood over Oswy's corpse.'

His lords also dismounted; the whole Mercian host readied their spears and shields for a charge up the southwestern slope where the ground rose more gently.

It is easier to hurl spears downhill than upwards; also, the Bernicians had not been idle; they had collected great piles of stones which they hurled down on their enemies' skulls and faces like a giant's hailstorm. The first Mercian charge was broken; the attackers recoiled out of reach.

That was only a few minutes' respite for the defenders. They were outnumbered; they could not retrieve their spears; the rest of the Bernician army could not get across the Weneta to relieve them or make a diversion.

The Mercians regrouped cheerfully; the repulse had got their blood up and given zest to the baying of their victims. The subject kings had held their own war-bands in check, respecting Penda's right to first kill and waiting to see what luck he had. Now they pressed forward; they wanted to get a good view of the sport. So did Peada and Eadbert, bringing up the rear; they were also eager to take part in it. They came jostling through their allies with little thought of courtesy.

The main body of the army was in disarray and bunching

towards the mouth of the gorge when the men at the back began shouting. They went unheeded at first; when the Mercians knew what was happening they were already doomed.

There had been too much rain on the western hills, their ground could take no more. During the morning downpour, the moorland streams that fed the Weneta had swept down in spate. Now there was a surge of flood-water towards the gorge; as men felt the water round their ankles and looked down it was already at their knees, dragging their feet from under them.

Some of the allies fled south ahead of the spreading flood-waters and struggled back towards the road, making for Doneceaster. A few, helped by despair and powerful horses, even fought their way across the current and got to the northern side. This did not save their lives for much longer. Oswy's men held the ridge; and on the road, as the Elmet man had promised, they were being waited for. Alchfrid had advanced from Ceasterford. Meanwhile, the flower of the Mercian warriors was swept away in the gorge, choking in a hideous tangle of men, horses and uprooted trees.

Penda stood with a small group of his thanes on the lower slope of the ridge and watched his people die. He knew now what the sacrifice was that Woden had prepared, and which land he had given to the spear at Doneceaster.

He went down towards the Weneta and hurled his own battle-spear into its waters. Then he drew his great sword and stepped into the river, facing west, breasting the current as if he would hold it off from his drowning warriors by using his body as their shield. For a moment his huge strength kept him on his feet, knee-deep in the water. He saw Woden coming for him, the one-eyed merciless smiler on his eight-legged horse, the betrayer, poser of death-runes, Frea's lover, the one enemy worthy of his sword. He was laughing as he raised the mighty blade and waded forward to fight his god. Woden nodded a greeting, then drove his spear through him.

The Mercian thanes saw their king go down, swept away in the branches of a huge ash tree. Then they made their shield ring, as the Bernicians came down the slope towards them.

CHAPTER
25

Alchflaed, crowned, veiled and robed with sober dignity, as befitted a queen, left her bower and walked to the palace followed by two of her bower-maidens. The guard at the door raised their spears in salute to her. The King's reeve, Helmstan, who was keeping order in Leirceaster while the King was absent, stood up and waited until she had taken her place on the dais. Then he sat down beside her and the law-suit began.

When the King is absent the Queen holds the kingdom. Until Peada put her in chains and dragged her to judgement as a sorceress, Alchflaed was Queen in Leirceaster and made the folk there treat her so. She would not hide away in her bower, trembling and weeping for her fate, but walked proudly about her city in the eyes of all.

Her people, who saw her as one marked for death like all her family, gave her their whole-hearted approval. She was a fine woman; Woden would be pleased to have her and would reward them with his favour. All her orders were obeyed. When she told Winefride to get out of her bower and live in her sister's hall, the girl had to go. If Winefride had harmed the Queen now by act or word, she would have been torn in pieces. Everyone was looking forward to seeing how Alchflaed died; she was sure to do them credit.

She had thought of trying to escape but had decided against it. She believed she could pass outside the walls easily enough. She could get into the great bath-house drain. But once outside, where would she go, alone in Mercia? Likely she would be caught and brought back roped with all her dignity lost. If she got to the Lady's Bower she would find it deserted after Peada's attack; she might bring trouble on Freawynn. Still, the thought that she could leave the city if she chose and was only there by her own will was a source of strength. It added to the pride of her bearing.

The main case that day was a complicated claim for wergild. Everyone was absorbed in it when there was a disturbance at the door. One of the guards came in with a stranger. His arm was across the guard's shoulder, the guard was holding him round the waist as his legs were buckling. His shirt and breeches were filthy and tattered but he had a new cloak and boots. His hair and beard were clotted with blood; the rag round his head was fairly clean. Someone had tended him on his way.

He got to the dais and slumped forward on to his knees.

'Lost—we're lost—the King's dead!'

Alchflaed suddenly saw Peada riding on the sands of Wirheale, laughing in the sunlight. She put her hand to her heart; a spear seemed to have struck her.

'There's been a battle? Has our army been beaten?' Helmstan could hardly put the question; it should not be thought, much less spoken.

'Our army's destroyed. Penda's lost. All lost—the river took them. Oswy's troops'll be across the Treanta by now. They're heading for Tomeworthig—we haven't the men to stop them—Mercia's gone.'

He crumpled forward, sobbing. The other folk in the hall were silent. The disaster was too great to hold in their minds. Then one of the women in the law-suit, whose son had ridden out with Peada, began to wail, softly at first, then rising to a howl as she pulled off her head veil and began to rip the neck of her gown. Alchflaed stood up.

'Stop that!'

The woman gasped and fell silent. Everyone was watching Alchflaed. She turned to Helmstan. 'Have wagons harnessed and get an escort ready to come with me.'

'As you will, lady. There aren't many wagons in the city, most of them were taken north with—' his voice shook a little—'with the King.'

Helmstan's sister's son had also gone north with the King; he had trained the boy himself and loved him as his own child.

'Will you have pack-horses, or would you rather ride to Northumbria at once and we'll send your goods after you?'

He spoke respectfully; he always had done, like all the rest. Looking at them, she now saw fear as well. She was Oswy's daughter; if she wanted blood to pay for her wrongs, she only had to ask Oswy for it.

'I don't believe the whole army has been destroyed, not all at once. There were too many of them. There must be some of our men left alive, wounded perhaps, exhausted and starving, scattered all the way to—where did it happen?' She bent over the messenger.

'The Weneta.'

She thought back along the road she had come on her wedding journey.

'We'll follow Peada's line of march to the Don. I want wagons for the wounded; perhaps we can get more from the farms on the way. Put some cloaks and blankets in them and what food you can spare but not too much, don't overload.'

She turned to Helmstan. 'See to it as quickly as possible. Choose me an escort and someone to lead it.'

'I'll come with you myself.'

'Very well. Then name someone to leave in charge here.'

She went back to the bower and got into her riding clothes and a thick hooded cloak. When she came out again, Helmstan had got six wagons harnessed and a dozen spearmen to ride with them, besides the drivers. It was a pitiful group to rescue what might be left of the greatest army that had marched in Britain since Roman times. A small crowd was standing by in silence: Leofred, the man Helmstan had picked to act as king's reeve while he was away, what remained of the garrison, the women and old men who had been loading the wagons.

She spoke to Leofred, raising her voice so that everyone could hear what she said.

'Now, listen. You may defend yourselves against any attempt to attack or rob you. Don't try fighting Oswy. If any of his troops come here, say that the city belongs to Alchflaed, Oswy's daughter, Queen of Mercia, and that I shall hold them to account for any wrong or loss you suffer. Now, let's be off.'

They had a bleak journey north, through the wintry land with its homesteads of frightened grieving folk, but at least she had the satisfaction of being proved right. They met fugitives and gleaned a little news of others. Eadbert had got away south with most of his own war-band. He had gone towards Lindesse, making for the Fens. Others were scattered about the countryside, heading for their homes by roundabout ways, lurking as outlaw bands in the forest, hiding in friendly farms.

The first survivors they met had been hungry and tired but not too badly injured. Then they began to come across those who had been half-drowned, battered by floating logs or crushed among corpses, then dragged to safety by the devoted courage of their sword-friends. She gave them such tending as she could, sending them back in the wagons one by one. It was now the beginning of December. Her heart ached when she thought of those who would never be found, dying of wounds and cold out in the wastes. No one could give her any word of Peada.

News of their coming had gone ahead of them by the mysterious ways of the countryfolk. They had crossed the River Idle with their last wagon and four of the spearmen and were about six miles south of Doneceaster when they saw a woman sitting by the road, huddled in a cloak. She had been waiting for them; she beckoned them on to a track that led off among the trees to the east.

They came to a small farm. An injured man was lying by the hearth with two bedraggled serfs keeping watch. Helmstan cried out at the sight of him—it was his young nephew Guthlac, with his hip and leg bones smashed and fever coming. His two companions had got him so far: his brother-in-law and a farm churl who had served as his groom. They could not go on any farther with him and he ought not to be moved but the farmwoman was frightened.

'I don't want to be hard on him, but if they found him here—'

'He should do well enough in the wagon.' Alchflaed looked troubled. 'But if there are any others still on the road behind you—'

'There aren't,' said the brother-in-law. 'We're the last. We've been going so slowly a blind beggar of ninety could have overtaken us. Our men would need to be moving fast out of Doneceaster—a Welshman from Elmet's got it. Any Mercians or Deirans there will be dead ones.'

They put Guthlac into the wagon and settled him as comfortably as possible. When they got back on the road she took Helmstan's hand.

'Farewell and God be with you.'

'Aren't you coming with us, lady?'

'My husband is somewhere up there to the north. If he's alive he'll need my help.'

'I'm coming with you.'

'No. Thank you with all my heart. But you couldn't protect me—as Oswy's daughter I'd have to shield you!'

'But that Welshman in Doneceaster—'

'I'm not afraid of Elmet folk. I speak their language, my mother was a great queen of their race. Now, be on your way—get Guthlac safely home. I'll pray to Christ to heal him.'

There goes a fine woman, thought Helmstan, watching her ride away to the north. She would have been a great queen herself if her fate had been kinder. A pity she followed that meek-spirited god. She deserved to have been given to Woden.

Alchflaed's fate seemed at last to have turned kinder. She was caught by a band of Bledri's men who had got bored collecting loot from the corpses in the Weneta and were out for some fun hunting runaways. Seeing she was a woman, they loyally took her back to their chief to have first use of her. She told him her name and he had her escorted with all honour to Eoforwic. Alchfrid was in control there, keeping order and some kind of peace between Bernicians, Deirans and Cumbrians, while Oswy raced down to Mercia to take Tomeworthig and find his younger son.

Alchfrid was truly glad to see her; he had heard from Bledri about Penda's vow to sacrifice the whole Bernician House and had been heart-sick for her. She had never seen him so moved; he caught her in his arms, crying, 'Oh, my dearest sister! Thank God, you're safe!'

This was a great comfort; but he had even better to give her. Peada was alive. He had been captured in Elmet and given to Alchfrid, whom the folk seemed to look on as one of their own princes, because of his mother's blood. Peada had been badly wounded and lost much blood; he had also suffered from days of starvation and shelterless nights in the marshes of Loidis. Alchfrid said kindly that he would surely get better now with his wife to tend him and sent a servant to lead her to his bedside.

She had been thinking about Peada all the while she had been helping the survivors of his army. She saw him in each one of the wretched men whose wounds she had cleaned and bound up, praying while she gave them food that someone else might be doing the same for him. Her anger and bitterness had been washed away in the flood-waters of the Weneta. Surely that sullen bully who had taken Peada's shape would have drowned there. She would meet again the sunny-tempered young man who had laughed with her and loved her in Legaceaster.

That was the man she saw when she leaned over his bed to look at him. He was asleep. He looked young and innocent with his brown lashes resting on his gaunt cheekbones. His flesh was very much wasted; under the beard his face was hollow. She touched it gently and stroked his curly hair; she could feel her throat tightening.

Peada stirred and turned towards her, opening his eyes. She could see that he knew her; he lifted his arm towards her but it fell back weakly on the bed; there were tears in his eyes. It was a moment before she took in that he had been trying to hit her and was weeping because he had not got the strength to do it.

Meilyr's eyes were weary; he laid aside the manuscript he had been studying and looked up towards the couch. His uncle had spent many days mostly in sleep. He had been exhausted almost to death by his ordeal, with barely strength to swallow a little wine or broth and murmur his thanks. Morfran was watching him and smiled.

'So you got my call. I was afraid you didn't hear—I couldn't reach you.'

He looked distressed. Meilyr wanted to humour him but decided that truth would be kinder; they had both played too long with dreams of power.

'You didn't. Our loyal friend Stephanos brought me word you were ill and needed me. It doesn't matter how I got the news, I'm here.'

'There was something I had to tell you—I can't remember—' He put his hand to his forehead. Meilyr didn't want him to remember. If he looked again, even in memory, into those ghastly waters, he might fall in and drown.

'You were ill and so you called for me. And I came. That's all.'

He made himself sound cheerful but Morfran knew him too well and had shared his thoughts.

'What did you tell Penda?'

'Nothing. He was drunk when I left, keeping up one of their festivals. He'll have thought I'd gone to hurry the Powys warband on its way to join him. By now he'll know it won't be on its way and never meant to.'

Morfran looked worried. 'But what will that do to your own plan—getting him to give Alchflaed to you as a war-prize?'

'Nothing; because he won't be giving her to anyone as a warprize. She's for death. Either he'll drown her as an offering to Woden or his Christian son will drown her as a witch.' He laughed. 'It's a pity Taliesin's in his grave. Only the greatest of all the bards could sing of a heroic feat like mine—raising the armies of all England to kill one helpless girl who never did me anything but good.'

'You love her, don't you?'

Meilyr bowed his head. 'Yes, I love her—and I've destroyed her, for the ghost of a dead hatred.'

'Go and get her. Go now, while the armies are in the north. You

279

can pass as a minstrel, you've done it before. You've got the wits to spirit her out of Leirceaster and the skill to dodge the hunters across Mercia.' He took the key from his neck. 'Go to my upper room and bring me the ivory casket on the shelf.'

When Morfran had it open, he sorted through its contents and poured something into a small leather phial. 'Sometimes music and a glib tongue alone can't lull guards or hunters. Be careful with this. One drop gives sleep for a day and a night—two for a very strong man. Three drops give the sleep that has no waking.'

He smiled at Meilyr, pointing to a wooden chest against the wall. 'And now for the strongest spell of all.'

Meilyr raised the lid.

'Hand me that leather bag.'

It clinked as it was lifted. Morfran took out a golden neck chain hung with pendants. Each one was a coin: bezants, Frankish pieces, solidi with the heads of Maxen and Theodosius.

'Wear that under your shirt. Armed with music, gold and secret lore, you could outmatch a war-host.'

Meilyr set out in good heart. He called at Llangollen, to thank the Abbot for the care he had given to Morfran, and to ask for a blessing. Sulien showed him a letter he had just received from a priest in Elmet, telling what had happened two weeks since at the Weneta.

He listened with polite interest while Sulien was reading it. He joined in the Abbot's relief at the destruction of the heathen; his thankfulness that Powys had not been drawn into the disaster.

He knew now why Morfran had been calling for him; that his uncle had tried to take his place and drown instead of him, offering his own life as a sacrifice. He had drawn Meilyr away from the deep waters, just as Meilyr had done for him. And neither of them could have saved the other if Stephanos had not pitied them both. It was strange that a slave's pity had proved stronger than war or flood.

He went back the way he had come, across the river and up the hill. There would be no call now for his skills in music and hunting, no use for his uncle's philtre or his gold. He had no chance left of spiriting Alchflaed out of Leirceaster and bringing her home to Dinas Brân. Her fate, like everything else in England, was now in the hands of Oswy, the Bretwalda.

A black-robed woman with a little girl in her arms walked up to one of the Bernician guards outside the Queen's bower in Tomeworthig. She told him quietly that she had come to speak to

Queen Cynwise. She had great dignity and seemed to expect to be obeyed. She must be the widow of one of Penda's thanes, drowned in the Weneta with most of his men. The grey-beard holding her horse was tall and strongly-built but far beyond the age of war-service.

The guard saw no reason to stop her. Oswy had left orders that Penda's widow should be treated with every courtesy. He stepped aside from the door; then called a groom to show her man the way to the stables and get him a bite and a sup.

Wulfrun walked up the hall, noting that the wall-hangings had been taken down and that some chests and bundles had been stacked by the door. Cynwise was in the chamber, with her children and bower-women. Wulfrun was greeted warmly; when she asked for a private talk, the Queen signed to the women to take the children out into the hall.

The door shut behind them. Wulfrun laid the little girl, who was fast asleep, on a couch. She looked around the room. The Queen had another chest by her side, half filled with robes.

'You're going?'

'You've heard that Oswy has split Mercia? He's taken all our land north of the Treanta. South Mercia's been given to Peada, he'll be coming to hold court here.'

'With that Bernician bitch to watch his every move. Is it she or Oswy who's turning you out?'

'I don't want to stay. I'm going to Alchfrid and Cyneburg. They've found a place for me in a house of their priestesses who worship the Mother of God. I can have my children with me.'

'You're going to *Christians?*'

'The Mother is the Mother, whatever they call her. And my children will be safe.'

'The girls, yes. And the younger boys—they're too small to be a danger to Oswy. There's plenty of time for the Christians to work on them and have them in monks' gowns before they're grown, turn them into women. But Wulfhere—he's ten, he'll be a man in three years. He won't be allowed to live.'

Cynwise looked alarmed. 'Oswy wouldn't kill a child?'

'He didn't kill his cousin Oswine. Oswine's best friend did, then vanished. He didn't kill Penda. A river rose and destroyed him and most of our fighting men. He hasn't killed Peada—just turned him into a traitor and made him into his daughter's kept man. Peada will have to die; he doesn't deserve to live since he laid down his sword between that witch's legs. We'll get rid of the pair of them but we need to have our new king safe. That's why I've come for Wulfhere.'

'Would that make him any safer? Where would you take him —you're just a helpless widow like me.'

'Eadbert isn't dead—and he got most of his men away into the Fenland. Oswy won't come after him. Our rivers are bigger than the Weneta, and he can't sack and burn the Fens. Eadbert's out there with the horses. He said he wouldn't have his wife coming into danger that he didn't share.'

She gripped the Queen's hand. 'He'll teach Wulfhere to be a great warrior like his father and I—you can trust me, I'll care for him as if he were my own.'

'How will you get him out of here?'

She pointed to the girl on the bed. 'I came with a child and I'll go with a child. She won't wake up for hours, I got a drink for her from a wise-woman in Charnwood. Call Wulfhere in to speak to his kinswoman and we'll change his clothes.'

'Who is that child?'

'Daughter of one of my farmwomen. I paid the mother well. I know you'll see she's cared for.'

Wulfhere was angry and stubborn. 'I'm not going to be a girl. I'm going to be a warrior.'

Wulfrun smiled. 'A warrior has to be cunning to trick his enemies. We're going to break our way out through the Bernicians. Let's see how well you can sham sleeping and make fools of them.'

Put like that the plan was worthy of Penda's son. Wulfhere played his part zestfully as Wulfrun carried him outside and Eadbert held him while she mounted her horse. He was patient and uncomplaining during the cold rough ride to the east, day-long and far into the night under the waxing mid-winter moon. He got to feel quite at home in Wulfrun's arms.

A week later he was asleep, snuggled into her cloak while she sat in a boat being rowed down the long Fenland reaches and across the broad meres towards Eadbert's island stronghold. An icy wind rustled in the reeds, frost sparkled on the bare alder boughs, but the child was warm under the cloak and her body was warm under the child. With his brown curls and soft round cheek resting against her breast, he looked like Peada come back to her, the child who had been given into her care. Now she could love him without shame or pain and show her love proudly to the world.

And he'll love me. I'll be his mother and his sister. Oh, I'll do my duty to Cynwise. I'll teach him always to show her respect. But I'll have him. I'll know everything he thinks and feels. I'll be the one he tells about his first hunting, his first fighting, his first girl. I'll be the one he loves best. He's mine, he's mine.

She lifted her face to the moon, smiling. Old age had come on her during this last year, there were lines deeply scored round her mouth, her eyes were hollow. Eadbert, watching her as he steered, thought his wife had never looked so beautiful.

We'll never be beaten, he told himself. *While we've still got a prince of Penda's blood, while we can breed women like her, Mercia will rise again.*

CHAPTER
26

If Alchflaed had not been so heartsick she could have laughed at the fairground juggler's skill that Oswy showed in handling his subjects when he came back to Eoforwic. The old city had suddenly become the capital of all Britain, as it had been on the day when Constantine was proclaimed Emperor. Kings hurried to send envoys to the new Bretwalda or came themselves to congratulate him on his overwhelming victory. His scops had already named it the *Winwaed*, with cruel wit, because hearts' blood had been poured like wine into the Weneta when Penda's host came to the ford.

Oswy left Alchfrid to deal with the folk of Elmet and their new ealdorman, Bledri. They saw themselves as having avenged their wrongs and won back their freedom from Deira, in alliance with a prince of ancient British race. Alchfrid spent most of his time riding over the Long Hills and through the forest of Loidis, talking to them. Cyneburg had sent him a message asking him to look for her father's body and give it burial.

'You can look for it,' said Oswy when Alchfrid told him, 'but I don't think you'll find it.' He added with no change of tone, 'I don't expect you to find it.'

'He's my wife's father.'

'What would you do with him if you found him?' Oswy was

reasonable and pleasant. 'You can't give him Christian burial. You won't give him heathen burial. And I'm not sending him down to Mercia to be laid in a mound and have every surviving Mercian riding round it chanting his great deeds and working themselves up to battle-frenzy again. You could only put him in a hole in the ground and that would be an insult to him and his people. Let the marches of Loidis be his tomb and the Weneta sing his death-song. That's a fitting burial for the greatest warrior England is ever likely to see.'

Alchfrid looked startled. Oswy laughed and added, 'You can tell Cyneburg I said so; it may ease her heart. She's a good woman, I don't want her hurt.'

Oswy left Deira to Eanfled, staying discreetly in the background. He was merely the Queen's husband, the foreign warrior brought in to help an orphan heiress hold her lands. It was Eanfled's task to reward the loyal and forgive repentant rebels.

Eanfled was very proud of her courage in rallying Deira and saving the north for Christ. She took her peace-weaving just as seriously. Since it was mostly wearing beautiful robes with many jewels and being queenly to people in front of crowds of admiring Deirans, she did it very well. This was the fate she was born for; she was pleased with Oswy for giving her her due. She was so charmingly gracious to him that he was able quietly to share in her popularity and govern Deira as he liked behind her back.

Mercia was the hardest problem, so Oswy dealt with it himself. He did not want to humiliate the Mercians or drive them desperate by harsh treatment. That would only be making future trouble for himself. But he had conquered them and had to be seen as conqueror. They, and the rest of England, would be watching to see if he had a strong hand. Also, his own loyal Bernicians and his allies from Elmet and Deira expected to be rewarded with enemy loot and lands. Any king who failed to do that would not have loyal warriors or allies much longer.

So he divided Mercia, taking the northern half into his kingdom and giving the rest to Peada. If Peada were reconciled, the lost lands might be put back under his rule after a few years. He was quite willing to accept Peada as an under-king, Alchfrid's friend. Luckily, Peada was bed-ridden during the victory feasts, so he would not hear the songs of triumph over his people. Alchflaed could win him round while she was nursing him.

The first words Peada spoke to Alchflaed were, 'So you've come to gloat over me.'

'I came to find you. I wanted to help you. I'll go, if you can't bear to see me.'

'Oh yes, you can't get away quick enough. Go and flaunt yourself in Oswy's feasting-hall. Give rings and brooches to the scop, after he's sung how bravely the Bernicians stood and watched my father drown.'

Alchflaed shut her mouth on the question: *What would you be doing now if you'd killed my father?* He'd been beaten, he was grieving, he was hurt in body and spirit. She stayed with him, waiting on him when he ate or drank. She had a servant's pallet brought into the room for her bed. He watched her undressing; when she took her shift off he said, 'Oswy's sent you to snare me again with your harlot's tricks. You won't trick me a second time, you can tell him.'

'I'll find somewhere else to sleep.'

'And someone else to sleep with. Who's Alchfrid going to offer you to this time? That Welsh spy from Elmet? He'll find you a bit cracked with use but I don't suppose he's very particular.'

Alchflaed had her bed made up in a store-room, telling the servants that Peada was sleeping badly and easily disturbed.

When other people were present he behaved decently. When she was alone with him he kept up a stream of abuse and taunts. He always ended by inviting her to report what he said to Oswy, as she was there to spy on him. Twice, he struck her, telling her to go and complain to Oswy, who would be glad of the excuse to hang him.

The second time, Alchflaed raised her clenched fist back at him.

'I don't need to complain to anyone. I'm quite ready to deal with you myself. Or if that's too much for you to face,' she added bitterly, remembering how Penda had broken his word to her, 'I'll give you your ancestor Offa of Angeln's choice. Find another Mercian as brave as yourself and I'll fight the two of you!'

Then she saw he was crying and felt sick. She was more disgusted with herself than him. *He's ill; I might just as well punish a sick child for hitting out at me in a fever.*

It was a relief when he was well enough to travel. She hoped that when he was busy with his kingdom, enlarged now with half Penda's land, he would get back some of his self-respect. There was one more ordeal they had to face before they could get away. However tolerant Oswy might be, he would not let Peada leave Eoforwic without swearing loyalty to him as overlord.

The ritual took place after the Nativity feast, when the whole

285

court was assembled in the great basilica. Oswy was seated on the gift-stool. Each of the subject kings in turn knelt before him, laying head and hands on Oswy's knee and vowing to be his true man. Alchfrid went first, then Peada. He waited till he was alone with Alchflaed to ask, 'Did you feel proud to see your husband walking at your brother's heels to grovel at your father's feet? He doesn't see Mercia as even the chief of his allies.'

'Every king swears loyalty to the Bretwalda. It's no disgrace. Oswy made even his own son kneel and take the vow. We thought it would be easier for you if you saw Alchfrid—'

'So I need to have things made easy for me? Do you think I'm a child?'

She did think so. Only by making herself think so could she keep herself from hating him. His sunny good humour and generosity had owed too much to his father's greatness and his own place as heir to the most powerful kingdom in England. He did not know how to deal with defeat.

When she got to Leirceaster, her life was better because she hardly saw him. He bustled about his kingdom, asserting himself. He spent most of his time at Tomeworthig or his monastery at Medeshamsted. He passed through Leirceaster on his way from the one to the other. He only stopped to see the progress of his new church that was being built in front of the palace gateway. He and his wife only spoke to each other formally and in public during these visits. She was never asked to visit the monastery or the Mercian capital.

For the rest, her life was almost the same as before the battle. She was queen in Leirceaster; her orders were obeyed; she was the Bretwalda's daughter. But the brief kindness they had felt for her while she was facing death or caring for their wounded had died away. She was now a living sign of the Bernician victory, feared and resented. Only Helmstan and some of his spearmen showed any liking for her.

January passed. There was no snow but the air was bleak and frost-nipped. The earth seemed dead. Then Nest's child was born, like a little herald of new life to come. He was a big baby with great dark eyes and the promise of dark hair. He would probably be like Nest; at any rate, he was not like anyone in the garrison or the palace household, which was a relief to some.

Nest came easily through the birth time and was soon up and about. She adored her son. She named him Gwalchmai, after Arthur's nephew and most brilliant warrior. She loved to suckle him and spent hours rocking him and singing to him. Her lullabies were all spring songs:

> Blow, northern wind,
> Send thou me my sweeting—

and one above all that she swore Gwalchmai knew and liked best:

> Maiden in the moor lay—

The maids laughed at her but agreed that he was a fine, forward child.

Nest's songs were the only hints of spring so far as the year had gone. The east wind still kept the land dry and barren through February. In the Old Religion it was Solmonath when certain cakes were offered to the gods. They were offered to Mother Earth above all, to get her strength up after the winter and make her fertile when the seeds came into her womb. Mercian earth needed to be strong; she had to bear and feed a new generation of warriors.

One morning, Nest got a message to ask her advice about cloth-dyeing. She kissed Gwalchmai, covered him warmly in his cradle and went off to the vat. When she came back, the cradle was empty. At first she thought that one of the maids had taken him to cuddle, but none of them had him. Then she thought she was being teased and passed through coaxing to storming and threatening, then sobbing and pleading. As the hours went by she got frantic, running about the city and catching strangers' hands, begging them to tell her where they had put her baby, clawing the neck of her shift to show her swollen breasts. Some folk pitied her, some were scared and tried to drive her away with curses. Alchflaed ordered Helmstan to make a search. Every house was entered, everyone was questioned, travellers were stopped at the gates but the child could not be found.

Winefride was on her way to Charnwood. Wulfrun rode with her. She had come back quietly to her hall the night before, entering the city on foot and wrapped in a coarse cloak like a farmwoman come to market. Neither she nor Eadbert had seen or spoken to Peada since the defeat; he felt this as a reproach and blamed that on Alchflaed like everything else.

The women were making for Aino's earth-house. The entrance was barred against the east wind by a heavy oak door. When Aino drew the bolts, Wulfrun said, 'We've come to make the cakes.'

'Have you brought what's needed?'

Wulfrun lifted a bundle she was carrying. Aino nodded but

instead of inviting them in, she came out wrapped in a heavy cloak and locking the door behind her. She led the way down the rocky slope and through the oak wood towards the north. Not far away, the trees parted in a glade where there was a ring of small stones with a slab of rock in the middle.

Wulfrun laid her bundle on the grass and opened the wrappings, lifting Gwalchmai out and laying him on the slab. Nest had given him a good feed just before she left him and he had been warmly swaddled so he had slept on the journey. The evil trinity bent over him—the corrupt virgin, the barren wife and the wise-woman who sold untimely death for gain.

Gwalchmai bubbled with his mouth and pushed out his arms and legs like a starfish. Finding nothing but hard rock instead of his warm shawl and a biting wind instead of Nest's warm breast, he opened his big dark eyes in amazement, then screwed them up and wailed his protest till Aino cut his throat. Wulfrun held and tipped his body; Winefride caught the blood in a bowl she had brought. Then Gwalchmai was wrapped up again and the three went back to the earth-house. This time Aino let her visitors in.

The chamber was neat and homely. Its one decoration was a hanging over the inner door leading to the heart of the barrow, where only Aino went. Whatever she did in there, her front room showed her to be decent and hardworking. Her hearth was swept, the cauldron hanging over it was bright, there was a mortar and pestle on the table, bunches of herbs hanging to dry.

The next hour was busy and housewifely: boiling, mincing, grinding, mixing, rolling. Then they sat comfortably round the hearth, watching the cakes bake to a golden brown. When they were ready, Aino picked out four and handed them to Wulfrun wrapped in a cloth.

'East, South, West, North—here you are.'

Winefride picked up one for herself; Wulfrun turned on her sharply.

'What are you going to do with that?'

Winefride giggled. 'I'm going to give it to her—a nice new-baked cake. I'll tell her what it is when she's eaten it and watch her face.'

Aino snatched her wrist and twisted it as she took away the cake.

'You fool! A mother's curse with *that* to strengthen it—she'd blight you, she could wither us all!'

Winefride pouted; then her face brightened again. 'Well, I'm going to have these—you don't need them.'

She picked up a tiny skull, boiled clean, and a little scalp with a

288

down of dark hair on it. Aino made no objection and the two women went back to Leirceaster. Wulfrun rested in her hall, then set off as secretly as she had come, back to the Fens. Winefride left with her; but first she went to the Queen's bower and into Nest's room when she was sure the coast was clear. She put the skull and the scalp into the cradle, tucking the blankets round so that the downy hair peeped out at the top.

Nest had kept coming back to the cradle between her frantic searchings and pleadings, drawn by the belief that Gwalchmai must appear in his rightful place sooner of later. She would find that the horror had been a mistake, a joke, a dream. When she saw the dusky hair over the edge of the blanket she knew that the horror was over. She ran forward and pulled back the blanket.

Her scream was heard through the palace. When folk ran in, they found her lying like a felled tree. They got her body back to life in the end, but her spirit was dead.

Alchflaed's furious questioning found no answers. The palace servants seemed truly shocked and sorry for Nest but could give no hint of what had happened. Helmstan's men went through Leirceaster again at the Queen's orders. He told her, 'I do not think those who did it are still in the city, lady,' but could not, or would not, tell her who they might be.

Towards dusk of that unhappy day, Alchflaed took the pitiful remains, wrapped in a piece of embroidered silk, and went out. She wanted to lay them where Nest would not see them again and where they might be safe from any further desecration. Beyond the framework of Peada's new church was a patch of waste ground where a few thorn bushes were growing. Christians called the may tree Mary's Tree, but it was holy to the Mother in the Old Faith as well. Nobody would harm one.

She cut a square of the rough turf, deepened the hole underneath and laid all that was left of Gwalchmai there wrapped in his silken shroud. She repeated all she could remember of the office for Childermas and commended the child's soul to Our Lady. She would have liked to set up a cross but feared that even twigs bound with a stalk might draw hostile eyes. She had a very beautiful necklet of gold and garnet with a cross pendant. Peada had given it to her at their wedding; she laid it on the earth in a protecting circle round the skull. Gwalchmai could wait in the hope of the Resurrection; there would be none for her marriage.

There was a rustling in the bushes behind her; she swung round in alarm to see Nest staring at her. She held out her arms; prayer and human pity might heal Nest or give her some comfort. But Nest ran away. She had to stop and fit back the square of turf before she could go to look for her.

Nest was crazed. Alchflaed tried to keep her in the bower as much as possible but she would not have her chained up or locked in a room, so she got out to wander round the city. She seemed to think it was springtime; she twisted trails of withered bindweed and Old Man's Beard round her head and kept offering herself to men in honour of the Goddess. Many who saw her thought this was a good joke at first. Children followed her, women smilingly offered her bits of straw or chicken's feathers to add to her crown, or got her to dance in ale-houses, clapping out the beat of *Maiden in the moor lay*. Some of the rougher men, farm serfs or traders' grooms, took her offer and pulled her into alleys or behind bushes. The warriors of the guard, especially those who had known her kindness, turned their eyes away from her and angrily bade folk to leave her alone.

Even the best jokes grow stale, though, with too much repeating. In a week or two she hardly got more notice than any other mad beggar-woman and drifted about Leirceaster unheeded as a withered leaf from last autumn.

Near the end of March, Peada came to the city. He was visiting one of his thanes at Brantestun and was coming to hold court in Leirceaster next day to hear law suits. He rode over, not meaning to stay long, to see how the work was going on his new church. Peada enjoyed church affairs and the company of churchmen; he did not feel that they were forever holding him up against his father and Woden to see how small he looked.

A message was brought that the Queen wished to speak to him. Since their return to Mercia, Peada treated her decently in public at the rare moments they met. There were Bernicians in his kingdom, come from Oswy to check tribute and military service. Also, Alchfrid was just over the border in Deira, and he was still in some awe of his brother-in-law's manners. He would cheerfully kill Alchfrid but would have hated to be despised by him.

He went to Alchflaed's bower. He found her in the peacock room, robed and veiled in state. She had sent her maids out of earshot as the talk would be painful.

'A child has been murdered. He was the son of my bower-woman, Nest of Elmet. She has been driven out of her mind. I have been told that the killers are no longer in the city. I demand that they should be found and brought to trial.'

290

Peada was unconcerned. 'Is that all? A Welsh whore's bastard—tell her to get another where that came from. I daresay she overlaid it herself to be rid of the trouble of tending it.'

The child was murdered and I believe his body was used in some heathen rite. His mother is a member of your queen's household. And if she were the poorest serf in the kingdom, it's your duty as King to give her justice.'

'Don't try to tell me my duty as King. Attend to your duties as a wife, if you know what they are. Don't meddle in matters that only befit a man.'

'Don't you talk to me about what befits a man. How would you know?'

Her voice seemed to have taken a life of its own. She stood and listened to it saying things she had been thinking for a long time but should never have spoken aloud.

'The only man in your family died at the Winwaed. You're not a man and you don't want a wife. You want a wet-nurse with a warm lap to grovel in and big teats to plug your wailing mouth—'

She got so far because Peada had been stunned that anyone could speak to him like that. Recovering, he hit her across the mouth with such force that he knocked her down. Then he stood over her and thrashed her with his belt till his arm grew tired and he was breathless.

'You've been asking for that for a long time. You're going to get plenty more, it's what you need.'

She heard his footsteps going away. Then there was silence. She lay on the beautiful mosaic, blood oozing from her mouth. Her body was not in pain, it was pain. Her throat felt parched; she longed for a drink of water but her mouth hurt too much to call her maids. No one would come anyway. She bore the marks of the King's anger; she was a stranger in an enemy land. The household servants had gone away and would stay away. There would not be a hand stretched to help her.

But the hand was already there, easing her cheek gently from the stones. Nest's arms lifted her head and held it against her breast. Pity and anger had shocked her back into her wits; she knew what to do.

'Oh, my dear, what has he done to you? Oh, never mind—never mind!'

Nest got Alchflaed on to the couch, washed her mouth where the flesh had been cut against her teeth, got her to swallow a little wine. She was dazed and oddly sleepy; she just wanted to lie with her eyes closed. Nest sat beside her, holding her hand, stroking her forehead and making soft little murmuring noises as if she were hushing Gwalchmai. No one else came near the bower.

Towards evening, when she stirred and sat up, Nest made her eat some cake sopped in wine. Then she asked if it would hurt too much to take off her clothes and see what harm she had taken from Peada's beating.

The heavy woollen robes had saved her from the worst injuries but he had struck with the buckle and struck hard. Her body showed some ugly weals and bruises. Her lip had also swollen and her cheek was discoloured and sore inside.

Nest got some salve and touched it delicately onto the sore places. Once when Alchflaed gasped and winced Nest turned to her with a fierce smile that was nearly a snarl.

'Don't you fret, my love. He won't live long enough to do that to you again.'

She caught Nest's hand. 'Nest, I forbid you! You mustn't even think—'

'I'll be thinking of it every moment. But I'm not going to dirty my hands on him—leave that to his own people, they've got it all planned. He's marked for death.'

Alchflaed stared at her. 'How do you know this?'

Nest laughed. 'I'm mad, aren't I? I count for no more than a piece of straw mucked out of a byre. Folk don't see me any more. They go on talking and I hear them—though I haven't paid much heed since—since—' She put her hand to her head.

'What do you hear?'

'Some of them got away from the Winwaed. There's a great chief heading them—he's in the Fens. They hate Peada for kneeling to Oswy. No Mercian likes it much. The Fenmen have sworn to kill Peada, they got a witch-woman to put a death curse on him.'

'I must get away at once.'

'Indeed you must, my love. They'll kill you too.'

Alchflaed hardly noticed this. 'He wouldn't believe me if I tried to warn him. And when those others saw I knew, they'd kill me or get him to imprison me before I could get word to Alchfrid. Oh, God! Even if I escape and get to Eoforwic, can we possibly come back in time to save him?'

Nest looked startled; she opened her mouth to protest, then shut it again. Her only wish was to get Alchflaed to safety; she told herself that there was no danger of Bernicians losing their breath rushing to rescue Peada. If she said that to Alchflaed, her dear mistress might give up her life in some crazy loyalty of dying by his side.

'Your brother's not in Eoforwic. He came down to Loidis two weeks ago. They didn't tell you in case you took it into your head to visit him and he got some idea how things were with you. There's a great gathering in Loidis, more than enough to keep you safe. King Edwin had a church in Doneceaster that Penda and Cadwallon burned in the old days. Only the stone altar wouldn't burn, so our priests took it and kept it hidden in the forest. Bledri told your brother and invited him to come down and keep the Resurrection in honour of Elmet.'

Alchflaed gave a hopeless sigh. 'I know how to get past the walls but I'll never get to Loidis in time without a horse. I can't take one without giving myself away.'

'It's mild weather and the land's at peace. They've started leaving the horses out in the pastures. If you can get past the walls, you can see to take one by moonlight—it's just coming to full. You'll have to ride without a saddle. I'll get you a bridle. No one heeds what I do.'

'If it's moonlight the night watch might see me from the walls, a stranger skulking round the horses.'

'If they're awake at all, they'll see Nest roving round moon-struck. You can wear my rags over your riding clothes.'

'And what's to become of you when they find I'm gone?'

'How soon do you think they'll start looking? I told you, I'm mad. If a queen takes a fancy to a poor madwoman's robes and garlands, and changes clothes with her, why should a poor madwoman say no? At worst, it'll only be a beating and you took one for me and my son. It won't hurt me, I can't suffer any more.'

Alchflaed embraced her. 'I wouldn't go if it wasn't to save a life. I'll come back for you, with my brother, then we'll go away together to my aunt's convent in the north. You won't be here much longer.'

'Not much longer.'

She made Alchflaed have a meal before she got into her riding clothes. Nest went off to steal a bridle and put up some food and a flask for the journey. When she came back with them, Alchflaed cried out in horror. Nest had cut off her long black hair; she twisted a plait of it round Alchflaed's head, letting the rest hang down in elf-locks. She put her tattered gown over the leather jerkin and breeches, then decked her lady's hair with the dirty veil and withered garlands. Alchflaed took an oil lamp and a strike-a-light to see her way along the drainage tunnel, then kissed Nest goodbye. The two of them must not be seen outside together.

Nest held the door ajar for her and watched her glide away into the shadows. Then she came back to the Queen's room; she had preparations of her own to make. There was no need to hurry, dawn was some hours away. She heated some water and washed herself. Then she went to the Queen's chests and trinket boxes to choose what she liked best. A fine shift and hose neatly cross-gartered. Shoes of soft leather. A splendid green gown from the very bottom of a chest. She had never seen Alchflaed wearing it; the hem was thick with silver embroidery, the thirteen moons of the year and all the Lady's flowers in their seasons. A heavy green mantle with silver brooches to pin at her shoulders. A coronet trimmed at each side with ropes of pearl hanging to her shoulders, such as Roman ladies had worn in the days of the Empire. A thickly embroidered veil.

The head-dress gave Nest some trouble at first. Her cropped head was too small for it; and even veiled, the shape showed nothing like Alchflaed's mass of brown tresses. Then she remembered some hanks of wool that had been dyed brown ready for weaving. She made a thick plait of it to coil and pin round her head, fixing the coronet firmly on top of it and throwing the veil over her face and shoulders.

She looked like the Queen of the Wood when she came out of the bower into the early morning sunlight and walked slowly across the palace courtyard, under the great arched doorway, past the new church where the workmen were already busy, and so down the road towards the western gate. No one came near her, though there were many pairs of eyes on her, some admiring and some angry, from half-open doors, hall-porches and alleyways. All Leirceaster had known before last nightfall that Peada had beaten Alchflaed like a slave-woman, yet there she was, going to confront him on the highway before all his men, as he rode back into the city, like the proud queen she was—or like the shameless Northumbrian bitch she was.

Nest felt the eyes on her and held her veiled head high, taking her time on the way to the gate.

I am Honesta, a noblewoman of Elmet. I bore a child to a bard, in honour of the Lady of the Springtime. Take a good look at me. My people were lords of this land before the Romans came. Damn you all, you're not fit to lick my shoes clean.

So Nest, Honesta, a noblewoman of Elmet, walked like a queen

294

through Leirceaster, out under the western gateway, and was never seen there again.

She strolled across the bridge over the Soar, as if she were taking the air for her pleasure, glancing idly at the fisherman in his punt by the bank, the farmwoman gathering coltsfoot in the skirts of the forest. She was wording what she was going to say to Peada when she met him, loud enough for his men to hear, remember and repeat. She hoped to get through a fair amount of it before he killed her; she thought she would be laughing as she watched her death-blow coming.

But when the blow came it was from behind. As she entered the forest, she was struck with a club on the back of her skull. She pitched forward under folds of veiling and mantle to be bundled head first into a sack by the two men who had stalked her. Wine-fride, who had been making a show of gathering coltsfoot, came out from under the trees. She looked pleased and excited, like a child whose nameday gift has bettered her hopes but is still looking forward to more treats.

The plotters had decided to remove Alchflaed before Peada's murder. 'Get her outside the walls,' Wulfrun had said. 'Make sure you're out of sight in the forest. Her body mustn't be found. Let folk think she's run off. We're not ready for trouble with Oswy yet.'

Prompted by her sister, Winefride had cobbled up a story to be delivered by one of the churls, about a rider from Alchfrid come with an urgent message that he had to give her secretly. They hoped the bait would be tempting enough to make her slip out of Leirceaster without a word to her women, unseen except by those who were dogging her. Then Peada could be told she had run away to Oswy in Bernicia to complain about his unkindness. The beating she had got last night would give more likelihood to that part of the tale.

Still, they could not be quite sure that she would swallow their bait. But the gods had turned kind to Mercia at last; they must have found their Solmonath cakes tasty and were inclined to help their worshippers. Woden and his waelcyriges had put Alchflaed into such a fury that she had shamed her husband by deserting him pub-licly, walking insolently out of his palace and city under the eyes of all the folk. She had left them no more to do but take her, hide her corpse and set a story going about Bernician horsemen lurking in the woods to help the flight that she must have been planning for weeks.

In her mind, Winefride was already wording obscene little hints about the Queen's furtive assignations, to spice the story. Her cheeks dimpled.

'Carry her to the riverside. Helmstan's waiting with the boat. If you see a good big piece of rock, pick it up. It'll do to weight the sack.'

One of the men humped the sack over his shoulder, the other walked behind to share the weight. Winefride led the way among the trees to a place on the riverbank, out of sight from the walls of Leirceaster. Helmstan, grim-faced and muffled in a black cloak, was waiting with the boat. As the sack was swung down there was a faint moan from inside it. Helmstan turned on Winefride.

'She's alive!'

'All the better, we won't have killed her.' Winefride giggled. 'There's no reason why she shouldn't undo the sack and swim!' She stopped laughing and added, 'Get well downstream and choose a good deep pool. Make sure you weight the sack. Remember, you're drowning Mercia's evil fortune—it must never rise up again.'

She turned back, followed by the servants. Helmstan began to pole slowly downstream. He wished with all his heart that Winefride had been in the sack, not Alchflaed. She was a fine woman, worth a hundred of that vicious little slut. He owed her the life of Guthlac, his sister's son. But he was loyal to his lord, Eadbert—and there was no doubt that Mercia had met with nothing but disaster since she had married Peada and turned him from his father's gods. Helmstan did not believe she had cursed them, as Lady Wulfrun said. More like she was one of those ill-fated folk who have bad luck on them and bring it wherever they go. He wished he could save her, for Guthlac's sake, but he had to lift the bad luck from his land.

Then he began to see dimly how he might do both. The idea came with thinking of Guthlac and ill-luck together, remembering how the boy came to be born.

Helmstan had been an orphan, brought up by his elder sister and her husband, a decent man. He made no complaint when his wife miscarried of her first child. She brought the second to full term but he died on his road out of the womb. Still, the husband was good-humoured; he told his wife she was young yet; there would be other babes. The wife stayed sad and silent; then, soon after she was up and about, she had come cloaked to Helmstan and gripped his shoulders.

'You must come and keep me company. Have you got your knife? Now remember, don't speak one word whatever you see me do and never turn your head to look over your shoulder.'

They had gone first to the place where the baby was buried. His sister cut a clod of earth from the grave and wrapped it in a piece of black cloth. Then she set off beyond their village towards the ford. A beggarman was loitering on the other bank. His sister called across, 'Do you want to buy anything?'

'Do you want to sell anything?'

'This.' She held out the clod of earth wrapped in black cloth and laid her best bracelet on top. The beggar held out a rusty iron pin.

'I'll pay you this for it.'

'Done.'

She stepped into the ford; the beggar came to meet her and they made the exchange over running water as she said:

> *I sell it, you must sell it,*
> *This black wool and the seeds of this sorrow.'*

Then she walked back the way she had come, gripping Helmstan's arm as she passed him and pushing him in front of her so that he could not look back. He had been too scared to ask questions; but next year after Guthlac had been born, a fine healthy boy, she had laughed and told him that this was a never-failing way to rid yourself of bad luck. There was always someone too poor or sick to mind about buying it if you put in a make-weight.

Helmstan thought of all this as he poled down the Soar, past several deep pools overshadowed by trees, with marshy land behind them where no one was ever likely to come. He went on till he came to a ford where a track crossed from east to west. He drove in his pole, fastened the boat and loosened the neck of the sack without looking inside.

I'll leave it to Woden and Frea, he thought. *I'll give her till midday. If no one's come by then, that'll prove she's fated and nothing can save her. I'll take her back to a pool. I won't leave her to drown in the dark, though. I'll cut her throat before I put her in, I owe her that much.*

Before the sun had reached its noon, Helmstan heard the clattering of hoofs on the eastern side of the track. He took off his black cloak and laid it over the sack. A string of four pack ponies came in sight, led by a servant armed with a spear. The trader rode behind. Helmstan hailed him, offering his flask.

'Where away?'

'West to the British kingdoms.'

'How's trade?'

'Bad. Mercia's almost beggared. The Elmet folk have collected so much loot after Winwaed, they don't need to buy or sell.'

'Could you use a woman—young, fair, well-taught?'

The trader looked round. 'Where is she?'

'In there.' Helmstan pointed to the sack. The trader drew back, shaking his head.

'Oh no. I'm not covering up for your murder—'

'She's alive.'

'Or rape. If she's sick, leave her to die. If she's got the plague, burn her.'

'It's not like that.' Helmstan had got his story ready while he waited. 'I took her in a raid on Elmet. She's beautiful and high-born—says she's a king's daughter, but they all say that. I liked her well enough, but my wife—you know how it is. She had a miscarriage and took it into her head that the girl had cursed her. It's a fact, I've had nothing but bad luck this past year—but you could say the same for all Mercia. Now my wife's with child again and well-nigh demented. Today she grabbed a cloth-beater and nearly stove the girl's skull in. She could have killed herself and the child. I don't wish the girl any harm but I want to rid myself of the bad luck. Will you buy?'

The trader still looked suspicious but bent to open the sack. Helmstan carefully turned his eyes away; you must never see your bad luck again after you'd wrapped it up. The trader satisfied himself that the girl was alive and had no signs of plague or fever. He decided that the story was likely true—why make up such an odd lie? The girl's hair was cropped like a slave's but her hands were soft and the dress she was wearing was worth a fortune— this poor devil with the mad shrew for wife must have really loved her. He opened his pouch and took out a cheap bronze brooch.

'I'll give you this for her.'

He called his servant and they hauled out the sack, still draped in the black cloak while Helmstan recited:

> *I sell it, you must sell it,*
> *This black wool and the seeds of this sorrow.'*

Then he pulled up the pole and took the boat upstream without looking back. He had sold the bad luck out of Mercia—to the Welsh, which was an added satisfaction. If Alchflaed's wits recovered from that crack on the head and she managed to get herself ransomed, still the bad luck had gone over running water and could not get back. He could truthfully tell Winefride that he had got rid of Alchflaed downstream in the river.

CHAPTER
27

The leaves were just beginning to unfold. Below Dinas Brân along the valley and east towards the plain of Mercia, the woodlands looked as if a green mist was rising after a green rain. Meilyr felt the same cold lightness inside him. Most of the ties that had bound his mind and spirit for the last four years had been broken.

He crossed the courtyard, where the servants were bringing out bundles to load on the pack-ponies, and went into the tower. Morfran was propped up on his couch by the table. He was putting some documents into a small casket; the carved box where he kept certain herbs and extracts stood beside it; there was a little pile of books and scraps of manuscript on the floor.

Morfran tapped the lid of the casket, smiling. 'Dinas Brân is yours. I'll give this to the Abbot to keep for you. He'll see that the farms are tended; your brother has given his pledged word to guard them for you.'

'Are you happy about this, Uncle? Do you truly want to go back to Llangollen?'

'Yes. I've lived above the world too long. We all need our fellow men, to stay human. And the Abbot is overjoyed—a real Greek scholar coming to his house!' He laughed. 'I've often heard Stephanos saying that it's an honour to serve a man of learning, so perhaps he'll take me as assistant librarian. We'll have a fine collection to show you when you come back from Ireland.'

'I may not come back as soon as I've finished my studies. I've a mind to see Constantinople, after hearing Stephanos talk about it.'

'God be with you, wherever you go.'

'Do you want me to have those books parcelled up?'

'No. I've asked Stephanos to burn them and to destroy this,' he touched the carved box. Then sharply, 'What are you doing?'

Meilyr had drawn his dagger and was putting it to his left wrist.

'Just prising the catch open.' He pointed the dagger to his bracelet of hair. 'I haven't moved it for years, it's stiff. Stephanos can destroy it with the rest. If there's any power in it—if I haven't been tricking myself with dreams and illusions—I don't want to hold her on a leash. Let her be free of me.'

Morfran put his hand on Meilyr's. 'I should have told you. It didn't bind her—you bound yourself.'

Meilyr laughed. 'Then let it go. I don't need it.' He began to attack the bracelet more fiercely; the dagger point slipped and pricked the plait of hair. He saw Morfran's face and stopped.

'Will destroying it harm her?'

Morfran sighed. 'I'm not sure. We don't know as much as we think we do. It came from her body, it's been against your flesh for years while you've thought about her, desired her, schemed to get her. These things create a bond. Let me have it. I'll give it to the Abbot to sain it and keep it under the cross. That should keep it safe.'

Meilyr looked hard at his uncle. 'Safe from what?'

'The night you first showed the hair to me and told me what you planned to do with it, I used its image and called her name. I only wanted her to come into sight for a moment so that I would know what she was like.'

'And did she come?'

'No.' Even after years, Morfran shuddered at the memory of what had come.

'I saw somewhere in England. There was treachery and some terrible evil. The picture came when I called her name. From all you've told me about her, I cannot believe that the evil came from Alchflaed herself—it must have been some crime done by one of her family—God knows there have been enough to choose from in every royal House. But after the picture—the evil broke through. It took me all my strength to banish it. And I only banished it for a time, I couldn't lay it.' He winced. 'It was drawn here. It was drawn by the hair.'

He looked at Meilyr; his eyes were haunted with remorse. 'Such beings—they can be the unhappy dead or those elementals that suck their life from human evil, from hate and pain and fear. They take a grip wherever they can. Meilyr, I watched your father fixing his hatred on Riemmelth and her marriage year after year. I watched you inherit the hatred. And I never warned you because I was too taken up with hating my own fate. The greatest sin was mine. Whatever came here looking for Alchflaed found a rich feast to glut it and give it strength.'

Meilyr sheathed his dagger. His uncle reached for the hair, imploring, 'Give it to me. Let me take it to the Abbot.'

'I'm going away, across running water. But if there is any evil

300

drawn by it, I'm the one who chose that it should be so. Let it come to me, not to her.'

In the dusk, the guard at the southern gate of Doneceaster heard the hoofbeats before he saw the rider. Only one, pushing a tired horse. He readied his spear as the stranger came up.

'Is the King here?'

'He is. What do you want?'

'I must speak to him at once. There's trouble in Mercia.'

The guard looked at him, exhausted and travel-stained. Very young, no sign of a beard yet. That was so surprise; there were few men of fighting age left in Mercia. He told the other men at the gate to keep good watch, called a groom to take the traveller's horse to the stables and led him towards the halls.

Doneceaster was crowded with nobles and their escorts. There were dark hill-men from Elmet. Alchflaed caught a glimpse of some of her brother's Cumbrian bodyguard. She kept her face shrouded in her cloak. The great hall was ablaze with torches, servants were hurrying in and out; clearly a feast was toward. Her guide led her into a smaller building, saying, 'A message for the King,' to the men keeping the doors.

While she followed him up the hall, which was deserted, she tried to word what she would say to Alchfrid. He would not be inclined to interfere in the affairs of Peada's kingdom, the more so now that he had responsibility for Elmet and the borders of Deira. She must be very calm, so as not to disgust him and make him dismiss her as a silly, frightened woman, but she must make him come back with her at once and in force.

The guard knocked at the door of the inner room. A voice told him to enter, there were a few murmured words, then he beckoned her to come in. He stood aside for her to enter; the man reading at the hearth looked up from his book. It was Oswy.

She gasped and stopped dead. The guard, alarmed, reached for his sword. Oswy stood up, saying, 'All's well, Leofgar, I know the man. You can leave us.'

When the door had shut again, Oswy said, 'Why are you so shocked to see me?'

'I thought it would be Alchfrid.'

'I've come to keep Passiontide with him and reverence that altar. It's a great time for Elmet, we want to show them as much honour as possible. Don't waste time telling me how pleased you are to see me, what's the matter?'

'The Mercians are going to kill Peada.'

'I'm not surprised. Clever girl, to get out in time; you've saved me a lot of worry. You must be tired out. I'll have a bower got ready, Bledri will find some women to attend you. Have a meal and a good night's sleep. We'll have you on the road to Eoforwic tomorrow. I'll get you a litter so you can travel in comfort.'

'Thank you, Father, but I'd rather wait here while you go for Peada; I'll get the news sooner.'

He shook his head, smiling. She stared at him.

'Aren't you going to get Peada out?'

'They'd kill him as soon as I invaded and say I'd ordered the killing in advance. And all Britain would believe it.'

'Send Alchfrid. His brother-in-law twice over, no one would say—'

'No. I've always kept Alchfrid out of these feuds, it's his greatest strength.'

'Then give me troops. He's my husband, I'll go myself.'

'No.'

She stepped up to him, her eyes wide with anger.

'You want Peada dead.'

'If I told you I'd break my heart to hear of his death, you wouldn't believe me. Why should I insult you by lying?'

She felt cold. 'Have you planned this killing—the way you killed Oswine?'

'What a dutiful question. No, I haven't planned it and I don't particularly want it at this time. A few more years and Mercia would have got used to my rule. Habit is a great healer and most folk only want a quiet life. But if they've planned to kill him now, they can get on with it. Now, it's just between Mercians. If I try to stop it, I'll only get dragged into worse trouble, and that I don't want at this moment.'

Alchflaed turned to the door. He caught her arm and pulled her back. 'Where are you going?'

'To warn Peada. Likely he won't believe me but—'

'No. Now you're here you'll stay. Then I won't have to send a war-band in to try to rescue you.'

'I'll denounce you to all Britain. You've no right to keep me from him.'

'Why are you ready to go all lengths to save him—risk your life? I'm not blind or deaf. I know how things were between you in Eoforwic and I don't suppose they're any better now. What happened to your mouth?'

302

There was no use in lying; he'd only think her more of a fool.

'Whatever happens between Peada and me, we've become one flesh. Is it so unnatural that I should care whether he lives or dies?'

'It's not in the least unnatural. He's your brother.'

She stared; then shook her head, smiling.

'Oh no, Father. Don't try that—it's an unworthy trick. You didn't think I'd believe you?'

'I don't play tricks with your mother's memory. I never meant to say the words as long as I lived. Only the direst need makes me say them now.'

She was beyond thought or speech. He put her into his chair by the hearth, drew up a stool and sat down facing her.

'I'll say it once and for all. Penda took Gefrin by surprise while I was away. He gave the place and everything in it to Woden, so there were no witnesses of what happened. Your mother fought him in armour, warrior to warrior, as you've heard. Her spirit was stronger than her body—but no man ever defeated Penda in fight. He took her, but her brain and her courage remained unbroken—like her honour. She escaped and made her way back to me. There was no one like her; she was as far above other women as the moon is over the earth. She told me everything, didn't try to pretend she'd been with child already and you were mine.'

'And knowing that, you let me—'

'I didn't let you. I tried everything I knew to stop you. I even made conditions that could have had Penda making war on me when I wasn't ready to face him. Anyway, it was already too late to stop you sleeping with Peada. That was your choice. Remember what I said to you: "*Whatever happens to you now, you'll have done it to yourself.*" '

'How you must hate me.'

'I don't hate you. I wish you were my daughter. I wish still more you were my son. If you'd been begotten by your mother's wish—if you'd been the child of some lover she'd had before she met me—or even some man she'd chosen to take for light-heartedness at a spring revel—' he sighed—'or even come as you did, if she'd lived on, loving you and happy with you, I could have loved you. But she suffered in your begetting and she's dead.'

She could hardly move her lips. 'You're saying I killed my mother.'

'Marsh-fever killed your mother. She was as strong as a well-forged sword. Love doesn't come with wishing. I'm sorry.'

He looked at her deathly face. 'I like you, Alchflaed. I pity you with all my heart. And I respect you. You'll have all the protection and honour I can give you. Go back to Ebbe. You love her and you were happy there. We always meant you to succeed her as Abbess—or if you want to found a house of your own, I'll give you lands and gold. You could go to Cumbria, your mother's country. Alchfrid will need a counsellor when I'm gone, to stop him trying to refound the Roman Empire. He'll listen to a royal Abbess, everybody does, you'll have far more power than a queen—'

He stopped and touched her cheek. 'This is too much for you all at once. You can eat and sleep here, I won't be coming back tonight—it's Bledri's feast, we'll all sleep where we drop. I'll have food sent in—I won't say who you are, just a trusted messenger. Tomorrow I'll send you off in a litter as if you were ill after your ride from Mercia. When I get back to Eoforwic, we'll talk.'

He smiled at her kindly. 'Keep up your heart, my dear. There's always hope.'

He went out. She sat staring at the fire. Some time later, a servant brought broth, grilled fish, bread and wine. She thanked him pleasantly and made herself eat it. Then she put on her cloak and went out by the side door of the chamber.

It was nearly dark now; there was torchlight from the hall and singing. She made her way to the stables and asked for a fresh horse; the King had another errand for his trusted messenger. The stable grooms brought her a fine mount as befitted one who was riding on the King's business. This time she left by the western gate and was swallowed up in the darkness.

At first the Mercian forest pressed round her but after about twelve miles the road began to climb and she came out on to the moors. The wind swept over the desolate heights. It was not more homeless than she was. There was nowhere on earth that she belonged by right because she should never have been born. She was nothing but the ghost of her mother's sorrow and shame, haunting her kinsfolk and destroying their peace. Riemmelth, Oswy, Peada.

'*A woman who mates in a tomb—what else could she bear but a corpse?*' Wherever she went, death had gone with her.

Her horse's feet beat on the stones; the beats turned into words hammering in her mind, the most terrible words in all the Scriptures. She had always shuddered when she read them and tried to

304

forget them, wondering why God had allowed them to be written and handed down. Now she knew that they had been spoken over her before time began.

Quare non in vulva mortua sum?—Why did I not die in the womb, why did I not perish when I came out of the belly . . . as a hidden, untimely birth I should not be . . .

I should not be.

That could be put right and no one need be troubled, accused, called to account for her death.

'If you should need shelter and all else has failed you, come back here.'

Unlike Job or Nicodemus, she knew the way back to the Mother's Womb and this time she would not come out.

CHAPTER
28

The waterfront at Legaceaster was as lively as ever after its change of masters. The King of Powys had quietly taken the city while Mercia's grip was slack. Oswy did not argue with him; he had enough to do in England and did not want trouble with Powys. Powys wanted no trouble with Oswy. So Welsh and English still met on the quays, round the booths and in the ale-houses with no more brawling than you get at any port. Traders and packmen still came in from the east to meet the merchant captains of the western sea-board.

Meilyr strolled along the quayside in the mild spring dusk— free, well-born and rich—with the same cold lightness of spirit he had felt ever since he heard the news of Winwaed. It was ebb-tide, the mud flats were beginning to gleam under the western sky. Tomorrow he would sail for Ireland to study, a good way of passing the time while he made up his mind what he wanted to do. At the moment, what he wanted was a woman; not love, not spring ecstasy, just a pair of thighs and a hole to ease himself.

He turned towards Mother Godelif's. Some girls were squatting by a pile of bales near one of the ships, waiting to be loaded. Nothing to interest him there. They were farm-churls taken in a raid on Mercia, dirty and ungraceful. He wanted a lively portqueen who took a pride in her trade. Looking carelessly at the sullen faces he saw that the dark-haired one was his spring girl from last year. He wondered how she came to be there, thinking bitterly that he and she together made a good picture of the British race, aimless and hopeless.

On an impulse he bought her; she had shown good sport. The trader tried to push her price up, saying she was a king's daughter. Meilyr laughed at him—'Aren't they all?'—and got her quite reasonably after a spirited haggle.

She was wearing a coarse woollen shift. He took her along to the booths and with cold amusement got her ready for a seaman's night in port. He bought her a red dress, purple slippers and a green shawl embroidered with yellow; a wristful of gaudy glass bracelets, some viciously-scented oil that claimed to have sprung from violets, a box of face-paint and a metal mirror. The woman silently took the things behind a corner in an alley and came out looking like a quayside whore.

He took her up to the northern end of the waterfront, into a dark little ale-house and bargained with the frowsy hag inside for a bed. She jerked her head to a row of grubby hangings; he insisted on a room. She overcharged him, then showed him up a ladder into the loft, which was divided by wattle-and-daub walls each with a rickety door.

When some weak-looking ale had been brought up to them, with a plate of greasy sausages and some bread, he barred the door and put the room's one stool in front of it. He hadn't shown his gold but the hag had seen that he was free-spending. He didn't want any of her friends coming in uninvited with their knives ready.

The woman began to take her clothes off. She was so stony-faced, so clearly without the least glimmer of pleasure, that his temper flared.

'God, girl, haven't I spent enough on you? Can't you even give me a smile in return? I know this isn't the Emperor's palace at Constantinople but it's better than the ship's hold where you were going to spend the night. And don't tell me you're the High King of Ireland's daughter, carried off by wicked pirates, I've heard it before.'

'Then I won't tell you. I could tell you I bore you a son, but I daresay you've heard that before too.'

Meilyr looked at her in horror: her slave-cropped hair, the despair in her face, her sagging breasts.

I brought her to this. Her husband or her keeper killed our child and sold her out of spite. And there's nothing I can do about it except let her cry her heart out, and get her to some decent refuge.

He took her in his arms. 'My poor girl, I'm sorry. Tell me all about it.'

Nest told him.

When she had finished he sighed; then looked up to the cracks in the roof.

'It's hours yet to dawn. Eat some of that foul food. I don't think she's poisoned it except with her cooking. We'll need our strength for the morning.'

'What are you going to do?'

'Get Alchflaed out of Mercia if she's still alive. If she's escaped to her own people, well and good. Let the Mercians do her one good turn and may God guide their daggers.' He took Nest's hand. 'But I won't go without seeing you safe. My brother's the prince of Iâl. I'm going to take you to his court and dower you. You're young and beautiful. He'll make a good marriage for you.'

Nest shook her head. 'I've done with courts and palaces. I never want to see one again. And I don't care for marrying. I don't care for anything now, except Alchflaed. I'd give my life for her safety. It's all I've got left to give.'

He gripped her shoulders. 'You're not to do that, Nest. I forbid you, for her sake as well as yours. You offered your life once and it was accepted. You were brought here to meet me. The task has passed from you to me. If you kill yourself now—'

Nest burst out laughing. 'I'm not going to. I never had much heroism and I've used it all up. When I said my life, I meant my name—who I am. If you do find her and bring her to Powys, she'll need a name. Alchflaed of Northumbria, Oswy's daughter! That'll bring every Mercian knifeman and,' her mouth twisted, 'hel-runing witch on her track. And it won't earn her many friends in Powys either, will it? But Honesta, a noblewoman from Elmet, that you saved in the east during Penda's wars. She'd be safe enough like that. She can have my name. I never did much credit to it.'

'But who will you be, Nest?'

'It doesn't matter any more.'

'Yes it does. It matters to me, for what that's worth. And it matters to Alchflaed. What am I to tell her about you if I ever meet her again?'

Nest shrugged.

'Look, Nest, I'm a poet and something of a magician. My brother's a prince and my uncle's a man of learning. Between us, we can surely make a spell strong enough to grant a wish. What would you be, if you could choose?'

Nest thought for a moment. 'I'd be an ale-wife. I'd be good at it; I was mistress to the palace steward in Eoforwic. Not in a pig-sty like this,' she looked round scornfully. 'I'd keep a decent house: my beds would be soft and my bedding would be clean and sunbleached. My ale would be strong-brewed, my bread freshbaked. I'd have pretty maid-servants—not worn-out slaves, hearty country girls who enjoyed their work and took their pleasure. And all the fine men would come to my house, the bold sea-captains and the wise merchants who walk the world. The singing there'd be in the evenings and the telling of stories! And wherever they were, afterwards, tossing in storms, or in fleabiting hovels all down the western sea-board, they'd say "We fared better when we were with—with Lleucu!" That's what I'd call myself—Lleucu at the sign of the Harbour Beacon!'

She stopped, out of breath. 'You think that's a whore's wish, don't you?'

'I think it's a poem. If I ever come back to your house, I'll make it into a song for you that they'll be singing in every port from Strathclyde to the Pillars of Hercules.'

So they got through the night, dozing as best they could on the straw mattress in one another's arms for warmth and company.

Next morning they paid another visit to the booths and Nest transformed herself again in a decent dark robe and cloak with a black veil over her head. She gave him her finery, knotted up in a bundle in the green-and-yellow shawl.

'Take these with you in your saddle bag. If you find her, you can hardly escort her out of the country as Queen Alchflaed of Mercia. But a harper can go anywhere and he can take his woman with him.'

They went to the maer, who listened respectfully and with every sign of belief while Prince Meilyr of Iâl introduced his widowed foster-sister whom he was setting up in Legaceaster. He swore to be accountable for her well-doing and for the pouch of gold Meilyr left with her.

Nest kissed him goodbye and he set off. He paused before he passed under the gateway, taking the dragon ring of Cumbria from a chain round his neck to put on his finger. He left by the east gate, going towards Manceinion, because so far as he knew, she was somewhere in England heading north—and that was all he did know.

Alchflaed dismounted on the hill-slope facing Mam Tor. She had ridden all night on the Roman road over the moors and followed the well-known valley up from the Noue in the early dawn. She patted the weary horse and slapped his flank. He ambled off down the valley; he would find grass and running water down there; sooner or later some farmer would take him.

She found her line from Mam Tor to the narrow cave mouth; inside, in the niche of rock, were the candles and lantern. She lit a candle and set it in the lantern, then imagined Freawynn standing at her left shoulder.

'Thrice to thine and thrice to mine
And thrice again to make up nine.'

The twisting path had a different look when it was trod backwards. As she got deeper and no more light came through the cracks, she was not sure she was going the same way. It need not have mattered; she was not going to come out again; it should make no odds which dark tunnel was her grave. But she had set her mind on reaching the Mother's Womb; it was the last task she had set herself to accomplish.

Meilyr hesitated at the east gate of Manceinion. Commonsense, so far as that had any share in his actions, told him to go north-east, over the Long Hills. Then he could easily keep on to Eoforwic, or south through Elmet and try to pick up news about her from Alchfrid's court before going down into Mercia.

Yet every nerve in his body urged him to take the other road, southeast towards the Lady's Bower as he had done last year. The bracelet of hair round his wrist felt warm. He felt drawn to the south—but then, he had felt drawn that way last year, sure that he would meet Alchflaed and nothing had come of it.

No. Nest had come of it. Because of what had happened there last year, Nest had saved Alchflaed's life and had been brought to Legaceaster to warn him of her danger. He had learned from Nest that Alchflaed had been in the Lady's Bower last spring though he had not met her. He had been wrong about the meeting—then he remembered how Morfran had tried to take his place in the Weneta three weeks before it overflowed its banks. Perhaps he had been told last spring about a meeting now.

He made the huntsman's choice; he did what his body told him and set off for the southeast.

He was benighted but got a lodging in a shepherd's hut and came along the valley towards Mam Tor in the late morning. It was very quiet. The land felt deserted as if all the folk had fled. Then he saw a man coming towards him leading a horse. It was Brid, the farmer who had lodged him last year. They greeted each other; Meilyr remarked on the silence.

'Eostre will be late coming this year. Peada's men came to destroy the shrine, so the priestesses took the holy things and fled.'

Meilyr's heart sank. He'd come for nothing, and lost a day.

'The shrine's destroyed?'

'No. They didn't find anything—they were too scared to look far. Not that they'd have found anything if they'd looked for a hundred years. The Lady's on her way; she'll be here in a sennight. I saw one of her bower maidens a while back, she came over the Doneceaster road in the dawn twilight. I'm looking after her horse.'

Meilyr tensed. 'Where is she?'

'She went into the hollow hill.'

'I've got to speak to her.'

'It'll be a while before she comes out. You can wait at my place.' Brid moved up the track beside the stream, heading towards his farm. 'You may want to speak to her but it depends whether she wants to speak to you. If she does she'll send a token. If not, you won't get sight or sound of her.'

'Brid, I came to speak to her. I was called. I must see her at once. You must show me the way into the hollow hill.'

Brid looked at him doubtfully, almost angrily. 'You can't do that. You've not been called. You'd have a token and they'd send a guide. No one but a priestess can go alone into the hollow hill. It's death for anyone else.'

Meilyr touched his harp bag. 'This is my token to you. Times are different. You know what Peada tried to do. Things will be worse now, since his father's dead and he's King of Mercia.' He lowered his voice. 'They took a child who was begotten here for the Goddess last spring and killed him to make a death magic.'

Brid looked horrified. Meilyr went on earnestly. 'No wonder Eostre's late this year. If Peada has his way, she might not be able to come at all. So you see why I've got to get to the priestess, to give her my message.'

Brid believed him. He called a boy to take Meilyr's horse and baggage, with the horse he had found; then went on up the track past his farm towards the cliff.

The limestone wall rose up sheer in front of them. Trees and ferns clung to the rock hundreds of feet above their heads. The track hugged the foot of the cliff with the stream at its side. The water disappeared under a crack in the rock-face but the track turned suddenly to the right. Meilyr gasped.

In front of him was a huge arch in the rock, the Gate of Birth. Meilyr felt his skin crawl as he went beneath it; he understood why it was forbidden except to the priestesses and those whom they chose to hallow. This was a path that no mortal should tread backwards. Yet he could not turn away. He was on a leash and it was tightening.

He followed Brid into a cave-hall. The Emperor's throne-room in Constantinople would be a churl's hovel beside it; it could have held a village.

Brid had gone to the side of the arch and came back with a lantern holding a large candle. 'Have you got a strike-a-light?'

Meilyr lit the lantern. Brid led him to the far end where there was a low tunnel in the rock. He laughed.

'Peada's men stopped here. They were scared enough when they came up the gorge and under the arch. They took one look and said, "There's nothing here" and got out quick. They were up and down the valley, though, for months on end, ransacking our homes, pouncing on wayfarers, bullying the children with threats and questions, so nobody could come for worship. Keep your head down now, or you'll crack your skull.'

Meilyr followed him with his back bent till he felt he would never walk straight again. When the roof lifted from over his head and he could stand up, he saw that their way was barred by a pool, black as death, that stretched to a low arch and vanished underneath it. There were two small flat-bottomed boats drawn up half out of the water by their feet. Brid put the lantern in one of them.

'You can paddle, lying down, or push your way under with your hands against the roof. It's shallow enough to wade through, but you don't want to be soaked.'

He waded out himself to push the boat under the rock and called 'Farewell' as Meilyr went into the world of the dead and the unborn.

Beyond the reach of his lantern, the darkness was not mere lack of light, it was a force. It knew nothing of light or life and closed in to crush them. His mind said the words of the Abbot's psalm, *'Let not the pit shut her mouth on me.'*

He came out into another great cave. Once the sound of ripples had stopped the silence was as complete as the blackness the other side of his candle. He raised the lantern to look around and saw a high passage leading off into the rocks. Just at the entrance there was a hook with a lantern hanging. He stood underneath it and looked along the passage. Almost at the edge of darkness he saw another lantern.

This was clearly the right direction. The priestesses would not be playing hide-and-seek. This was the Lady's House, the way that Eostre's procession led her to her bridal. But was it the way Alchflaed had come—if she had come—and if so, how had she crossed the water without a boat? Had someone ferried her? How many other passages were there?

Suddenly he threw back his head and yelled, 'Alchflaed! Where are you?' His voice clanged against the rock; then silence came back.

He was being a fool, forgetting all his teaching. That was not the way to call her. He set his lantern down at the entrance to the passage and put his fingertips on the bracelet of her hair. He rubbed it gently, thinking of the brown mass of waves and curls flowing free, the autumn glints in it, the silky warmth coiling round his fingers. He made himself see her, sending out his mind to her powered with the memory of all he knew about her, her laughter, her dancing body, her ready lies and stratagems. All the while he was murmuring insistently, 'Alchflaed, Alchflaed, Alchflaed . . .'

He had not lost the art of sending out a summons. He felt a stir in the darkness, an answer. Somewhere ahead, what he had called up was waiting for him.

He would have liked to light the lanterns as he passed and have a path of light behind him. He decided not to. The candles would be wasting down like the one he carried. They might be used up just when he needed one on his way back. He went on, using the lanterns as markers, walking easily enough on a fine wide track, awe-stricken at the wonder of the caves glimpsed by the light of his lantern. Once there was a delicate cascade falling like rain in the heart of the earth. The river reappeared, glimmering by the side of the path. The roof rose in five high arches and a dome such as he had seen in Roman pictures. Yet all these mighty works were cut out of the living rock and had been shaped by no mortal hands.

He had been carried along so far in an almost light-hearted mood, as if he were going to a feast. He was pleased with himself for having made the right choice by coming to the Lady's Bower. He savoured the sense of mastery that had come when he sent out the summons and felt the answer. He swung the lantern to enjoy the glitter of the ripples over the stony river bed and make the shadows dance among the rocks, birds swooping across the cave roof, tree branches beckoning from the crannies.

Then the track ended under a soaring cliff where two streams flowed together across his way.

To his left, the river filled the cavern from side to side, going off into invisible reaches. To the right, a narrow, boulder-strewn footway edged the water; he followed it some way but it was soon clear that he would have to crawl or wade. No procession would have come this way.

He went back to the watersmeet. Clambering had made him sweat; his skin felt damp and cold. His heart sank at the thought of going back. But those lanterns had not been set up for nothing; the priestesses would not come here just to look at an underground river. Where did Eostre stay during her night in the earth before she came up for her bridal?

He walked back under the dome, looking carefully at the rockface. This time, coming from the opposite direction, he saw the lantern hidden behind a jutting outcrop of rock, hiding another entry.

As he turned he took a last glance back along the cavern, under the shadows, as far as his lantern would reach. Just at the edge of the darkness there was a patch of darker shadow on its own, away from the wall. At the very moment Meilyr looked back, it slid round the bend in the track. He thought he saw the flutter of a cloak.

He felt his heart beating hard. He had likely made the shadow, as he made the others, by moving his lantern. Yet he felt a slight tremor of his nerves, that he knew from hunting when some creature was close on his track. He nearly called, 'Who's there?' but stopped himself. It might be one of the priestesses. He should not be inside the shrine and after their harrying by Peada's men they would be angry and suspicious. There might be more of them ahead. He didn't want a knife in his heart before he had a chance to explain.

It might be Alchflaed, wary and terrified. She would not think of his being here; if he called out or came after her, she might take flight and lose herself in the rock tunnels.

He decided to go on, cautiously, letting whoever was behind follow him till he reached the inner shrine, or temple, or whatever lay at the end of this strange path.

The next part was a twisting climb up the rocky cleft, where juts and crevices had been roughly chiselled into steps. He did not like it; the steps were uneven; he found his lantern a nuisance; he did not know what might be lurking over his head each turn of the stairway; and he could hear by scrabbling sounds below that someone else was climbing behind him.

Anger began to well up in him. What selfish folly in Alchflaed to draw him into this dark maze! Why was he here, when he could have been out in the sunlight, on the open sea on his way to Ireland? What was it to him that some stupid Englishwoman was at odds with her husband or if she got beaten to death in the course of a quarrel? Why should he lose his time and risk his life scrambling about underground?

He heard his own voice speaking to Morfran; he wasn't sure if he was remembering the words or saying them aloud. If it was really Alchflaed down there on the stairway, he hoped she could hear him.

They've taken too much from us—the English. Our rich eastern lands, our great cities—even our name taken from us, called "Welsh"—foreigners—in our own country. It's not to be forgotten or forgiven . . .'

He was breathless when he got to the top, from resentment as much as from the climb. He lit the lantern he found at the top of the stairs and when he was sure there was no one near him in the long gallery that opened ahead of him, he backed slowly down it with one hand against the rock, ready to challenge his pursuer. The passage was high and wide, yet he was beginning to feel hemmed in and stifled, as if the rocks were closing in on him with the weight of all the earth and stone that was over him, burying him alive.

Nothing had come up the stairway by the time he had reached the end of the gallery. There was another great arch here, leading into what seemed to be a higher and wider chamber. He stepped inside and waited behind the rocks, still watching the head of the stairs.

Something moved there; a shadowy figure climbed up and

paused under the dim lantern light. Meilyr craned forward to see it more clearly; his own lantern swung forward and gleamed in the darkness. The figure darted back down the stairway; in the brief glimpse, Meilyr saw that his tracker was very thin and was wearing man's clothes that seemed to be in tatters.

He had darted back himself when he knew his light had been seen, he turned just in time to save himself stepping over the edge of a crack. For one terrible moment he looked down into what seemed to be a bottomless pit, he felt the gulf drawing him down. He could hear water rushing below; the rushing in his head answered it. He was dizzy and nearly fell but threw himself backwards, staggering till he hit the cave wall. He pressed himself against it, sobbing for breath, while the cave spun round outside him.

He was frightened, and furious with himself for being frightened, for knowing that he could not force himself to go back to the stairway. The fury centred on Alchflaed. Waves of hatred for her washed through him as he cautiously circled the pit and made his way along the next tunnel. It seemed to be endless, like his rage, like his hunger for revenge on Alchflaed and all her race. When the tunnel widened into a cavern that seemed to end in a ledge over emptiness, his hatred swelled to fill it. All the old dreams of tricking her and shaming her came flocking round him like crows to a corpse, while he heaped the old reproaches on her.

'—let her find out what it is to be a foreigner, lost in an alien land—alone—with not a friendly hand lifted to save her from the whip—'

He stopped, appalled, reminding himself that this was exactly what she had found out; and that the whip had been laid upon her for the sake of his lover and his son.

Did I make her fate? Did I bring the evil on her by wishing it so often?

He felt the sweat beginning to trickle down his forehead and put up his hand to wipe his eyes. He touched slime. He jerked his arm away with a cry of disgust as fingers brushed across his cheek, groping for his eyes and throat. He spun round, dropping the lantern, and the light flickered and dimmed as he tripped or was knocked down. He was blind and suffocating, feeling his chest and his heart crushed by the weight of the darkness pressing on them, his nose and throat choked in a foul stench, his hands bruised with battering on the rocks as they closed on him, his mind cracking under the beat of the curse that was trying to scream itself through his mouth against Alchflaed.

May she be trapped into living death. May she die alone in terror. May her name be blotted out from memory and may her soul be eaten . . .

Still he fought like a wildcat, while his breaking mind tried to hold off the curse.

No. It isn't true, I love her. I've loved her with all my hate.

There was a sudden slackening in the assault. The attacker drew away from him. The last guttering of the candle lit the face for a moment before he was left in total darkness but that was enough. That face had looked at him every time he stooped to a pool to drink.

God forgive me! It's myself!

He recoiled in horror, pushing out his arms to hold it away from him and rolled off the ledge.

CHAPTER 29

At last Alchflaed came back to the Mother's Womb. It was in darkness, except for the faint amber glow of the pillars and the crystal shimmer on the walls when she lifted her candle. There was no sign of the priestesses, no flowers or green leaves; yet the shrine had not been sacked. Whatever Peada's men had done in the valley, they had clearly not reached the sanctuary. The couch was made up, the candles and braziers were ready for lighting.

She had meant to step out on to the Sword Bridge and throw herself down. Yet if she did that, her body would be passed out into the world again. She had come back to die in the womb like a hidden untimely birth and here she would stay.

She went round the cave lighting all the candles, kindling every brazier. The holy place blazed out in all its beauty. She sat on the couch, enjoying it for a while, but then her eyelids began to droop. She was very tired from her ride over the moors, coming after the dreadful scene with Oswy and her desperate race to the north before that. She lay down among the sheepskins and closed her eyes. Once or twice she opened them, like a child wanting to make sure that its mother has left a candle by its bed. Remembering Ebbe's teaching she murmured dutifully, 'Holy Mary, Mother of God, pray for us sinners now and in the hour of our death.' Then she nestled her cheek against a fleece and let the darkness take her.

His enemy was trying to hack his body apart but the sword was too blunt. Meilyr was annoyed; he wanted to die quickly. He opened his eyes to curse the man and tell him to borrow a better weapon. He shut them again because he was looking at a river flowing above his head several hundred feet up and it made him feel sick. The sword-hacking went on but did not seem to be getting anywhere. He opened his eyes in desperation and realised that he was lying across a narrow spur of rock about five feet below the ledge of the cavern.

Far below him, a river rushed through a gorge between sheer cliffs. The sight made him so giddy he had to turn his eyes away. He gripped the rock where he was lying and looked hopelessly at the ledge. To get back, he would have to stand up on the rocky spur and balance while he tried to pull himself up. He knew that at the moment he had neither the strength or the steadiness to do it and he would not get any better the longer he lay where he was.

Something nagged at his mind, there was an oddity apart from the hopeless dread of his fate. It seemed stupid to ask himself what was strange; yet he kept puzzling till he realised that he was seeing without a lantern.

Gripping the rock, he turned his head to look along the end of the spur and saw that it arched like a bridge over the gulf and reached the other side. Here it came in level with the edge of the cliff so that if he could get across he would reach a firm footing. The light was from that side, not the dim point made by a candle in a lantern but a widespread radiance. His soul longed for it.

Getting his body over to it was not going to be easy. First he had to turn himself so that he was lying along the the rocky spine of the arch. If he slipped he could not save himself. He moved inch by inch, one limb at a time. It seemed hours till he was ready to try the crossing.

He had to crawl, holding on with hands, knees and feet, watching his hands, scared to look down. It was hellishly painful, as the spine was sharp. Twice he stopped with his eyes shut, resting his cheek against the rock, but he was so tired he was afraid he might fall asleep and lose his grip.

When at last he got to the other side and crawled on to the

317

smooth stone of the cavern floor, he lay face down for some time, half-fainting, half-dozing, before he was able to push himself up to his knees and look around him. What he saw startled him back into wakefulness.

He was in a hall of amber and jewels. Strangely-shaped pillars of amber stood all round him, amber icicles hung from the roof, amethyst, sapphire and emerald glittered on the walls. He had come to the shrine in the earth's dark womb where Eostre lay before rising again with the spring-time. The young priestess who embodied her had already arrived, she was asleep on the couch in a circle of fire and light. Awe-stricken, he walked softly over to look at her; she was Alchflaed.

He sat down on the couch and touched her hair, drawing a strand of it through his fingers, feeling the silky curls, watching the bracken and beech-leaf tints shine in the candle light. He saw that her face was pinched, with dark shadows under the eyes, that her mouth was bruised and swollen. Peada's handiwork.

She stirred and opened her eyes. His face was the first thing she saw; her greeting chilled him more than the dark caves.

'Are you dead too?'

Her wits were crazed and no wonder; he'd nearly gone out of his mind in the darkness and silence and he hadn't suffered beforehand as she had. He made his voice as easy as if they'd just met at a fair.

'No, we're both alive. Let's be on our way. This is a very pretty place to sleep in but it isn't meant for mortals like you and me.'

'If you're alive you must go at once. This place is for the unborn and the dead.'

'Just as soon as you're ready.'

'I'm dead. I should never have been born.'

She spoke gently from somewhere very far away. He was terrified but kept up his cheerful manner. He put his arm round her and drew her close.

'No, love, you're just very tired and I startled you awake. Rest a little more if you like, but not too long or the candles will burn out, then we really will die.'

'Go now. I've got to stay here. I don't belong under the sun.'

He thought he understood. 'If Peada caught you again and you knifed him, it was self-defence.'

She shook her head.

'Or put something in his drink. Why should a delicate girl be broken by some fist-heaving lout? You've a right to use your own weapons.'

'I've no right to live.'

'He meant to kill you, didn't you know? I've listened to him boasting while I was with the Mercian army. He'd have tied you to a hurdle and drowned you in the Fenland mud.'

'I wish he had.'

Meilyr had seen her dancing for joy. What had Peada done to her to bring her to this?

'Well, his own folk are going to save me the trouble of cutting his throat. I hope he fries in Hell to the end of time.'

'There's no need to damn him, I've done that for both of us. He's my brother.'

Meilyr blessed the hours he'd spent hunting. No catch of the breath or tightening of his arm betrayed a surprise that she would have felt as horror or disgust.

'Well, now, we all want to curse our brothers sometimes. I often damn Madoc.'

She took no notice and went on in the same flat voice as if she were talking to herself in the darkness.

'Penda took my mother when he sacked Gefrin and gave it to Woden. She escaped and my fa—and Oswy let me be known as his.'

The ghost of Riemmelth, that had haunted Meilyr so long, as it had haunted his father, dissolved like a wisp of smoke. It had never been Riemmelth, the living, suffering woman. The luxury-loving traitress they had cursed had been begotten by themselves out of evil will and hoarded grudges.

Alchflaed's dead voice was saying, 'Peada is my brother and I married him.'

'Don't let that turn you off marriage. I'm going to marry you as soon as I can.'

'You're not my brother.'

'I'm your cousin, far off on the mother's side. And if your mother had married my father, as she meant to once, I would have been your brother. Thank God they didn't.'

She looked at him; turned her mind back for a moment from the land of the dead.

'My mother and your father?'

'They loved each other when they were young. It came to nothing, but once she sent him this ring.' He showed her the ruby on his hand; he was glad to see that she was listening and watching. 'It's the royal ring of Cumbria. You gave it to me and I've worn it ever since, just as your mother wanted my father to wear it.'

He smiled at her. 'So you see, you didn't marry Peada. He's as free of you as you are of him. You could never have married him, whoever he was, because you were betrothed to me first and I'm going to hold you to it.'

He wasn't sure what canon law would say to this and didn't care. Any tie would do to bind her. He had to weave a web of words round her and draw her back into the land of the living.

'I know it's what Riemmelth and my father would have wanted. That's why I came north for you over four years ago.'

She touched the ruby with her finger.

'You came for me?'

It was the perfect opening. He'd been planning how to seduce her for years; he had all the words ready, though he'd never dreamed that his rival would be death. And here they were together on a bed.

'What do you think I was doing in Penda's army? I've got no quarrel with your people. I came to find you. I fell in love with you at first sight.' He showed her the bracelet on his arm.

'Look, I cut a lock of your hair as a love-token,' he lied. Then he realised that all his lies were coming true. God must be laughing.

'My uncle's a monk. He'll speak to Abbot Sulien. We'll be married in my country —'

She rested her cheek against his shoulder. 'If only I'd known in time, while I was still a maiden. I'm not fit for you to marry —'

'So you've had a lover. So did your mother. So have I, many times. That poor child you gave Christian burial — and got flogged for — he was my son!'

That really startled her. 'Nest told me. Don't worry about her, I've seen her safe. I've been unfaithful to you since you gave me your ring, and with your own maid, too. Will you forgive me?'

She smiled but her eyes were sad. He kept up the attack.

'And what about Nest? She offered her life for your escape — they tried to murder her instead of you. I'll tell you all about it when we've got out of here. What could I say to her when I met her again, if you'd thrown away her gift and I'd let you do it?'

'I love her. I love you both. You've made me feel that my life wasn't all worthless. But it's too late for me now —'

Meilyr fell back on the last unfair trick that men can play on tender-hearted women.

'Very well, my dearest. If death is what you want I won't go against your will. I won't be unfaithful to you again. What more could I ask than to die in your arms?'

He swung his legs on to the couch and drew the sheepskin over them. She pushed him away.

'No, not you! I couldn't bear it! Please, please go!'

'It was hopeless from the first,' he sighed. 'I could never have got you back over that rock-bridge. Don't send me away to die alone in the dark.' He looked pleadingly at her.

'You don't have to. There's another way out. Listen carefully — see that crack in the cave wall? — you say,

> *"Thrice to mine and thrice to thine*
> *And thrice again to make up nine"*

and then you take the third —'

Meilyr bowed his head in his hands. 'I don't know what you're talking about. It's no good. I'm beaten.'

His shoulders drooped, all his courage had drained out of him. It was pitiful. It worked.

Alchflaed got up from the couch. 'Take down one of the lanterns. I'll show you the way.'

It was good for her to have to count the turns and check every crevice so that she did not lead him carelessly to his death. He left her to be leader, to do all the thinking and give the orders.

When they came out of the low cave on the hill-side it was already evening. The bulk of Mam Tor was black against the northwestern sky. He remembered last year when it had been ablaze with fires and torches. Alchflaed said nothing more about going back into the hollow hill. They strolled together down the valley without any talk until they came to the meadow and the track that led up beside the stream to the great cavern. Brid was leaning over his gate; he opened it and they went into the farmhouse.

Brid's wife took one look at Alchflaed and got her settled by the hearth with a good bowl of broth; then bedded her down with her own daughters. Meilyr sat up later, out of regard for his hosts. His hands were not fit to touch his harp but he gave them the story of *The Wooing of Olwen* and they felt well repaid.

He was glad to see Alchflaed had a better colour after her night's sleep. Her eyes were brighter; she talked cheerfully to Brid's wife while they were breaking their fast. The woman made them up some food and filled Meilyr's flask. Brid brought their horses and they rode to the fort on the Noue, where three ways met. Meilyr set off at once towards the northwest, back to

Manceinion. She reined in her horse by the road that went south. Surprised, Meilyr stopped; she held out her hand smiling.

'Farewell, my dear, and God be with you.'

'What are you talking about?'

'You've given me my life. Thank you for that and God bless you for ever. I've got to go and warn Peada if he's still alive.'

Meilyr gasped with shock and anger.

'You cheat! You love him!'

'No. It's because I don't love him. He hasn't even got that. He'd never have married me if I hadn't put it in his head. I brought him nothing but bitterness. I meant to be a peace-weaver and I've woven his shroud. He's lost everything. He thinks he's failed his father and his land. And now he's going to die by the hands of his own folk.' Her eyes filled with tears. 'He'll be so lonely.'

Meilyr looked at her in despair. He could have knocked her senseless and tied her on her horse, arguing with some justice that she was crazed and he was acting to save her life. So he would have got her body and broken her spirit as men have done to captive women since war began. Or he could have wept and begged her to pity his love for her, and torn her apart between her loyalties. What he could not do was change her. She was as she was.

He turned his horse.

'What are you doing?'

'Coming with you, of course. You don't think I've been tracking you across Britain for four years just to say, "Goodbye. I enjoyed our meeting"?' He gave her a mocking smile. Which of them was madder?

'Besides, you could never handle this by yourself. No English wits are sharp enough. It needs the Cymric mind.'

CHAPTER
30

Peada had been feeling happier ever since Alchflaed had left him, going brazenly out of Leirceaster in all her finery, so they told him, to meet some of Oswy's Bernicians and take herself off. He felt healthier too, as if some suppurating flesh had been cut away from a wound.

I can cast her off now, he told himself. *I'll denounce her to the*

Archbishop as a runaway wife and a witch. Oswy won't be able to stop me or defend her if he values his own name as a Christian. Then I'll marry Winefride, she's a true-bred Mercian. I'll win back my people's good word. Give me three years till the next crop of boys is ready for war and I'll dare Oswy to fight me for all my father lost.

The Lenten fast had left him light and pure. He had kept the Feast of the Resurrection in his new church. And Wulfrun had come back. She had arrived in her hall with Eadbert on Holy Thursday. They wouldn't come to the church, of course, but they were waiting to greet him as he came towards the great gateway of his palace. He felt forgiven and approved. He would bid them to his feast; there'd be such a revel as Leirceaster had not seen since he made it his city. He'd call in every singer and tumbler for miles.

There was a minstrel waiting to beg for his custom, a harper carrying his instrument in an otter-skin bag. He had a dancing woman with him, showing the hem of a red dress and purple slippers. They were not well-to-do; their coarse cloaks were worn and travel-stained. He'd call them over and startle them by a promise of gold if they amused his guests.

The usual group of beggars had been crouching on the watch for his coming out of the church. He waited for them to come up to him, ready to scatter alms for them, smiling and free-handed as a king should be. When the knife went in, he was puzzled. He stepped back, putting his hand to his side and looking at the blood on his fingers as if he could not understand what it was. He knew death in battle, but this was different. His knees buckled, his eyes were growing dim. He blinked and tried to guess what was happening to him, looking bewildered and very young.

The killers hesitated, taken aback, not sure what to do next. The bystanders had been caught by surprise. They did not know whether to cheer for the death of a traitor who had yielded to Northumbria or to howl for the death of their king, Penda's son. Old habits are strongest. Rage for the shedding of Penda's blood began to rise in them, while Peada groped feebly for something to cling to, lost in his gathering darkness.

Then arms were clasped round him, and the face that had always meant comfort was looking down at him through the shadows. Everything would be all right now. He smiled.

'Dear Wulfrun, you've always been a kind sister to me.'

He laid his head against her breasts and died.

Pain seared through Wulfrun like a poisoned spear from Hel. She rocked Peada in her arms as she did when he was a little boy, looking round wildly for something that would show her that this was just a nightmare and she would wake up in her mother's house with Peada sleeping beside her.

Eyes were watching her from the shadow of a hooded cloak, eyes wide with pain and horror. Grief knows its kin. Wulfrun knew the eyes, though they were in a heavily-painted face under a bush of frizzed hair. She wanted to denounce the Bernician witch, whose evil spells had driven her to kill what she loved better than her own life. She wanted to give orders how the creature should be killed: torn to pieces slowly so that nothing should remain of her woman's shape by the time she died, mad with agony. She opened her mouth to tell people but her voice would only scream and scream: 'Bernician—kill—kill!' She struggled to order her words, but she had ruled herself too harshly for too long. There was no Wulfrun any more, and would never be again, only a screaming.

Eadbert had sensed the movement of anger in the crowd. Another moment and they might tear him apart. He thanked the gods for his wife's quick brain and good acting. Following her lead, he drew his sword.

'Murder! The Bernicians have slain our king!'

He drove his sword through one of Oswy's tax assessors who had been in the church. His men cut down the Bernician's servants. The hired knifemen saw their danger and turned to run but were not quick enough. The crowd swooped joyfully and tore them to death, then rampaged off to look for more Bernicians. There were not many of them in Leirceaster but the mob was not biased. Any foreigner would do.

Meilyr grabbed Alchflaed's arm, shouting 'Kill, kill!' and went with the tide of bodies until he got the chance to pull her into an alley and double back towards their ale-house, a little hovel down by the southwest angle of the walls. He had already seen one Frisian trader's booth go up in flames. Judging by the screaming, the Frisian had gone with it.

The ale-house was deserted; all the folk had gone off earlier to see the King come out of his fine church. Meilyr paused by the door. Alchflaed swayed; he caught her before she hit the ground and held her propped against the wall. Her hood slipped back; she looked to be in agony. She was in no state to save herself unless he could give her some comfort.

324

'God was merciful to him. He'd just taken the sacrament and he died in the arms of the one who loved him best. That woman— she's always loved him, I saw it years ago.'

She caught his hand. 'Wulfrun knew me.'

'Then when she's stopped screaming long enough to talk, they'll be looking for us. We wouldn't get past the gates even if we had time to get there. Any foreigner will be game for the mob and they'll be searching the ale-houses first.'

Alchflaed looked towards the market-place. 'They're on their way now.'

He pulled her inside the ale-house and shut the door. There were no windows; it was dark except for the hearth-fire. He caught her by the shoulders.

'Listen, Alchflaed. No need to tell you not to show fear. You mustn't even feel fear or think fear, when they come. When men are killing-mad they can smell fear as wolves smell blood. But if their evil can't get a hold, the fear and rage can be turned back on themselves.' He smiled at her. 'Remember how you held those churls at Bebbanburh? Lie down on that bench and be fast asleep. Then just follow my lead.'

She did as she was told. Meilyr had time to pull the table closer to the hearth and light a candle. He was drawing some Greek letters on the table-top with a bit of burnt stick when the door was flung open and some of the townsfolk pushed into the low dark room, led by a smith.

Meilyr went on writing for a second or two, while they had time to be taken aback by his quietness and the fact that he was disregarding them. Then he raised his head and looked at them over the candle-flame.

'Yes? What do you want?'

'We want you, filthy murderer!'

'You'll pay for killing our king!'

'Did you hear his voice?' screeched one of the women. 'He's a cursed Welshman—one of those who left our men to drown in the Weneta.'

Mailyr raised his eyebrows and looked at them scornfully. 'My name is Stephanos Maleinos. I'm a man of learning, come from the Emperor's court at Constantinople to offer you the benefit of my skills. You're making too much noise, you'll wake my woman. I shall have to call my servants to put you out.'

He kicked the charred logs on the hearth to make them blaze brighter. Then he picked up his piece of stick and began drawing with it, taking no more notice of them. They looked at him uneasily, finding his lack of fear frightening.

'Your servants!' The smith looked scornful. 'Lodging in a hole like this and you say you've got servants! Where are they?'

'In Constantinople, of course, waiting till I call them. They don't need eyes to find me or ships to bring them oversea.' Meilyr fixed his dark eyes on them; the candle light was reflected in them so that the watchers saw three flames. He spoke very softly.

'They're stirring now, they know I want them, lifting up their muzzles to catch the scent.'

Alchflaed stirred and raised herself on the bench. Her eyes were shut, she moved her head from side to side, sniffing, her face blank. Meilyr was staring at the candle. 'Look! They're unfolding their wings, great black pinions. In Constantinople the sun's hidden, the sky darkens.'

Alchflaed stretched her arms. Meilyr began to chant softly, 'Hismael . . . Barzabel . . . Sorath . . . Kedemel . . . Chasmodai . . .'

The listeners felt how dark the ale-house was. The crowd jammed by the low door kept out the daylight; inside there was only the candle, with the two eyes behind it, and the glow from the flames moving on the walls. The shadow of the girl's arms seemed to stretch across the walls and round the room, great black hands groping for them.

Suddenly, a knot in one of the logs cracked and burst into flames; the shadows leaped up on black wings. Alchflaed threw back her head with an eerie howl. The rioters' nerve broke; there was a scuffle at the door as they pushed through and fled. Meilyr laughed and blew out the candle.

'Good girl! They won't come back in a hurry.'

'There'll be others. Or those will talk and Eadbert will send his spearmen.'

'Can you think of anywhere we could hide till sundown? If I could steal a rope we could try to go over the walls after nightfall.'

'Better. I know how we can go under the walls by daylight. There's a good Roman drain under a hut near the Queen's bower. Nobody will have stayed there since Nest and I went, they all thought it was ill-omened.'

'Oh God, not another tunnel.'

'Only a short one. And we needn't be afraid of meeting any ghosts down there. Whoever heard of a haunted drain?'

*   *   *

Word of Peada's death reached Oswy within the octave of the Resurrection. He was still in Elmet, keeping the feast with Bledri. Alchfrid came to his father, cloaked and booted for riding.

'This is terrible news. They say Alchflaed quarrelled with him just before Passion Week and walked out.'

Oswy said nothing.

'The Mercians are claiming she ordered his death.'

'That's better than saying I ordered it. I shall have to bring Mercia under my rule. I don't want a rebellion on my hands.'

'I'm riding for Leirceaster at once. They may have taken her already.'

'No, they haven't. If they had, she'd be dead and the Mercians would be shouting to all Britain how she confessed before she died. She may have had him killed; I wouldn't blame her. Leave her alone—if she's kept out of their clutches for so long, she's probably well away.'

'Whatever she's done, she's my sister. I'm going to look for her.'

'Where will you look? With the start she's had, you've got all Britain to choose from. At this very moment, while we're talking here, a pilgrim bound for Rome may be bargaining with a Frisian shipman in Lundenburh or Dofras. An English embroidress may be offering her skills to the Queen of Strathclyde. An Irish abbess may be taking in a postulant, or a bawd on the Legaceaster water-front may be bringing a customer to her newest girl—'

Alchfrid was outraged.

'My lord, she's your *daughter!*'

'Yes. Breeding counts as much as birth. She hasn't lived under my roof for nothing; she's my daughter too.' He smiled at his indignant son. 'Which means she could be doing anything, any-where.'

At that moment, while they were talking, she was lost somewhere in Mercia, as she and Meilyr harped and danced, begged and lied their way across country in a seemingly hopeless attempt to escape. No one who knew the odds would have backed them, the forces against them were too great. If the Mercians guessed who they were, they would kill Alchflaed as Peada's murderess and Meilyr as one of the Welsh who had deserted them. If the North-umbrians found them, they would kill Meilyr as one of the Welsh who had fought for Penda. He suspected that they might kill Alchflaed too, to stop any scandal of being caught with him; or at best, pen her in a nunnery. The land was full of outlaw bands

327

after the war, who would gladly cut Meilyr's throat for the chance of stealing his harper's takings and his woman. The countryfolk, wary by nature and more suspicious of strangers than ever now with so many thieves about, were just as likely to knife them as welcome them.

They knew this, so they did not have to talk about it. Having no hope, they had nothing to worry about and gave themselves up to the enjoyment of each other and of the springtime, which grew warmer and lovelier all the way from Resurrection to Pentecost.

They became lovers on the second night after leaving Leirceaster. The farm folk who lodged them bedded them together as a matter of course. Meilyr had meant to let her alone for a while, however much he wanted her, and only hold her for comfort; but she'd turned to him, pulling him close and he'd entered her as naturally as breathing. After that, they took joy of each other as much as they liked, snuggled down on straw under rough blankets in farmhouses or lying in the young grass in the sunlight. Every time it seemed sweeter because every time might be the last.

Yet strangely, they felt none of the panic haste that drives hunted creatures when time is running out for them. They had gone inside Meilyr's story, the web he had spun so carelessly in the Eoforwic tavern to trap her long ago.

'. . . you'd come to a farmstead or a shepherd's hut and take your place in the ring round the hearth. You'd get your share of the broth in the cauldron, your hunk of cheese and oatcake. And then, over the ale, you'd spin your tales of adventure and enchantment till the folk would swear they saw the wizards and elf-women you told about, floating out of the peat-smoke . . .'

One night at a farmer's hearth, Meilyr gave them the story of King Arthur and the Loathly Bride, while Alchflaed danced it to his harping. The farm folk loved it, especially her acting of the amorous hag.

Afterwards the talk moved on enjoyably to witch-wives in general, with the trouble they brought, and then to the King's murder. Everyone there was sure the Queen had plotted it. She had come invisibly into Leirceaster with a Greekland sorcerer to see the King die and to destroy the Lady Wulfrun's wits. Then the two of them had changed into huge black ravens and flown away under the very eyes of the men who had tried to seize them.

The farm folk shook their heads at the wickedness of the Northumbrian queen.

'I saw her once,' said the farm-wife's cousin, who was staying overnight on the way to a niece's wedding.

Alchflaed yawned, crossing her legs and showing most of their length under her red skirt.

'She seemed a quiet, drab creature to look at her, not much spirit. I like 'em with a bit more colour.' He winked at Alchflaed. 'I wouldn't have said she had it in her to kill anyone.'

'It was Oswy who got her to do it. He's got it in him all right.' The farmer was bitter.

'I daresay,' said the cousin. 'But my brother-in-law—he was in Peada's war-band—he swears she was a witch. Look how she vanished into thin air over a week before Peada died. You'd have met my brother-in-law if you came along with me tomorrow,' he added to Meilyr. 'It's my niece's wedding—pity you're not coming my way, you'd have been very welcome. My brother-in-law could have told you what Queen Alchflaed was like when she ruled in Leirceaster.'

Next morning, Alchflaed and Meilyr were walking through the dappled light and shade of the oakwoods, where drifts of blue-bells were like patches of cloudless sky fallen on the grass. Earth and heaven melted into each other; the pools and quietly gliding forest rivers were full of sunlit boughs and butterflies. It seemed they had found the Land of Youth—

'*Winter never comes there, or old age or sorrow. The apple-trees bear flowers and fruit together. Centuries pass like hours, time goes by so lightly with music and dancing and laughter—*'

They were both thoughtful; but by now they were so much at peace with each other that they could keep silence without uneasiness or grudging.

Alchflaed was thinking: *This is lovely but it can't go on. We've been lucky this month. It's been like finding that lost Land of Youth Meilyr told me about. But this isn't the Land of Youth, it's the world of time. The longer we keep moving, the likelier I'll be to meet someone who knows me. The hunt will pick up our trail. We'll draw enemies after us into Meilyr's country and there'll be more deaths. It's time to stop wandering. We'll find a farm where the man was killed in the war and offer to stay and help. Meilyr can still make his harp music. I can grow herbs and practise healing. We'll make a home somewhere soon . . .*

Meanwhile, Meilyr was near to despair. Since his boyhood he had lived close to death by his own choice and had enjoyed it,

329

getting extra zest for life and more pleasure in his daring and skill with every risk he took. His love for Alchflaed was teaching him the fear of death.

He had always been drawn to Alchflaed, first by her bodily beauty and vivid life, that pleased all his poet's demanding senses. Then, he had been charmed and amused by her ready wit, her artistry in lying. As a bard, a maker himself, he admired her craftswoman's skill with colour, form and rhythm, that matched his own skill with words and music, so that she could make his songs visible to him by her dancing. Nest had taught him something of her courage and kindness; he had seen the heart of them in her pitying loyalty to her wretched, unloved husband. Now she was growing dearer to him every day they spent together, dearest of all when she slept in his arms after love-making and he took care to shield her from the cold and the hard ground.

If they were trapped, he might not be able to save her, even if he gave his own life in the attempt. He was terrified of dying before he had time to kill her, terrified that she would be taken away to face torture and death alone at the hands of the Mercians or made a slave by some outlaw pack.

Then, as the days went by and their luck still held, another fear began to grow in him. He had never expected to be scared of dying; but now he dreaded that escape and freedom might bring the worst horror of all.

He had no idea where they were. The forest was all around them, it seemed to stretch to the ends of the world. They had been circling and doubling back on their tracks, avoiding Roman roads, staying at lonely farms. The farm-folk's world ended at the next village or steading; they had little idea what lay beyond, except that there were Welsh lands 'somewhere to the west'. Often, in the depths of the forest, following winding tracks, they hardly knew for hours which way they were going. Yet, mile by mile, they were moving northwest. For the first time, Meilyr let himself look at the likelihood that he would win his way home.

If, against all the odds, he got her over the border into Powys, what would her life be like there? She would have a name—Nest, now shining brightly as a beacon to sailors across the sands of Dee, had given her that. He could invent something of a history for her: Honesta, a noblewoman of ancient British blood, rescued from the east during the Mercian wars. It was true as far as it went, like all the best lies. But how would she feel when she was cut off for ever from her home and her kin? How would she feel if she heard her people being cursed; if the English made war on Powys, killing or enslaving his people; if English captives were brought back from raids, cursing the Britons in their heartbreak and slavery? Wouldn't his own curse against her come true at last: '*She'll wake up and find that she's put herself into life-long exile for nothing.*'

Then he saw another picture, bright against the dreary vision. Dinas Brân, lifted high above the world's petty squabbles and feuds. The hall with its hearth circled by oak pillars and Alchflaed on her couch beside it, with the wonderful tapestries hanging round her: the glory of the Sun and Moon, and all the colours of the four elements. She would find peace there, beauty to fill her eyes and her mind, work that would be worthy of her skills. She could make embroideries even lovelier than the one Peada had slashed to rags, paint books for the monastery. They could go down to Llangollen to talk with Morfran and Stephanos and the Abbot; if she wanted pastime he could make harp-music for her; there would be singing and board-games for battles of wits.

He couldn't hold the picture; it faded like a rainbow into the greyness of rain clouds. Their happiness had flourished on adventure and laughter and shared escapes from danger. Could laughter and love ever hold out against other people's hatreds? He knew he could not bear to watch her joy dying slowly.

Meilyr was very tired; he had used up all his strength; the dread of hurting her defeated him at last. He thought longingly of the phial in his pouch, the sleeping draught that Morfran had given him when he first set out to rescue her. He had never bothered to give it back; now it was the only remnant of his uncle's potions that had not been destroyed when Morfran renounced his magic. It could still be used to rescue Alchflaed, though not even Morfran had foreseen how he would do it.

'*Three drops give the sleep that has no waking.*'

Meilyr pictured Alchflaed as he had watched her while they lay together, asleep in the circle of his arm, happy and safe. He wanted to keep her safe for ever. It was time to stop wandering.

Next day brought a thick summer mist that hung low under the trees and would not lift. They were warm enough in their heavy woollen cloaks. They did not come upon any homestead but they had food for that day. Towards dusk the track they were following came to a river; they had lost all sense of direction in the mist and could not tell which way it was flowing. They crossed it at a

331

ford. The land began to rise on the other side. They followed the river upstream but in the gathering darkness they left it and moved further up the slope among the trees to find a drier place to sleep.

Tomorrow, Meilyr decided; as soon as the mist lifted. They'd climb up above the woods into the sunlight and go to sleep for ever in each other's arms before her heart could be broken by exile.

But when he woke up next morning he saw he had left it too late to escape into the gentle sleep of death. They were trapped now. The mist still lay around the tree boles and along the river, though it was thinning as the sun rose; but Dinas Brân was so high, the hill was so steep, that travellers coming westward along the valley could see it for miles.

Alchflaed, drowsing in his arms under the cloaks, felt him start and grow tense. She opened her eyes and saw him staring at what was waiting for them, blocking their path to the west.

The hill rose out of the mist into the dawn sunlight. It was cone-shaped and circled with green ramparts. The tower was gilded by the rising sun. The vision that had haunted her since the siege of Bebbanburh, that had drawn her along a strange road through the shadows of death, had taken solid form at last, rock and earth, tree and grass. The mist swayed like a dancer's veil to the music of rustling leaves and the cool voice of the river.

Meilyr heard her gasp; looking at her face he saw that, unbelievable as it seemed, she knew the place. Whatever else she would find at Dinas Brân, it would not be exile.

She turned to him, glowing with wonder and pleasure; she caught his arm and pointed.

'Look! We're home!'

LANGUAGES AND PLACE NAMES

England, Scotland and Wales did not exist politically in the seventh century. The island of Britain contained lands of the British, English, Picts and Scots, divided into many kingdoms and lordships. These fought briskly among themselves, or tried to take over each other's dynasties by marriage or murder.

The earlier inhabitants of the island were the Picts and the Britons. The strongest Pictish tribes were north of the Clyde and Forth; they had never been under Roman rule and had preserved a very ancient language and culture. The rest of the island—in modern times, southern Scotland, England and Wales— belonged to the Britons. They spoke a Celtic language, the ances- tor of modern Welsh, but during the four hundred years while Britain was a province of the Roman Empire they absorbed the classical culture of the south, without forgetting their own. Even after the imperial government lost control of the northern prov- inces, the Britons continued to trade with the Mediterranean lands via the western sea-routes, put Latin inscriptions on their tombstones and dated by the names of the Roman consuls. In their historical writings they proudly called themselves the "*cives*"—the citizens, the *civilised*.

During the last century of the Empire and afterwards, there was heavy Irish immigration all down the western seaboard. Latin writers called these Gaelic-speaking people the "Scots". One powerful group had set up a kingdom in Argyll. The English came from the east; they were Europeans, mainly from north Germany, Frisia and Denmark. Some of the earliest had come officially as federate troops; the Roman government, with over- extended frontiers to guard and desperate for man-power, had recruited heavily among the German tribes. Other English had taken to the sea, ready for freebooting, mercenary service or settlement as chance offered. There was never an organised Eng- lish military invasion.

Faced with increasing Scottish and English immigration, the Britons began to call themselves the "Cymry" in their native language—fellow-countrymen. The English called them "Brettas"—Britons, or "Wealas"—foreigners, a name they also applied to the Romans and seemed to associate with exotic luxuries: vermilion dye, gerfalcons, walnuts.

When the central Roman government finally lost control, the most powerful local man took over in different parts of the country. In the east, he would be a commander of federate troops or a sea-raider with a crew of warriors. When he was strong enough to call himself king, then he would found an English kingdom. Elsewhere the local chief would be a Romano-British noble, possibly descended from the old tribal kings; then there would be a Welsh kingdom. These Welsh-speaking kingdoms were established in what are now Scotland and England as well as modern Wales. Strathclyde, Cumbria, Elmet and Devon survived longest. Since at that time most people must have had at least a smattering of another language, a large number of "English" place names are Welsh or Latin. That is why some of the places in this story have two, sometimes three names.

PLACE NAMES

BERNICIA AND CUMBRIA

At Wall	a royal estate on the Roman Wall near Newcastle
Bebbanburh	Bamburgh
Caer Luel	Carlisle
Coludesburh	St Abb's Head
Eamot	River Eamont
Englawud	Inglewood Forest
Gatesheafod	Gateshead
Hagustaldesham	Hexham
Idon	River Eden
Lonceaster	Lancaster
Stony Moor	Stainmore
Suala	River Swale
Tina	River Tyne
Tuidimuth	Tweedmouth

DEIRA

Calcaceaster (Caer Galch)	Tadcaster
Caldre	River Calder
Ceasterford	Castleford

Doneceaster	Doncaster
Eoforwic (Caer Efrog, Eboracum)	York
Getlingas	Gilling
Haethfeld	Hatfield Chase
Loidis	the Leeds district
Perscbrig	Piercebridge
Tese	River Tees
Weneta	River Went
Weorf	River Wharfe
Yr	River Aire
The Long Hills	the Pennines

MERCIA

Arnemeton (The Buckstones)	Buxton
Brantestun	Braunestone
Caer Legion (Legaceaster)	Chester
Ceastertun	Chesterton
Leirceaster	Leicester
Maersea	River Mersey
Manceinion	Manchester
Medeshamsted	Peterborough
Northworthig	Derby
Noue	River Noe
Peaclond	the Peak District
Tomeworthig	Tamworth
Treanta	River Trent
The Lady's Bower	Castleton and the Hope Valley, Derbyshire

THE SOUTH

Cantwaraburh	Canterbury
Dofras	Dover
Lundenburh (Llundain, Londinium)	London

Note; the names in italics are hypothetical forms as there is no record of what they were called at this period and two of the modern names contain Romance elements.